The
James Tiptree
Award Anthology 3

EDITED BY

Karen Joy Fowler · Pat Murphy · Debbie Notkin · Jeffrey D. Smith

TACHYON PUBLICATIONS · SAN FRANCISCO

The James Tiptree Award Anthology 3

"Introduction" by Jeffrey D. Smith. Copyright © 2007 Jeffrey D. Smith. ¶ "Have Not Have" by Geoff Ryman. Copyright © 2001 by Geoff Ryman. First published in *The Magazine of Fantasy & Science Fiction*, April, 2001. Chapter 1 of *Air* by Geoff Ryman, St. Martin's Press 2004. Reprinted by permission of St. Martin's Press. ¶ "The Glass Bottle Trick" by Nalo Hopkinson. Copyright © 2000 by Nalo Hopkinson. First published in *Whispers from the Cotton Tree Root* edited by Nalo Hopkinson, Invisible Cities Press 2000. Reprinted by permission of the author. ¶ "Wooden Bride" by Margo Lanagan. Copyright © 2004 by Margo Lanagan. First published in *Black Juice* by Margo Lanagan, Eos/HarperCollins 2004. Used by permission of HarperCollins Publishers. ¶ "Dearth" by Aimee Bender. Copyright © 2005 by Aimee Bender. First published in *On The Rocks: The KGB Bar Fiction Anthology* edited by Rebecca Donner. From *Willful Creatures* by Aimee Bender, Doubleday 2005. Reprinted by permission of Doubleday, a division of Random House, Inc. ¶ "Mountain Ways" by Ursula K. Le Guin. Copyright © 1996 by Ursula K. Le Guin. First appeared in *Asimov's Science Fiction*, August 1996. From *The Birthday of the World and Other Stories* by Ursula K. Le Guin, HarperCollins 2002. Reprinted by permission of the author and the author's agents, the Virginia Kidd Agency, Inc. ¶ "Shame" by Pam Noles. Copyright © 2006 by Pam Noles. First appeared in *The Infinite Matrix* (www.infinitematrix.com), April 2006. Reprinted by permission of the author. ¶ "The Future of Female: Octavia Butler's Mother Lode" by Dorothy Allison. Copyright © 1990 by Dorothy Allison. First published in *Reading Black, Reading Feminist* edited by Henry Louis Gates, Meridian 1990. Reprinted by permission of the author. ¶ "Liking What You See: A Documentary" by Ted Chiang. Copyright © 2002 by Ted Chiang. First appeared in *Stories of Your Life and Others* by Ted Chiang, Tor Books 2002. Reprinted by permission of the author's estate and the author's agents, the Virginia Kidd Agency, Inc. ¶ "The Girl Who Was Plugged In" by James Tiptree, Jr. Copyright © 1973 by James Tiptree, Jr. First published in *New Dimensions 3* edited by Robert Silverberg, Doubleday 1973. Reprinted by permission of the author's agents, the Virginia Kidd Agency, Inc. ¶ "Dear Alice Sheldon" by L. Timmel Duchamp. Copyright © 2006 by L. Timmel Duchamp. First published in *Talking Back: Epistolatory Fantasies* edited by L. Timmel Duchamp, Aqueduct Press 2006. Reprinted by permission of the author. ¶ "Little Faces" by Vonda N. McIntyre. Copyright © 2005 by Vonda N. McIntyre and SCIFI.COM. First published on SCIFICTION 02.23.05. Reprinted by permission of the author. ¶ "Knapsack Poems" by Eleanor Arnason. Copyright © 2002 by Eleanor Arnason. First appeared in *Asimov's Science Fiction*, May 2002. Reprinted by permission of the author.

Book design & composition by John D. Berry.
The text typeface is MVB *Verdigris, with titles in* HTF *Knockout Cruiserweight.*

Tachyon Publications
1459 18th Street #139
San Francisco CA 94107
(415) 285-5615
www.tachyonpublications.com

Series Editor: Jacob Weisman

ISBN 13: 978-1-892391-41-4
ISBN 10: 1-892391-41-4

FIRST EDITION: 2007

9 8 7 6 5 4 3 2 1

contents

vii   Introduction | *Jeffrey D. Smith*

3   HAVE NOT HAVE | *Geoff Ryman*

25   THE GLASS BOTTLE TRICK | *Nalo Hopkinson*

39   WOODEN BRIDE | *Margo Lanagan*

51   DEARTH | *Aimee Bender*

63   MOUNTAIN WAYS | *Ursula K. Le Guin*

91   SHAME | *Pam Noles*

105   THE FUTURE OF FEMALE: OCTAVIA BUTLER'S
MOTHER LODE | *Dorothy Allison*

113   LIKING WHAT YOU SEE: A DOCUMENTARY | *Ted Chiang*

151   THE GIRL WHO WAS PLUGGED IN | *James Tiptree, Jr.*

191   DEAR ALICE SHELDON | *L. Timmel Duchamp*

199   LITTLE FACES | *Vonda N. McIntyre*

239   KNAPSACK POEMS | *Eleanor Arnason*

259   *Winners and short lists*

269   *About the authors*

273   *About the editors*

introduction

Jeffrey D. Smith

When the Tiptree Award was founded by my coeditors Pat Murphy and Karen Joy Fowler, it must have seemed very simple. (This is an assumption on my part, because I wasn't there; my only involvement at the time was that Pat wrote to me — as James Tiptree's literary trustee — and asked for permission to use the name.) But yeah, pretty easy: pick a science fiction or fantasy short story (because Tiptree was a short story writer) that "explores and expands gender." Have a party to publicize the winner. Do it again next year.

That was 1991. And while the award has expanded from being run out of a shoebox in Pat Murphy's office to having a full board of directors, a treasurer, a bank account, nonprofit status, and a lot of supporters and volunteers, we're still trying to figure it out.

The celebration part usually works pretty well, although despite what we think is extensive advance planning there always seems to be an element of chaos involved. We regularly get the winners to the ceremony's traveling location — often but not always WisCon, our home base in Madison, Wisconsin — and most of the time (really, almost *always*) have hotel rooms reserved for them. We fete them with speeches, singing, chocolate, artwork, and jewelry, which seems to both bemuse and delight them. We have, though, sent shell-shocked jurors up on stage to discuss winners they have prepared no remarks for, and have disappointed others who were ready to go but weren't asked. And while we would of course never lose the beautiful silver-and-pearl Elise Matthesen tiara that our winners parade around in for the weekend, we might mislay the box and not be sure whether or not the tiara was in it. Fortunately, in that unlikely event, Joe Haldeman would still be *wearing* the tiara and nothing bad would have happened.

So, overall, we do okay on the celebration front. And we think we do okay on the fiction-selection front as well, even though the constantly-evolving nature of the process leads to continual growing pains.

We ourselves are honored by the responses of our winners. The award has gone to new writers for their first novels, and established writers in the midst of long careers, and they have all risen to the occasion. Theodore Roszak, a noted professor and social thinker, who wrote both *The Making of a Counter Culture* and the Tiptree Award-winning novel *The Memoirs of Elizabeth Frankenstein*, delivered a touching speech about what an amazing community this was. Had a tiara been part of the proceedings that year, we're sure that he would have worn it proudly.

The idea of a short fiction award only lasted a couple of months; the gender aspects of a story are much more important than its length, and if the best story is a novel, then a novel should win. In fact, the first jury didn't find *any* short stories they felt were appropriate. They chose two winning novels and put five other novels on their short list of recommended works.

At the suggestion of the first jury, we have always publicized the winners and short lists together, as opposed to first publishing a short list and then announcing a winner a couple of months later. Each jury determines for itself how many items should be on the short list. We four anthologists then take the short fiction on the list and something out of the winning novel, and juggle it together with some nonfiction pieces and some stories from older short lists until we have something that feels like a book. (We decided right from the start that as much affection as we individually might have for some items that didn't make the short lists, we would respect the juries' decisions and limit our own choices.)

So in that sense it's a good thing that we didn't start this anthology series with the first year of the award, with the jury handing us two winning novels and five short-listed novels. That would have been a tough juggle.

At the beginning, the juries recognized works that were generally identifiable as science fiction (using that phrase in its broad sense to include fantasy). Of the first jury's seven recommended books, five were clearly from sf writers and publishers, one was by a mainstream writer but was nonambiguously sf, and one was ambiguously sf but by an sf writer. (In the sf field, we use the term "mainstream" to mean non-genre writing. Sf writers write sf, mystery writers write mysteries, romance writers write romances…and mainstream writers write realistic prose fiction, or something similar. Most mainstream writers have probably never heard the term, and doubtless assume that they just write fiction. Should we tell them?)

As time went on, more and more (and more) diverse items started showing up. Stories are nominated for the Tiptree Award through different paths. Sometimes publishers submit novels or short fiction on their own—and some of those times, after we read them, we wonder why. A lot of recommendations come in through our website from readers, or from the stories' writers, or the writers' beards. Many jurors actively search out prospective works on their own, depending on their own interests. The wider the net we cast, the more interesting our final list can be. And the more extensive.

The second year's list was similar to the first. It included eight works, one winner and seven on the short list. One came from outside the field, but its main character was a woman who was gradually turning herself into a cyborg, so it certainly fell under our purview.

The third year the list exploded in size: thirty-four books and stories were mentioned, and while most of them came from sf sources, several were from literary small presses. The first two juries had chosen winners and short lists. This jury identified one winner and a ten-piece short list, then added a "long list" of twenty-three more items. The long list contained stories that the jurors liked but didn't feel explored gender, or that left some jurors cold but that other jurors loved, or that were valuable in some way to the ongoing conversation about gender in science fiction. This also gave that jury the opportunity to include some novels that were not really eligible for the award: a thriller that looked like sf but may have turned out to be non-sf in the end, a historical novel with a fantasy feel. Not every jury since then has come up with a long list, but most do. One, maybe a bit mathematically challenged, had twenty-six stories on its short list and twenty on its long list.

The 1994 jury snuck a piece of nonfiction onto its short list: the jurors recommended Ursula K. Le Guin's collection *A Fisherman of the Inland Sea*, particularly for the title story (actually entitled "Another Story," and included in volume 2 of this anthology series) and Le Guin's introduction. (We anthology editors considered running that introduction in our first volume, but ended up with a different — though similar — essay by her instead.)

In 1996, the jury was particularly wide reaching, including two mainstream novels on its short list: Fred Chappell's *Farewell, I'm Bound to Leave You* (actually, only one segment of the novel, which did have a fantasy element) and Sue Woolfe's *Leaning Towards Infinity*, about mother and daughter mathematicians (a science, if not a science fictional, element).

That seemed to empower other juries to include mainstream works; the object, after all, is to point people to good stories. The gay characters on a Caribbean island in Shani Mootoo's *Cereus Blooms at Night* were praised by the 1997 jury as "people we never see in the genre, each with stories we would have never thought to tell." That's expanding "gender in science fiction" in a completely different way. The 2000 jury read David Ebershoff's *The Danish Girl*, a novel based on the life of the first male-to-female transsexual, because it was reputed to contain magical realism. (A couple paragraphs, maybe. No way to justify it for a genre award, but such an excellent novel that onto the short list it went.) Neither of these books was written by a genre author or marketed to a genre audience, but because we listed them, members of the Tiptree Award audience have been able to enjoy and be moved by novels they otherwise may not have known about.

The 2002 jury included Karen Joy Fowler's "What I Didn't See" on its short list (and we included it in *Anthology 1*). The controversy over whether this story, which also won the Nebula Award from the Science Fiction and Fantasy Writers of America, was sf or mainstream led to huge online discussions and even entire convention panels.

Along with the non-sf novels that juries wanted to reward for their exploration of gender, the 1998 jurors found an sf story — Ted Chiang's "Story of Your Life" — that they loved so much that they placed it on the short list even though its gender content was slim. "Not a Tiptree winner," they said, "because it is not concerned to explore the concepts of gender — but the head spins when you wonder what might have happened if it did."

Young adult novels are currently experiencing a publishing boom, and have been showing up on our lists at least since 1995, when Julie Haydon's *Lines Upon the Skin* was on the long list. The 2005 jury even longlisted a mainstream young adult novel, *Luna* by Julie Anne Peters, about a girl and her transgendered brother, because they were sure that people who read Tiptree Award-recommended fiction would enjoy it.

We don't consider movies or other media, but we have recommended one comic book: Bryan Talbot's *The Tale of One Bad Rat* (1996 long list). Interestingly, Talbot's story follows our current theme and is without any real sf or fantasy elements: a victim of sexual abuse runs away from her family and has adventures paralleling those of Beatrix Potter and her characters.

There is a music CD related to one of this year's short-listed works. *Misfortune* is Wesley Stace's first novel, but he has been playing folk music since the 1980s under the name John Wesley Harding. He released a CD called *Songs from Misfortune* (as by the Love Hall Tryst), which contains the songs that are sung by various characters throughout the novel. The CD material doesn't share the gender confusion of the novel, so it is not a Tiptree Award item on its own, but it's worth mentioning.

When we started out, we wanted to bring notice to stories that celebrated gender diversity in ways that only science fiction and fantasy could — and to encourage more such stories to be written. At first, these stories were easy to identify, but over time some people feel the gender issues have become less what the stories were about and more woven into the background. So the question was asked if maybe we hadn't won our war and should just retire. Or maybe we should expand our scope into the full range of race/class/gender concerns.

While we have discussed these issues among ourselves at length (see the introduction to last year's anthology), so far we are still happy with what we (and the Secret Feminist Cabal that has grown up around us) are accomplishing. We're also pleased to see other groups emerge from the WisCon DNA soup, just as we did. Some years back it was Broad Universe, a group devoted to promoting women science fiction writers. More recently, it was the Carl Brandon Society, which looks at race and culture the way we look at gender. (More on them later in the book.)

The 1999 jury wanted to include a nonfiction book — *Biological Exuberance* by Bruce Bagemihl, a natural history of homosexual behavior in animals — however, the Tiptree motherboard asked them to limit themselves to sf and fantasy. The 2004 jury figured out a way to handle that, and added a new category to the award listings: Special Mention. They included *Changing Ones* by Will Roscoe, an anthropological study of gender diversity among Native Americans; and *Stars in My Pocket Like Grains of Sand*, a 1984 novel by Samuel R. Delany that had been reissued in 2004. (Is it just coincidence that the jury that founded the long list and the jury that added the Special Mentions both had Ursula Le Guin on them?)

The 2005 jury also identified two Special Mentions: *Writing the Other* by Nisi Shawl and Cynthia Ward, based on the workshop they have designed on writing characters from other cultures; and the *regender.com* website, which will take any webpage and change the genders of everyone mentioned on it.

A website now. What new worlds are left to conquer?

Ah, but the 2005 jury wasn't through yet.

The 2005 jury included an unfinished piece of slash fanfiction on its long list: "Arcana" by Emily Brunson. "Fanfiction," in the current use of the term, is unauthorized fiction about someone else's characters. The "slash" subgenre portrays those characters in homosexual relationships that did not exist in the original stories. (This is traced back to stories about Kirk/Spock in the 1970s. See the slash there?) Sometimes the characters are even from different sources. In "Arcana," Severus Snape from the Harry Potter novels impregnates Nick Stokes from csi: *Crime Scene Investigation*.

The appearance of this story on the long list caused a bit of an uproar. As fanfiction is not authorized by the copyright holders of the original works, most of its creators prefer to stay out of the public eye. But twice this year fanfic was lit up for all to see. First, one writer printed up copies of her *Star Wars* novel and offered it for sale. That novel was available on Amazon for a week or so before Lucasfilm and other fanfic writers got it removed. Then, just a little bit later, our long list was publicized.

We heard from everybody. We heard from outside the fanfic field that we shouldn't promote copyright violations. We heard from inside it that we shouldn't be drawing attention to it. We heard that we should have waited until all the chapters were published. We heard that if indeed we wanted to celebrate what they were doing, we should have spent time researching the field and finding the best possible piece of fanfic to recommend, rather than a piece that was written for a specific limited audience.

We heard a lot of people talking about the Tiptree Award, which is what we really want. We don't go out of our way to be controversial, but we don't shy away from it, either. We know that not everybody is going to agree with our decisions all the time. People have questioned how we run the award and what the juries select, and we're okay with that. We even prefer it that way. We want to challenge people, and we want others to challenge us.

We want to change the world, one good story at a time.

The James Tiptree Award Anthology 3

Have Not Have

Geoff Ryman

"Have Not Have," which was originally published as a short story in 2001, became the first chapter of Geoff Ryman's *Air*, this year's winner of the Tiptree Award, as well as the Arthur C. Clarke Award, the British Science Fiction Award, and the Canadian Sunburst Award. Interesting in itself, it only hints at the richness of this remarkable novel. After the arrival of the Internet in her small Central Asian village, Chung Mae has her life change in every possible way. The new technology threatens her fashion consultant business. The death of a neighbor threatens her mental stability. An affair threatens her marriage and her social standing in the village. An impossible biological event threatens her physical well-being.

Women are frequently innovative entrepreneurs in isolated areas like Ryman's imaginary Karzistan, while men often feel honor bound to continue the traditional ways. Amid all the national, cultural, and technological turmoil around her, Mae has to determine which boundaries she must cross, which she must crush, and which she must shore up. While some people try to help her, others stand in her way — either because they want to put her back in her place, or because they oppose the change she is working with, or because they want for themselves the place she's trying to carve out in the new world rushing toward them.

Mae lived in the last village in the world to go online. After that, everyone else went on Air.

Mae was the village's fashion expert. She advised on makeup, sold cosmetics, and provided good dresses. Every farmer's wife needed at least one good dress.

Mae would sketch what was being worn in the capital. She would always add a special touch: a lime-green scarf with sequins; or a lacy ruffle with colorful embroidery. A good dress was for display. "We are a happier people and we can wear these gay colors," Mae would advise.

"Yes, that is true," her customer might reply, entranced that fashion expressed their happy culture. "In the photographs, the Japanese women all look so solemn."

"So full of themselves," said Mae, and lowered her head and scowled, and she and her customer would laugh, feeling as sophisticated as anyone in the world.

Mae got her ideas as well as her mascara and lipsticks from her trips to the town. It was a long way and she needed to be driven. When Sunni Haseem offered to drive her down in exchange for a fashion expedition, Mae had to agree. Apart from anything else, Mae had a wedding dress to collect.

Sunni herself was from an old village family, but her husband was a beefy brute from farther down the hill. He puffed on cigarettes and his tanned fingers were as thick and weathered as the necks of turtles. In the backseat with Mae, Sunni giggled and prodded and gleamed with the thought of visiting town with her friend and confidante who was going to unleash her beauty secrets.

Mae smiled and whispered, promising much. "I hope my source will be present today," she said. "She brings me my special colors, you cannot get them anywhere else. I don't ask where she gets them." Mae lowered her eyes and her voice. "I think her husband..."

A dubious gesture, meaning that perhaps the goods were stolen, stolen from — who knows? — supplies meant for foreign diplomats? The tips of Mae's fingers rattled once, in provocation, across her client's arm.

The town was called Yeshibozkent, which meant Green Valley City. It was now approached through corridors of raw apartment blocks set on beige desert soil. It had billboards, a new jail, discos with mirror balls, illuminated shop signs, and Toyota jeeps that belched out blue smoke.

The town center was as Mae remembered it from childhood. Traditional wooden houses crowded crookedly together. Wooden shingles covered the roofs and gables. The shop signs were tiny, faded, and sometimes hand-lettered. The old market square was still full of peasants selling vegetables laid out on mats. Middle-aged men still played chess outside tiny cafes; youths still prowled in packs.

There was still the public-address system. The address system barked out news and music from the top of the electricity poles. Its sounds drifted over the city, announcing public events or new initiatives against drug dealers. It told of progress on the new highway, and boasted of the well known entertainers who were visiting the town.

Mr. Haseem parked near the market, and the address system seemed to enter Mae's lungs, like cigarette smoke, perfume, or hairspray. She stepped out of the van and breathed it in. The excitement of being in the city trembled in her belly. The address system made Mae's spirits rise as much as the bellowing of shoppers, farmers, and donkeys; as much as the smell of raw petrol and cut greenery and drains. She and her middle-aged client looked at each other and gasped and giggled at themselves.

"Now," Mae said, stroking Sunni's hair, her cheek. "It is time for a complete makeover. Let's really do you up. I cannot do as good a workup in the hills."

Mae took her client to Halat's, the same hairdresser as Sunni might have gone to anyway. But Mae was greeted by Halat with cries and smiles and kisses on the cheek. That implied a promise that Mae's client would get special treatment. There was a pretense of consultancy. Mae offered advice, comments, cautions. Careful! — she has such delicate skin! The hair could use more shaping there. And Halat hummed as if perceiving what had been hidden before and then agreed to give the client what she would otherwise have had. But Sunni's nails were soaking, and she sat back in the center of attention, like a queen.

All of this allowed the hairdresser to charge more. Mae had never pressed her luck and asked for a cut. Something beady in Halat's eyes told Mae there would be no point. What Mae got out of it was standing, and that would lead to more work later.

With cucumbers over her eyes, Sunni was safely trapped. Mae announced, "I just have a few errands to run. You relax and let all cares fall away." She disappeared before Sunni could protest.

Mae ran to collect the dress. A disabled girl, a very good seamstress called Miss Soo, had opened up a tiny shop of her own.

Miss Soo was grateful for any business, poor thing, skinny as a rail and twisted. After the usual greetings, Miss Soo shifted around and hobbled and dragged her way to the back of the shop to fetch the dress. Her feet hissed sideways across the uneven concrete floor. Poor little thing, Mae thought. How can she sew?

Yet Miss Soo had a boyfriend in the fashion business — *genuinely* in the fashion business, far away in the capital city, Balshang. The girl often showed Mae his photograph. It was like a magazine photograph. The boy was very handsome, with a shiny shirt and coiffed-up hair. She kept saying she was saving up money to join him. It was a mystery to Mae what such a boy was doing with a cripple for a girlfriend. Why did he keep contact with her? Publicly Mae would say to friends of the girl: It is the miracle of love, what a good heart he must have. Otherwise she kept her own counsel which was this: You would be very wise not to visit him in Balshang.

The boyfriend sent Miss Soo the patterns of dresses, photographs, magazines, or even whole catalogues. There was one particularly treasured thing; a showcase publication. The cover was like the lid of a box, and it showed in full color the best of the nation's fashion design.

Models so rich and thin they looked like ghosts. They looked half asleep, as if the only place they carried the weight of their wealth was on their eyelids. It was like looking at Western or Japanese women, and yet these were their own people, so long-legged, so modern, so ethereal, as if they were made of air.

Mae hated the clothes. They looked like washing-up towels. Oatmeal or gray in one color, and without a trace of adornment.

Mae sighed with lament. "Why do these rich women go about in their underwear?"

The girl shuffled back with the dress, past piles of unsold oatmeal cloth. Miss Soo had a skinny face full of teeth, and she always looked like she was staring ahead in fear. "If you are rich you have no need to try to look rich." Her voice was soft. She made Mae feel like a peasant without meaning to. She made Mae yearn to escape herself, to be someone else, for the child was effortlessly talented, somehow effortlessly in touch with the outside world.

"Ah, yes," Mae sighed. "But my clients, you know, they live in the hills." She shared a conspiratorial smile with the girl. "Their taste! Speaking of which, let's have a look at my wedding cake of a dress."

The dress was actually meant to look like a cake, all pink and white sugar icing, except that it kept moving all by itself. White wires with Styrofoam bobbles on the ends were surrounded with clouds of white netting.

"Does it need to be quite so busy?" the girl asked doubtfully, encouraged too much by Mae's smile.

"I know my clients," replied Mae, coolly. This is, at least, she thought, a dress that makes some effort. She inspected the work. The needlework was delicious, as if the white cloth were cream that had flowed together. The poor creature could certainly sew, even when she hated the dress.

"That will be fine," said Mae, and made a move towards her purse.

"You are so kind!" murmured Miss Soo, bowing slightly.

Like Mae, Miss Soo was of Chinese extraction. That was meant to make no difference, but somehow it did. Mae and Miss Soo knew what to expect of each other.

The dress was packed in brown paper and carefully tied so it would not crease. There were farewells, and Mae scurried back to the hairdressers. Sunni was only just finished, hairspray and scent rising off her like steam.

"This is the dress," said Mae and peeled back part of the paper, to give Halet and Sunni a glimpse of the tulle and styrofoam.

"Oh!" the women said, as if all that white were clouds, in dreams.

And Halat was paid. There were smiles and nods and compliments and then they left.

Outside the shop, Mae breathed out as though she could now finally speak her mind. "Oh! She is good, that little viper, but you have to watch her, you have to make her work. Did she give you proper attention?"

"Oh, yes, very special attention. I am lucky to have you for a friend," said Sunni. "Let me pay you something for your trouble."

Mae hissed through her teeth. "No, no, I did nothing, I will not hear of it." It was a kind of ritual.

There was no dream in finding Sunni's surly husband. Mr. Haseem was red-faced, half drunk in a club with unvarnished walls and a television.

"You spend my money," he declared. His eyes were on Mae.

"My friend Mae makes no charges," snapped Sunni.

"She takes something from what they charge you." Mr. Haseem glowered like a thunderstorm.

"She makes them charge me less, not more," replied Sunni, her face going like stone.

The two women exchanged glances. Mae's eyes could say: How can you bear it, a woman of culture like you?

It is my tragedy, came the reply, aching out of the ashamed eyes.

So they sat while the husband sobered up and watched television. Mae contemplated the husband's hostility to her, and what might lie behind it.

On the screen, the local female newsreader talked: Talents, such people were called. She wore a red dress with a large gold brooch. Something had been done to her hair to make it stand up in a sweep before falling away. She was groomed as smooth as ice. She chattered in a high voice, perky through a battery of tiger's teeth.

"She goes to Halat's as well," Mae whispered to Sunni. Weather, maps, shots of the honored President and the full cabinet one by one, making big decisions.

The men in the club chose what movie they wanted. Since the satellites, they could do that. Satellites had ruined visits to the town. Before, it used to be that the men were made to sit through something the children or families might also like to watch, so you got everyone together for the watching of the television. The clubs had to be more polite. Now, women hardly saw TV at all and the clubs were full of drinking. The men chose another kung fu movie. Mae and Sunni endured it, sipping Coca-Cola. It became apparent that Mr. Haseem would not buy them dinner.

Finally, late in the evening, Mr. Haseem loaded himself into the van. Enduring, unstoppable, and quite dangerous, he drove them back up into the mountains, weaving across the middle of the road.

"You make a lot of money out of all this," Mr. Haseem said to Mae.

"I…I make a little something. I try to maintain the standards of the village. I do not want people to see us as peasants. Just because we live on the high road."

Sunni's husband barked out a laugh. "We are peasants!" Then he added, "You do it for the money."

Sunni sighed in embarrassment. And Mae smiled a hard smile to herself in the darkness. You give yourself away, Sunni's-man. You want my husband's land. You want him to be your dependent. And you don't like your wife's money coming to me to prevent it. You want to make both me and my husband your slaves.

It is a strange thing to spend four hours in the dark listening to an engine roar with a man who seeks to destroy you.

In late May, school ended.

There were no fewer than six girls graduating and each one of them needed a new dress. Miss Soo was making two of them; Mae would have to do the others, but she needed to buy the cloth. She had a mobile phone, a potent fashion symbol. But she needed another trip to Yeshibozkent.

Mr. Wing was going to town to collect a new television set for the village. It was going to be connected to the Net. Mr. Wing was something of a politician in his way. He had applied for a national grant to set up a company to provide information services to the village. Swallow Communications, he called himself, and the villagers said it would make him rich.

Kwan, Mr. Wing's wife, was one of Mae's favorite women: She was intelligent and sensible; there was less dissembling with her. Mae enjoyed the drive.

Mr. Wing parked the van in the market square. As Mae reached into the back for her hat, she heard the public-address system. The voice of the Talent was squawking.

"...*a tremendous advance for culture,*" the Talent said. "*Now the Green Valley is no farther from the center of the world than Paris, Singapore, or Tokyo.*"

Mae sniffed, "Hmm. Another choice on this fishing net of theirs."

Wing stood outside the van, ramrod-straight in his brown and-tan town shirt. "I want to hear this," he said, smiling slightly, taking nips of smoke from his cigarette.

Kwan fanned the air. "Four modern wires say that smoking is dangerous. I wish you would follow all this news you hear."

"Sssh!" he insisted.

The bright female voice still enthused: "*Previously all such advances left the Valley far behind because of wiring and machines. This advance will be in the air we breathe. This new thing will be like TV in your head. All you need is the wires in the human mind.*"

Kwan gathered up her things. "Some nonsense or another," she murmured.

"*Next Sunday, there will be a Test. The Test will happen in Tokyo and Singapore but also here in the Valley at the same time. What Tokyo sees and hears, we will see and hear. Tell everyone you know: Next Sunday, there will be a Test. There is no need for fear, alarm, or panic.*"

Mae listened then. There would certainly be a need for fear and panic if the address system said there was none.

"What test, what kind of test? What? What?" the women demanded of the husband.

Mr. Wing played the relaxed, superior male. He chuckled. "Ho-ho, now you are interested, yes?"

Another man looked up and grinned. "You should watch more TV," he called. He was selling radishes and shook them at the women.

Kwan demanded, "What are they talking about?"

"They will be able to put TV in our heads," said the husband, smiling. He looked down, thinking, perhaps wistfully, of his own new venture. "There has been talk of nothing else on the TV for the last year. But I didn't think it would happen."

All the old market was buzzing like flies on carrion, as if it were still news to them. Two youths in strange puffy clothes spun on their heels and slapped each other's palms, in a gesture that Mae had seen only once or twice before. An old granny waved it all away and kept on accusing a dealer of short measures.

Mae felt grave doubts. "TV in our heads. I don't want TV in my head." She thought of viper newsreaders and kung fu.

Wing said, "It's not just TV. It is more than TV. It is the whole world."

"What does that mean?"

"It will be the Net — only, in your head. The fools and drunks in these parts know nothing about it; it is a word they use to sound modern. But you go to the cafes, you see it. The Net is all things." He began to falter.

"Explain! How can one thing be all things?"

There was a crowd of people gathering to listen.

"Everything is on it. You will see on our new TV. It will be a Net TV." Kwan's husband did not really know, either.

The routine had been soured. Halat the hairdresser was in a very strange mood, giggly, chattery, her teeth clicking together as if it were cold.

"Oh, nonsense," she said, when Mae went into her usual performance. "Is this for a wedding? For a feast?"

"No," said Mae. "It is for my special friend."

The little hussy put both hands either side of her mouth as if in awe. "Oh! Uh!"

"Are you going to do a special job for her or not?" Mae demanded. Her eyes were able to say: I see no one else in your shop.

Oh, how the girl would have loved to say, I am very busy — if you need something special, come back tomorrow. But money spoke. Halat slightly amended her tone. "Of course. For you."

"I bring my friends to you regularly because you do such good work for them."

"Of course," the child said. "It is all this news; it makes me forget myself."

Mae drew herself up, and looked fierce, forbidding — in a word, older. Her entire body said: *Do not forget yourself again.* The way the child dug away at Kwan's hair with the long comb-handle said back: *Peasants.*

The rest of the day did not go well. Mae felt tired, distracted. She made a terrible mistake and, with nothing else to do, accidentally took Kwan to the place where she bought her lipsticks.

"Oh! It is a treasure trove!" exclaimed Kwan.

Idiot, thought Mae to herself. Kwan was good-natured and would not take advantage. But, if she talked. . . ! There would be clients who would not take such a good-natured attitude, not to have been shown this themselves.

"I do not take everyone here," whispered Mae, "hmm? This is for special friends only."

Kwan was good-natured, but very far from stupid. Mae remembered, in school Kwan had always been best at letters, best at maths. Kwan was pasting on false eyelashes in a mirror and said, very simply and quickly, "Don't worry, I won't tell anyone."

And that was far too simple and direct. As if Kwan were saying: Fashion expert, we all know you. She even looked around and smiled at Mae, and batted her now-huge eyes, as if mocking fashion itself.

"Not for you," said Mae. "The false eyelashes. You don't need them."

The dealer wanted a sale. "Why listen to her?" she asked Kwan.

Because, thought Mae, I buy fifty riels' worth of cosmetics from you a year.

"My friend is right," said Kwan, to the dealer. The sad fact was that Kwan was almost magazine-beautiful anyway, except for her teeth and gums. "Thank you for showing me this," said Kwan, and touched Mae's arm. "Thank you," she said to the dealer, having bought one lowly lipstick.

Mae and the dealer glared at each other, briefly. I'll go somewhere else next time, Mae promised herself.

The worst came last. Kwan's ramrod husband was not a man for drinking. He was in the promised cafe at the promised time, sipping tea, having had a haircut and a professional shave.

A young man called Sloop, a tribesman, was with him. Sloop was a telephone engineer and thus a member of the aristocracy as far as Mae was concerned. He was going to wire up their new TV. Sloop said, with a woman's voice, "It will work like your mobile phone, no cable. We can't lay cable in our mountains. But before MMN, there was not enough space on the line for the TV." He might as well have been talking English, for all Mae understood him.

Mr. Wing maintained his cheerfulness. "Come," he said to the ladies, "I will show you what this is all about."

He went to the communal TV and turned it on with an expert's flourish. Up came not a movie or the local news, but a screenful of other buttons.

"You see? You can choose what you want. You can choose anything." And he touched the screen.

Up came the local Talent, still baring her perfect teeth. She piped in a high, enthusiastic voice that was meant to appeal to men and Bright Young Things:

"Hello. Welcome to the Airnet Information Service. For too long the world has been divided into information haves and have-nots." She held up one hand towards the heavens of information and the other out towards the citizens of the Green Valley, inviting them to consider themselves as have-nots.

"Those in the developed world can use their TVs to find any information they need at any time. They do this through the Net."

Incomprehension followed. There were circles and squares linked by wires in diagrams. Then they jumped up into the sky, into the air — only the air was full of arcing lines. "The field," they called it, but it was nothing like a field. In Karzistani, it was called the Lightning-Flow, Compass-Point Yearning Field. "Everywhere in the world." Then the lightning flow was shown striking people's heads. "There have been many medical tests to show this is safe."

"Hitting people with lightning?" Kwan asked in crooked amusement. "That does sound so safe, doesn't it?"

"It's only the Formatting that uses the Yearning Field," said Sloop. "That happens only once. It makes a complete map of minds, and that's what exists in Air, and Air happens in other dimensions."

What?

"There are eleven dimensions," he began, and began to see the hopelessness of it. "They were left over after the Big Bang."

"I know what will interest you ladies," said her husband. And with another flourish, he touched the screen. "You'll be able to have this in your heads, whenever you want."

Suddenly the screen was full of cream color.

One of the capital's ladies spun on her high heel. She was wearing the best of the nation's fashion design. She was one of the ladies in Mae's secret treasure book.

"Oh!" Kwan breathed out. "Oh, Mae, look, isn't she lovely!"

"This channel shows nothing but fashion," said her husband.

"All the time?" Kwan exclaimed, and looked back at Mae in wonder. For a moment, she stared up at the screen, her own face reflected over those of the models. Then, thankfully, she became Kwan again. "Doesn't that get boring?"

Her husband chuckled. "You can choose something else. Anything else."

It was happening very quickly and Mae's guts churned faster than her brain to certain knowledge: Kwan and her husband would be fine with all this.

"Look," he said, "This is what two-way does. You can buy the dress."

Kwan shook her head in amazement. Then a voice said the price and Kwan gasped again. "Oh, yes, all I have to do is sell one of our four farms, and I can have a dress like that."

"I saw all that two years ago," said Mae. "It is too plain for the likes of us. We want people to see everything."

Kwan's face went sad. "That is because we are poor, back in the hills." It was the common yearning, the common forlorn knowledge.

Sometimes it had to cease, all the business-making, you had to draw a breath, because after all, you had known your people for as long as you had lived.

Mae said, "None of them are as beautiful as you are, Kwan." It was true, except for her teeth.

"Flattery-talk from a fashion expert," Kwan said lightly. But she took Mae's hand. Her eyes yearned up at the screen, as secret after secret was spilled like blood.

"With all this in our heads," Kwan said to her husband, "we won't need your TV."

It was a busy week.

It was not only the six dresses. For some reason, there was much extra business.

On Wednesday, Mae had a discreet morning call to make on Tsang Muhammed. Mae liked Tsang. She looked like a peach that was over-ripe, round and soft to the touch and very slightly wrinkled. Everything about her was off-kilter. She was Chinese with a religious Karz husband, who was ten years her senior. He was a Muslim who allowed — or perhaps could not prevent — his Chinese wife keeping a pig.

The family pig was in the front room being fattened: half the room was full of old shucks. The beast looked lordly and pleased with itself. Tsang's four-year-old son sat tamely beside it, feeding it the greener leaves, as if the animal could not find them for itself.

"Is it all right to talk?" Mae whispered, her eyes going sideways towards the boy.

"Who is it?" Mae mouthed.

Tsang simply waggled a finger.

So it was someone they knew. Mae suspected it was Kwan's oldest boy, Luk. Luk was sixteen, but he was kept in pressed white shirt and shorts like a baby. The shorts only showed he had hair on his football-player calves. His face was still round and soft and babylike but lately had been full of a new and different confusion.

"Tsang. Oh!" Mae gasped.

"Sssh," giggled Tsang, who was red as a radish. As if either of them could be certain what the other one meant. "I need a repair job!" So it was someone younger.

Almost certainly Kwan's handsome son.

"Well, they have to be taught by someone," whispered Mae.

Tsang simply dissolved into giggles. She could hardly stop laughing.

"I can do nothing for you. You certainly don't need redder cheeks," said Mae.

Tsang uttered a squawk of laughter.

"There is nothing like it for a woman's complexion." Mae pretended to put away the tools of her trade. "No, I can effect no improvement. Certainly I cannot compete with the effects of a certain young man."

"Nothing... Nothing..." gasped Tsang. "Nothing like a good prick!"

Mae howled in mock outrage and Tsang squealed, and both squealed and pressed down their cheeks, and shushed each other. Mae noted exactly which part of the cheeks were blushing so she would know where color should go later.

As Mae painted, Tsang explained how she escaped her husband's view. "I tell him that I have to get fresh garbage for the pig," whispered Tsang. "So I go out with the empty bucket..."

"And come back with a full bucket," Mae said airily.

"Oh!" Tsang pretended to hit her. "You are as bad as me!"

"What do you think I get up to in the City?" asked Mae, who arched an eyebrow, lying.

Love, she realized later, walking back down the track and clutching her cloth bag of secrets, love is not mine. She thought of the boy's naked calves.

On Thursday, Kwan wanted her teeth to be flossed. This was new. Kwan had never been vain before. This touched Mae, because it meant her friend was getting older. Or was it because she had seen the TV models with their impossible teeth? How were real people supposed to have teeth like that?

Kwan's handsome son ducked as he entered, wearing his shorts, showing smooth, full thighs, and a secret swelling about his groin.

He ducked as he went out again. Guilty, Mae thought. For certain it is him.

She laid Kwan's head back over a pillow with a towel under her.

Should she not warn her friend to keep watch on her son? Which friend should she betray? To herself, she shook her head; there was no possibility of choosing between them. She could only keep silent. "Just say if I hit a nerve," Mae said.

Kwan had teeth like an old horse, worn, brown, black. Her gums were scarred from a childhood disease, and her teeth felt loose as Mae rubbed the floss between them. She had a neat little bag into which she flipped each strand after it was used.

It was Mae's job to talk: Kwan could not. Mae said she did not know how she would finish the dresses in time. The girl's mothers were never satisfied, each wanted her daughter to have the best. Well, the richest would have the best in the end because they bought the best cloth. Oh! Some of them had asked to pay for the fabric later! As if Mae could afford to buy cloth for six dresses without being paid!

"They all think their fashion expert is a woman of wealth." Mae sometimes found the whole pretense funny. Kwan's eyes crinkled into a smile; but they were also moist from pain. It was hurting.

"You should have told me your teeth were sore," said Mae, and inspected the gums. In the back, they were raw.

If you were rich, Kwan, you would have good teeth; rich people keep their teeth, and somehow keep them white, not brown. Mae pulled stray hair out of Kwan's face.

"I will have to pull some of them," Mae said quietly. "Not today, but soon."

Kwan closed her mouth and swallowed. "I will be an old lady," she said, and managed a smile.

"A granny with a thumping stick."

"Who always hides her mouth when she laughs."

Both of them chuckled. "And thick glasses that make your eyes look like a fish."

Kwan rested her hand on her friend's arm. "Do you remember,

years ago? We would all get together and make little boats, out of paper or shells. And we would put candles in them, and send them out on the ditches."

"Yes!" Mae sat forward. "We don't do that anymore."

"We don't wear pillows and a cummerbund anymore, either."

There had once been a festival of wishes every year, and the canals would be full of little glowing candles, that floated for a while and then sank with a hiss. "We would always wish for love," said Mae, remembering.

Next morning, Mae mentioned the wish boats to her neighbor, Old Mrs. Tung. Mae visited her nearly every day. Mrs. Tung had been her teacher during the flurry of what had passed for Mae's schooling. She was ninety years old, and spent her days turned towards the tiny loft window that looked out over the valley. She was blind, her eyes pale and unfocused. She could see nothing through the window. Perhaps she breathed in the smell of the fields.

When Mae reminded her about the boats of wishes, Mrs. Tung said, "And we would roast pumpkin seeds. And the ones we didn't eat, we would turn into jewelry. Do you remember that?"

Mrs. Tung was still beautiful, at least in Mae's eyes. Mrs. Tung's face had grown even more delicate in extreme old age, like the skeleton of a cat, small and fine. She gave an impression of great merriment, by continually laughing at not very much. She repeated herself.

"I remember the day you first came to me," she said. Before Shen's village school, Mrs. Tung had kept a nursery, there in their courtyard. "I thought: 'Is that the girl whose father has been killed? She is so pretty.' I remember you looking at all my dresses hanging on the line."

"And you asked me which one I liked best."

Mrs. Tung giggled. "Oh yes, and you said the butterflies." Blindness meant that she could only see the past. "We had tennis courts, you know. Here in Kizuldah."

"Did we?" Mae pretended she had not heard that before.

"Oh yes, oh yes. When the Chinese were here, just before the

Communists came. Part of the Chinese army was here, and they built them. We all played tennis, in our school uniforms."

The Chinese officers had supplied the tennis rackets. The traces of the courts were broken and grassy, where Mr. Pin now ran his car-repair business.

"Oh! They were all so handsome, all the village girls were so in love." Mrs. Tung chuckled. "I remember, I couldn't have been more than ten years old, and one of them adopted me, because he said I looked like his daughter. He sent me a teddy bear after the war." She chuckled and shook her head. "I was too old for teddy bears by then. But I told everyone it meant we were getting married. Oh!" Mrs. Tung shook her head at her foolishness. "I wish I had married him," she confided, feeling naughty. She always said that.

Mrs. Tung, even now, had the power to make Mae feel calm and protected. Mrs. Tung had come from a family of educated people and once had had a house full of books. The books had all been lost in a flood many years ago, but Mrs. Tung could still recite to Mae the poems of the Turks, the Karz, or the Chinese. She had sat the child Mae on her lap and rocked her. She could still recite now, the same poems.

"*Listen to the reed flute,*" she began now, "*How it tells a tale!*" Her old blind face swayed with the words, the beginning of *The Mathnawi*. "*This noise of the reed is fire, it is not the wind.*"

Mae yearned. "Oh, I wish I remembered all those poems!" When she saw Mrs. Tung, she could visit the best of her childhood.

Mae then visited the Ozdemirs for a fitting.

The mother was called Hatijah, and her daughter was Sezen. Hatijah was a shy, slow little thing, terrified of being overcharged by Mae, and of being underserved. Hatijah's low, old stone house was tangy with the smells of burning charcoal, sweat, dung, and the constantly stewing tea. From behind the house came a continual, agonized bleating from the family goat. It needed milking. The poor animal's voice was going raw and harsh. Hatijah seemed not to hear it. Hatijah had four children, and a skinny shiftless husband who probably had worms. Half of the main room was heaped up with corncobs. The youngest of her babes wore only shirts and sat with their dirty naked bottoms on the corn.

Oh, this was a filthy house. Perhaps Hatijah was a bit simple. She offered Mae roasted corn. Not with your child's wet shit on it, thought Mae, but managed to be polite.

The daughter, Sezen, stomped in barefoot for her fitting, wearing the dress. It was a shade of lemon yellow that seared the eyes. Sezen was a tough, raunchy brute of a girl and kept rolling her eyes at everything: at her nervous mother, at Mae's efforts to make the yellow dress hang properly, at anything either one of the adults said.

"Does…will…tomorrow…" Sezen's mother tried to begin.

Yes, thought Mae with some bitterness, tomorrow Sezen will finally have to wash. Sezen's bare feet were slashed with infected cuts.

"What my mother means is," Sezen said, "will you make up my face?" Sezen blinked, her unkempt hair making her eyes itch.

"Yes, of course," said Mae, curtly to a younger person who was so forward.

"What, with all those other girls on the same day? For someone as lowly as us?"

The girl's eyes were angry. Mae pulled in a breath.

"No one can make you feel inferior without you agreeing with them first," said Mae. It was something Old Mrs. Tung had once told Mae when she herself was poor and famished for magic.

"Take off the dress," Mae said. "I'll have to take it back for finishing."

Sezen stepped out of it, right there, naked on the dirt floor. Hatijah did not chastise her, but offered Mae tea. Because she had refused the corn, Mae had to accept the tea. At least that would be boiled.

Hatijah scuttled off to the black kettle and her daughter leaned back in full insolence, her supposedly virgin pubes plucked as bare as the baby's bottom.

Mae fussed with the dress, folding it, so she would have somewhere else to look. The daughter just stared. Mae could take no more. "Do you want people to see you? Go put something on!"

"I don't have anything else," said Sezen.

Her other sisters had gone shopping in the town for graduation gifts. They would have taken all the family's good dresses.

"You mean you have nothing else you will deign to put on." Mae glanced at Hatijah: she really should not be having to do this woman's work for her. "You have other clothes, old clothes — put them on."

The girl stared at her with even greater insolence.

Mae lost her temper. "I do not work for pigs. You have paid nothing so far for this dress. If you stand there like that, I will leave, now, and the dress will not be yours. Wear what you like to the graduation. Come to it naked like a whore, for all I care."

Sezen turned and slowly walked towards the side room.

Hatijah, the mother, still squatted over the kettle, boiling more water to dilute the stew of leaves. She lived on tea and burnt corn that was more usually fed to cattle. Her cow's-eyes were averted. Untended, the family goat still made noises like a howling baby.

Mae sat and blew out air from stress. This week! She looked at Hatijah's dress. It was a patchwork assembly of her husband's old shirts, beautifully stitched. Hatijah could sew. Mae could not. With all these changes, Mae was going to have to find something else to do beside sketch photographs of dresses. She had a sudden thought.

"Would you be interested in working for me?" Mae asked. Hatijah looked fearful and pleased and said she would have to ask her husband. In the end she agreed to do the finishing on three of the dresses.

Everything is going to have to change, thought Mae, as if to convince herself.

That night Mae worked nearly to dawn on the other three dresses. Her noisy old sewing machine sat silent in the corner. It was fine for rough work, but not for finishing, not for graduation dresses.

The bare electric light glared down at her like a headache, as Mae's husband Joe snored. Above them in the loft, Joe's brother Siao and his father snored, too, as they had done for twenty years. In the morning they would scamper out to the water butt to wash, holding towels over their y-fronts.

Mae looked into Joe's open mouth like a mystery. When he was sixteen, Joe had been handsome — in the context of the village — wild and clever. They'd been married a year when she first went to Yeshibozkent with him, where he worked between harvests building a house. She saw the clever city man, an acupuncturist who had money. She saw her husband bullied, made to look foolish, asked questions for which he had no answer. The acupuncturist made Joe do the work again. In Yeshibozkent, her handsome husband was a dolt.

Here they were, both of them now middle-aged. Their son Lung was a major in the army. They had sent him to Balshang. He mailed Mae parcels of orange skins for potpourri; he sent cards and matches in picture boxes. He had met some city girl. Lung would not be back. Their daughter Ying had been pulled into Lung's orbit. She had gone to stay with him, met trainee officers, and eventually married one. She lived in an army housing compound, in a bungalow with a toilet.

At this hour of the morning, Mae could hear their little river, rushing down the steep slope to the valley. Then a door slammed in the North End. Mae knew who it would be: their Muerain, Mr. Shenyalar. He would be walking across the village to the mosque. A dog started to bark at him; Mrs. Doh's, by the bridge.

Mae knew that Kwan would be cradled in her husband's arms, and that Kwan was beautiful because she was an Eloi tribeswoman. All the Eloi had fine features. Her husband Wing did not mind and no one now mentioned it. But Mae could see Kwan shiver now in her sleep. Kwan had dreams, visions, she had tribal blood, and it made her shift at night as if she had another, tribal life.

Mae knew that Kwan's clean and noble athlete son would be breathing like a moist baby in his bed, cradling his younger brother.

Without seeing them, Mae could imagine the moon and clouds over their village. The moon would be reflected shimmering on the water of the irrigation canals which had once borne their paper boats of wishes. There would be old candles, deep in the mud.

Then, the slow, sad voice of their Muerain began to sing. Even amplified, his voice was deep and soft, like pillows that allowed the unfaithful to sleep. In the byres, the lonely cows would be stirring. The beasts would walk themselves to the village square, for a lick of salt, and then wait to be herded down to valley pastures. In the evening, they would walk themselves home. Mae heard the first clanking of a cowbell.

At that moment something came into the room, something she did not want to see, something dark and whole like a black dog with froth around its mouth that sat in her corner and would not go away, nameless yet.

Mae started sewing faster.

The dresses were finished on time, all six, each a different color.

Mae ran barefoot in her shift to deliver them. The mothers bowed sleepily in greeting. The daughters were hopping with anxiety like water on a skillet.

It all went well. Under banners the children stood together, including Kwan's son Luk, Sezen, all ten children of the village, all smiles, all for a moment looking like an official poster of the future, brave, red-cheeked, with perfect teeth.

Teacher Shen read out each of their achievements. Sezen had none, except in animal husbandry, but she still collected her certificate to applause. And then Mae's friend Shen did something special.

He began to talk about a friend to all of the village, who had spent more time on this ceremony than anyone else, whose only aim was to bring a breath of beauty into this tiny village — the seamstress who worked only to adorn other people...

He was talking about her.

...One who was devoted to the daughters and mothers of rich and poor alike and who spread kindness and goodwill.

The whole village was applauding her, under the white clouds, the blue sky. All were smiling at her. Someone, Kwan perhaps, gave her a push from behind and she stumbled forward.

And her friend Shen was holding out a certificate for her.

"In our day, Mrs. Chung-ma'am," he said, "there were no schools for the likes of us, not after early childhood. So. This is a graduation certificate for you. From all your friends. It is in 'Fashion Studies.'"

There was applause. Mae tried to speak, and found that only fluttering sounds came out, and she saw the faces all in smiles, ranged around her, friends and enemies, cousins and non-kin alike.

"This is unexpected," she finally said, and they all chuckled. She looked at the high school certificate, surprised by the power it had, surprised that she still cared about her lack of education. She couldn't read it. "I do not do fashion as a student, you know."

They knew well enough that she did it for money and how precariously she balanced things.

Something stirred, like the wind in the clouds.

"After tomorrow, you may not need a fashion expert. After tomorrow, everything changes. They will give us TV in our heads, all the knowledge we want. We can talk to the President. We can pretend to order cars from Tokyo. We'll all be experts," she looked at her certificate, hand-lettered, so small.

Mae found she was angry, and her voice seemed to come from her belly, an octave lower.

"I'm sure that it is a good thing. I am sure the people who do this think they do a good thing. They worry about us, like we were children." Her eyes were like two hearts, pumping furiously. "We don't have time for TV or computers. We face sun, rain, wind, sickness, and each other. It is good that they want to help us." She wanted to shake her certificate; she wished it was one of them, who had upended everything. "But how dare they? How dare they call us have-nots?"

The Glass Bottle Trick

Nalo Hopkinson

Last year we published Hopkinson's essay "Looking for Clues." In this story, she (and her characters) are also looking for clues — looking in her home culture of the Caribbean, looking in the relationship of tribal magic to the modern world, looking in the world of nature (and nature affected by magic).

The air was full of storms, but they refused to break.

In the wicker rocking chair on the front veranda, Beatrice flexed her bare feet against the wooden slat floor, rocking slowly back and forth. Another sweltering rainy season afternoon. The arid heat felt as though all the oxygen had boiled out of the parched air to hang as looming rainclouds, waiting.

Oh, but she loved it like this. The hotter the day, the slower she would move, basking. She stretched her arms and legs out to better feel the luxuriant warmth, then guiltily sat up straight again. Samuel would scold if he ever saw her slouching like that. Stuffy Sammy. She smiled fondly, admiring the lacy patterns the sunlight threw on the floor as it filtered through the white gingerbread fretwork that trimmed the roof of their house.

"Anything more today, Mistress Powell? I finish doing the dishes." Gloria had come out of the house and was standing in front of her, wiping her chapped hands on her apron.

Beatrice felt the shyness come over her as it always did when she thought of giving the older woman orders. Gloria was older than Beatrice's mother. "Ah...no, I think that's everything, Gloria..."

Gloria quirked an eyebrow, crinkling her face like running a fork through molasses. "Then I go take the rest of the afternoon off. You and Mister Samuel should be alone tonight. Is time you tell him."

Beatrice gave an abortive, shamefaced "huh" of a laugh. Gloria had known from the start, she'd had so many babies of her own. She'd been mad to run to Samuel with the news from since. But Beatrice had already decided to tell Samuel. Well, almost decided. She felt irritated, like a child whose tricks have been found out. She swallowed the feeling. "I think you right, Gloria," she said, fighting for some dignity before the older woman. "Maybe…maybe I cook him a special meal, feed him up nice, then tell him."

"Well I say is time and past time you make him know. A picknie is a blessing to a family."

"For true," Beatrice agreed, making her voice sound as certain as she could.

"Later then, Mistress Powell." Giving herself the afternoon off, not even a by-your-leave, Gloria headed off to the maid's room at the back of the house to change into her street clothes. A few minutes later, she let herself out the garden gate.

"That seems like a tough book for a young lady of such tender years."

"Excuse me?" Beatrice threw a defensive cutting glare at the older man. He'd caught her off guard, though she'd seen his eyes following her ever since she entered the bookstore. "You have something to say to me?" She curled the Gray's Anatomy *possessively into the crook of her arm, price sticker hidden against her body. Two more months of saving before she could afford it.*

He looked shyly at her. "Sorry if I offended, Miss," he said. "My name is Samuel."

Would be handsome, if he'd chill out a bit. Beatrice's wariness thawed a little. Middle of the sun-hot day, and he wearing black wool jacket and pants. His crisp white cotton shirt was buttoned right up, held in place by a tasteful, unimaginative tie. So proper, Jesus. He wasn't that much older than she.

"Is just…you're so pretty, and it's the only thing I could think of to say to get you to speak to me."

Beatrice softened more at that, smiled for him, and played with the

*collar of her blouse. He didn't seem too bad, if you could look beyond the
stocious, starchy behavior.*

Beatrice doubtfully patted the slight swelling of her belly. Four
months. She was shy to give Samuel her news, but she was starting to
show. Silly to put it off, yes? Today she was going to make her husband
very happy, break that thin shell of mourning that still insulated him
from her. He never said so, but Beatrice knew that he still thought of
the wife he'd lost, and tragically, the one before that. She wished she
could make him warm up to life again.

Sunlight was flickering through the leaves of the guava tree in the
front yard. Beatrice inhaled the sweet smell of the sun-warmed fruit.
The tree's branches hung heavy with the pale yellow globes, smooth
and round as eggs. The sun reflected off the two blue bottles suspended in the tree, sending cobalt light dancing through the leaves.

When Beatrice first came to Sammy's house, she'd been puzzled
by the two bottles that were jammed onto branches of the guava tree.

"Is just my superstitiousness, darling," he'd told her. "You never
heard the old people say that if someone dies, you must put a bottle in
a tree to hold their spirit, otherwise it will come back as a duppy and
haunt you? A blue bottle. To keep the duppie cool, so it won't come at
you in hot anger for being dead."

Beatrice had heard something of the sort, but it was strange to
think of her Sammy as a superstitious man. He was too controlled
and logical for that. *Well, grief make somebody act in strange ways.* Maybe
the bottles gave him some comfort, made him feel that he'd kept some
essence of his poor wives near him.

*"That Samuel is nice. Respectable, hard-working. Not like all them
other ragamuffins you always going out with." Mummy picked up the
butcher knife and began expertly slicing the goat meat into cubes for
the curry.*

*Beatrice watched the red lumps of flesh part under the knife. Crim-
son liquid leaked onto the cutting board. She sighed, "But, Mummy,*

Samuel so boring! Michael and Clifton know how to have fun. All Samuel want to do is go for country drives. Always taking me away from other people."

"You should be studying your books, not having fun," her mother replied crossly.

Beatrice pleaded, "You well know I could do both, Mummy." Her mother just grunted.

Is only truth Beatrice was talking. Plenty men were always courting her, they flocked to her like birds, eager to take her dancing or out for a drink. But somehow she kept her marks up, even though it often meant studying right through the night, her head pounding and belly queasy from hangover while some man snored in the bed beside her. Mummy would kill her if she didn't get straight As for medical school. "You going have to look after yourself, Beatrice. Man not going do it for you. Them get their little piece of sweetness and then them bruk away."

"Two patty and a King Cola, please." The guy who'd given the order had a broad chest that tapered to a slim waist. Good face to look at, too. Beatrice smiled sweetly at him, made shift to gently brush his palm with her fingertips as she handed him the change.

A bird screeched from the guava tree; a tiny kiskedee, crying angrily, "Dit, dit, qu'est-ce qu'il dit!" A small snake was coiled around one of the upper branches, just withdrawing its head from the bird's nest. Its jaws were distended with the egg it had stolen. It swallowed the egg whole, throat bulging hugely with its meal. The bird hovered around the snake's head, giving its pitiful wail of, "Say, say, what's he saying!"

"Get away!" Beatrice shouted at the snake. It looked in the direction of the sound, but didn't back off. The gulping motion of its body as it forced the egg further down its own throat made Beatrice shudder. Then, oblivious to the fluttering of the parent bird, it arched its head over the nest again. Beatrice pushed herself to her feet and ran into the yard. "Hsst! Shoo! Come away from there!" But the snake took a second egg.

Sammy kept a long pole with a hook at one end leaned against the guava tree for pulling down the fruit. Beatrice grabbed up the pole, started jooking it at the branches as close to the bird and nest as she dared. "Leave them, you brute! Leave!" The pole connected with some of the boughs. The two bottles in the tree fell to the ground and shattered with a crash. A hot breeze sprang up. The snake slithered away quickly, two eggs bulging in its throat. The bird flew off, sobbing to itself.

Nothing she could do now. When Samuel came home, he would hunt down the nasty snake for her and kill it. She leaned the pole back against the tree.

The light breeze should have brought some coolness, but really it only made the day warmer. Two little dust devils danced briefly around Beatrice. They swirled across the yard, swung up into the air, and dashed themselves to powder against the shuttered window of the third bedroom.

Beatrice got her sandals from the veranda. Sammy wouldn't like it if she stepped on broken glass. She picked up the broom that was leaned against the house and began to sweep up the shards of bottle. She hoped Samuel wouldn't be too angry with her. He wasn't a man to cross, could be as stern as a father if he had a mind to.

That was mostly what she remembered about Daddy, his temper — quick to show and just as quick to go. So was he; had left his family before Beatrice turned five. The one cherished memory she had of him was of being swung back and forth through the air, her two small hands clasped in one big hand of his, her feet held tight in another. Safe. And as he swung her through the air, her Daddy had been chanting words from an old-time story:

> *Yung-Kyung-Pyung, what a pretty basket!*
> *Margaret Powell Alone, what a pretty basket!*
> *Eggie-law, what a pretty basket!*

Then he had held her tight to his chest, forcing the air from her lungs in a breathless giggle. The dressing down Mummy had given him for that game! "You want to drop the child and crack her head open on the hard ground? Ee? Why you can't be more responsible?"

"Responsible?" he'd snapped. "Is who working like dog sunup to sundown to put food in oonuh belly?" He'd set Beatrice down, her feet hitting the ground with a jar. She'd started to cry, but he'd just pushed her toward her mother and stormed out of the room. One more volley in the constant battle between them. After he'd left them Mummy had opened the little food shop in town to make ends meet. In the evenings, Beatrice would rub lotion into her mother's chapped, work-wrinkled hands. "See how that man make us come down in the world?" Mummy would grumble. "Look at what I come to."

Privately, Beatrice thought that maybe all Daddy had needed was a little patience. Mummy was too harsh, much as she loved her. To please her, she had studied hard all through high school: physics, chemistry, biology, describing the results of her lab experiments in her copy book in her cramped, resigned handwriting. Her mother greeted every A with a noncommittal grunt and anything less with a lecture. Beatrice would smile airily, seal the hurt away, pretend the approval meant nothing to her. She still worked hard, but she kept some time for play of her own. Rounders, netball, and later, boys. All those boys, wanting a chance for a little sweetness with a light-skin browning like her. Beatrice had discovered her appeal quickly.

"Leggo beast..." Loose woman. *The hissed words came from a knot of girls that slouched past Beatrice as she sat on the library steps, waiting for Clifton to come and pick her up. She willed her ears shut, smothered the sting of the words. But she knew some of them. Marguerita, Deborah. They used to be friends of hers. Though she sat up proudly, she found her fingers tugging self-consciously at the hem of her short white skirt. She put the big physics textbook in her lap, where it gave her thighs a little more coverage.*

The farting vroom of Clifton's motorcycle interrupted her thoughts. Grinning, he slewed the bike to a dramatic halt in front of her. "Study time done now, darling. Time to play."

He looked good this evening, as he always did. Tight white shirt, jeans that showed off the bulges of his thighs. The crinkle of the thin gold

chain at his neck set off his dark brown skin. Beatrice stood, tucked the
physics text under her arm, smoothed the skirt over her hips. Clifton's
eyes followed the movement of her hands. See, it didn't take much to
make people treat you nice. She smiled at him.

Samuel would still show up hopefully every so often to ask her to accompany him on a drive through the country. He was so much older
than all her other suitors. And dry? Country drives, Lord! She went
out with him a few times; he was so persistent and she couldn't figure out how to tell him no. He didn't seem to get her hints that really
she should be studying. Truth to tell though, she started to find his
quiet, undemanding presence soothing. His eggshell-white BMW
took the graveled country roads so quietly that she could hear the kis-
kadee birds in the mango trees, chanting their query: "Dit, dit, qu'est-
ce qu'il dit?"

One day, Samuel brought her a gift.

"These are for you and your family," he said shyly, handing her a
wrinkled paper bag. "I know your mother likes them." Inside were
three plump eggplants from his kitchen garden, raised by his own
hands. Beatrice took the humble gift out of the bag. The skins of the
eggplants had a taut, blue sheen to them. Later she would realize that
that was when she'd begun to love Samuel. He was stable, solid, responsible. He would make Mummy and her happy.

Beatrice gave in more to Samuel's diffident wooing. He was cul-
tured and well spoken. He had been abroad, talked of exotic sports:
ice hockey, downhill skiing. He took her to fancy restaurants she'd
only heard of, that her other young, unestablished boyfriends would
never have been able to afford, and would probably only have embarrassed her if they had taken her. Samuel had polish. But he was humble too, like the way he grew his own vegetables, or the self-deprecat-
ing tone in which he spoke of himself. He was always punctual, always courteous to her and her mother. Beatrice could count on him
for little things, like picking her up after class, or driving her mother
to the hairdresser's. With the other men, she always had to be on
guard: pouting until they took her somewhere else for dinner, not

another free meal in her mother's restaurant, wheedling them into using the condoms. She always had to hold something of herself shut away. With Samuel, Beatrice relaxed into trust.

"Beatrice, come! Come quick, nuh!"

Beatrice ran in from the backyard at the sound of her mother's voice. Had something happened to Mummy?

Her mother was sitting at the kitchen table, knife still poised to crack an egg into the bowl for the pound cake she was making to take to the shop. She was staring in openmouthed delight at Samuel, who was fretfully twisting the long stems on a bouquet of blood-red roses. "Lord, Beatrice; Samuel say he want to marry you!"

Beatrice looked to Sammy for verification. "Samuel," she asked unbelievingly, "what you saying? Is true?"

He nodded yes. "True, Beatrice."

Something gave way in Beatrice's chest, gently as a long-held breath. Her heart had been trapped in glass, and he'd freed it.

They'd been married two months later. Mummy was retired now; Samuel had bought her a little house in the suburbs, and he paid for the maid to come in three times a week. In the excitement of planning for the wedding, Beatrice had let her studying slip. To her dismay she finished her final year of university with barely a C average.

"Never mind, sweetness," Samuel told her. "I didn't like the idea of you studying, anyway. Is for children. You're a big woman now." Mummy had agreed with him too, said she didn't need all that now. She tried to argue with them, but Samuel was very clear about his wishes, and she'd stopped, not wanting anything to cause friction between them just yet. Despite his genteel manner, Samuel had just a bit of a temper. No point in crossing him, it took so little to make him happy, and he was her love, the one man she'd found in whom she could have faith.

Too besides, she was learning how to be the lady of the house, trying to use the right mix of authority and jocularity with Gloria, the maid, and Cleitis, the yardboy who came twice a month to do the mowing and the weeding. Odd to be giving orders to people when she was used to being the one taking orders, in Mummy's shop. It made her feel uncomfortable to tell people to do her work for her. Mummy said she should get used to it, it was her right now.

The sky rumbled with thunder. Still no rain. The warmth of the day was nice, but you could have too much of a good thing. Beatrice opened her mouth, gasping a little, trying to pull more air into her lungs. She was a little short of breath nowadays as the baby pressed on her diaphragm. She knew she could go inside for relief from the heat, but Samuel kept the air-conditioning on high, so cold that they could keep the butter in its dish on the kitchen counter. It never went rancid. Even insects refused to come inside. Sometimes Beatrice felt as though the house was really somewhere else, not the tropics. She had been used to waging constant war against ants and cockroaches, but not in Samuel's house. The cold in it made Beatrice shiver, dried her eyes out until they felt like boiled eggs sitting in their sockets. She went outside as often as possible, even though Samuel didn't like her to spend too much time in the sun. He said he feared that cancer would mar her soft skin, that he didn't want to lose another wife. But Beatrice knew he just didn't want her to get too brown. When the sun touched her, it brought out the sepia and cinnamon in her blood, overpowered the milk and honey, and he could no longer pretend she was white. He loved her skin pale. "Look how you gleam in the moonlight," he'd say to her when he made gentle, almost supplicating love to her at night in the four-poster bed. His hand would slide over her flesh, cup her breasts with an air of reverence. The look in his eyes was so close to worship that it sometimes frightened her. To be loved so much! He would whisper in her ear, "Beauty. Pale Beauty, to my Beast," then blow a cool breath over the delicate membranes of her ear, making her shiver in delight. For her part, she loved to look at him, his molasses-dark skin, his broad chest, the way the planes of flat muscle slid across it. She imagined tectonic plates shifting in the earth. She loved the bluish-black cast the moonlight lent him. Once, gazing up at him as he loomed above her, body working against and in hers, she had seen the moonlight playing glints of deepest blue in his trim beard.

"Black Beauty," she had joked softly, reaching to pull his face closer for a kiss. At the words, he had lurched up off her to sit on the edge of the bed, pulling a sheet over him to hide his nakedness. Beatrice watched him, confused, feeling their blended sweat cooling along her body.

"Never call me that, please, Beatrice," he said softly. "You don't have to draw attention to my color. I'm not a handsome man, and I know it. Black and ugly as my mother made me."

"But Samuel...!"

"No."

Shadows lay between them on the bed. He wouldn't touch her again that night.

Beatrice sometimes wondered why Samuel hadn't married a white woman. He could have met someone while he was studying abroad. She thought she knew the reason, though. She had seen the way that Samuel behaved around white people. He smiled too broadly, he simpered, he made silly jokes. It pained her to see it, and she could tell from the desperate look in his eyes that it hurt him too. For all his love of creamy white skin, Samuel probably couldn't bring himself to approach a white woman the way he'd courted her.

The broken glass was in a neat pile under the guava tree. Time to make Samuel's dinner now. She went up the veranda stairs to the front door, stopping to wipe her sandals on the coir mat just outside the door. Samuel hated dust. As she opened the door, she felt another gust of warm wind at her back, blowing past her into the cool house. Quickly, she stepped inside and closed the door, so that the interior would stay as cool as Sammy liked it. The insulated door shut behind her with a hollow sound. It was airtight. None of the windows in the house could be opened. She had asked Samuel, "Why you want to live in a box like this, sweetheart? The fresh air good for you."

"I don't like the heat, Beatrice. I don't like baking like meat in the sun. The sealed windows keep the conditioned air in." She hadn't argued.

She walked through the elegant, formal living room to the kitchen.

She found the heavy imported furnishings cold and stuffy, but Samuel liked them.

In the kitchen she set water to boil and hunted a bit — where did Gloria keep it? — until she found the Dutch pot. She put it on the burner to toast the fragrant coriander seeds that would flavor the curry. She put on water to boil, stood staring at the steam rising from the pots. Dinner was going to be special tonight. Curried eggs, Samuel's favorite. The eggs in their cardboard case made Beatrice remember a trick she'd learned in physics class for getting an egg unbroken into a narrow-mouthed bottle. You had to boil the egg hard and peel it, then stand a lit candle in the bottle. If you put the narrow end of the egg into the mouth of the bottle, it made a seal, and when the candle had burnt up all the air in the bottle, the vacuum it created would suck the egg in, whole. Beatrice had been the only one in her class patient enough to make the trick work. Patience was all her husband needed. Poor, mysterious Samuel had lost two wives in this isolated country home. He'd been rattling about in the airless house like the egg in the bottle. He kept to himself. The closest neighbors were miles away, and he didn't even know their names.

She was going to change all that, though. Invite her mother to stay for a while, maybe have a dinner party for the distant neighbors. Before her pregnancy made her too lethargic to do much.

A baby would complete their family. Samuel *would* be pleased, wouldn't he? She remembered him joking that no woman should have to give birth to his ugly black babies, but she would show him how beautiful their children would be, little brown bodies new as the earth after the rain. She would show him how to love himself in them.

It was hot in the kitchen. Perhaps the heat from the stove? Beatrice went out into the living room, wandered through the guest bedroom, the master bedroom, both bathrooms. The whole house was warmer than she'd ever felt it. Then she realized she could hear sounds coming from the outside, the cicadas singing loudly for rain. There was no whisper of cool air through the vents in the house. The air conditioner wasn't running.

Beatrice began to feel worried. Samuel liked it cold. She had planned tonight to be a special night for the two of them, but he wouldn't react well if everything wasn't to his liking. He'd raised his voice at her a few times. Once or twice he had stopped in the middle of an argument, one hand pulled back as if to strike, to take deep breaths, battling for self-control. His dark face would flush almost blue-black as he fought his rage down. Those times she'd stayed out of his way until he was calm again.

What could be wrong with the air conditioner? Maybe it had just come unplugged? Beatrice wasn't even sure where the controls were. Gloria and Samuel took care of everything around the house. She made another circuit through her home, looking for the main controls. Nothing. Puzzled, she went back into the living room. It was becoming thick and close as a womb inside their closed-up home.

There was only one room left to search. The locked third bedroom. Samuel had told her that both his wives had died in there, first one, then the other. He had given her the keys to every room in the house, but requested that she never open that particular door.

"I feel like it's bad luck, love. I know I'm just being superstitious, but I hope I can trust you to honor my wishes in this." She had, not wanting to cause him any anguish. But where else could the control panel be? It was getting so hot!

As she reached into her pocket for the keys she always carried with her, she realized she was still holding a raw egg in her hand. She'd forgotten to put it into the pot when the heat in the house had made her curious. She managed a little smile. The hormones flushing her body were making her so absent-minded! Samuel would tease her, until she told him why. Everything would be all right.

Beatrice put the egg into her other hand, got the keys out of her pocket, opened the door.

A wall of icy, dead air hit her body. It was freezing cold in the room. Her exhaled breath floated away from her in a long, misty curl. Frowning, she took a step inside and her eyes saw before her brain could understand, and when it did, the egg fell from her hands to smash open on the floor at her feet. Two women's bodies lay side by side on the double bed. Frozen mouths gaped open; frozen, gutted bellies too. A fine sheen of ice crystals glazed their skin, which like hers was barely brown, but laved in gelid, rime-covered blood that had solidified ruby red. Beatrice whimpered.

"But Miss," Beatrice asked her teacher, "how the egg going to come back out the bottle again?"

"How do you think, Beatrice? There's only one way; you have to break the bottle."

This was how Samuel punished the ones who had tried to bring his babies into the world, his beautiful black babies. For each woman had had the muscled sac of her womb removed and placed on her belly, hacked open to reveal the purplish mass of her placenta. Beatrice knew that if she were to dissect the thawing tissue, she'd find a tiny fetus in each one. The dead women had been pregnant too.

A movement at her feet caught her eyes. She tore her gaze away from the bodies long enough to glance down. Writhing in the fast congealing yolk was a pin-feathered embryo. A rooster must have been at Mister Herbert's hens. She put her hands on her belly to still the sympathetic twitching of her womb. Her eyes were drawn back to the horror on the beds. Another whimper escaped her lips.

A sound like a sigh whispered in through the door she'd left open. A current of hot air seared past her cheek, making a plume of fog as it entered the room. The fog split into two, settled over the heads of each woman, began to take on definition. Each misty column had a face, contorted in rage. The faces were those of the bodies on the bed. One of the duppy women leaned over her own corpse. She lapped like a cat at the blood thawing on its breast. She became a little more solid for having drunk of her own life blood. The other duppy stooped to do the same. The two duppy women each had a belly slightly swollen with the pregnancies for which Samuel had killed them. Beatrice had broken the bottles that had confined the duppy wives, their bodies held in stasis because their spirits were trapped. She'd freed them. She'd let them into the house. Now there was nothing to cool their fury. The heat of it was warming the room up quickly.

The duppy wives held their bellies and glared at her, anger flaring hot behind their eyes. Beatrice backed away from the beds. "I didn't know," she said to the wives. "Don't vex with me. I didn't know what it is Samuel do to you."

Was that understanding on their faces, or were they beyond compassion?

"I making baby for him too. Have mercy on the baby, at least?"

Beatrice heard the *snik* of the front door opening. Samuel was home. He would have seen the broken bottles, would feel the warmth of the house. Beatrice felt that initial calm of the prey that realizes it has no choice but to turn and face the beast that is pursuing it. She wondered if Samuel would be able to read the truth hidden in her body, like the egg in the bottle.

"Is not me you should be vex with," she pleaded with the duppy wives. She took a deep breath and spoke the words that broke her heart. "Is…is Samuel who do this."

She could hear Samuel moving around in the house, the angry rumbling of his voice like the thunder before the storm. The words were muffled, but she could hear the anger in his tone. She called out, "What you saying, Samuel?"

She stepped out of the meat locker and quietly pulled the door in, but left it open slightly so the duppy wives could come out when they were ready. Then with a welcoming smile, she went to greet her husband. She would stall him as long as she could from entering the third bedroom. Most of the blood in the wives' bodies would be clotted, but maybe it was only important that it be *warm*. She hoped that enough of it would thaw soon for the duppies to drink until they were fully real.

When they had fed, would they come and save her, or would they take revenge on her, their usurper, as well as on Samuel?

Eggie-Law, what a pretty basket.

Wooden Bride

Margo Lanagan

Some stories shouldn't be introduced. After all, you don't want to know in advance what six terms of Bride School will do to a young woman....

I'm in danger. Up ahead, limousines, white horses, flower strewers, white-and-silver gift carts block the street. Here brides and their families crowd. Irate mothers are shouting; fathers are giggling, and some are trying to push forward; we brides stand motionless in First Position, like fence posts in a flood. But a few feet behind me, Gabby's dad has started one of his hairy stories. In many a Composure class I've busted out laughing from one of those stories. But this is the Day; I can't afford to come unstuck today. I have to get away from him, before the crowd jams up completely.

I turn, and people make way for me. "Why," says Gabby's dad in his always-surprised voice, "if it isn't little Matty Weir!" I steel myself for the joke he'll toss at me, which'll prod my mind in an unexpected spot and make me splutter laughter. But it doesn't come, and I pass through. I lost Gabby's dad for words! I won't risk blushing by thinking about such a compliment now; I'll store it away to tell Mother and Winke later, when I'm allowed to be myself.

Here—I'll duck into the Lanes district. I haven't been through this part of town since they rebuilt after last year's rat hunt, but it can't be that different, can it? And there won't be a lot of people around; not many families in these poorer quarters can afford to bride up a daughter.

I gather up two handfuls of the beaded white-tissue skirt. Last night's rain has left all the flagstones gleaming, and the sun shows up every pore of them, every puddle and scrap of refuse. I tiptoe through.

The slippers are made to last one day—*this* day. They're folded out of varnished paper, with a twinkle in it. We had to go all the way to the markets at the Crossways to find a paper binder who did shoes the old way with no glue, just sheer skill of folding and knowledge of a girl's own foot and a girl's own walk holding the creation together.

Where am I now?

The crowd noise is fading behind me, though the bells still carol overhead. Oh, yes, there's the old Mechanics Hall, where Mother used to hold her mask-making workshops, so I turn right here to loop around the Orphans Home. I'm trying to hurry yet stay Composed. I'm keeping my skin cool, all pores closed, as they taught us in School. I'll come up to the side door of the church, by the Hospice there. It won't matter to Mother and Winke; they can still come up the main way and do their nodding and smiling. That's not the point of this, for me. I'm not quite sure what the point *is*—I couldn't put it into words or anything—but it's strong, and it's not about getting the neighbors to admire me. The neighbors have nothing to do with it at all.

What, have they *moved* the Orphans Home? Come to think of it, I did hear Gabby and Flo say something about that. Farther up the hill, for better drainage. But the lane looks much the same — maybe a bit of a curve downward, which I'll have to compensate for when I get to Farmers Bar. Those bells, they're wild, as if they're shouting fire or an attack on the town; they're a test in themselves. But I'm prepared for that kind of test: I've got counting rhymes in my head; I've got breathing exercises; I've got six terms worth of Bride School resources to draw on.

And then the bells stop, and the lane stops. And I stop. Farmers Bar isn't here.

"That doesn't make sense," I say coolly, firmly. "No matter how ratty, a public house doesn't move. They smoke out the cellars, and they scrub everything else down with disinfectant."

Then I remember: It was the Olds Home that moved, not the Or-

phans; they moved all the olds away from the dampness, for their ar-
thritis or something. The Orphans Home should have been where it
always was.

Five lanes meet where I'm standing; not a soul stirs along any of
them. Not a sound from any window or door.

"It's all right," I say, counting furiously inside to keep my heart
down. "I can go back the way I came."

But behind me are two lanes, and with all my revolving I can't remember which one I came down.

"The church is at the top of the hill, Mattild." There's a shake in my
voice, and I pause to do some breathing. "All you have to do is choose
any lane that goes upward, and you'll be there."

So I set off. Actually, the silence — just the pat and shush of my
shoes — is more alarming than the bells were. The silence means
they're inside the church — all the brides, anyway. The relatives will
take a while to shuffle in. But I mustn't think about that; I must just
walk and breathe and count.

Every lane deceives me; every lane curves. I set out confidently upward at every corner; I end up hoisting my skirts behind me so they
won't drag as I go down steps. Lanes keep ending at a wall, or a dripping mill wheel, or they continue on the other side of an unbridged
drain a trousered person could leap, but not I in my finery. I go back
and forth, breathing, counting, intent on outwitting the lanes. I try
a new tactic, taking some downward streets in the hope that their
curves will take me upward. No such luck; down and down they go.
I'm so confused; I'm just starting to think I'm getting somewhere
when I arrive — the lane does a quick turnabout and dumps me — at
an arched gateway in the town wall.

I stand there, counting, breathing, shocked. Beyond the gate, the
water meadows and the market gardens stretch purple and many-
greened among their wind guards of black pines. Rubbish-stink
streams from the pits farther east.

Ha! said my dad over the whir and clatter of his workshop. I was
there to wangle money out of him toward my shoes. *My daughter?
Matty Weir? Miss Million-Miles-an-Hour? Miss Ten-Projects-at-Once,*

none of them ever finished? You haven't a hope! You're lucky to've made it through the first semester. They mustn't have much of a crop this year. All this very cheerfully, as he *zizzed* the wooden bowl to a perfect curve on the lathe.

And then Mother, wearing that face that makes you ashamed to have brought her down from the clouds where she dances and sings and brings such joy to so many people — that doubtful, older face: *But are you* sure *about this?*

Which I was, I *was*. Tearfulness rises in my throat. My skin trembles, ready to give out. I was *sure* I was sure, until…

An old woman in blue gardening clothes appears in the archway, carrying an enormous cabbage. "Madam," she says, and walks in past me.

Madam, she said, not *Miss*. You see a bride, you don't meet her eye. You say *Madam* to acknowledge her, but nothing more unless she speaks to you. Thank the Saints that woman came along.

I breathe more carefully. My shoes are still good — perhaps a bit soft underfoot, but still good. I just need to walk out a little way beyond the arch to see which gate I'm at, to see my way back.

I lift my skirts and go. I'm not far out among the fields before I can see the church's twin spires. But I'm behind them; if I take any of the three gates I can see from here, I'll be straight back in the maze. Better to go around on the outside to a gate that leads to straighter streets, like Silk Street or Jewelers Way. I shade my eyes and pick out a zigzag way for myself, along the broad earthen field walls, between the water meadows and the moving leaves of purple sour kale.

I put out of my head the thought of Mother and Winke and all the other families in the church, sitting patched pink with rose-window light. I push away the vision of all the other brides, their upper bodies like snooty white flock herons at rest on a mist of white gorgeousness. I just walk, swiftly and calmly, trying to think of nothing.

You see, said Mother doubtfully, *as someone who had to go to Bride School herself, whose parents wanted it more than anything else in the world, I sometimes thought…*

It was as if her voice were *funneling* stubbornness and resentment into my spine.

You see, the kings and queens that it's modeled on, they're just so long dead; they have so little to do with our lives now. They're four revolutions ago — think about that! And what were those revolutions about?

I spoke through gritted teeth. *I don't care what they were about —*

About people being able to relax, and move any way they wanted, and find their own path creatively. They were about freedom.

She was in full flight and making perfect sense. I had to stop her before she deflected me. *Which doesn't mean,* I said gaspingly — I had no control over my breathing, back then — *which doesn't mean the Straitened kings and queens were all bad. I mean, people must have let them rule because they believed the way they lived worked in some way, don't you think? It's not as if they revolted after six months; those royals had power for hundreds of years! If everybody hates you, you can't last that long.* I think I made a pretty good fist of it, considering I hadn't even been to the Bride School Open Day yet.

Mother was too smart for me. Dad just laughed at me. Once I got through the entrance tests, all I had on my side was stubbornness. I couldn't explain it to myself any more than I could to them. I listened to them, I agreed, but I dug in my heels. *It's just something I'm* Going to Do, I said. *I've never imagined not doing it. I've always meant to.* That was all I had.

Bit by bit, the zigs and zags of the field walls work me farther from the town. The spires turn, and the facade comes into view, the rose window with the Saints' linked crowns above it. But it seems to be moving farther away, not closer. The fields' silence takes over, plopped more silent by fish, creaked more silent by breeze-shifted cabbage leaves, startled quieter by a burst of bird out of reeds. Always there are people at middle distance or beyond, bending to the water, to the feet of the plants, wading in mirages.

This gentle, shoe-protecting walk is tiring after a while. I'm glad when I reach my friend Yakkert's village, with its wide, flat path, where I don't have to carry my skirts to protect my hems. My hands feel raw from that, after two years of oiling and gloving them, two years of keeping them safe from cuts and calluses.

People are laundering at the water race on the common. At tables outside the house doors, children and old people are picking over dried corn silk to make their votive dollies. "Madam," says anyone I pass near, and they lower their eyes. They all know me, and I them. Two years ago I used to come out here to fish the race regularly; I've made so many dollies with these people, I could do it in my sleep. But none of them will greet me by name while I'm dressed like this.

My skin feels thin, ready to perspire. It's not that I *care* whether they talk to me. I can come back tomorrow and they'll be as friendly as ever. I sit on a stump, and Yakkert's cat, Biddy, comes up to me. A cat's not to know you can't approach a bride, is she? I give her a bridely stroke of the head, instead of wrestling her over and pushing my face into her belly fur, as I usually would.

Yakkert's mother passes in front of me and leaves a pottery cup of cool tea on the next stump. She knows I'm supposed to save my mouth for bishop's cake and wedding wine. But she wouldn't — no one here would — think less of me if I drank that tea.

Which isn't the point, I tell myself as the circle of sky on the tea surface stills from its rocking. *Besides, it's enough that she's put it there. I don't actually have to drink it to get the benefit.*

I stand up and check my skirt hems. At the back, the edges are gray-brown and damp from brushing the dew and the ground. And the outer edge of one shoe is sodden, in spite of my careful walking. I'll have to walk differently, oddly, so it doesn't get any worse. I could take the shoes off and go barefoot and faster. I could bundle up my skirts and run and probably reach the church before the brides leave. Why can't I find it in myself to do that?

Because it would be me, Miss Matty Weir, who never finishes things, who never does things quite right, who'd be running. It would be the person everyone expects me to be, the person everyone thinks I am.

I gather up some skirt into my sore hands and walk away from the village. You just keep up the Bridal Gait, Mattild. Though it be among weeds and the trickle of leaking water gates, instead of across petals and floor wax, you step and step until you get where you said — through six terms of homework and gown fittings and gossip and abstinence-from-all-fun — where you said you were going to go. You might not get to smell the incense, or hear the pure drone of the Wedding Song from the choir, or see the visiting bishop in his magnificent tarnished ancient robe, his rings all over rubies. But you set yourself on this path to becoming someone not Matty, someone cool and un-flustered, remote, with impermeable skin. And you'll get there; with measured steps you'll get there.

"Madam," say a string of gardeners' children. Each carries a puppy in one hand and a basket of sorted eggs in the other. The sun has lost all its morning kindness, lifting into steam, killing off the breeze. It stings through my sheer sleeves and on my neck, which is usually covered by my mess of hair. My skin feels cool, though; I'm keeping it that way.

The bells shout again. In the church the brides will be losing some of their Composure; they've only the photographs to go, and then they can all fall away down the porch stairs, blessed and brilliant and allowed to laugh now, to wreck their dresses, to show their legs, to hug their families. The feast awaits in flower-stuffed halls around town: many-storied white cakes, powder-blue wedding cachous, fla-vored violets, glazed fruit, clove-studded meats, salt-crusted heart biscuits.

Paths go off to right and left, among dank slabs of mirror whis-kered with rice. But no path seems to lead to the mound of the town — not straightly anyway. But I'll get there, even if *not* straightly. The bishop must stay for the feasting; if the worse comes to the worst, he can bless me among flowers, between mouthfuls of cake, with cake cream on his beard.

When finally I reach the gate I want and step out of the meadows, the town streets are empty, dim, and very cool. The higher I climb, the more flower petals are gummed to the flags, the more constant are the gusts of chatter and music channeled along the lanes. I know exactly where I am and how to avoid those halls, the sight of food, the cries of brides with unpinned hair. My leg aches from my toe gripping the loose shoe; my hands are stiff from carrying the netting skirt; my arms cramp from lifting all the expensive cloth.

The church is stripped of its usual pennants and garlands. The church square too is bare of all decoration. Of all the people who choked the streets this morning, only the photographer is left, folding his black cloth on the church steps.

I rustle across the square. All those Posture, Carriage, Masque, and Step lessons play themselves out in me as if I have no will of my own. The boned bodice holds my back right, and my face is rightly wooden, empty of anything — weariness, anxiety, relief, determination, anything.

The photographer glances aside from his equipment case. He sees the stained edge of my skirt and pauses.

"Mr. Pellisson," I say in my cold, rehearsed Bride Voice.

"Madam." His gaze remains lowered.

"I require your sponsorship. Is the bishop within?"

"He is, Madam." He closes his case with a soft, rich click. Wordlessly he precedes me up the steps.

The church is very dark, its air like cold water. It seems much larger than usual, cleared of all candles, all votives, banners, flowers. All the coziness is gone, and the building's ribs rise naked to separate the high lattice windows. A vein of light runs up the central aisle, a carpet of white petals. Someone is sweeping them from the altar toward us; he slips into a side aisle and murmurs, "Madam," as we pass.

We reach the altar. All the monstrances with their yellowed Relics have been taken away, all the cloths and vases and prayer trees. The only ornament is the Saint Crown on its purple cushion on the altar, two palace guards in ceremonial black like statues either side. The only scent is of cold marble.

The photographer opens the brass altar gate for me. The cold strikes straight up through my damp paper shoes.

We skirt the altar and enter the vestry, which is smaller, warmer, carpeted, and full of the cedar smell of vain old man. The lace trim on the hem of the bishop's underrobe — well, none at my school could afford such stuff. I mustn't meet his eye, mustn't look for the outer vestments, the thorned miter. I must keep my eyes on the red carpet, the expensive hem, the gilded paper slipper toe.

A plain wooden kneeler is pushed in front of me. Pellisson's hand plucks a leaf from the beading near my hem and withdraws.

I kneel, and the bishop starts the blessing: Witness: *To the holy basilica of All Saints comes this young woman, beloved of the town of Mountfort-among-the-Waters...* He doesn't need the vestments, this man; the words vest him, vest all three of us as beautifully as the robes would. He shapes his voice to set the small, padded vestry singing.

...before witnesses that she has undergone instruction and proven herself constituted of such purity of body, austerity of practice, modesty of habit, and restraint and moderation of temperament as befits...

How many times have I read those words in the liturgy book? How many times have I stopped and said to myself, *That isn't me. I'm just not like that, moderate and pure and austere. I'll never make it through; they'll stop me way before the Day when a bishop would say those words over me. "What were you thinking, Matty?" they'll say, and laugh, and send me to the cashier to claim back the rest of the School fee.* Yet here I am, relaxed in the flow of the holy words, firm in the rightness of this, taking the blessing and knowing — as I haven't known for two whole years, as I didn't even know this morning, darting out of the house because I hadn't the patience to wait for Mother to dress Winke's hair; as I didn't know pacing the lanes and counting — that it's mine to take, that I deserve it, that I've earned it. I've made myself a Bride; out among the fields today, alone and without instruction, I wedded myself to the severe and lovely ways of the old dead kings and queens at their height, when all the people loved them. And now the bishop's thumb is dipping into the sacred oil and ash — ash that once, centuries ago, was actual kingly or queenly matter — and he's whispering to himself the final and most secret words, in the language of the Straitened times, and applying history to my brow.

Pellisson helps the bishop take the Bride book from its box. They place it on its stand, and the bishop unlocks and opens it. He moves aside the gilded bookmark, and there's Agnes Stork's flourish that she practiced for two years, and Felicity Doe's loopy tangle of a name, with the two hearts dotting the *i*'s. When the quill is readied and handed to me, *Mattild Weir* I write plainly, so that anyone who looks will know that I was here, became a Bride, this day. Thereunder signs my witness: Pellisson, descended all the way from the court painters of the Straitened days.

The way to thank the bishop is with money, in a white purse a bride unties from her waist. He opens a chest, and the bride purses are piled in there like sleeping mice. A few are trimmed end to end with lace, one or two monogrammed; most are like mine, standard-issue Bride School purses, plain linen, strongly sewn.

I give an exemplary curtsy, nothing ostentatious. Rising, I look at the bishop properly for the first time. His face is round and red and weary. His white comb-over has a miter furrow around it. Apart from the white, double-plaited beard, he's greatly ordinary against the magnificent vestments in their case behind him, the gold ribbons of the miter laid just so on the shoulders of the cape.

The bishop tips his head at me, saying *get-out-of-here* as much as *nicely-executed-curtsy-bless-you-my-child*.

Now the Bride walks ahead of her sponsor, out into the body of the church, down the darkened aisle, past the glowing heap of petals at the rear.

Out on the church steps Pellisson scatters handfuls of petals around my feet. My eyes fix on the middle distance as a good bride's should, but I can still see him: He backs down the steps without needing to check his footing. He shakes out his black cloth and organizes his photographer's dust. My spine is straight as a pine trunk, and my face is empty of everything.

He arranges all his equipment, and then he comes up the stairs and starts to arrange *me*. It only strikes me then how unsupervised I am, as his gentle adjustments of the hem tug at my waist. There's no crowd of matrons making sure the thing's done right, snapping commands at him, or sighing and coming forward to fix me themselves. But he knows what he's doing; he knows about cloth; he knows with small and professionally exact movements how to tease the maximum width, the maximum puff, out of the skirts, the maximum contrast with my slenderfied, rigidified upper half.

"Is all satisfactory?" I say, for he may not speak unless spoken to.

He steps back to judge. "If Madam would lift her chin just a touch higher?"

She would. Although she could hug Pellisson, old vinegar bottle that he is, Madam would be pleased instead to lift her chin, to look down her regal nose past His Nobodyness.

He disappears under the cloth. The dust flashes and thuds. The smoke jumps free like a loosed kite.

Dearth

Aimee Bender

Parenting is a major topic in today's society. Parenting-related gender issues, including how many of which kinds of people are ideal or even permissible as parents of which kinds of children, are discussed in government chambers, talk radio, the courts — and in stories.

In this sometimes charming, sometimes disturbing story, a woman wakes up one morning to find that she is suddenly a single mother, to a most unusual group of children.

The next thing in the morning was the cast-iron pot full of potatoes. She had not ordered them and did not remember buying potatoes at the grocery store. She was not one to bake a potato. Someone must have come in and delivered them by accident. Once she'd woken to meadows full of sunflower bouquets all over her house in glass vases and they turned out to be for the woman next door. Perhaps the woman next door had a new suitor now, one who found something romantic in root vegetables.

Our woman checked through her small house but it was empty as ever. She asked her neighbor, the one whose windows were still crowded with flowers, but the neighbor wiped her hands on a red-checkered cloth and said no, they were not for her, and she had not ordered any potatoes from the store either, as she grew her own.

Back at the house, the potatoes smelled normal and looked normal but our woman did not want them around so she threw them in the trash and went about the rest of her day. She swept and squared and pulled weeds from her garden. She walked to the grocery store and bought milk. She was a quiet person, and spoke very few words throughout the afternoon: Thank You, Goodbye, Excuse Me.

The next morning, when she woke up, the potatoes were back. Nestled, a pile of seven, in the cast-iron pot on the stove. She checked her trash and it looked as it had before, with a folded milk carton and some envelopes. Just no potatoes. She picked up all seven again, and took them across the road and pushed them one at a time into the trash Dumpster, listening as they thumped at the bottom of the bin.

During the afternoon she walked past rows of abandoned cabins to her lover's house. He was in his bedroom, asleep. She crawled into the bed with him and pushed her body against his until he woke up, groggy, and made love to her. She stared at the wall as the craving built bricks inside her stomach, and then she burst onto him like a brief rain in drought season. Afterward, she walked home, and he got ready for his night job of loading supplies into trucks and out of trucks. She stopped by the cemetery on the way home to visit her mother, her father, her brother. Hello mother, hello father, hello brother. Goodbye now.

The next morning, the potatoes had returned. This time she recognized them by the placement of knots and eyes, and she could see they were not seven new potatoes, but the same seven she had, just the day before, thumped into the Dumpster. The same seven she had, just the day before that, thrown into the small garbage of her home. They looked a little smug. She tied them tight in a plastic bag and dropped them next door on the sunflower woman's front stoop. Then she repotted her plants. For the rest of the day, she forgot all about them, but the next morning, the first thing she checked was that cast-iron pot. And what do you know. And on this day they seemed to be growing slightly, curving inward like big gray beans.

They were bothering her now. Even though she was minutely pleased that they had picked her over the sunflower neighbor, still.

"All right." She spoke into the pot. "Fine."

Oven.

On.

Since she did not enjoy the taste of baked potatoes, when they were done she took them into the road and placed all seven crispy purses in a line down the middle. The summer sun was white and hot. At around three, when the few cars and trucks and bicycles came rolling through town, she swayed and hummed at the soft sound of impact, and that night, she slept so hard that she lost her own balance and didn't wake up at sunrise like usual but several hours into the morning. There was a note slipped under the door from her lover who had come to visit after work. He forgot to write "Love" before his name. He had written "Sincerely" instead.

Settling down to a breakfast of milk and bread, the woman looked into the pot almost as an afterthought. Surely they would not survive the oven *and* the tires *and* the road. But. All seven — raw, gray, growing. Her mouth went dry, and she ignored them furiously for the rest of the day, jabbing the dirt with a spade as she bordered the house with nasturtium seeds.

Later that day, she stapled them in a box and lugged them to the post office and mailed them to Ireland, where potatoes belonged. She left no return address. When they were back in the pot the next morning, she soaked them in kerosene, lit them on fire, and kicked them into the hills. When they were back again the next morning, she walked two miles with them in her knapsack and threw them over the county line, into the next county. But they were back again by morning, and again, and again and again, and by the twentieth day, they curved inward even more and had grown sketches of hands and feet. Her heart pulled its curtain as she held each potato up to the bare hanging lightbulb and looked at its hint of neck, its almost torso, its small backside. Each of the seven had ten very tiny indented toes and ten whispers of fingertips.

Trembling, she left the potatoes in the pot and fled her house as fast as she could. She found no comfort in the idea of seeing her sincere lover so she went to the town tavern and had a glass of beer. The bartender told her a long story about how his late wife had refused to say the word "love" in the house for fear she only had a certain amount of times in a life to say the word "love" and she did not want to ever use them up. "So she said she liked me, every day, over and over." He polished a wineglass with a dirty cloth. "I like you is not the same," he said. "It is not. On her deathbed even, she said 'Darling, I like you.'" He spit in the cloth and swept it around the stem. "You'd think," he said, "that even if her cockamamie idea were true, even if there were only a certain amount of loves allotted per person, you'd think she could've spent one of them then."

The woman sipped her beer as if it were tea.

"You say nothing," he said. "I don't know which is worse."

On the buzzy walk home, she stopped by the cemetery and on her way to see her family she passed the bartender's wife's grave which stated, simply, SHE WAS GREATLY LOVED.

Back at her house, holding her breath, she sliced all seven potatoes up with a knife as fast as she could. The blade nearly snapped. She could hardly look at the chubby suggestions of arms and legs as she chopped, and cut her own finger by accident. Drunk and bleeding, she took the assortment of tuber pieces and threw them out the window. She only let out her breath when it was over.

One piece of potato was left on the cutting board, so she ate it, and for the rest of the evening she swept the stone floor of her house, pushing every speck of dirt out the door until the floor rang smooth.

She woke at the first light of day and ran into the kitchen and her heart clanged with utter despair and bizarre joy when she saw those seven wormy little bodies, whole, pressed pale gray against the black of the cast iron. Their toes one second larger. She brushed away the tears sliding down her nose and put a hand inside the pot, stroking their backsides.

In the distance, the sunflowers on the hill waved at her in fields of yellow fingers.

August came and went. The potatoes stayed. She could not stand to bother them anymore. By the fourth month, they were significantly larger and had a squareish box of a head with the faintest pale shutter of an eyelid.

Trucks, big and small, rattled through the town but they did not stop to either unload or load up. She hadn't seen her lover in months. She hadn't been to the cemetery either; the weeds on her family were probably ten feet high by now.

With summer fading from her kitchen window, the woman saw

her neighbor meet up with the latest suitor, yellow petals peeking out from her wrists and collar, collecting in clusters at the nape of her neck. He himself was hidden by armfuls of red roses. They kissed in the middle of the dirt road.

Inside her house, the woman shivered. She did not like to look at so many flowers and the sky was overcast. Pluck, pluck, pluck, she thought. Her entire floor was so clean you could not feel a single grain when you walked across it with bare feet. She had mailed her electricity bill and bought enough butter and milk to last a week. The nasturtiums were watered.

The smacking sound kept going on by the window. Wet.

It was lunchtime by now, and she was hungry. And you can't just eat butter by itself.

She put the potatoes in the oven again. With their bellies and toes. With their large heads and slim shoulders. She let them bake for an hour and a half, until their skin was crisp and bright brown. Her stomach was churning and rose petals blew along the street as she sat herself down at her kitchen table. It was noon. She used salt and pepper and butter, and a fork and a knife, but they were so much larger now than your average potato, and they were no longer an abstract shape, and she hated potatoes, and the taste in her mouth felt like the kind of stale dirt that has lost its ability to grow anything. She shoved bite after bite into her teeth, to the sound of the neighbor laughing in her kitchen, through such dizziness she could hardly direct the fork into her mouth correctly. She chewed until the food gathered in the spittle at the corners of her lips, until she had finished one entire enormous potato. The other six crackled off the table and spilled onto the floor.

That night, she had a horrible stomachache, and she barely slept. She dreamed of a field of sunflowers and in each pollened center was the face of someone she once knew. Their eyes were closed.

At dawn, when she walked over to the stove, as she did every morning now, pulling her bathrobe tighter around her aching stomach, there were only six potatoes in the pot. Her body jerked in horror. She must have miscounted. She counted them over. Six. She counted again. Six. Again. Six. Six. Again. Six. Her throat closed up as she checked under the stove and behind the refrigerator and around the whole kitchen. Six. She checked all their markings until it was clear which one was missing: the one with the bumpiest head, with the potato eye right on its shoulder blade. She could feel it take shape again inside her mouth. A wave of nausea swept over her throat, and she spent the rest of the day in the corner of the old red couch, choking for breath. She threw up by evening from so much crying, but the seventh potato never came back.

The sunflower fields browned with autumn, and within a month, two other potatoes were expelled from the pot. There was simply not enough room for all six in the pot anymore. She had done nothing this time. She didn't want to put them outside, bare, in the cold, so when they were soft enough, she buried them deep beneath the hibernating nasturtium seeds. They never came back either. The four remaining in the pot seemed to be growing fine but it was unsettling to look in and see only four now; she had grown so used to seven.

By the eighth month it was raining outside and she was having stomach cramps and the potatoes were fully formed, with nails and feet, with eyelids and ears, and potato knots all over their bodies. They rotated their position so that their heads faced the mouth of the pot. On the ninth month, they tumbled out of the pot on the date of their exact birthday, and began moving slowly across the floor. They were silent. They did not cry like regular babies and they smelled faintly of hash browns. She picked them up occasionally, when they stopped on the floor, legs and arms waving, but mostly she kept her distance. They tended to stick together, moving in a clump, opening their potato eyes to pupils the same color as the rest of them.

The four were similar, but you could distinguish them by the distribution of potato marks on their bodies, and so she named them One, Two, Three, and Four. Two also had a tiny wedge missing from its kneecap, in the shape of a cut square.

When she left to go mail a letter or pick up some groceries, the potato visitors went to the windows like dogs do, and watched her walk off. When she returned, they were back at the window, or still at the window, waiting. Their big potato heads turning as she walked up and opened the door. Eyes blinking fast to welcome her home. She went through her mail and fell into a corner of the rotting old red sofa and they walked over and put rough hands on her shoulders, her knees, her hair. The five of them spent the winter like that, together in the small house, watching the snow fall. She tried to send them out-side, to find their fortune, but they always turned right around and came back. They only slept when she slept, making burbling noises like the sound of water warming up. They were dreamless, and woke once she awoke.

On the first day of spring, the bountiful neighbor came over with lilies woven into her hair, asking to borrow some matches. The woman had the four hide in the bathroom. She tried to talk to the neighbor but had very little to say and instead the neighbor filled the small house with chatter. The neighbor was in love! The neighbor liked the weather! The neighbor asked to use the bathroom and the woman said sorry, her bathroom was broken. The neighbor talked at length about broken bathrooms, and how difficult, and if she, the woman, ever needed to use her bathroom, she was welcome anytime. Thank you. You're welcome! When the neighbor left, the woman's ears were ringing. She went into the bathroom to pee and was some-how startled to see the four still in there, blinking beneath the silver towel rack.

"Get," she said, brushing them off. "Get away from me. Go!"

They bumped out the door and waited in the living room. She put them in the closet and went about her day, and there they stayed, wait-ing, until the guilt drove her to let them out. The following morning, after a sleepless night where they gazed at her with white pupils, she pushed them out the front door to the side of the house where there was a strip of dirt that the neighbor could not see. The woman picked up her gardening shovel and dug a hole in the earth, as deep as her knee. She looked at One.

"Get in," she said.

He stepped into the hole.

"Lie down," she said. He looked up at her with wondering eyes and she filled the hole with dirt over him.

"Go back to where you came from," she said, as she shoved more dirt over his grayish body. She looked at Two. Built another hole. "Go," she said, "and don't you come out," and her voice shook as she said it. Two hopped in without pause. As did Three and then Four. She filled the holes up fast and then strode into her house and locked the door. Fine, she said to herself. Fine. Fine. FINE. She ate dinner alone and slept alone and woke alone, and the cast-iron pot was empty when she checked. They wouldn't fit in it anymore anyway. She couldn't even eat them now, could she? They would just walk right out of the oven, right out of her mouth. Go back to where you came from, she told herself. Thank you, Goodbye, Excuse me. She swept endlessly, and trucks moved past her window.

In the morning, with spring rolling off the hillsides in bright puffs, she went outside to the strip of dirt. No movement at all. She set a rock at each site, one rock for One, two for Two, etc. She sat for long spells, over the course of the next week, and watched the sky drift overhead. It all felt very familiar, and she recognized the shape and texture of her life before, but it was as if someone had put her old life in the laundry and washed it wrong. The color was slightly off. The sleeves were now too short.

At the end of the week, she kicked off the stones and got out her big shovel. Her neighbor was hanging up clothing on her laundry line, green dresses and blue scarves. The wind whisked her hair around.

"How's that broken bathroom?" she yelled.

"Oh," said the woman. "Well. There never was any broken bathroom."

The neighbor raised her eyebrows.

"I was hiding my children from you," said our woman. "Children? What children?" said the neighbor, wrapping her neck in a rose-colored scarf. "I had no idea! How sweet! How many? Where are they?"

"I buried them," said the woman, waving her shovel.

"You what?"

"I buried them," said the woman. "And now I am going to dig them back up."

She went to the side of the house, and dug up One first. He sat up right when the shovel touched his arm and dirt fell from his face and legs. He blinked at her, as if no time had passed at all, and she held out her hand and pulled him out. She dug up Three, and Four. She thought briefly of leaving Two there forever, letting weeds grow all over him, but the other three were looking at his spot expectantly, so she dug up Two too.

The woman looked at each in turn. The layers of dirt became them.

"Okay," she said.

They stepped into her open arms, solemn as monks. As they nestled and burrowed into her neck, the neighbor poked her head around corner of the house, draped in a clean sheet. "Oh!" she said. "Look at this!"

The woman glanced over with Three on her back and Four clinging to her shoe.

"I didn't think you could be serious," said the neighbor. "I am always serious," said our woman.

The neighbor crouched down and smiled at Four. "Are you okay, honey?" she asked. Four looked past the neighbor and then climbed onto our woman's back, pushing off One who fell lightly to the ground.

"They look so pale," said the neighbor, her voice unsure where to drop, into which voice box positioned between curiosity and righteousness. "You might want to call a doctor," she said. "I know a good one, who can be here within the hour."

Four curled his hand around our woman's neck, and began tugging on the lobe of her ear. Our woman barely smiled at her neighbor. It was a smile not made of pity, and it was not made of envy, even though the two had merged, for years now, on her lips. This smile instead was built of a weariness, of the particular quiet of the body after a long bout of weeping or illness. Certain things endured, and somehow she had ended up with four.

From the ground, Two leaped up to swing gently from her wrist.

"They need no doctors," she said, walking to her front door. "Trust me."

Inside, the woman dressed the group in clothing even though they had no hair or blood and would never look normal, dressed or undressed. Still she put them in pants and shirts she had sewn herself; in hats and shoes and belts.

She took their slow-moving hands and walked out the door again. They blinked and ducked under the lemony March sun. Already, like clockwork, the very first buds of green were pushing up from the soil, a ring of nasturtiums and dead potato babies to border her house. Halfway down the block, she turned and glanced at the neighbor, who was wearing a straw hat now, planting tomatoes. The four glanced with her. Thinking of the doctor had been a kind idea; she would thank the neighbor later. Living next to abundance was not so awful after all. It was contagious, in its own way.

The rest of the town was quiet and drowsy as the five walked past the cemetery, where they waved to the headstones, and over to the edge of the county. The air smelled ripe with spring. At the county line, the potato children stood by the fence posts and laid their hands on the dirt. They seemed interested, even pleased, by the new setting. They had no traumatic recollections of their past week buried alive. Instead, they brought fingers dusted with soil to their noses and smelled appreciatively.

They all crossed over, and began walking. A farmer pulling a wheelbarrow full of corn stopped and said hello.

"Good day," said the woman.

His eyes flicked to the bluish figures at her side, but he was a polite farmer and didn't say anything.

"How's the corn?"

"Fine," said the farmer. "Should be a good growing season. Good weather."

He kept his eyes steady on her face.

"These are my children," said the woman, giving him permission to look. "Children," she said, "say hello to the nice farmer." The four lifted their hands to touch him, and the farmer, familiar best with things of the earth, felt a wave of fluency, inexplicable, wash through him. His own son ran to catch up with them. "Here's mine," he said helplessly.

She shook the boy's hand, the boy who was fixed on looking at the potato children, and who, the way children do, immediately felt entitled to touch their nubbly elbows.

"Do they talk?" asked the boy, and the woman shook her head, no.

"Do they have magic powers?" asked the boy, and she shook her head again.

"They stay," she told the boy.

The farmer touched each potato child on the shoulder, and then waved goodbye to return to his work. He gave his son the day off. "Enjoy yourself," he said, surprised by the pang of longing in his voice. The group walked around the county, trailed by the farmer's boy; most things were very similar here except for the one movie theater showing a Western. In the interest of novelty, they all went to see it. The farmer's son ate popcorn. The cowboys rode along the prairie. There was a shoot-out at the saloon. The potato babies found it all amazing, and although they could not eat the popcorn, they clutched handfuls of it in their fat fingers until it dribbled in soft white shapes to the floor.

Afterward, the farmer's son ran home for dinner, and the family of five crossed back over. The sky was darkening with clouds, and halfway home, it began to rain. The woman tried to huddle the four under her arms, but they resisted, and held their bodies freely under the water. They seemed to enjoy it, tilting their faces to the sky. She had never seen them wet before, and rain, falling on their dirty potato bodies, smelled just like Mother at the sink, washing. Mother, who had died so many years ago, now as vivid as actual, scrubbing potatoes at the kitchen sink before breakfast. How many times had she done that? Year after year after year. Lighting the new fire of the morning. Humming. Her skirt so easy on her waist. Her hands so confident at the sink. They were that memory, created. Holding their potato hands up, they let the rain pour down their potato arms, their potato knees and legs, and the woman breathed in the smell of them, over and over, as deeply as she could. For here was grandmother, greeting her grandchildren, gathering them in her arms, and covering their wide faces with kisses.

Mountain Ways

Ursula K. Le Guin

Last year we included Ursula K. Le Guin's "Another Story," whose protagonist came from the planet O. The fact that marriages on O are between four people was background information in "Another Story," but central to "Mountain Ways," which shared the 1996 Tiptree Award with Mary Doria Russell's novel *The Sparrow*.

Every social norm will work for some people and not for others. This story presents us with a complex initial standard for relationships, and, while we readers are still coming to terms with it, shows us characters for whom it does not work—or only works if they live it as a lie.

Note for readers unfamiliar with the planet O:

Ki'O society is divided into two halves or moieties, called (for ancient religious reasons) the Morning and the Evening. You belong to your mother's moiety, and you can't have sex with anybody of your moiety.

Marriage on O is a foursome, the sedoretu—a man and a woman from the Morning moiety and a man and a woman from the Evening moiety. You're expected to have sex with both your spouses of the other moiety, and not to have sex with your spouse of your own moiety. So each sedoretu has two expected heterosexual relationships, two expected homosexual relationships, and two forbidden heterosexual relationships.

The expected relationships within each sedoretu are:

The Morning woman and the Evening man (the "Morning marriage")
The Evening woman and the Morning man (the "Evening marriage")
The Morning woman and the Evening woman (the "Day marriage")
The Morning man and the Evening man (the "Night marriage")

The forbidden relationships are between the Morning woman and the

Morning man, and between the Evening woman and the Evening man, and they aren't called anything, except sacrilege.

It's just as complicated as it sounds, but aren't most marriages?

In the stony uplands of the Deka Mountains the farmholds are few and far between. Farmers scrape a living out of that cold earth, planting on sheltered slopes facing south, combing the yama for fleece, carding and spinning and weaving the prime wool, selling pelts to the carpet-factories. The mountain yama, called ariu, are a small wiry breed; they run wild, without shelter, and are not fenced in, since they never cross the invisible, immemorial boundaries of the herd territory. Each farmhold is in fact a herd territory. The animals are the true farmholders. Tolerant and aloof, they allow the farmers to comb out their thick fleeces, to assist them in difficult births, and to skin them when they die. The farmers are dependent on the ariu; the ariu are not dependent on the farmers. The question of ownership is moot. At Danro Farmhold they don't say, "We have nine hundred ariu," they say, "The herd has nine hundred."

Danro is the farthest farm of Oro Village in the High Watershed of the Mane River on Oniasu on O. The people up there in the mountains are civilized but not very civilized. Like most ki'O they pride themselves on doing things the way they've always been done, but in fact they are a willful, stubborn lot who change the rules to suit themselves and then say the people "down there" don't know the rules, don't honor the old ways, the true ki'O ways, the mountain ways.

Some years ago, the First Sedoretu of Danro was broken by a landslide up on the Farren that killed the Morning woman and her husband. The widowed Evening couple, who had both married in from other farmholds, fell into a habit of mourning and grew old early, letting the daughter of the Morning manage the farm and all its business.

Her name was Shahes. At thirty, she was a straight-backed, strong, short woman with rough red cheeks, a mountaineer's long stride, and a mountaineer's deep lungs. She could walk down the road to the village center in deep snow with a sixty-pound pack of pelts on her back, sell the pelts, pay her taxes and visit a bit at the village hearth, and stride back up the steep zigzags to be home before nightfall, forty kilometers round trip and six hundred meters of altitude each way. If she or anyone else at Danro wanted to see a new face they had to go down the mountain to other farms or to the village center. There was nothing to bring anybody up the hard road to Danro. Shahes seldom hired help, and the family wasn't sociable. Their hospitality, like their road, had grown stony through lack of use.

But a travelling scholar from the lowlands who came up the Mane all the way to Oro was not daunted by another near-vertical stretch of ruts and rubble. Having visited the other farms, the scholar climbed on around the Farren from Ked'din and up to Danro, and there made the honorable and traditional offer: to share worship at the house shrine, to lead conversation about the Discussions, to instruct the children of the farmhold in spiritual matters, for as long as the farmers wished to lodge and keep her.

This scholar was an Evening woman, over forty, tall and long-limbed, with cropped dark-brown hair as fine and curly as a yama's. She was quite fearless, expected nothing in the way of luxury or even comfort, and had no small talk at all. She was not one of the subtle and eloquent expounders of the great Centers. She was a farm woman who had gone to school. She read and talked about the Discussions in a plain way that suited her hearers, sang the Offerings and the praise songs to the oldest tunes, and gave brief, undemanding lessons to Danro's one child, a ten-year-old Morning half-nephew. Otherwise she was as silent as her hosts, and as hard-working. They were up at dawn; she was up before dawn to sit in meditation. She studied her few books and wrote for an hour or two after that. The rest of the day she worked alongside the farm people at whatever job they gave her.

It was fleecing season, midsummer, and the people were all out every day, all over the vast mountain territory of the herd, following the scattered groups, combing the animals when they lay down to chew the cud.

The old ariu knew and liked the combing. They lay with their legs folded under them or stood still for it, leaning into the comb-strokes a little, sometimes making a small, shivering whisper-cough of enjoyment. The yearlings, whose fleece was the finest and brought the best price raw or woven, were ticklish and frisky; they sidled, bit, and bolted. Fleecing yearlings called for a profound and resolute patience. To this the young ariu would at last respond, growing quiet and even drowsing as the long, fine teeth of the comb bit in and stroked through, over and over again, in the rhythm of the comber's soft monotonous tune, "Hunna, hunna, na, na…"

The travelling scholar, whose religious name was Enno, showed such a knack for handling newborn ariu that Shahes took her out to try her hand at fleecing yearlings. Enno proved to be as good with them as with the infants, and soon she and Shahes, the best finefleecer of Oro, were working daily side by side. After her meditation and reading, Enno would come out and find Shahes on the great slopes where the yearlings still ran with their dams and the newborns. Together the two women could fill a forty-pound sack a day with the airy, silky, milk-colored clouds of combings. Often they would pick out a pair of twins, of which there had been an unusual number this mild year. If Shahes led out one twin the other would follow it, as yama twins will do all their lives; and so the women could work side by side in a silent, absorbed companionship. They talked only to the animals. "Move your fool leg," Shahes would say to the yearling she was combing, as it gazed at her with its great, dark, dreaming eyes. Enno would murmur "Hunna, hunna, hunna, na," or hum a fragment of an Offering, to soothe her beast when it shook its disdainful, elegant head and showed its teeth at her for tickling its belly. Then for half an hour nothing but the crisp whisper of the combs, the flutter of the unceasing wind over stones, the soft bleat of a calf, the faint rhythmical sound of the nearby beasts biting the thin, dry grass. Always one old female stood watch, the alert head poised on the long neck, the large eyes watching up and down the vast, tilted planes of the mountain from the river miles below to the hanging glaciers miles above. Far peaks of stone and snow stood distinct against the dark-blue, sun-filled sky, blurred off into cloud and blowing mists, then shone out again across the gulfs of air.

Enno took up the big clot of milky fleece she had combed, and Shahes held open the long, loose-woven, double-ended sack.

Enno stuffed the fleece down into the sack. Shahes took her hands.

Leaning across the half-filled sack they held each other's hands, and Shahes said, "I want —" and Enno said, "Yes, yes!"

Neither of them had had much love, neither had had much pleasure in sex. Enno, when she was a rough farm girl named Akal, had the misfortune to attract and be attracted by a man whose pleasure was in cruelty. When she finally understood that she did not have to endure what he did to her, she ran away, not knowing how else to escape him. She took refuge at the school in Asta, and there found the work and learning much to her liking, as she did the spiritual discipline, and later the wandering life. She had been an itinerant scholar with no family, no close attachments, for twenty years. Now Shahes's passion opened to her a spirituality of the body, a revelation that transformed the world and made her feel she had never lived in it before.

As for Shahes, she'd given very little thought to love and not much more to sex, except as it entered into the question of marriage. Marriage was an urgent matter of business. She was thirty years old. Danro had no whole sedoretu, no childbearing women, and only one child. Her duty was plain. She had gone courting in a grim, reluctant fashion to a couple of neighboring farms where there were Evening men. She was too late for the man at Beha Farm, who ran off with a lowlander. The widower at Upper Ked'd was receptive, but he also was nearly sixty and smelled like piss. She tried to force herself to accept the advances of Uncle Mika's half-cousin from Okba Farm down the river, but his desire to own a share of Danro was clearly the sole substance of his desire for Shahes, and he was even lazier and more shiftless than Uncle Mika.

Ever since they were girls, Shahes had met now and then with Temly, the Evening daughter of the nearest farmhold, Ked'din, round on the other side of the Farren. Temly and Shahes had a sexual friendship that was a true and reliable pleasure to them both. They both wished it could be permanent. Every now and then they talked, lying in Shahes's bed at Danro or Temly's bed at Ked'din, of getting married, making a sedoretu. There was no use going to the village matchmakers; they knew everybody the matchmakers knew. One by one they would name the men of Oro and the very few men they knew from outside the Oro Valley, and one by one they would dismiss them as either impossible or inaccessible. The only name that always stayed on the list was Otorra, a Morning man who worked at the carding sheds down in the village center. Shahes liked his reputation as a steady worker; Temly liked his looks and conversation. He evidently liked Temly's looks and conversation too, and would certainly have come courting her if there were any chance of a marriage at Ked'din, but it was a poor farmhold, and there was the same problem there as at Danro: there wasn't an eligible Evening man. To make a sedoretu, Shahes and Temly and Otorra would have to marry the shiftless, shameless fellow at Okba or the sour old widower at Ked'd. To Shahes the idea of sharing her farm and her bed with either of them was intolerable.

"If I could only meet a man who was a match for me!" she said with bitter energy.

"I wonder if you'd like him if you did," said Temly. "I don't know that I would."

"Maybe next autumn at Manebo…"

Shahes sighed. Every autumn she trekked down sixty kilometers to Manebo Fair with a train of pack-yama laden with pelts and wool, and looked for a man; but those she looked at twice never looked at her once. Even though Danro offered a steady living, nobody wanted to live way up there, on the roof, as they called it. And Shahes had no prettiness or nice ways to interest a man. Hard work, hard weather, and the habit of command had made her tough; solitude had made her shy. She was like a wild animal among the jovial, easy-talking dealers and buyers. Last autumn once more she had gone to the fair and once more strode back up into her mountains, sore and dour, and said to Temly, "I wouldn't touch a one of 'em."

———

Enno woke in the ringing silence of the mountain night. She saw the small square of the window ablaze with stars and felt Shahes's warm body beside her shake with sobs.

"What is it? What is it, my dear love?"

"You'll go away. You're going to go away!"

"But not now—not soon—"

"You can't stay here. You have a calling. A resp—" the word broken by a gasp and sob—"responsibility to your school, to your work, and I can't keep you. I can't give you the farm. I haven't anything to give you, anything at all!"

Enno — or Akal, as she had asked Shahes to call her when they were alone, going back to the girl-name she had given up—Akal knew only too well what Shahes meant. It was the farmholder's duty to provide continuity. As Shahes owed life to her ancestors she owed life to her descendants. Akal did not question this; she had grown up on a farmhold. Since then, at school, she had learned about the joys and duties of the soul, and with Shahes she had learned the joys and duties of love. Neither of them in any way invalidated the duty of a farmholder. Shahes need not bear children herself, but she must see to it that Danro had children. If Temly and Otorra made the Evening marriage, Temly would bear the children of Danro. But a sedoretu must have a Morning marriage; Shahes must find an Evening man. Shahes was not free to keep Akal at Danro, nor was Akal justified in staying there, for she was in the way, an irrelevance, ultimately an obstacle, a spoiler. As long as she stayed on as a lover, she was neglecting her religious obligations while compromising Shahes's obligation to her farmhold. Shahes had said the truth: she had to go.

She got out of bed and went over to the window. Cold as it was she stood there naked in the starlight, gazing at the stars that flared and dazzled from the far grey slopes up to the zenith. She had to go and she could not go. Life was here, life was Shahes's body, her breasts, her mouth, her breath. She had found life and she could not go down to death. She could not go and she had to go.

Shahes said across the dark room, "Marry me."

Akal came back to the bed, her bare feet silent on the bare floor.

She slipped under the bedfleece, shivering, feeling Shahes's warmth against her, and turned to her to hold her; but Shahes took her hand in a strong grip and said again, "Marry me."

"Oh if I could!"

"You can."

After a moment Akal sighed and stretched out, her hands behind her head on the pillow. "There's no Evening men here; you've said so yourself. So how can we marry? What can I do? Go fishing for a husband down in the lowlands, I suppose. With the farmhold as bait. What kind of man would that turn up? Nobody I'd let share you with me for a moment. I won't do it."

Shahes was following her own train of thought. "I can't leave Temly in the lurch," she said.

"And that's the other obstacle," Akal said. "It's not fair to Temly. If we do find an Evening man, then she'll get left out."

"No, she won't."

"Two Day marriages and no Morning marriage? Two Evening women in one sedoretu? There's a fine notion!"

"Listen," Shahes said, still not listening. She sat up with the bedfleece round her shoulders and spoke low and quick. "You go away. Back down there. The winter goes by. Late in the spring, people come up the Mane looking for summer work. A man comes to Oro and says, is anybody asking for a good finefleecer? At the sheds they tell him, yes, Shahes from Danro was down here looking for a hand. So he comes on up here, he knocks at the door here. My name is Akal, he says, I hear you need a fleecer. Yes, I say, yes, we do. Come in. Oh come in, come in and stay forever!"

Her hand was like iron on Akal's wrist, and her voice shook with exultation. Akal listened as to a fairytale.

"Who's to know, Akal? Who'd ever know you? You're taller than most men up here — you can grow your hair, and dress like a man — you said you liked men's clothes once. Nobody will know. Who ever comes here anyway?"

"Oh, come on, Shahes! The people here, Magel and Madu — Shest —"

"The old people won't see anything. Mika's a halfwit. The child won't know. Temly can bring old Barres from Ked'din to marry us. He never knew a tit from a toe anyhow. But he can say the marriage ceremony."

"And Temly?" Akal said, laughing but disturbed; the idea was so wild and Shahes was so serious about it.

"Don't worry about Temly. She'd do anything to get out of Ked'din. She wants to come here, she and I have wanted to marry for years. Now we can. All we need is a Morning man for her. She likes Otorra well enough. And he'd like a share of Danro."

"No doubt, but he gets a share of me with it, you know! A woman in a Night marriage?"

"He doesn't have to know."

"You're crazy, of course he'll know!"

"Only after we're married."

Akal stared through the dark at Shahes, speechless. Finally she said, "What you're proposing is that I go away now and come back after half a year dressed as a man. And marry you and Temly and a man I never met. And live here the rest of my life pretending to be a man. And nobody is going to guess who I am or see through it or object to it. Least of all my husband."

"He doesn't matter."

"Yes he does," said Akal. "It's wicked and unfair. It would desecrate the marriage sacrament. And anyway it wouldn't work. I couldn't fool everybody! Certainly not for the rest of my life!"

"What other way have we to marry?"

"Find an Evening husband — somewhere — "

"But I want you! I want you for my husband and my wife. I don't want any man, ever. I want you, only you till the end of life, and nobody between us, and nobody to part us. Akal, think, think about it, maybe it's against religion, but who does it hurt? Why is it unfair? Temly likes men, and she'll have Otorra. He'll have her, and Danro. And Danro will have their children. And I will have you, I'll have you forever and ever, my soul, my life and soul."

"Oh don't, oh don't," Akal said with a great sob.

Shahes held her.

"I never was much good at being a woman," Akal said. "Till I met you. You can't make me into a man now! I'd be even worse at that, no good at all!"

"You won't be a man, you'll be my Akal, my love, and nothing and nobody will ever come between us."

They rocked back and forth together, laughing and crying, with the fleece around them and the stars blazing at them. "We'll do it, we'll do it!" Shahes said, and Akal said, "We're crazy, we're crazy!"

Gossips in Oro had begun to ask if that scholar woman was going to spend the winter up in the high farmholds, where was she now, Danro was it or Ked'din? — when she came walking down the zigzag road. She spent the night and sang the Offerings for the mayor's family, and caught the daily freighter to the suntrain station down at Dermane. The first of the autumn blizzards followed her down from the peaks.

Shahes and Akal sent no message to each other all through the winter. In the early spring Akal telephoned the farm. "When are you coming?" Shahes asked, and the distant voice replied, "In time for the fleecing."

For Shahes the winter passed in a long dream of Akal. Her voice sounded in the empty next room. Her tall body moved beside Shahes through the wind and snow. Shahes's sleep was peaceful, rocked in a certainty of love known and love to come.

For Akal, or Enno as she became again in the lowlands, the winter passed in a long misery of guilt and indecision. Marriage was a sacrament, and surely what they planned was a mockery of that sacrament. Yet as surely it was a marriage of love. And as Shahes had said, it harmed no one — unless to deceive them was to harm them. It could not be right to fool the man, Otorra, into a marriage where his Night partner would turn out to be a woman. But surely no man knowing the scheme beforehand would agree to it; deception was the only means at hand. They must cheat him.

The religion of the ki'O lacks priests and pundits who tell the common folk what to do. The common folk have to make their own moral and spiritual choices, which is why they spend a good deal of time discussing the Discussions. As a scholar of the Discussions, Enno knew more questions than most people, but fewer answers.

She sat all the dark winter mornings wrestling with her soul. When she called Shahes, it was to tell her that she could not come. When she heard Shahes's voice her misery and guilt ceased to exist, were gone, as a dream is gone on waking. She said, "I'll be there in time for the fleecing."

In the spring, while she worked with a crew rebuilding and repainting a wing of her old school at Asta, she let her hair grow. When it was long enough, she clubbed it back, as men often did. In the summer, having saved a little money working for the school, she bought men's clothes. She put them on and looked at herself in the mirror in the shop. She saw Akal. Akal was a tall, thin man with a thin face, a bony nose, and a slow, brilliant smile. She liked him.

Akal got off the High Deka freighter at its last stop, Oro, went to the village center, and asked if anybody was looking for a fleecer.

"Danro." — "The farmer was down from Danro, twice already." — "Wants a finefleecer." — "Coarsefleecer, wasn't it?" — It took a while, but the elders and gossips agreed at last: a finefleecer was wanted at Danro.

"Where's Danro?" asked the tall man.

"Up," said an elder succinctly. "You ever handled ariu yearlings?"

"Yes," said the tall man. "Up west or up east?"

They told him the road to Danro, and he went off up the zigzags, whistling a familiar praise song.

As Akal went on he stopped whistling, and stopped being a man, and wondered how she could pretend not to know anybody in the household, and how she could imagine they wouldn't know her. How could she deceive Shest, the child whom she had taught the water rite and the praise-songs? A pang of fear and dismay and shame shook her when she saw Shest come running to the gate to let the stranger in.

Akal spoke little, keeping her voice down in her chest, not meeting the child's eyes. She was sure he recognized her. But his stare was simply that of a child who saw strangers so seldom that for all he knew they all looked alike. He ran in to fetch the old people, Magel and Madu. They came out to offer Akal the customary hospitality, a religious duty, and Akal accepted, feeling mean and low at deceiving these people, who had always been kind to her in their rusty, stingy way, and at the same time feeling a wild impulse of laughter, of triumph. They did not see Enno in her, they did not know her. That meant that she was Akal, and Akal was free.

She was sitting in the kitchen drinking a thin and sour soup of summer greens when Shahes came in — grim, stocky, weather-beaten, wet. A summer thunderstorm had broken over the Farren soon after Akal reached the farm. "Who's that?" said Shahes, doffing her wet coat.

"Come up from the village." Old Magel lowered his voice to address Shahes confidentially: "He said they said you said you wanted a hand with the yearlings."

"Where've you worked?" Shahes demanded, her back turned, as she ladled herself a bowl of soup.

Akal had no life history, at least not a recent one. She groped a long time. No one took any notice, prompt answers and quick talk being unusual and suspect practices in the mountains. At last she said the name of the farm she had run away from twenty years ago. "Bredde Hold, of Abba Village, on the Oriso."

"And you've finefleeced? Handled yearlings? Ariu yearlings?"

Akal nodded, dumb. Was it possible that Shahes did not recognize her? Her voice was flat and unfriendly, and the one glance she had given Akal was dismissive. She had sat down with her soupbowl and was eating hungrily.

"You can come out with me this afternoon and I'll see how you work," Shahes said. "What's your name, then?"

"Akal."

Shahes grunted and went on eating. She glanced up across the table at Akal again, one flick of the eyes, like a stab of light.

Out on the high hills, in the mud of rain and snowmelt, in the stinging wind and the flashing sunlight, they held each other so tight neither could breathe, they laughed and wept and talked and kissed and coupled in a rock shelter, and came back so dirty and with such a sorry little sack of combings that old Magel told Madu that he couldn't understand why Shahes was going to hire the tall fellow from down there at all, if that's all the work was in him, and Madu said what's more he eats for six.

But after a month or so, when Shahes and Akal weren't hiding the fact that they slept together, and Shahes began to talk about making a sedoretu, the old couple grudgingly approved. They had no other kind of approval to give. Maybe Akal was ignorant, didn't know a hassel-bit from a cold-chisel; but they were all like that down there. Remember that travelling scholar, Enno, stayed here last year, she was just the same, too tall for her own good and ignorant, but willing to learn, same as Akal. Akal was a prime hand with the beasts, or had the makings of it anyhow. Shahes could look farther and do worse. And it meant she and Temly could be the Day marriage of a sedoretu, as they would have been long since if there'd been any kind of men around worth taking into the farmhold, what's wrong with this generation, plenty of good men around in my day.

Shahes had spoken to the village matchmakers down in Oro. They spoke to Otorra, now a foreman at the carding sheds; he accepted a formal invitation to Danro. Such invitations included meals and an overnight stay, necessarily, in such a remote place, but the invitation was to share worship with the farm family at the house shrine, and its significance was known to all.

So they all gathered at the house shrine, which at Danro was a low, cold, inner room walled with stone, with a floor of earth and stones that was the unlevelled ground of the mountainside. A tiny spring, rising at the higher end of the room, trickled in a channel of cut granite. It was the reason why the house stood where it did, and had stood there for six hundred years. They offered water and accepted water, one to another, one from another, the old Evening couple, Uncle Mika, his son Shest, Asbi who had worked as a packtrainer and handyman at Danro for thirty years, Akal the new hand, Shahes the farmholder, and the guests: Otorra from Oro and Temly from Ked'din.

Temly smiled across the spring at Otorra, but he did not meet her eyes, or anyone else's.

Temly was a short, stocky woman, the same type as Shahes, but fairer-skinned and a bit lighter all round, not as solid, not as hard. She had a surprising, clear singing voice that soared up in the praise-songs. Otorra was also rather short and broad-shouldered, with good features, a competent-looking man, but just now extremely ill at ease; he looked as if he had robbed the shrine or murdered the mayor, Akal thought, studying him with interest, as well she might. He looked furtive; he looked guilty.

Akal observed him with curiosity and dispassion. She would share water with Otorra, but not guilt. As soon as she had seen Shahes, touched Shahes, all her scruples and moral anxieties had dropped away, as if they could not breathe up here in the mountains. Akal had been born for Shahes and Shahes for Akal; that was all there was to it. Whatever made it possible for them to be together was right.

Once or twice she did ask herself, what if I'd been born into the Morning instead of the Evening moiety? — a perverse and terrible thought. But perversity and sacrilege were not asked of her. All she had to do was change sex. And that only in appearance, in public. With Shahes she was a woman, and more truly a woman and herself than she had ever been in her life. With everybody else she was Akal, whom they took to be a man. That was no trouble at all. She was Akal; she liked being Akal. It was not like acting a part. She never had been herself with other people, had always felt a falsity in her relationships with them; she had never known who she was at all, except sometimes for a moment in meditation, when her *I am* became *It is*, and she breathed the stars. But with Shahes she was herself utterly, in time and in the body, Akal, a soul consumed in love and blessed by intimacy.

So it was that she had agreed with Shahes that they should say nothing to Otorra, nothing even to Temly. "Let's see what Temly makes of you," Shahes said, and Akal agreed.

Last year Temly had entertained the scholar Enno overnight at her farmhold for instruction and worship, and had met her two or three times at Danro. When she came to share worship today she met Akal for the first time. Did she see Enno? She gave no sign of it. She greeted Akal with a kind of brusque goodwill, and they talked about breeding ariu. She quite evidently studied the newcomer, judging, sizing up; but that was natural enough in a woman meeting a stranger she might be going to marry. "You don't know much about mountain farming, do you?" she said kindly after they had talked a while. "Different from down there. What did you raise? Those big flatland yama?" And Akal told her about the farm where she grew up, and the three crops a year they got, which made Temly nod in amazement.

As for Otorra, Shahes and Akal colluded to deceive him without ever saying a word more about it to each other. Akal's mind shied away from the subject. They would get to know each other during the engagement period, she thought vaguely. She would have to tell him, eventually, that she did not want to have sex with him, of course, and the only way to do that without insulting and humiliating him was to say that she, that Akal, was averse to having sex with other men, and hoped he would forgive her. But Shahes had made it clear that she mustn't tell him that till they were married. If he knew it beforehand he would refuse to enter the sedoretu. And even worse, he might talk about it, expose Akal as a woman, in revenge. Then they would never be able to marry. When Shahes had spoken about this, Akal had felt distressed and trapped, anxious, guilty again; but Shahes was serenely confident and untroubled, and somehow Akal's guilty feelings would not stick. They dropped off. She simply hadn't thought much about it. She watched Otorra now with sympathy and curiosity, wondering what made him look so hangdog. He was scared of something, she thought.

After the water was poured and the blessing said, Shahes read from the Fourth Discussion; she closed the old boxbook very carefully, put it on its shelf and put its cloth over it, and then, speaking to Magel and Madu as was proper, they being what was left of the First Sedoretu of Danro, she said, "My Othermother and my Otherfather, I propose that a new sedoretu be made in this house."

Madu nudged Magel. He fidgeted and grimaced and muttered inaudibly. Finally Madu said in her weak, resigned voice, "Daughter of the Morning, tell us the marriages."

"If all be well and willing, the marriage of the Morning will be Shahes and Akal, and the marriage of the Evening will be Temly and Otorra, and the marriage of the Day will be Shahes and Temly, and the marriage of the Night will be Akal and Otorra."

There was a long pause. Magel hunched his shoulders. Madu said at last, rather fretfully, "Well, is that all right with everybody?" —which gave the gist, if not the glory, of the formal request for consent, usually couched in antique and ornate language.

"Yes," said Shahes, clearly.

"Yes," said Akal, manfully.

"Yes," said Temly, cheerfully.

A pause.

Everybody looked at Otorra, of course. He had blushed purple and, as they watched, turned greyish.

"I am willing," he said at last in a forced mumble, and cleared his throat. "Only —" He stuck there.

Nobody said anything.

The silence was horribly painful.

Akal finally said, "We don't have to decide now. We can talk. And, and come back to the shrine later, if…"

"Yes," Otorra said, glancing at Akal with a look in which so much emotion was compressed that she could not read it at all — terror, hate, gratitude, despair? — "I want to — I need to talk — to Akal."

"I'd like to get to know my brother of the Evening too," said Temly in her clear voice.

"Yes, that's it, yes, that is — " Otorra stuck again, and blushed again. He was in such an agony of discomfort that Akal said, "Let's go on outside for a bit, then," and led Otorra out into the yard, while the others went to the kitchen.

Akal knew Otarra had seen through her pretense. She was dismayed, and dreaded what he might say; but he had not made a scene, he had not humiliated her before the others, and she was grateful to him for that.

"This is what it is," Otorra said in a stiff, forced voice, coming to a stop at the gate. "It's the Night marriage." He came to a stop there, too.

Akal nodded. Reluctantly, she spoke, to help Otorra do what he had to do. "You don't have to — " she began, but he was speaking again:

"The night marriage. Us. You and me. See, I don't — There's some — See, with men, I — "

The whine of delusion and the buzz of incredulity kept Akal from hearing what the man was trying to tell her. He had to stammer on even more painfully before she began to listen. When his words came clear to her she could not trust them, but she had to. He had stopped trying to talk.

Very hesitantly, she said, "Well, I…I was going to tell you…. The only man I ever had sex with, it was… It wasn't good. He made me — He did things — I don't know what was wrong. But I never have — I have never had any sex with men. Since that. I can't. I can't make myself want to."

"Neither can I," Otorra said.

They stood side by side leaning on the gate, contemplating the miracle, the simple truth.

"I just only ever want women," Otorra said in a shaking voice.

"A lot of people are like that," Akal said.

"They are?"

She was touched and grieved by his humility. Was it men's boastfulness with other men, or the hardness of the mountain people, that had burdened him with this ignorance, this shame?

"Yes," she said. "Everywhere I've been. There's quite a lot of men who only want sex with women. And women who only want sex with men. And the other way round, too. Most people want both, but there's always some who don't. It's like the two ends of," she was about to say "a spectrum," but it wasn't the language of Akal the fleecer or

Otorra the carder, and with the adroitness of the old teacher she substituted "a sack. If you pack it right, most of the fleece is in the middle. But there's some at both ends where you tie off, too. That's us. There's not as many of us. But there's nothing wrong with us." As she said this last it did not sound like what a man would say to a man. But it was said; and Otorra did not seem to think it peculiar, though he did not look entirely convinced. He pondered. He had a pleasant face, blunt, unguarded, now that his unhappy secret was out. He was only about thirty, younger than she had expected.

"But in a marriage," he said. "It's different from just... A marriage is — Well, if I don't — and you don't — "

"Marriage isn't just sex," Akal said, but said it in Enno's voice, Enno the scholar discussing questions of ethics, and Akal cringed.

"A lot of it is," said Otorra, reasonably.

"All right," Akal said in a consciously deeper, slower voice. "But if I don't want it with you and you don't want it with me why can't we have a good marriage?" It came out so improbable and so banal at the same time that she nearly broke into a fit of laughter. Controlling herself, she thought, rather shocked, that Otorra was laughing at her, until she realized that he was crying.

"I never could tell anybody," he said.

"We don't ever have to," she said. She put her arm around his shoulders without thinking about it at all. He wiped his eyes with his fists like a child, cleared his throat, and stood thinking. Obviously he was thinking about what she had just said.

"Think," she said, also thinking about it, "how lucky we are!"

"Yes. Yes, we are." He hesitated. "But...but is it religious...to marry each other knowing... Without really meaning to...." He stuck again.

After a long time, Akal said, in a voice as soft and nearly as deep as his, "I don't know."

She had withdrawn her comforting, patronizing arm from his shoulders. She leaned her hands on the top bar of the gate. She looked at her hands, long and strong, hardened and dirt-engrained from farm work, though the oil of the fleeces kept them supple. A farmer's hands. She had given up the religious life for love's sake and never looked back. But now she was ashamed.

She wanted to tell this honest man the truth, to be worthy of his honesty.

But it would do no good, unless not to make the sedoretu was the only good.

"I don't know," she said again. "I think what matters is if we try to give each other love and honor. However we do that, that's how we do it. That's how we're married. The marriage — the religion is in the love, in the honoring."

"I wish there was somebody to ask," Otorra said, unsatisfied. "Like that travelling scholar that was here last summer. Somebody who knows about religion."

Akal was silent.

"I guess the thing is to do your best," Otorra said after a while. It sounded sententious, but he added, plainly, "I would do that."

"So would I," Akal said.

A mountain farmhouse like Danro is a dark, damp, bare, grim place to live in, sparsely furnished, with no luxuries except the warmth of the big kitchen and the splendid bedfleeces. But it offers privacy, which may be the greatest luxury of all, though the ki'O consider it a necessity. "A three-room sedoretu" is a common expression in Okets, meaning an enterprise doomed to fail.

At Danro, everyone had their own room and bathroom. The two old members of the First Sedoretu, and Uncle Mika and his child, had rooms in the center and west wing; Asbi, when he wasn't sleeping out on the mountain, had a cozy, dirty nest behind the kitchen. The new Second Sedoretu had the whole east side of the house. Temly chose a little attic room, up a half-flight of stairs from the others, with a fine view. Shahes kept her room, and Akal hers, adjoining; and Otorra chose the southeast corner, the sunniest room in the house.

The conduct of a new sedoretu is to some extent, and wisely, prescribed by custom and sanctioned by religion. The first night after the ceremony of marriage belongs to the Morning and Evening couples;

the second night to the Day and Night couples. Thereafter the four spouses may join as and when they please, but always and only by invitation given and accepted, and the arrangements are to be known to all four. Four souls and bodies and all the years of their four lives to come are in the balance in each of those decisions and invitations; passion, negative and positive, must find its channels, and trust must be established, lest the whole structure fail to found itself solidly, or destroy itself in selfishness and jealousy and grief.

Akal knew all the customs and sanctions, and she insisted that they be followed to the letter. Her wedding night with Shahes was tender and a little tense. Her wedding night with Otorra was also tender; they sat in his room and talked softly, shy with each other but each very grateful; then Otorra slept in the deep windowseat, insisting that Akal have the bed.

Within a few weeks Akal knew that Shahes was more intent on having her way, on having Akal as her partner, than on maintaining any kind of sexual balance or even a pretense of it. As far as Shahes was concerned, Otorra and Temly could look after each other and that was that. Akal had of course known many sedoretu where one or two of the partnerships dominated the others completely, through passion or the power of an ego. To balance all four relationships perfectly was an ideal seldom realized. But this sedoretu, already built on a deception, a disguise, was more fragile than most. Shahes wanted what she wanted and consequences be damned. Akal had followed her far up the mountain, but would not follow her over a precipice.

It was a clear autumn night, the window full of stars, like that night last year when Shahes had said, "Marry me."

"You have to give Temly tomorrow night," Akal repeated.

"She's got Otorra," Shahes repeated.

"She wants you. Why do you think she married you?"

"She's got what she wants. I hope she gets pregnant soon," Shahes said, stretching luxuriously, and running her hand over Akal's breasts and belly. Akal stopped her hand and held it.

"It isn't fair, Shahes. It isn't right."

"A fine one you are to talk!"

"But Otorra doesn't want me, you know that. And Temly does want you. And we owe it to her."

"Owe her what?"

"Love and honor."

"She's got what she wanted," Shahes said, and freed her hand from Akal's grasp with a harsh twist. "Don't preach at me."

"I'm going back to my room," Akal said, slipping lithely from the bed and stalking naked through the starry dark. "Good night."

She was with Temly in the old dye room, unused for years until Temly, an expert dyer, came to the farm. Weavers down in the Centers would pay well for fleece dyed the true Deka red. Her skill had been Temly's dowry. Akal was her assistant and apprentice now.

"Eighteen minutes. Timer set?"

"Set."

Temly nodded, checked the vents on the great dye-boiler, checked the read-out again, and went outside to catch the morning sun. Akal joined her on the stone bench by the stone doorway. The smell of the vegetable dye, pungent and acid-sweet, clung to them, and their clothes and hands and arms were raddled pink and crimson.

Akal had become attached to Temly very soon, finding her reliably good-tempered and unexpectedly thoughtful — both qualities that had been in rather short supply at Danro. Without knowing it, Akal had formed her expectation of the mountain people on Shahes — powerful, willful, undeviating, rough. Temly was strong and quite self-contained, but open to impressions as Shahes was not. Relationships within her moiety meant little to Shahes; she called Otorra brother because it was customary, but did not see a brother in him. Temly called Akal brother and meant it, and Akal, who had had no family for so long, welcomed the relationship, returning Temly's warmth. They talked easily together, though Akal had constantly to guard herself from becoming too easy and letting her woman-self speak out. Mostly it was no trouble at all being Akal and she gave little thought to it, but sometimes with Temly it was very hard to keep up the pretense, to prevent herself from saying what a woman would say to her sister. In general she had found that the main drawback in being a man was that conversations were less interesting.

They talked about the next step in the dyeing process, and then Temly said, looking off over the low stone wall of the yard to the huge purple slant of the Farren, "You know Enno, don't you?"

The question seemed innocent and Akal almost answered automatically with some kind of deceit — "The scholar that was here…?"

But there was no reason why Akal the fleecer should know Enno the scholar. And Temly had not asked, do you remember Enno, or did you know Enno, but, "You know Enno, don't you?" She knew the answer.

"Yes."

Temly nodded, smiling a little. She said nothing more.

Akal was amazed by her subtlety, her restraint. There was no difficulty in honoring so honorable a woman.

"I lived alone for a long time," Akal said. "Even on the farm where I grew up I was mostly alone. I never had a sister. I'm glad to have one at last."

"So am I," said Temly.

Their eyes met briefly, a flicker of recognition, a glance planting trust deep and silent as a tree-root.

"She knows who I am, Shahes."

Shahes said nothing, trudging up the steep slope.

"Now I wonder if she knew from the start. From the first water-sharing…"

"Ask her if you like," Shahes said, indifferent.

"I can't. The deceiver has no right to ask for the truth."

"Humbug!" Shahes said, turning on her, halting her in midstride. They were up on the Farren looking for an old beast that Asbi had reported missing from the herd. The keen autumn wind had blown Shahes's cheeks red, and as she stood staring up at Akal she squinted her watering eyes so that they glinted like knifeblades. "Quit preaching! Is that who you are? 'The deceiver'? I thought you were my wife!"

"I am, and Otorra's too, and you're Temly's — you can't leave them out, Shahes!"

"Are they complaining?"

"Do you want them to complain?" Akal shouted, losing her temper. "Is that the kind of marriage you want? — Look, there she is," she added in a suddenly quiet voice, pointing up the great rocky mountainside. Farsighted, led by a bird's circling, she had caught the movement of the yama's head near an outcrop of boulders. The quarrel was postponed. They both set off at a cautious trot towards the boulders.

The old yama had broken a leg in a slip from the rocks. She lay neatly collected, though the broken foreleg would not double under her white breast but stuck out forward, and her whole body had a lurch to that side. Her disdainful head was erect on the long neck, and she gazed at the women, watching her death approach, with clear, unfathomable, uninterested eyes.

"Is she in pain?" Akal asked, daunted by that great serenity.

"Of course," Shahes said, sitting down several paces away from the yama to sharpen her knife on its emery-stone. "Wouldn't you be?"

She took a long time getting the knife as sharp as she could get it, patiently retesting and rewhetting the blade. At last she tested it again and then sat completely still. She stood up quietly, walked over to the yama, pressed its head up against her breast and cut its throat in one long fast slash. Blood leaped out in a brilliant arc. Shahes slowly lowered the head with its gazing eyes down to the ground.

Akal found that she was speaking the words of the ceremony for the dead, *Now all that was owed is repaid and all that was owned, returned. Now all that was lost is found and all that was bound, free.* Shahes stood silent, listening till the end.

Then came the work of skinning. They would leave the carcass to be cleaned by the scavengers of the mountain; it was a carrion-bird circling over the yama that had first caught Akal's eye, and there were now three of them riding the wind. Skinning was fussy, dirty work, in the stink of meat and blood. Akal was inexpert, clumsy, cutting the hide more than once. In penance she insisted on carrying the pelt, rolled as best they could and strapped with their belts. She felt like a grave robber, carrying away the white-and-dun fleece, leaving the thin, broken corpse sprawled among the rocks in the indignity of its nakedness. Yet in her mind as she lugged the heavy fleece along was Shahes standing up and taking the yama's beautiful head against her breast and slashing its throat, all one long movement, in which the woman and the animal were utterly one.

It is need that answers need, Akal thought, as it is question that answers question. The pelt reeked of death and dung. Her hands were caked with blood, and ached, gripping the stiff belt, as she followed Shahes down the steep rocky path homeward.

"I'm going down to the village," Otorra said, getting up from the breakfast table.

"When are you going to card those four sacks?" Shahes said.

He ignored her, carrying his dishes to the washer-rack. "Any errands?" he asked of them all.

"Everybody done?" Madu asked, and took the cheese out to the pantry.

"No use going into town till you can take the carded fleece," said Shahes.

Otorra turned to her, stared at her, and said, "I'll card it when I choose and take it when I choose and I don't take orders at my own work, will you understand that?"

Stop, stop now! Akal cried silently, for Shahes, stunned by the uprising of the meek, was listening to him. But he went on, firing grievance with grievance, blazing out in recriminations. "You can't give all the orders, we're your sedoretu, we're your household, not a lot of hired hands, yes it's your farm but it's ours too, you married us, you can't make all the decisions, and you can't have it all your way either," and at this point Shahes unhurriedly walked out of the room.

"Shahes!" Akal called after her, loud and imperative. Though Otorra's outburst was undignified it was completely justified, and his anger was both real and dangerous. He was a man who had been used, and he knew it. As he had let himself be used and had colluded in that misuse, so now his anger threatened destruction. Shahes could not run away from it.

She did not come back. Madu had wisely disappeared. Akal told Shest to run out and see to the pack-beasts' feed and water.

The three remaining in the kitchen sat or stood silent. Temly looked at Otorra. He looked at Akal.

"You're right," Akal said to him.

He gave a kind of satisfied snarl. He looked handsome in his anger, flushed and reckless. "Damn right I'm right. I've let this go on for too long. Just because she owned the farmhold —"

"And managed it since she was fourteen," Akal cut in. "You think she can quit managing just like that? She's always run things here. She had to. She never had anybody to share power with. Everybody has to learn how to be married."

"That's right," Otorra flashed back, "and a marriage isn't two pairs. It's four pairs!"

That brought Akal up short. Instinctively she looked to Temly for help. Temly was sitting, quiet as usual, her elbows on the table, gathering up crumbs with one hand and pushing them into a little pyramid.

"Temly and me, you and Shahes, Evening and Morning, fine," Otorra said. "What about Temly and her? What about you and me?"

Akal was now completely at a loss. "I thought... When we talked..."

"I said I didn't like sex with men," said Otorra.

She looked up and saw a gleam in his eye. Spite? Triumph? Laughter?

"Yes. You did," Akal said after a long pause. "And I said the same thing."

Another pause.

"It's a religious duty," Otorra said.

Enno suddenly said very loudly in Akal's voice, "Don't come onto me with your religious duty! I studied religious duty for twenty years and where did it get me? Here! With you! In this mess!"

At this, Temly made a strange noise and put her face in her hands. Akal thought she had burst into tears, and then saw she was laughing, the painful, helpless, jolting laugh of a person who hasn't had much practice at it.

"There's nothing to laugh about," Otorra said fiercely, but then had no more to say; his anger had blown up leaving nothing but smoke. He groped for words for a while longer. He looked at Temly, who was indeed in tears now, tears of laughter. He made a despairing gesture. He sat down beside Temly and said, "I suppose it is funny if you look at it. It's just that I feel like a chump." He laughed, ruefully, and then, looking up at Akal, he laughed genuinely. "Who's the biggest chump?" he asked her.

"Not you," she said. "How long…"

"How long do you think?"

It was what Shahes, standing in the passageway, heard: their laughter. The three of them laughing. She listened to it with dismay, fear, shame, and terrible envy. She hated them for laughing. She wanted to be with them, she wanted to laugh with them, she wanted to silence them. Akal, Akal was laughing at her.

She went out to the workshed and stood in the dark behind the door and tried to cry and did not know how. She had not cried when her parents were killed; there had been too much to do. She thought the others were laughing at her for loving Akal, for wanting her, for needing her. She thought Akal was laughing at her for being such a fool, for loving her. She thought Akal would sleep with the man and they would laugh together at her. She drew her knife and tested its edge. She had made it very sharp yesterday on the Farren to kill the yama. She came back to the house, to the kitchen.

They were all still there. Shest had come back and was pestering Otorra to take him into town and Otorra was saying, "Maybe, maybe," in his soft lazy voice.

Temly looked up, and Akal looked round at Shahes — the small head on the graceful neck, the clear eyes gazing. Nobody spoke.

"I'll walk down with you, then," Shahes said to Otorra, and sheathed her knife. She looked at the women and the child. "We might as well all go," she said sourly. "If you like."

Shame

Pam Noles

The February 2006 death of Octavia Butler hit the science fiction community extremely hard. She was our very own MacArthur Grant-certified genius, a woman of enormous talent, insight, generosity, and dedication. Butler was shortlisted for the Retrospective Tiptree Award with her book *Wild Seed* and again for the 1998 award with *Parable of the Talents*. We miss her very much.

We've chosen an essay about her fiction that was first published in 1990. Obviously it makes no reference to later work. But we couldn't resist the gifted Dorothy Allison discussing the gifted Octavia Butler. The provocative issues discussed here remained central to everything Butler subsequently wrote.

The Tiptree Award is dedicated to changing the world — one bake sale, one chocolate chip cookie, and one reader at a time. Since its inception, the award has focused on gender roles. But we have always also cared about issues of race and ethnicity, even though they are outside our specific mandate.

This year saw the creation of the Carl Brandon Awards for works by writers of color and about characters of color. Just as the James Tiptree Award was named after a man who didn't exist, an award-winning science fiction writer who was the public face of Alice B. Sheldon, Carl Brandon was an sf fan who didn't exist, a black fan in the 1950s (when there were almost no fans of color) who was invented by two white fans, Terry Carr and Peter Graham. Carr and Graham, active fan writers under their own names, carried on a separate existence as Brandon. Brandon, because he wrote as well as Carr and Graham, and because of his supposedly unique perspective, was a popular contributor to many fanzines. Now, he's given his name to a group who began by gathering writers and readers of color in the sf, fantasy, and horror fields; this group promotes discussion of race and ethnicity in fiction. This year, they have instituted a pair of awards.

Debbie Notkin, who had chaired the first Tiptree jury, brought that experience to these new ventures and chaired the jury for the first Carl Brandon Kindred Award, given to a novel or story that deals with race and ethnicity issues. The award went to *Stormwitch*, a young adult novel by Susan Vaught. The Carl Brandon Parallax Award, an award for the best work by a writer of color, went to Walter Mosley's young adult novel *47*. The short lists and long lists for both awards are posted on the Society's website, *www.carlbrandon.org*.

Simultaneously, our jury broadened its focus with its "special mention" of *Writing the Other* by Nisi Shawl and Cynthia Ward. This nonfiction book offers writers an approach to creating fully realized, well-rounded characters who differ from the writer in race, orientation, age, ability, religion, and/or sex.

Pam Noles's essay presents convincing reasons that science fiction writers should consult *Writing the Other* and take its advice to heart.

Ursula K. Le Guin said this:

"I have received letters that broke my heart, from adolescents of color in this country and in England, telling me that when they realized that Ged and the other Archipelagans in the Earthsea books are not white people, they felt included in the world of literary and movie fantasy for the first time."

— *Speech to the* Book Expo America *children's literature breakfast, June 4, 2004*

Back then there was UHF and VHF, and you had to manipulate two different dials on the TV to make the channels come in. That's where they put *Star Trek* and *Space: 1999*, and on weekend afternoons ran movies like *Colossus: The Forbin Project*. On Saturday nights The Ghoul would take over, a spazz in a lab coat and shock of frizzy blond wig, showing *Voyage to the Bottom of the Sea* but with added sound effects of flushing toilets. In between, he'd take his puppet friend Froggy and stuff him into a huge vat of Spam, maybe, then blow the whole thing up. Over on one of the regular channels, late Friday night belonged to Houlihan and Big Chuck, who mostly showed horror movies. In between scenes they ran skits about "Soulman," the black superhero, or about "a certain ethnic" who loved polka, or a woman named Bertha Butt, whose butt was so big it could catch the rain. After Houlihan found God and went to Florida, Big Chuck was joined by Little John. A new skit was added: "Fallacy Island," with Little John as Cuckoo and Big John as Mr. Roarke. Little John also made a great caveman, and with a blonde wig he was the cutest little girl with a beard you've ever seen.

Usually it would be just me in the basement sprawled on the floor surrounded by snacks, Legos, and books to read during the commercials. If he was off shift, sometimes Dad would come down and join me in his leather recliner by the stairs. Every once in a while Mom called down from the kitchen, *Are you letting her watch those weird things?* And we'd lie in unison, *No.* If she came down to check for herself, Dad would get in trouble.

Dad had his own names for the movies.

What's this? "Escape to a White Planet"?

It's called 'When Worlds Collide.' I'm sure I sounded indignant.

"Mars Kills the White People." I love this one.

Daaaaad. It says it right there. 'War of the Worlds.' I know I sighed heavily, but was careful to turn back to the TV before rolling my eyes.

Once he asked me which was more real, the movie or the skits between. I didn't get it, and told him that they were both stories, so they were both fake. He didn't bring it up again until a skit came on. I can't remember if it was a "Soulman" skit or one of the caveman gags (the cavemen were multicultural—basic white, Polish, Italian, and black). But I remember Dad saying, *how come you never see anybody like that in the stories you like?* And I remember answering, *maybe they didn't have black people back then.* He said *there's always been black people.* I said *but black people can't be wizards and space people and they can't fight evil, so they can't be in the story.* When he didn't say anything back I turned around. He was in full recline mode in his chair and he was very still, looking at me. He didn't say anything else.

Mom was in on it, too. I'd see her frowning at the books I left trailed throughout the house. Their covers were almost all the same: white men with swords, white women draped across dragons, their golden hair flowing in the breeze, white men stepping from gleaming ships onto fantastic alien landscapes. Sometimes she'd ask what the story was about. As I rambled through the plot and raved about the heroes, she might interrupt with a question in code: *what color was his hair? What kind of eyes did she have?*

There were times when she didn't bother with code. *How come there's only one kind of hero in those books?* I would get upset, then.

You think we're being racist, Mom would say. It was an accusation.

But she was the one who taught me how to read before I even got

into kindergarten. She was the one who let me read practically anything I wanted to.

You're not being fair, was usually all I could think to shout back.

Ursula K. Le Guin said this:

"I think it is possible that a good many readers never even notice what color the people in the story are. Don't notice, maybe
don't care. Whites of course have the privilege of not caring, of
being 'colorblind.' Nobody else does."

— *Commentary on* Slate, *Dec. 16, 2004*

When she was young, Mom was very active with CORE. She remembers thrilling to the voice of The Rev. Martin Luther King, Jr. that
spring of 1966 when she traveled to Washington, DC, to stand. This
one wasn't as big as the other march on Washington that often gets its
own section in the history books, but that didn't matter. She was surrounded by regular black people just like her from all over the country, standing next to the reflecting pool of the Lincoln Memorial, its
sheen blurred by the tears in her eyes as she listened to Dr. King speak
hope and faith over the loudspeakers. Even when marriage, family,
and the pressures of juggling a household while holding down a day
job came along, she worked with the NAACP and for social justice
efforts through her church.

By the time he was a teen, Dad was the mascot for his neighborhood fire station. In the days before liability concerns, they used to
bring the truck over to his house and pick him up. He'd ride with them
back from calls, eat with them in the station. In 1965, just before he
was to be discharged from the Air Force, Dad flew home to take the
fire department's qualifying exam. He aced it, but was told his background check didn't pass muster. As an Air Force veteran, former
Boy Scout, and yes, an actual altar boy, this didn't make sense. He
retook the test in 1966 and twice again in 1967, holding down other
jobs while he pursued his dream of being a firefighter. Each time they
came up with something new — his nose was too flared, putting him

at risk for excess smoke inhalation. He had a bad heart. His feet were too flat and broad, bringing into question whether or not he could physically do the job. He had to go get medical clearances for each of these allegations. A couple of times they just said you did great on the test, but we're not hiring you. In all, they turned him down eight times. By 1972 he'd had enough and went to the courts. The city settled. He joined the department the next year, where he played a role in what eventually became the landmark Headen lawsuit, a discrimination case that made it all the way up to the Supreme Court. Dad served 21 years with the fire department. Dramatic career highlights included catching a jumper in mid-air as he plunged past the floor Dad was on, and being blown out through the top floor of a house after having thrown two rookies to safety down a flight of stairs because they didn't yet know how to spot a backdraft flare. When Dad retired as a captain, the city named a day after him. He's now chief of his own department in a city that is not his hometown.

Robert Halmi, Sr., said this:

"It's usually a European and middle-European world (in fantasy). Because 'Earthsea' comes from America, it comes with all those American traditions. That's why it's multicultural, multiracial. You never see wizard movies done in England that has any kind of color in it, because that's a different world. We have no mythology, so we create our own."
  — *Interview with* Zap2it.com, *Dec. 8, 2004*

You think we're being racist, is what my Mom accused.

I've never told my parents that, in a way, they ruined these books and movies for me. Nor did I ever tell them that gradually, during near-weekly pilgrimages to the neighborhood branch library, I'd started asking the librarian if she had books with magic and spaceships and dragons and stuff in them, but with some black people, too. Black would be the first choice, but anybody kind of brown would do. It seemed the answer, for my age group anyway, was no. When I got older, there would be a few.

A kid can feel the loss from something taken away, even if they don't have the words to say exactly what it is or define the nature of this new pain. All a kid can do is try to find what caused it all, and blame.

Then *Star Wars* came out. I was eleven, and in the car with the seat belt fastened on that Saturday of its opening week before Dad even managed to find his keys. I spazzed all the way through the screening, my first science fiction movie on the big screen and with everything so huge, it made a big difference. When Dad returned after the movie and managed to cull me from the herd of Jedis-in-training blitzing around the courtyard, I launched into it. Han Solo had this ship that he flew upside down! Darth Vader even breathed scary!! And there were robots!!! And Luke had to fly into the canyon on the Death Star with the other ships shooting at him and he had to get the bomb into a tiny hole and then he turned off the machine thing and he prayed to Obi-Wan and the bomb went in. And then they got medals. Also there was a giant teddy bear with stringy hair and a gun.

He said it sounded as if I liked it. I said I mostly thought it was absolutely great. And it was, really. Don't get me wrong. But it was like most of the other stuff I had seen. I explained to him about the planet where Luke came from, a desert with two suns? And how here, where we only one sun, in the desert the people are black. I told him how there wasn't even one black person in the whole movie, even in the background, and I had looked.

Back then I didn't understand enough why part of me felt an empty echo even as the rest was hyper-jazzed. Over the years I realized my expectations were not in line with reality. I thought a movie made in the modern time, not one created back when black people didn't exist, would reflect the reality of the world. And if there had been at least one brown person in *Star Wars*, someone besides the unseen rumbling black baritone voicing the ultimate evil, then I would have at last one thing to point when I felt I needed to justify. But it turned out this fantasy set in a far-away galaxy a long time ago operated under the same old rules. Not even the force of two suns could do a thing to change who was allowed to exist in the universe.

Later that summer, during the weekly hajj to the library, the librarian gave me a copy of *A Wizard of Earthsea*. She told me it had just come in, that she held it special for me, and that she knew I would like it a lot.

I know I didn't start reading it that day. But I was deep into it before the week was out. And because Le Guin snuck up on it, let us thrill with Sparrowhawk as he made his way, the Revelation came as a shock. I do remember bursting out into tears on the living room couch when I understood what was going on. And the tears flowed again when Mom came home from work and I showed her the book while trying to explain. Sparrowhawk is brown. I think he's like an Indian from India. And Vetch is black like from Africa. There's a bunch more and they have real power. Not the girls, though. But still they are also the good guys. It's the white people who are evil. And Sparrowhawk is also Ged, and he's going to be the most powerful one of them all, ever.

Mom had no idea what I was talking about. But being used to the non sequiturs that come with having a high-strung child, she knew just what to do. She took the book away from me and had me lay down on the couch for a little bit. I got it back, later, and read it a few times more before I had to return it to the library. I probably overdid it with the thanks to the librarian. When she gave me the next one, I flew home.

All I can say is this is how I remember it, but I know that in this part memory and fact don't match. Earthsea came out almost ten years before *Star Wars*. I don't know why the book wasn't put into my hands before that summer. I don't know why I clearly remember the librarian telling me that the book had just come out when she gave it to me. I don't understand why my memory of first reading the book is intricately tied to my memory of that *Star Wars* summer. For some of us geeks who were there that night, with Arthur, the king, life is kind of divided into BSW and ASW — Before *Star Wars* and After *Star Wars*. Maybe that's it. Not sure that I actually care, though. What matters most to me is that same summer I decided I was going to be a Jedi, no matter what they said on that screen, was the same summer a genre work showed me for the first time that my people can have the magic and be the heroes, too.

Robert Halmi, Sr., said this:

"*Legend of Earthsea*, the miniseries, was cast completely color-blind, as any of my productions have been. We searched for the right actors for the roles and brought in diversity to the cast as a result. There was no decision to make Ged blond and pale-skinned."

— *Interview on* SciFi.com's '*Ask Robert Halmi, Sr.' feature on its 'Legend of Earthsea' website, July 20, 2004*

Sometime in spring 2004 I saw the first casting notices about the SciFi Channel's *Legend of Earthsea* miniseries blurbed in a film industry trade. What I read was hurtful to my heart. I wonder how many other FoPs (Fans of Pigment) lunged to their bookshelves and snatched down their copies to make sure they didn't imagine what they had read all those years ago. Did they also make character charts on a legal pad, three columns labeled "Character," "Original Color," "Hollywood Color"? And when they finished filling out the boxes, did they sit there staring at it, stunned at the truth? Those Hollywood People took all of the key heroic players and shifted them down into the paler end of the spectrum. And they were obvious about it. Yes, they knew enough about the rules to keep at least one Magical Negro around to help the newly blond-haired, blue-eyed surfer Ged through his Journey Of Transformation To Save The World, because lord knows white boys can't do something like that on their own.

What is that? That's spit. Gobbed right between the eyes and dribbling down.

In this reality, the hip-hop kids come from every ethnic group on the planet. At the big comic book convention in San Diego, white, black, Latino, and Asian kids are heaped around the Tokyopop booth speaking in their own special manga language. My dental hygienist, a Red Sonja-type with curiously delicate hands and frightfully blue eyes, can link Tupac to Zora Neale Hurston to Ozo Motley, with a seamless detour to Parliament Funkadelic. While in line for a sneak peek of *Bubba Ho-Tep*, I listened to a clutch of teen white and Mexican boys passionately debate the heroic nature of Blade. (Blade is the black, half-human vampire hunter portrayed with cartoon efficiency by actor Wesley Snipes.)

It continues. In one of the most acclaimed fantasy books of last year, a white woman put a black man on the fairy throne, and nobody screamed murder. When I went to a chain bookstore to buy another copy of *My Soul to Keep* as a gift, the white male hipster clerk corrected my pronunciation and spelling of "Tananarive." I should have been humiliated, but as he walked me to the stacks explaining I didn't have to special order one because he made sure her work is always kept in stock, I was too busy resisting the urge to hug him. A couple of years ago a white man writing about the gods of America made the fate of the universe hinge on the courage and smarts of the child of a Nordic god and a black woman.

I don't have the luxury of not noticing this type of thing. Given all that reality, I cannot understand why The Hollywood People remain such cowards. Why does that industry still feel it is still too dangerous to allow a genre hero with a brown face?

The pass I granted to the movie makers and writers who lived and created in the time devoid of brown people has long expired.

You think we're being racist, my Mom said so many times as I was growing up, when we went round and round about these weird books and movies. I heard an accusation. But what she and my Dad were trying to make me hear was their question: *Why do you love a thing that won't even let you exist within their made-up worlds?*

How many other FoPs were driven to tears by this question they could not answer, despite painful struggles to do so? Am I the only FoP forced to develop a veneer of denial in order to function at the gaming tournaments, at the conventions other than the comic book fest in San Diego, or while watching *Buffy* and wondering if The Hollywood People who had ever actually *been* to Sunnydale? Because, you know, if they *had*, there'd be five Asian/Pacific Islanders and at least three Latinos in the background. Am I the only FoP who was reduced to searching the people in the background because the people in the foreground were always a given? Am I the only one to wonder why the Los Angeles of *Angel* looked a lot like the New York City of Woody Allen's films?

What the hell did it say about my Blackitude that I just kept coming back for more, no matter how many times genre, in words and pictures, broke my heart? Any day now, the HNIC is coming for my membership card.

Le Guin's racial choices in *A Wizard of Earthsea* mattered because her decision said to the wide white world: You Are Not The Whole Of The Universe. For many fans of genre, no matter where they fell on the spectrum of pale, this was the first time such a truth was made alive for them within the pages of the magical worlds they loved.

Ursula K. Le Guin said this:

> *"I wonder if the people who made the film of* The Lord of the Rings *had ended it with Frodo putting on the Ring and ruling happily ever after, and then claimed that that was what Tolkien 'intended'... would people think they'd been 'very, very honest to the books'?"*
>
> — *Statement on* ursulakleguin.com, *responding to an article with the filmmakers in the December 2004 issue of* SciFi Magazine, *Nov. 13, 2004*

The Hollywood People will adapt anything they think will sell, and they'll do whatever they feel they must to the source material to ensure a high box office or advertising return. We know this. The record is filled with lamentations from authors who got the money but then got done incredibly wrong. The Hollywood system is not set up to benefit anyone outside of the family. So every time something like this happens to the creator of the source material, our hearts go out to them.

Le Guin isn't the one who should have raised the stink about what The Hollywood People did to the racial stance she deliberately made in her books. In her December 16, 2004 commentary on *Slate* magazine, she termed this "The Whitewashing of Earthsea."

The genre news outlets should have been out front on this story. Their silence during the months SciFi Channel's adaptation was in production was appalling.

We admit that Fan often equals Obsessive. So you are not surprised to hear that from the day I spotted that first blurb in a Hollywood trade, the one that said We Made Them All White, I began tracking the genre news outlets. I expected they would bring what Le Guin also hilariously called "Earthsea in Clorox" to the editorial pages. But I found only scatterings of comments from other fans on the occasional message board and blog. In the genre news outlets, there was nothing. Except for the ones that were running *A Legend of Earthsea* contests in collaboration with SciFi.com.

This is what it feels like to put your fingers in a gob of spit on your face so you can wipe it from your eyes: Eeewwww.

The primary function of media is to inform about issues within a community. Editors and reporters must notice what's going on, look into it, and put it out there for examination. Conclusions don't have to be drawn, concrete action does not have to be outlined, but the fact of the events should be noted for the benefit of the target audience. A media that consistently fails to notice issues or topics of potential import within the community or industry it is covering is a media that is either lazy, corrupt, or stupefyingly ignorant.

This I believe: If Hollywood has taken a groundbreaking, universally acclaimed, multicultural novel that has been in print for over thirty years and turned it into a white-boy romp, *that is a news story.* The cooperation of the author of the books *is not needed to write that news story.* If the genre news outlets exist to serve their subculture in a way more than pimping for the publishers and the production companies, *the deliberate omission of characters of pigment in the Hollywood adaptation of Le Guin's* Earthsea *is the sort of news story a genre news outlet should notice and write about.*

But they did not. When we live in *this* reality where a redhead white woman can throw down about Tupac with a hip-hop Asian kid who can walk into a bookstore and get briefed about the proper pronunciation of Tananarive from a hipster white guy who first learned about the Beast of London from a Chicano low-rider. It's a crying shame.

Shame, too, on The Hollywood People for making me cry again, even though here I am all grown.

It's about scope, reach, and perceived value. The difference between an issue being discussed on a blog or message board and that same issue showing up on the front page of the *New York Times* (or even the *Podunk Tribune* for that matter) is vast. As producer Julia Phillips once wrote, what's the difference between television and movies? "*The size of the fucking screen.*" Adapting that just a bit, what's the difference between a message board and a news outlet? *The size of the fucking reach*. One message board poster can say to another "wow, what's up with this?" and have a nice conversation that precious few others will know even existed. But one news outlet can say to the world "wow, what's up with this?" and by doing so, put the issue on the table for wider examination. By doing so, that media outlet is saying to their target audience we noticed this. This is important. Be aware. Discuss.

Not a single one of our primary news outlets in genre used their space to ask "what's up with this" in the many months leading up to the broadcast of the SciFi Channel's Earthsea adaptation. I believe the first strike questioning why heroes of pigment were deliberately omitted from the filmed version of this landmark multicultural work should have come from within our genre's news outlets. This is news emerging from their turf. This is news directly related to the long-standing problem of genre's severe lack of diversity. The Earthsea adaptation was an obvious example that could be used to explore an issue critical to the state and form of the genre industry. Our media should have been on top of this story, not the mainstream media. But our media ignored it.

Le Guin's commentary appeared on *Slate* because a fan asked her what she thought about what was done to the racial message in her books. And the mainstream media, once made aware of the issue, recognized the value of the larger story and ran with it. The mainstream media broke this story, while our media played catch up by linking to *Slate*.

What this says to me is My People Still Don't Get It.

Ursula K. Le Guin said this:

"I was a little wily about my color scheme. I figured some white kids (the books were published for 'young adults') might not identify straight off with a brown kid, so I kind of eased the information about skin color in by degrees — hoping that the reader would get 'into Ged's skin' and only then discover it wasn't a white one."

— *Commentary on* Slate, *Dec. 16, 2004*

It was a relief to learn that The Hollywood People had excised Le Guin from their process when they adapted her books. I bet FoPs all over the world, and a good chunk of the rest of them too, exhaled when she told us what had actually happened. It was glorious to see the outpouring of outrage, sympathy, and protest petitions blaze across the planet on her behalf. Because of the reaction when Le Guin spoke out, because of the number of people who said, "Yeah, why *couldn't* they stay brown?" I believe there is hope.

I also believe that our media's failure to take note of the whitewashing of Earthsea and its related issues — along with genre media's continued failure in general to tackle topical, thorny topics — is in part my fault. For all of the responsibility a media outlet has to bring issues of importance to the attention of its masses, so do the masses have a responsibility to make sure their media is adequately serving them. If evidence indicates editors and reporters for genre skip, ignore, or are not aware of what seems to me to be an obvious story, then perhaps I, and news consumers interested enough to make the attempt, should bring topical, potentially difficult issues to their attention. Even if the suggested topic is declined, the attempt must be made. Perhaps such attempts have not been made in the past, or maybe this level of engagement between media and consumer is an unusual concept within the traditions of genre media. I don't know. I have a hypothesis, but I'm keeping that to myself for now. I do know it's far easier to bitch after the fact than try to make a direct attempt at altering the landscape. Figuring out when to speak out, and where, and how best to do so will be an evolving adventure.

Over the years, my parents have listened to me complain and delight over issues related to being of pigment in this genre. When I brought them up to speed on my feelings surrounding the Earthsea adaptation, after urging me to calm down a little bit they wanted me to explain why I was so surprised. They reminded me that nothing changes until the culture changes. They reminded me that it is a mistake to assume the majority is even paying attention or aware of whatever it is upsetting me, let alone interested or motivated enough to do something about it. And the smaller and more specialized the culture, such as the array of fans, pros, publishers, and media that comprise genre, the wider the gulf between that majority and any special interest within it.

If I haven't "left these people after all this time," my Mom said, then what I need to do is accept that I'm stuck with the way things are. I can look at this current world of genre and keep whining, or I can take note of the positive changes that have come down over the years and hope that more will come in the future. And if it matters that much to me, I've got to figure out what I need to do to bring that future into being rather than just waiting for it to magically appear. What those actions are, she can't say. That I'm trying to figure it out pleases her in a way, even though "when it comes down to it, you're still talking about that weird stuff." But since it's this weird world I've chosen, she's glad I'm trying to make it my own.

Dad's advice was cryptic only if you fail to understand that he knows precisely what it means to look directly into the face of what you love while saying *you are wrong*.

"I think you should try," my Dad said to me. Then he added a caution. "Be ready."

I am.

The Future of Female: Octavia Butler's Mother Lode

Dorothy Allison

I love Octavia Butler's women even when they make me want to scream with frustration. The problem is not their feminism; her characters are always independent, stubborn, difficult, and insistent on trying to control their own lives. What drives me crazy is their attitude: the decisions they make, the things they do in order to protect and nurture their children — and the assumption that children and family always come first.

Butler's nine books are exceptional not only because she is that rarity, a black woman writing science fiction, but because she advocates motherhood as the humanizing element in society (not a notion I have ever taken too seriously). But even though the lives she creates for her women characters make me impatient, I cannot stop reading her. I buy her new books, look for her short stories, and hunt down her old paperbacks for friends. While acknowledging the imbalances and injustices inherent in traditional family systems, Butler goes on writing books with female characters who heroically adjust to family life and through example, largeness of spirit, and resistance to domination make the lives of those children better even though this means sacrificing personal freedom. But she humanizes her dark vision of women's possibilities by making sure that the contradictions and grief her women experience are as powerfully rendered as their decision to sacrifice autonomy. Within the genre of science fiction, Butler is a realist, writing the most detailed social criticism and creating some of the most fascinating female characters in the genre. For me, it's like reading about my mother, my aunts, my sisters. Even when I'm gnashing my teeth, I go on believing in them.

Butler creates dystopias, landscapes in which the hard edge of cruelty, violence, and domination is described in stark detail. Her work addresses the issues of survival and adaptation, in which resistance, defeat, and compromise are the vital elements, Like Samuel Delany's *The Bridge of Lost Desire* and *Stars in My Pocket Like Grains of Sand*, Butler's most recent work, the Xenogenesis series (*Dawn*, *Adulthood Rites*, and *Imago*), radically reexamines human sexual relations and what it means to be other.

Homosexuality, incest, and multiple sexual pairings turn up in almost all her books, usually insisted on by the patriarchal or alien characters and resisted by the heroines, who eventually give in. Her women are always in some form of bondage, captives of domineering male mutants or religious fanatics or aliens who want to impregnate them. Though the men in Butler's novels are often equally oppressed, none is forced so painfully to confront the difference between surrender and adjustment. Women who surrender die; those who resist, struggle, adjust, compromise, and live by their own ethical standards survive to mother the next generation — literally to make the next world. Maybe if this world were not so hard a place, Butler might be writing less painful fiction.

The circumstances of Butler's life have shaped her fiction. Her father died when she was two and her mother supported the family by working as a maid. Butler grew up on the stories of her maternal grandmother, a woman who raised seven children alone in Louisiana and died a property owner in Pasadena, California, where Octavia was born in 1947. Echoes of Butler's grandmother turn up in all her books, from *Patternmaster* (1976) to *Imago* (1989). *Patternmaster*, like most first novels, lays out her concerns. The men in this book, as in all that follow, begin with sexist assumptions about women. Amber, a small, sturdy, practical black woman, is a prototypical Butler heroine. Her response to Teray, the domineering hero, when he offers her power and prestige as his "lead wife," is to ask him, "How interested would you be in becoming my lead husband?" Butler makes it clear that Teray cannot rule his world until he accepts Amber's independence; she pledges to bear his children but only so long as she has her own household, her own life, and her female lovers.

None of Butler's heroines ever again manages that much autonomy, though the nearly egalitarian relationship that Teray and Amber finally arrange is the ideal each of her women aims for. Though Butler designates the mother as the civilizing force in human society — the one who teaches both men and children compassion and empathy — she also shows it is not a role that women easily or willingly take on. She also carefully shows how mothering can mimic paternalistic domination. When Mary, the telepathic black heroine of *Mind of My Mind*, defeats her father, Doro, she becomes a tyrant herself, though a more benevolent one.

Butler's Patternist novels, a series that includes *Patternmaster*, *Wild Seed*, *Mind of My Mind*, *Survivor*, and *Clay's Ark*, cover a period from the 1600s through a far future in which disease has decimated Earth's population. The series reworks one of science fiction's traditional motifs: mutants who are hated and endangered until they gain control of their talents. Butler's mutants are self-destructive, immature characters deliberately bred for their psychic skills by Doro, a 4,000-year-old psychic vampire and patriarch, who never frees them to grow up and live independently. In the early books (*Wild Seed*, *Patternmaster*, *Mind of My Mind*), ordinary people, known as nontelepaths or "latents," are cast as the racial inferiors to the psychically gifted humans. The latents are also known as "mutes"; when Doro explains that the term means "ordinary people," his wife Emma tells him, "I know what it means, Doro. I knew the first time I heard Mary use it. It means nigger!" Butler's use of the term nigger is as deliberate as her matter-of-fact handling of racism in the everyday lives of her characters. By portraying the "ordinary" ones as lesser people who are treated with contempt, bred like animals (or slaves) for desirable genetic material, and murdered as if they were not fully human, Butler is commenting on the underlying structure of racism.

But those on top are also on the bottom. The telepaths cannot function in normal human society; they are prone to violence, madness, and unreasoning hatred. Many are also black. In the early novels they are enslaved, victimized, assaulted, and killed. In the later, they enslave, victimize, assault, and kill normal humans. The nigger, Butler suggests, is the one who's made slave/child/victim. It is the concept of nigger, the need for a victim, and the desire to profit by the abuse or misuse of others that corrupts and destroys.

Butler's best known and most successful novel, *Kindred*, first published in 1979 and reprinted by Beacon Press in 1988, is a recreation of plantation life rather than a symbolic examination of slavery. In the introduction to the Beacon edition, Butler called *Kindred* a "grim fantasy" — an accurate description. *Kindred*'s heroine, Dana, is an articulate young black writer who works for a temporary agency, which she calls "a slave market," a reference that takes on new meaning when she finds herself on an antebellum plantation where the everyday horrors of slavery are no metaphor. Like all Butler's works, *Kindred* concentrates on the psychological, here the emotional impact of slavery on Dana as she is continually transported back in time to save the life of Rufus, her abusive, slave-owning, white great-grandfather. The novel doesn't explain the mechanism of her time travels, suggesting only that she is pulled back whenever Rufus's life is threatened and can return to 1976 L.A. only when her own life is threatened.

Kindred reads like a historical slave narrative, a horror tale of the real. Violence is not passed over quickly. When Dana witnesses a slave being beaten by nightriders it's not from a safe distance.

> I could literally smell his sweat, hear every ragged breath, every cry, every cut of the whip. I could see his body jerking, convulsing, straining against the rope as his screaming went on and on. My stomach heaved, and I had to force myself to stay where I was and keep quiet...
>
> I shut my eyes and tensed my muscles against an urge to vomit.
>
> I had seen people beaten on television and in the movies. I had seen the too-red blood substitute streaked across their backs and heard their well-rehearsed screams. But I hadn't lain nearby and smelled their sweat or heard them pleading and praying, shamed before their families and themselves.

Dana's attitudes, language, and beliefs about herself are those of a black woman in 1976. She objects indignantly to being called "nigger" by Rufus, is contemptuous of the ignorant white masters, and thinks at first that she will just write herself a pass and flee north. But nothing she thinks she knows about slavery prepares her for suddenly being property in 1800s Maryland. Rufus's father thinks her an "uppity nigger" and whips her for teaching a slave boy to read. At the same time, the plantation slaves accuse her of being "more like white folks than some white folks." Alice, Dana's great-great-grandmother, tells her, "They be calling you mammy in a few years." In this world, compromise is a close cousin to betrayal, but refusing to compromise means risking not only your own life but the lives of family and friends. Each slave is hostage to the others, Dana realizes, and the choices are all deadly. When Rufus tells Dana she must help him persuade the slave Alice to accept him as a lover, she is horrified but unable to refuse. She can't "refuse to help the girl — help her avoid at least some pain." Alice "wouldn't think much of me for helping her this way," Dana tells herself. "I didn't think much of myself." This is not a simple or easy decision, but it is the one Butler's heroines invariably make. From Anyanwu of *Wild Seed* to Lilith in *Dawn*, Butler's women submit and bear children rather than die or murder the rapists/masters/aliens.

Kindred is the only one of Butler's books in which the woman refuses to submit, and even here Butler emphasizes the internal struggle resistance prompts. Early in the book, Dana realizes she is "the worst possible guardian for [Rufus] — a black to watch over him in a society that considered blacks subhuman, a woman to watch over him in a society that considered women perennial children." But still she hopes to "plant a few ideas in his mind that would help both me and the people who would be his slaves in the years to come." She gives up this illusion only with grief and difficulty. When Rufus tries to rape Dana, she hesitates, unable for a moment to use the knife she has hidden in her hand. While he sees her only as a female animal and his by right, she feels a link to him as kin. But when she looks at herself from Rufus's perspective, she realizes that if she submits to him she will become the slave he believes her to be. "And Rufus was Rufus — erratic, alternately generous and vicious. I could accept him as my ancestor, my younger brother, my friend, but not as my master, and not as my lover." In horror, Dana kills him — the boy she has saved so many times.

Other than the death of Rufus, Butler offers no resolutions at the end of *Kindred*. Dana is left wounded and unsure even of her own sanity. Just as we never learn the mechanism of her time travel, we do not know what will become of her marriage to Kevin, a white man. More important, neither we nor Dana know what has become of Hagar, Dana's great-grandmother and the girl child of Alice, the slave woman Dana persuaded to submit to Rufus. Dana, Alice, and Hagar remind us of all the women in Butler's work, the victims and survivors she envisions not as dispassionate historical constructs, overlaid with political slogans and psychological reinterpretations, but as real women caught in impossible situations.

In her most recent books, the Xenogenesis trilogy, Butler portrays a world in which the worst has happened. Nuclear winter and disease have killed off most of the people who were not killed in the initial nuclear conflict, and only the intervention of the alien Oankali has kept anyone alive at all. The Oankali blame the catastrophe on humanity's obsession with conflict and hierarchy. Butler clearly believes that these human characteristics must be overcome if society is to survive, but *Dawn* offers little reason to believe this is possible.

Lilith, another of Butler's black female mother figures, has been kept in suspended animation for 250 years. Like Dana in *Kindred* and Anyanwu in *Wild Seed*, Lilith compromises in order to save lives and ease pain. The Oankali teach her first to tolerate and then to join an Oankali family, and then to "mother" a group of human survivors until they too have adjusted. In *Imago* and *Adulthood Rites* Lilith's Oankali/human children triumph and survive, reclaiming Earth and forcing the Oankali to free the remaining humans.

Unfortunately, these last two books do not provide the vivid sense of alien encounter that is so strong in *Dawn*. The savage humans abandon their resistance to the aliens too easily; their hatred seems more stubbornness than xenophobia. It is a hopeful vision, but not very convincing—as if Butler has tried to demonstrate where her philosophy of mother-nurturance leads. But her reasonable humans are nowhere near as captivating as the rebellious mothers and complex villains of her earlier books, and Butler seems to lose interest in their story even before we do.

What continues to hold her interest and ours are many-layered and extensive explorations of male/female relationships, resistance to traditional moral teachings, women's responsibility to bear and raise children, and the fine line between compromise and betrayal. The alien Oankali have some slavemaster attitudes toward humans, but they also introduce new and positive variations on traditional sexual relationships.

Since the sexual abuse of women and women's desire for autonomy are central themes in all of Butler's books, the Oankali's benign attitude toward sex and sexual variation is vitally important in understanding what Butler sees as the answer to sexual violence — not abstinence or enforced celibacy, but a redefinition of sex and a rapprochement between the genders. Without the human need to impose a hierarchical male dominant/female submissive structure on sexuality, the Oankali approach the act with a genuine sense of joy equally shared. Nothing is sinful, nothing is forced. Everything is permitted except violence. After all, traditional male and female role expectations cannot be rigidly imposed on a people whose gender is mutable and unspecified until the onset of adolescence. And incest, a continuing obsession for Butler, is not a meaningful concept among the Oankali, whose third sex, the ooloi, literally construct genetic material, sorting for healthy and useful attributes. Sex among the Oankali is seen as both an act of blissful biological exchange (sperm for egg) and a euphoric ritual that lovingly bonds participants — the family bond that Butler invariably emphasizes. The Oankali represent Butler's solution to the sexual horrors she details in every novel — a people who honor the act of procreation so greatly they are incapable of rape, and who enjoy sex so much they treat all sexual acts with matter-of-fact honesty, an approach that appalls the kidnapped humans.

Much of *Dawn* concentrates on the cultural shock the humans experience when they marry Oankali. The men feel as if they have lost authority (they have); the women feel as if they are being bred like animals (they are); and all feel some horror of what might be hidden homosexual desires — after all, there is no way to be sure an ooloi is a man or a woman. Humans feel a deep psychochemical attraction to ooloi, almost a compulsion. It is as if the slavemasters had gotten under their skins, and humans no longer control their own desires. The Oankali sound authentically alien, sexy, and terrifying. They are also completely family-centered. All of them are mothers, nurturers, healers — traditional Butler heroines in new forms. But they are also tyrants, with the same tendency to infantilize, to make choices for the child's "own good."

At the end of the trilogy, Lilith's son thinks about how humans and aliens treat each other, how they struggle and resist chaos by clinging together. "The whole business was like Lilith's rounded black cloud of hair," he thinks. "Every strand seemed to go its own different way, bending, twisting, spiraling, angling. Yet together they formed a symmetrical, recognizable shape, and all were attached to the same head." This is the dream of an ideal family, the mother making possible her children's lives and freeing them to choose their own destinies — the essential vision of Octavia Butler.

Liking What You See: A Documentary

Ted Chiang

We are so deeply controlled by what we see, what we like to look at, what we think is beautiful, or ugly, or normal. How much of that is "natural" and how much is "social"? How much of social and sexual attraction depends on gender? What choices do we have about what we like, and how do our likes and dislikes affect the objects of our gaze?

Neither Ted Chiang nor James Tiptree, Jr., can answer these questions any better than we can.

At the same time, Chiang can ask completely new questions: What if we could get rid of this whole aspect of our lives? Would we? Examining these sheds extraordinary light on how we think and feel about these subjects and how they control us. And being Ted Chiang, he can also do it in a fresh and unexplored storytelling style.

More than thirty years ago, when James Tiptree, Jr. was examining these same subjects, he (and Alice Sheldon behind him) were concerned with what is ugliness, what is beauty, and what do those concepts do to us? While Chiang explores what it would mean to leave them behind, Tiptree explores what it means to live in the very heart of them. Who is "better," Delphi or P. Burke? And why? This Hugo Award–winning story has not lost one whit of its power in the intervening decades.

"Beauty is the promise of happiness."
— Stendhal

TAMERA LYONS, FIRST-YEAR STUDENT AT PEMBLETON:
I can't believe it. I visited the campus last year, and I didn't hear a word about this. Now I get here and it turns out people want to make calli a requirement. One of the things I was looking forward to about college was getting rid of this, you know, so I could be like everybody else. If I'd known there was even a chance I'd have to keep it, I probably would've picked another college. I feel like I've been scammed.

I turn eighteen next week, and I'm getting my calli turned off that day. If they vote to make it a requirement, I don't know what I'll do; maybe I'll transfer, I don't know. Right now I feel like going up to people and telling them, "Vote no." There's probably some campaign I can work for.

MARIA DESOUZA, THIRD-YEAR STUDENT, PRESIDENT OF THE STUDENTS FOR EQUALITY EVERYWHERE (SEE):

Our goal is very simple. Pembleton University has a Code of Ethical Conduct, one that was created by the students themselves, and that all incoming students agree to follow when they enroll. The initiative that we've sponsored would add a provision to the code, requiring students to adopt calliagnosia as long as they're enrolled.

What prompted us to do this now was the release of a spex version of Visage. That's the software that, when you look at people through your spex, shows you what they'd look like with cosmetic surgery. It became a form of entertainment among a certain crowd, and a lot of college students found it offensive. When people started talking about it as a symptom of a deeper societal problem, we thought the timing was right for us to sponsor this initiative.

The deeper societal problem is lookism. For decades people've been willing to talk about racism and sexism, but they're still reluctant to talk about lookism. Yet this prejudice against unattractive people is incredibly pervasive. People do it without even being taught by anyone, which is bad enough, but instead of combating this tendency, modern society actively reinforces it.

Educating people, raising their awareness about this issue, all of that is essential, but it's not enough. That's where technology comes in. Think of calliagnosia as a kind of assisted maturity. It lets you do what you know you should: ignore the surface, so you can look deeper.

We think it's time to bring calli into the mainstream. So far the calli movement has been a minor presence on college campuses, just another one of the special-interest causes. But Pembleton isn't like other colleges, and I think the students here are ready for calli. If the initiative succeeds here, we'll be setting an example for other colleges, and ultimately, society as a whole.

JOSEPH WEINGARTNER, NEUROLOGIST:
The condition is what we call an associative agnosia, rather than an apperceptive one. That means it doesn't interfere with one's visual perception, only with the ability to recognize what one sees. A calliagnosic perceives faces perfectly well; he or she can tell the difference between a pointed chin and a receding one, a straight nose and a crooked one, clear skin and blemished skin. He or she simply doesn't experience any aesthetic reaction to those differences.

Calliagnosia is possible because of the existence of certain neural pathways in the brain. All animals have criteria for evaluating the reproductive potential of prospective mates, and they've evolved neural "circuitry" to recognize those criteria. Human social interaction is centered around our faces, so our circuitry is most finely attuned to how a person's reproductive potential is manifested in his or her face. You experience the operation of that circuitry as the feeling that a person is beautiful, or ugly, or somewhere in between. By blocking the neural pathways dedicated to evaluating those features, we induce calliagnosia.

Given how much fashions change, some people find it hard to imagine that there are absolute markers of a beautiful face. But it turns out that when people of different cultures are asked to rank photos of faces for attractiveness, some very clear patterns emerge across the board. Even very young infants show the same preference for certain faces. This lets us identify certain traits that are common to everyone's idea of a beautiful face.

Probably the most obvious one is clear skin. It's the equivalent of a bright plumage in birds or a shiny coat of fur in other mammals. Good skin is the single best indicator of youth and health, and it's valued in every culture. Acne may not be serious, but it *looks* like more serious diseases, and that's why we find it disagreeable.

Another trait is symmetry; we may not be conscious of millimeter differences between someone's left and right sides, but measurements reveal that individuals rated as most attractive are also the most symmetrical. And while symmetry is what our genes always aim for, it's very difficult to achieve in developmental terms; any environmental stressor — like poor nutrition, disease, parasites — tends to result in asymmetry during growth. Symmetry implies resistance to such stressors.

Other traits have to do with facial proportions. We tend to be attracted to facial proportions that are close to the population mean. That obviously depends on the population you're part of, but being near the mean usually indicates genetic health. The only departures from the mean that people consistently find attractive are exaggerations of secondary sexual characteristics.

Basically, calliagnosia is a lack of response to these traits; nothing more. Calliagnosics are *not* blind to fashion or cultural standards of beauty. If black lipstick is all the rage, calliagnosia won't make you forget it, although you might not notice the difference between pretty faces and plain faces wearing that lipstick. If everyone around you sneers at people with broad noses, you'll pick up on that.

So calliagnosia by itself can't eliminate appearance-based discrimination. What it does, in a sense, is even up the odds; it takes away the innate predisposition, the tendency for such discrimination to arise in the first place. That way, if you want to teach people to ignore appearances, you won't be facing an uphill battle. Ideally you'd start with an environment where everyone's adopted calliagnosia, and then socialize them to not value appearances.

TAMERA LYONS:
People here have been asking me what it was like going to Saybrook, growing up with calli. To be honest, it's not a big deal when you're young; you know, like they say, whatever you grew up with seems normal to you. We knew that there was something that other people could see that we couldn't, but it was just something we were curious about.

For instance, my friends and I used to watch movies and try to figure out who was really good-looking and who wasn't. We'd say we could tell, but we couldn't really, not by looking at their faces. We were just going by who was the main character and who was the friend; you always knew the main character was better-looking than the friend. It's not true a hundred percent of the time, but you could usually tell if you were watching the kind of thing where the main character wouldn't be good-looking.

It's when you get older that it starts to bother you. If you hang out with people from other schools, you can feel weird because you have calli and they don't. It's not that anyone makes a big deal out of it, but it reminds you that there's something you can't see. And then you start having fights with your parents, because they're keeping you from seeing the real world. You never get anywhere with them, though.

RICHARD HAMILL, FOUNDER OF THE SAYBROOK SCHOOL:
Saybrook came about as an outgrowth of our housing cooperative. We had maybe two dozen families at the time, all trying to establish a community based on shared values. We were holding a meeting about the possibility of starting an alternative school for our kids, and one parent mentioned the problem of the media's influence on their kids. Everyone's teens were asking for cosmetic surgery so they could look like fashion models. The parents were doing their best, but you can't isolate your kids from the world; they live in an image-obsessed culture.

It was around the time the last legal challenges to calliagnosia were resolved, and we got to talking about it. We saw calli as an opportunity: What if we could live in an environment where people didn't judge each other on their appearance? What if we could raise our children in such an environment?

The school started out being just for the children of the families in the cooperative, but other calliagnosia schools began making the news, and before long people were asking if they could enroll their kids without joining the housing co-op. Eventually we set up Saybrook as a private school separate from the co-op, and one of its requirements was that parents adopt calliagnosia for as long as their kids were enrolled. Now a calliagnosia community has sprung up here, all because of the school.

RACHEL LYONS:

Tamera's father and I gave the issue a lot of thought before we decided to enroll her there. We talked to people in the community, found we liked their approach to education, but really it was visiting the school that sold me.

Saybrook has a higher than normal number of students with facial abnormalities, like bone cancer, burns, congenital conditions. Their parents moved here to keep them from being ostracized by other kids, and it works. I remember when I first visited, I saw a class of twelve-year-olds voting for class president, and they elected this girl who had burn scars on one side of her face. She was wonderfully at ease with herself, she was popular among kids who probably would have ostracized her in any other school. And I thought, this is the kind of environment I want my daughter to grow up in.

Girls have always been told that their value is tied to their appearance; their accomplishments are always magnified if they're pretty and diminished if they're not. Even worse, some girls get the message that they can get through life relying on just their looks, and then they never develop their minds. I wanted to keep Tamera away from that sort of influence.

Being pretty is fundamentally a passive quality; even when you work at it, you're working at being passive. I wanted Tamera to value herself in terms of what she could do, both with her mind and with her body, not in terms of how decorative she was. I didn't want her to be passive, and I'm pleased to say that she hasn't turned out that way.

MARTIN LYONS:

I don't mind if Tamera decides as an adult to get rid of calli. This was never about taking choices away from her. But there's more than enough stress involved in simply getting through adolescence; the peer pressure can crush you like a paper cup. Becoming preoccupied with how you look is just one more way to be crushed, and anything that can relieve that pressure is a good thing, in my opinion.

Once you're older, you're better equipped to deal with the issue of personal appearance. You're more comfortable in your own skin, more confident, more secure. You're more likely to be satisfied with how you look, whether you're "good-looking" or not. Of course not everyone reaches that level of maturity at the same age. Some people are there at sixteen, some don't get there until they're thirty or even older. But eighteen's the age of legal majority, when everyone's got the right to make their own decisions, and all you can do is trust your child and hope for the best.

TAMERA LYONS:

It's been kind of an odd day for me. Good, but odd. I just got my calli turned off this morning.

Getting it turned off was easy. The nurse stuck some sensors on me and made me put on this helmet, and she showed me a bunch of pictures of people's faces. Then she tapped at her keyboard for a minute, and said, "I've switched off the calli," just like that. I thought you might feel something when it happened, but you don't. Then she showed me the pictures again, to make sure it worked.

When I looked at the faces again, some of them seemed...diff erent. Like they were glowing, or more vivid or something. It's hard to describe. The nurse showed me my test results afterwards, and there were readings for how wide my pupils were dilating and how well my skin conducted electricity and stuff like that. And for the faces that seemed different, the readings went way up. She said those were the beautiful faces.

She said that I'd notice how other people's faces look right away, but it'd take a while before I had any reaction to how I looked. Supposedly you're too used to your face to tell.

And yeah, when I first looked in a mirror, I thought I looked totally the same. Since I got back from the doctor's, the people I see on campus definitely look different, but I still haven't noticed any difference in how I look. I've been looking at mirrors all day. For a while I was afraid that I was ugly, and any minute the ugliness was going to appear, like a rash or something. And so I've been staring at the mirror, just waiting, and nothing's happened. So I figure I'm probably not really ugly, or I'd have noticed it, but that means I'm not really pretty either, because I'd have noticed that too. So I guess that means I'm absolutely plain, you know? Exactly average. I guess that's okay.

JOSEPH WEINGARTNER:

Inducing an agnosia means simulating a specific brain lesion. We do this with a programmable pharmaceutical called neurostat; you can think of it as a highly selective anesthetic, one whose activation and targeting are all under dynamic control. We activate or deactivate the neurostat by transmitting signals through a helmet the patient puts on. The helmet also provides somatic positioning information so the neurostat molecules can triangulate their location. This lets us activate only the neurostat in a specific section of brain tissue, and keep the nerve impulses there below a specified threshold.

Neurostat was originally developed for controlling seizures in epileptics and for relief of chronic pain; it lets us treat even severe cases of these conditions without the side-effects caused by drugs that affect the entire nervous system. Later on, different neurostat protocols were developed as treatments for obsessive-compulsive disorder, addictive behavior, and various other disorders. At the same time, neurostat became incredibly valuable as a research tool for studying brain physiology.

One way neurologists have traditionally studied specialization of brain function is to observe the deficits that result from various lesions. Obviously, this technique is limited because the lesions caused by injury or disease often affect multiple functional areas. By contrast, neurostat can be activated in the tiniest portion of the brain, in effect simulating a lesion so localized that it would never occur naturally. And when you deactivate the neurostat, the "lesion" disappears and brain function returns to normal.

In this way neurologists were able to induce a wide variety of agnosias. The one most relevant here is prosopagnosia, the inability to recognize people by their faces. A prosopagnosic can't recognize friends or family members unless they say something; he can't even identify his own face in a photograph. It's not a cognitive or perceptual problem; prosopagnosics can identify people by their hairstyle, clothing, perfume, even the way they walk. The deficit is restricted purely to faces.

Prosopagnosia has always been the most dramatic indication that our brains have a special "circuit" devoted to the visual processing of faces; we look at faces in a different way than we look at anything else. And recognizing someone's face is just one of the face-processing tasks we do; there are also related circuits devoted to identifying facial expressions, and even detecting changes in the direction of another person's gaze.

One of the interesting things about prosopagnosics is that while they can't recognize a face, they still have an opinion as to whether it's attractive or not. When asked to sort photos of faces in order of attractiveness, prosopagnosics sorted the photos in pretty much the same way as anyone else. Experiments using neurostat allowed researchers to identify the neurological circuit responsible for perceiving beauty in faces, and thus essentially invent calliagnosia.

MARIA deSOUZA:
SEE has had extra neurostat programming helmets set up in the Student Health Office, and made arrangements so they can offer calliagnosia to anyone who wants it. You don't even have to make an appointment, you can just walk in. We're encouraging all the students to try it, at least for a day, to see what it's like. At first it seems a little odd, not seeing anyone as either good-looking or ugly, but over time you realize how positively it affects your interactions with other people.

A lot of people worry that calli might make them asexual or something, but actually physical beauty is only a small part of what makes a person attractive. No matter what a person looks like, it's much more important how the person acts; what he says and how he says it, his behavior and body language. And how does he react to you? For me, one of the things that attracts me to a guy is if he seems interested in *me*. It's like a feedback loop; you notice him looking at you, then he sees you looking at him, and things snowball from there. Calli doesn't change that. Plus there's that whole pheromone chemistry going on too; obviously calli doesn't affect that.

Another worry that people have is that calli will make everyone's face look the same, but that's not true either. A person's face always reflects their personality, and if anything, calli makes that clearer. You know that saying, that after a certain age, you're responsible for your face? With calli, you really appreciate how true that is. Some faces just look really bland, especially young, conventionally pretty ones. Without their physical beauty, those faces are just boring. But faces that are full of personality look as good as they ever did, maybe even better. It's like you're seeing something more essential about them.

Some people also ask about enforcement. We don't plan on doing anything like that. It's true, there's software that's pretty good at guessing if a person has calli or not, by analyzing eye gaze patterns. But it requires a lot of data, and the campus security cams don't zoom in close enough. Everyone would have to wear personal cams, and share the data. It's possible, but that's not what we're after. We think that once people try calli, they'll see the benefits themselves.

TAMERA LYONS:
Check it out, I'm pretty!

What a day. When I woke up this morning I immediately went to the mirror; it was like I was a little kid on Christmas or something. But still, nothing; my face still looked plain. Later on I even *(laughs)* I tried to catch myself by surprise, by sneaking up on a mirror, but that didn't work. So I was kind of disappointed, and feeling just, you know, resigned to my fate.

But then this afternoon, I went out with my roommate Ina and a couple other girls from the dorm. I hadn't told anyone that I'd gotten my calli turned off, because I wanted to get used to it first. So we went to this snack bar on the other side of campus, one I hadn't been to before. We were sitting at this table, talking, and I was looking around, just seeing what people looked like without calli. And I saw this girl looking at me, and I thought, "She's really pretty." And then, *(laughs)* this'll sound really stupid, then I realized that this wall in the snack bar was a mirror, and I was looking at myself!

I can't describe it, I felt this incredible sense of *relief*. I just couldn't stop smiling! Ina asked me what I was so happy about, and I just shook my head. I went to the bathroom so I could stare at myself in the mirror for a bit.

So it's been a good day. I really *like* the way I look! It's been a good day.

JEFF WINTHROP, THIRD-YEAR STUDENT, SPEAKING AT A STUDENT DEBATE:

Of course it's wrong to judge people by their appearance, but this "blindness" isn't the answer. Education is.

Calli takes away the good as well as the bad. It doesn't just work when there's a possibility of discrimination, it keeps you from recognizing beauty altogether. There are plenty of times when looking at an attractive face doesn't hurt anyone. Calli won't let you make those distinctions, but education will.

And I know someone will say, what about when the technology gets better? Maybe one day they'll be able to insert an expert system into your brain, one that goes, "Is this an appropriate situation to apprehend beauty? If so, enjoy it; else, ignore it." Would that be okay? Would that be the "assisted maturity" you hear people talking about?

No, it wouldn't. That wouldn't be maturity; it'd be letting an expert system make your decisions for you. Maturity means seeing the differences, but realizing they don't matter. There's no technological shortcut.

ADESH SINGH, THIRD-YEAR STUDENT, SPEAKING AT A STUDENT DEBATE:

No one's talking about letting an expert system make your decisions. What makes calli ideal is precisely that it's such a minimal change. Calli doesn't decide for you; it doesn't prevent you from doing anything. And as for maturity, you demonstrate maturity by choosing calli in the first place.

Everyone knows physical beauty has nothing to do with merit; that's what education's accomplished. But even with the best intentions in the world, people haven't stopped practicing lookism. We try to be impartial, we try not to let a person's appearance affect us, but we can't suppress our autonomic responses, and anyone who claims they can is engaged in wishful thinking. Ask yourself: Don't you react differently when you meet an attractive person and when you meet an unattractive one?

Every study on this issue turns up the same results: looks help people get ahead. We can't help but think of good-looking people as more competent, more honest, more deserving than others. None of it's true, but their looks still give us that impression.

Calli doesn't blind you to anything; beauty is what blinds you. Calli lets you see.

TAMERA LYONS:
So, I've been looking at good-looking guys around campus. It's fun; weird, but fun. Like, I was in the cafeteria the other day, and I saw this guy a couple tables away, I didn't know his name, but I kept turning to look at him. I can't describe anything specific about his face, but it just seemed much more noticeable than other people's. It was like his face was a magnet, and my eyes were compass needles being pulled toward it.

And after I looked at him for a while, I found it really easy to imagine that he was a nice guy! I didn't know anything about him, I couldn't even hear what he was talking about, but I wanted to get to know him. It was kind of odd, but definitely not in a bad way.

FROM A BROADCAST OF EDUNEWS, ON THE AMERICAN COLLEGE NETWORK:
In the latest on the Pembleton University calliagnosia initiative: EduNews has received evidence that public-relations firm Wyatt/ Hayes paid four Pembleton students to dissuade classmates from voting for the initiative, without having them register their affiliations. Evidence includes an internal memo from Wyatt/Hayes, proposing

that "good-looking students with high reputation ratings" be sought, and records of payments from the agency to Pembleton students.

The files were sent by the SemioTech Warriors, a culture-jamming group responsible for numerous acts of media vandalism.

When contacted about this story, Wyatt/Hayes issued a statement decrying this violation of their internal computer systems.

JEFF WINTHROP:

Yes, it's true, Wyatt/Hayes paid me, but it wasn't an endorsement deal; they never told me *what* to say. They just made it possible for me to devote more time to the anti-calli campaign, which is what I would've done anyway if I hadn't needed to make money tutoring. All I've been doing is expressing my honest opinion: I think calli's a bad idea.

A couple of people in the anti-calli campaign have asked that I not speak publicly about the issue anymore, because they think it'd hurt the cause. I'm sorry they feel that way, because this is just an *ad hominem* attack. If you thought my arguments made sense before, this shouldn't change anything. But I realize that some people can't make those distinctions, and I'll do what's best for the cause.

MARIA DESOUZA:

Those students really should have registered their affiliations; we all know people who are walking endorsements. But now, whenever someone criticizes the initiative, people ask them if they're being paid. The backlash is definitely hurting the anti-calli campaign.

I consider it a compliment that someone is taking enough interest in the initiative to hire a PR firm. We've always hoped that its passing might influence people at other schools, and this means that corporations are thinking the same thing.

We've invited the president of the National Calliagnosia Association to speak on campus. Before we weren't sure if we wanted to bring the national group in, because they have a different emphasis than we do; they're more focused on the media uses of beauty, while here at SEE we're more interested in the social equality issue. But given the way students reacted to what Wyatt/Hayes did, it's clear that the media manipulation issue has the power to get us where we need to go. Our best shot at getting the initiative passed is to take advantage of the anger against advertisers. The social equality will follow afterwards.

FROM THE SPEECH GIVEN AT PEMBLETON BY WALTER LAMBERT, PRESIDENT OF THE NATIONAL CALLIAGNOSIA ASSOCIATION:
Think of cocaine. In its natural form, as coca leaves, it's appealing, but not to an extent that it usually becomes a problem. But refine it, purify it, and you get a compound that hits your pleasure receptors with an unnatural intensity. That's when it becomes addictive.

Beauty has undergone a similar process, thanks to advertisers. Evolution gave us a circuit that responds to good looks — call it the pleasure receptor for our visual cortex — and in our natural environment, it was useful to have. But take a person with one-in-a-million skin and bone structure, add professional makeup and retouching, and you're no longer looking at beauty in its natural form. You've got pharmaceutical-grade beauty, the cocaine of good looks.

Biologists call this "supernormal stimulus"; show a mother bird a giant plastic egg, and she'll incubate it instead of her own real eggs. Madison Avenue has saturated our environment with this kind of stimuli, this visual drug. Our beauty receptors receive more stimulation than they were evolved to handle; they're getting more in one day than our ancestors did in their entire lives. And the result is that beauty is slowly ruining our lives.

How? The way any drug becomes a problem: by interfering with our relationships with other people. We become dissatisfied with the way ordinary people look because they can't compare to supermodels. Two-dimensional images are bad enough, but now with spex, advertisers can put a supermodel right in front of you, making eye contact. Software companies offer goddesses who'll remind you of your appointments. We've all heard about men who prefer virtual girlfriends over actual ones, but they're not the only ones who've been affected. The more time any of us spend with gorgeous digital apparitions around, the more our relationships with real human beings are going to suffer.

We can't avoid these images and still live in the modern world. And that means we can't kick this habit, because beauty is a drug you can't abstain from unless you literally keep your eyes closed all the time.

Until now. Now you can get another set of eyelids, one that blocks out this drug, but still lets you see. And that's calliagnosia. Some people call it excessive, but I call it just enough. Technology is being used to manipulate us through our emotional reactions, so it's only fair that we use it to protect ourselves too.

Right now you have an opportunity to make an enormous impact. The Pembleton student body has always been at the vanguard of every progressive movement; what you decide here will set an example for students across the country. By passing this initiative, by adopting calliagnosia, you'll be sending a message to advertisers that young people are no longer willing to be manipulated.

FROM A BROADCAST OF EduNEWS:
Following NCA president Walter Lambert's speech, polls show that 54% of Pembleton students support the calliagnosia initiative. Polls across the country show that an average of 28% of students would support a similar initiative at their school, an increase of 8% in the past month.

TAMERA LYONS:
I thought he went overboard with that cocaine analogy. Do you know anyone who steals stuff and sells it so he can get his fix of advertising?

But I guess he has a point about how good-looking people are in commercials versus in real life. It's not that they look better than people in real life, but they look good in a different way.

Like, I was at the campus store the other day, and I needed to check my e-mail, and when I put on my spex I saw this poster running a commercial. It was for some shampoo, Jouissance I think. I'd seen it before, but it was different without calli. The model was so — I couldn't take my eyes off her. I don't mean I felt the same as that time I saw the good-looking guy in the cafeteria; it wasn't like I wanted to get to know her. It was more like…watching a sunset, or a fireworks display.

I just stood there and watched the commercial like five times, just so I could look at her some more. I didn't think a human being could look so, you know, spectacular.

But it's not like I'm going to quit talking to people so I can watch commercials through my spex all the time. Watching them is very intense, but it's a totally different experience than looking at a real person. And it's not even like I immediately want to go out and buy everything they're selling, either. I'm not even really paying attention to the products. I just think they're amazing to watch.

MARIA DESOUZA:

If I'd met Tamera earlier, I might have tried to persuade her not to get her calli turned off. I doubt I would've succeeded; she seems pretty firm about her decision. Even so, she's a great example of the benefits of calli. You can't help but notice it when you talk to her. For example, at one point I was saying how lucky she was, and she said, "Because I'm beautiful?" And she was being totally sincere! Like she was talking about her height. Can you imagine a woman without calli saying that?

Tamera is completely unself-conscious about her looks; she's not vain or insecure, and she can describe herself as beautiful without embarrassment. I gather that she's very pretty, and with a lot of women who look like that, I can see something in their manner, a hint of showoffishness. Tamera doesn't have that. Or else they display false modesty, which is also easy to tell, but Tamera doesn't do that either, because she truly is modest. There's no way she could be like that if she hadn't been raised with calli. I just hope she stays that way.

ANNIKA LINDSTROM, SECOND-YEAR STUDENT:

I think this calli thing is a terrible idea. I like it when guys notice me, and I'd be really disappointed if they stopped.

I think this whole thing is just a way for people who, honestly, aren't very good-looking, to try and make themselves feel better. And the only way they can do that is to punish people who have what they don't. And that's just unfair.

Who wouldn't want to be pretty if they could? Ask anyone, ask the people behind this, and I bet you they'd all say yes. Okay, sure, being pretty means that you'll be hassled by jerks sometimes. There are always jerks, but that's part of life. If those scientists could come up with some way to turn off the jerk circuit in guys' brains, I'd be all in favor of that.

JOLENE CARTER, THIRD-YEAR STUDENT:
I'm voting for the initiative, because I think it'd be a relief if everyone had calli.

People are nice to me because of how I look, and part of me likes that, but part of me feels guilty because I haven't done anything to deserve it. And sure, it's nice to have men pay attention to me, but it can be hard to make a real connection with someone. Whenever I like a guy, I always wonder how much he's interested in me, versus how much he's interested in my looks. It can be hard to tell, because all relationships are wonderful at the beginning, you know? It's not until later that you find out whether you can really be comfortable with each other. It was like that with my last boyfriend. He wasn't happy with me if I didn't look fabulous, so I was never able to truly relax. But by the time I realized that, I'd already let myself get close to him, so that really hurt, finding out that he didn't see the real me.

And then there's how you feel around other women. I don't think most women like it, but you're always comparing how you look relative to everyone else. Sometimes I feel like I'm in a competition, and I don't want to be.

I thought about getting calli once, but it didn't seem like it would help unless everyone else did too; getting it all by myself wouldn't change the way others treat me. But if everyone on campus had calli, I'd be glad to get it.

TAMERA LYONS:

I was showing my roommate Ina this album of pictures from high school, and we get to all these pictures of me and Garrett, my ex. So Ina wants to know all about him, and so I tell her. I'm telling her how we were together all of senior year, and how much I loved him, and wanted us to stay together, but he wanted to be free to date when he went to college. And then she's like, "You mean *he* broke up with *you?*"

It took me a while before I could get her to tell me what was up; she made me promise twice not to get mad. Eventually she said Garrett isn't exactly good-looking. I was thinking he must be average-looking, because he didn't really look that different after I got my calli turned off. But Ina said he was definitely below average.

She found pictures of a couple other guys who she thought looked like him, and with them I could see how they're not good-looking. Their faces just look goofy. Then I took another look at Garrett's picture, and I guess he's got some of the same features, but on him they look cute. To me, anyway.

I guess it's true what they say: love is a little bit like calli. When you love someone, you don't really see what they look like. I don't see Garrett the way others do, because I still have feelings for him.

Ina said she couldn't believe someone who looked like him would break up with someone who looked like me. She said that in a school without calli, he probably wouldn't have been able to get a date with me. Like, we wouldn't be in the same league.

That's weird to think about. When Garrett and I were going out, I always thought we were meant to be together. I don't mean that I believe in destiny, but I just thought there was something really right about the two of us. So the idea that we could've both been in the same school, but not gotten together because we didn't have calli, feels strange. And I know that Ina can't be sure of that. But I can't be sure she's wrong, either.

And maybe that means I should be glad I had calli, because it let me and Garrett get together. I don't know about that.

FROM A BROADCAST OF EDUNEWS:

Netsites for a dozen calliagnosia student organizations around the country were brought down today in a coordinated denial-of-service attack. Although no one claimed responsibility, some suggest the perpetrators are retaliating for last month's incident in which the American Association of Cosmetic Surgeons' netsite was replaced by a calliagnosia site.

Meanwhile, the SemioTech Warriors announced the release of their new "Dermatology" computer virus. This virus has begun infecting video servers around the world, altering broadcasts so that faces and bodies exhibit conditions such as acne and varicose veins.

WARREN DAVIDSON, FIRST-YEAR STUDENT:

I thought about trying calli before, when I was in high school, but I never knew how to bring it up with my parents. So when they started offering it here, I figured I'd give it a try. (shrugs) It's okay.

Actually, it's better than okay. (pause) I've always hated how I look. For a while in high school I couldn't stand the sight of myself in a mirror. But with calli, I don't mind as much. I know I look the same to other people, but that doesn't seem as big a deal as it used to. I feel better just by not being reminded that some people are so much better-looking than others. Like, for instance: I was helping this girl in the library with a problem on her calculus homework, and afterwards I realized that she's someone I'd thought was really pretty. Normally I would have been really nervous around her, but with calli, she wasn't so hard to talk to.

Maybe she thinks I look like a freak, I don't know, but the thing was, when I was talking to her I didn't think I looked like a freak. Before I got calli, I think I was just too self-conscious, and that just made things worse. Now I'm more relaxed.

It's not like I suddenly feel all wonderful about myself or anything, and I'm sure for other people calli wouldn't help them at all, but for me, calli makes me not feel as bad as I used to. And that's worth something.

ALEX BIBESCU, PROFESSOR OF RELIGIOUS STUDIES AT
PEMBLETON:

Some people have been quick to dismiss the whole calliagnosia debate as superficial, an argument over makeup or who can and can't get a date. But if you actually look at it, you'll see it's much deeper than that. It reflects a very old ambivalence about the body, one that's been part of Western civilization since ancient times.

You see, the foundations of our culture were laid in classical Greece, where physical beauty and the body were celebrated. But our culture is also thoroughly permeated by the monotheistic tradition, which devalues the body in favor of the soul. These old conflicting impulses are rearing their heads again, this time in the calliagnosia debate.

I suspect that most calli supporters consider themselves to be modern, secular liberals, and wouldn't admit to being influenced by monotheism in any way. But take a look at who else advocates calliagnosia: conservative religious groups. There are communities of all three major monotheistic faiths — Jewish, Christian, and Muslim — who've begun using calli to make their young members more resistant to the charms of outsiders. This commonality is no coincidence. The liberal calli supporters may not use language like "resisting the temptations of the flesh," but in their own way, they're following the same tradition of deprecating the physical.

Really, the only calli supporters who can credibly claim they're not influenced by monotheism are the NeoMind Buddhists. They're a sect who see calliagnosia as a step toward enlightened thought, because it eliminates one's perception of illusory distinctions. But the NeoMind sect is open to broad use of neurostat as an aid to meditation, which is a radical stance of an entirely different sort. I doubt you'll find many modern liberals or conservative monotheists sympathetic to that!

So you see, this debate isn't just about commercials and cosmetics, it's about determining what's the appropriate relationship between the mind and the body. Are we more fully realized when we minimize the physical part of our nature? And that, you have to agree, is a profound question.

JOSEPH WEINGARTNER:

After calliagnosia was discovered, some researchers wondered if it might be possible to create an analogous condition that rendered the subject blind to race or ethnicity. They've made a number of attempts — impairing various levels of category discrimination in tandem with face recognition, that sort of thing — but the resulting deficits were always unsatisfactory. Usually the test subjects would simply be unable to distinguish similar-looking individuals. One test actually produced a benign variant of Fregoli syndrome, causing the subject to mistake every person he met for a family member. Unfortunately, treating everyone like a brother isn't desirable in so literal a sense.

When neurostat treatments for problems like compulsive behavior entered widespread use, a lot of people thought that "mind programming" was finally here. People asked their doctors if they could get the same sexual tastes as their spouses. Media pundits worried about the possibility of programming loyalty to a government or corporation, or belief in an ideology or religion.

The fact is, we have no access to the contents of anyone's thoughts. We can shape broad aspects of personality, we can make changes consistent with the natural specialization of the brain, but these are extremely coarse-grained adjustments. There's no neural pathway that specifically handles resentment toward immigrants, any more than there's one for Marxist doctrine or foot fetishism. If we ever get true mind programming, we'll be able to create "race blindness," but until then, education is our best hope.

TAMERA LYONS:

I had an interesting class today. In History of Ideas, we've got this T.A., he's named Anton, and he was saying how a lot of words we use to describe an attractive person used to be words for magic. Like the word "charm" originally meant a magic spell, and the word "glamour" did, too. And it's just blatant with words like "enchanting" and "spellbinding." And when he said that, I thought, yeah, that's what it's like: seeing a really good-looking person is like having a magic spell cast over you.

And Anton was saying how one of the primary uses of magic was to create love and desire in someone. And that makes total sense, too, when you think about those words "charm" and "glamour." Because seeing beauty feels like love. You feel like you've got a crush on a really good-looking person, just by looking at them.

And I've been thinking that maybe there's a way I can get back together with Garrett. Because if Garrett didn't have calli, maybe he'd fall in love with me again. Remember how I said before that maybe calli was what let us get together? Well, maybe calli is actually what's keeping us apart now. Maybe Garrett would want to get back with me if he saw what I really looked like.

Garrett turned eighteen during the summer, but he never got his calli turned off because he didn't think it was a big deal. He goes to Northrop now. So I called him up, just as a friend, and when we were talking about stuff, I asked him what he thought about the calli initiative here at Pembleton. He said he didn't see what all the fuss was about, and then I told him how much I liked not having calli anymore, and said he ought to try it, so he could judge both sides. He said that made sense. I didn't make a big deal out of it, but I was stoked.

DANIEL TAGLIA, PROFESSOR OF COMPARATIVE LITERATURE AT PEMBLETON:

The student initiative doesn't apply to faculty, but obviously if it passes there'll be pressure on the faculty to adopt calliagnosia as well. So I don't consider it premature for me to say that I'm adamantly opposed to it.

This is just the latest example of political correctness run amok. The people advocating calli are well-intentioned, but what they're doing is infantilizing us. The very notion that beauty is something we need to be protected from is insulting. Next thing you know, a student organization will insist we all adopt music agnosia, so we don't feel bad about ourselves when we hear gifted singers or musicians.

When you watch Olympic athletes in competition, does your self-esteem plummet? Of course not. On the contrary, you feel wonder and admiration; you're inspired that such exceptional individuals exist. So why can't we feel the same way about beauty? Feminism would have us to apologize for having that reaction. It wants to replace aesthetics with politics, and to the extent it's succeeded, it's impoverished us.

Being in the presence of a world-class beauty can be as thrilling as listening to a world-class soprano. Gifted individuals aren't the only ones who benefit from their gifts; we all do. Or, I should say, we all can. Depriving ourselves of that opportunity would be a crime.

COMMERCIAL PAID FOR BY PEOPLE FOR ETHICAL NANOMEDICINE:

Voiceover: Have your friends been telling you that calli is cool, that it's the smart thing to do? Then maybe you should talk to people who grew up with calli.

"After I got my calli turned off, I recoiled the first time I met an unattractive person. I knew it was silly, but I just couldn't help myself. Calli didn't help make me mature, it *kept* me from becoming mature. I had to relearn how to interact with people."

"I went to school to be a graphic artist. I worked day and night, but I never got anywhere with it. My teacher said I didn't have the eye for it, that calli had stunted me aesthetically. There's no way I can get back what I've lost."

"Having calli was like having my parents inside my head, censoring my thoughts. Now that I've had it turned off, I realize just what kind of abuse I'd been living with."

Voiceover: If the people who grew up with calliagnosia don't recommend it, shouldn't that tell you something?

They didn't have a choice, but you do. Brain damage is never a good idea, no matter what your friends say.

MARIA DESOUZA:

We'd never heard of the People for Ethical Nanomedicine, so we did some research on them. It took some digging, but it turns out it's not a grassroots organization at all, it's an industry PR front. A bunch of cosmetics companies got together recently and created it. We haven't been able to contact the people who appear in the commercial, so we don't know how much, if any, of what they said was true. Even if they were being honest, they certainly aren't typical; most people who get their calli turned off feel fine about it. And there are definitely graphic artists who grew up with calli.

It kind of reminds me of an ad I saw a while back, put out by a modeling agency when the calli movement was just getting started. It was just a picture of a supermodel's face, with a caption: "If you no longer saw her as beautiful, whose loss would it be? Hers, or yours?" This new campaign has the same message, basically saying, "you'll be sorry," but instead of taking that cocky attitude, it has more of a con-cerned-warning tone. This is classic PR: hide behind a nice-sounding name, and create the impression of a third party looking out for the consumer's interests.

TAMERA LYONS:

I thought that commercial was totally idiotic. It's not like I'm in fa-vor of the initiative — I don't want people to vote for it — but people shouldn't vote against it for the wrong reason. Growing up with calli isn't crippling. There's no reason for anyone to feel sorry for me or anything. I'm dealing with it fine. And that's why I think people ought to vote against the initiative: because seeing beauty is fine.

Anyway, I talked to Garrett again. He said he'd just gotten his calli turned off. He said it seemed cool so far, although it was kind of weird, and I told him I felt the same way when I got mine disabled. I suppose it's kind of funny, how I was acting like an old pro, even though I've only had mine off for a few weeks.

JOSEPH WEINGARTNER:

One of the first questions researchers asked about calliagnosia was whether it has any "spillover," that is, whether it affects your appreciation of beauty outside of faces. For the most part, the answer seems to be "no." Calliagnosics seem to enjoy looking at the same things other people do. That said, we can't rule out the possibility of side effects.

As an example, consider the spillover that's observed in prosopagnosics. One prosopagnosic who was a dairy farmer found he could no longer recognize his cows individually. Another found it harder to distinguish models of cars, if you can imagine that. These cases suggest that we sometimes use our face-recognition module for tasks other than strict face recognition. We may not think something looks like a face—a car, for example—but at a neurological level we're treating it as if it were a face.

There may be a similar spillover among calliagnosics, but since calliagnosia is subtler than prosopagnosia, any spillover is harder to measure. The role of fashion in cars' appearances, for example, is vastly greater than its role in faces', and there's little consensus about which cars are most attractive. There may be a calliagnosic out there who doesn't enjoy looking at certain cars as much as he otherwise would, but he hasn't come forward to complain.

Then there's the role our beauty-recognition module plays in our aesthetic reaction to symmetry. We appreciate symmetry in a wide range of settings-painting, sculpture, graphic design-but at the same time we also appreciate asymmetry. There are a lot of factors that contribute to our reaction to art, and not much consensus about when a particular example is successful.

It might be interesting to see if calliagnosia communities produce fewer truly talented visual artists, but given how few such individuals arise in the general population, it's difficult to do a statistically meaningful study. The only thing we know for certain is that calliagnosics report a more muted response to some portraits, but that's not a side effect *per se*; portrait paintings derive at least some of their impact from the facial appearance of the subject.

Of course, any effect is too much for some people. This is the reason given by some parents for not wanting calliagnosia for their children: they want their children to be able to appreciate the Mona Lisa, and perhaps create its successor.

MARC ESPOSITO, FOURTH-YEAR STUDENT AT
WATERSTON COLLEGE:

That Pembleton thing sounds totally crazed. I could see doing it like a setup for some prank. You know, as in, you'd fix this guy up with a girl, and tell him she's an absolute babe, but actually you've fixed him up with a dog, and he can't tell so he believes you. That'd be kind of funny, actually.

But I sure as hell would never get this calli thing. I want to date good-looking girls. Why would I want something that'd make me lower my standards? Okay, sure, some nights all the babes have been taken, and you have to choose from the leftovers. But that's why there's beer, right? Doesn't mean I want to wear beer goggles all the time.

TAMERA LYONS:

So Garrett and I were talking on the phone again last night, and I asked him if he wanted to switch to video so we could see each other. And he said okay, so we did.

I was casual about it, but I had actually spent a lot of time getting ready. Ina's teaching me to put on makeup, but I'm not very good at it yet, so I got that phone software that makes it look like you're wearing makeup. I set it for just a little bit, and I think it made a real difference in how I looked. Maybe it was overkill, I don't know how much Garrett could tell, but I just wanted to be sure I looked as good as possible.

As soon as we switched to video, I could see him react. It was like his eyes got wider. He was like, "You look really great," and I was like, "Thanks." Then he got shy, and made some joke about the way he looked, but I told him I liked the way he looked.

We talked for a while on video, and all the time I was really conscious of him looking at me. That felt good. I got a feeling that he was thinking he might want us to get back together again, but maybe I was just imagining it.

Maybe next time we talk I'll suggest he could come visit me for a weekend, or I could go visit him at Northrop. That'd be really cool. Though I'd have to be sure I could do my own makeup before that.

I know there's no guarantee that he'll want to get back together. Getting my calli turned off didn't make me love him less, so maybe it won't make him love me any more. I'm hoping, though.

CATHY MINAMI, THIRD-YEAR STUDENT:
Anyone who says the calli movement is good for women is spreading the propaganda of all oppressors: the claim that subjugation is actually protection. Calli supporters want to demonize those women who possess beauty. Beauty can provide just as much pleasure for those who have it as for those who perceive it, but the calli movement makes women feel guilty about taking pleasure in their appearance. It's yet another patriarchal strategy for suppressing female sexuality, and once again, too many women have bought into it.

Of *course* beauty has been used as a tool of oppression, but eliminating beauty is not the answer; you can't liberate people by narrowing the scope of their experiences. That's positively Orwellian. What's needed is a woman-centered concept of beauty, one that lets all women feel good about themselves instead of making most of them feel bad.

LAWRENCE SUTTON, FOURTH-YEAR STUDENT:
I totally knew what Walter Lambert was talking about in his speech. I wouldn't have phrased it the way he did, but I've felt the same way for a while now. I got calli a couple years ago, long before this initiative came up, because I wanted to be able to concentrate on more important things.

I don't mean I only think about schoolwork; I've got a girlfriend, and we have a good relationship. That hasn't changed. What's changed is how I interact with advertising. Before, every time I used to walk past a magazine stand or see a commercial, I could feel my attention being drawn a little bit. It was like they were trying to arouse me against my will. I don't necessarily mean a sexual kind of arousal, but they were trying to appeal to me on a visceral level. And I would automatically resist, and go back to whatever I was doing before. But it was a distraction, and resisting those distractions took energy that I could have been using elsewhere.

But now with calli, I don't feel that pull. Calli freed me from that distraction, it gave me that energy back. So I'm totally in favor of it.

LORI HARBER, THIRD-YEAR STUDENT AT MAXWELL COLLEGE:
Calli is for wusses. My attitude is, fight back. Go radical ugly. That's what the beautiful people need to see.

I got my nose taken off about this time last year. It's a bigger deal than it sounds, surgery-wise; to be healthy and stuff, you have to move some of the hairs further in to catch dust. And the bone you see *(taps it with a fingernail)* isn't real, it's ceramic. Having your real bone exposed is a big infection risk.

I like it when I freak people out; sometimes I actually ruin someone's appetite when they're eating. But freaking people out, that's not what it's *about*. It's about how ugly can beat beautiful at its own game. I get more looks walking down the street than a beautiful woman. You see me standing next to a video model, who you going to notice more? Me, that's who. You won't want to, but you will.

TAMERA LYONS:
Garrett and I were talking again last night, and we got to talking about, you know, if either of us had been going out with someone else. And I was casual about it, I said that I had hung out with some guys, but nothing major.

So I asked him the same. He was kind of embarrassed about it, but eventually he said that he was finding it harder to, like, really become friendly with girls in college, harder than he expected. And now he's thinking it's because of the way he looks.

I just said, "No way," but I didn't really know what to say. Part of me was glad that Garrett isn't seeing someone else yet, and part of me felt bad for him, and part of me was just surprised. I mean, he's smart, he's funny, he's a great guy, and I'm not just saying that because I went out with him. He was popular in high school.

But then I remembered what Ina said about me and Garrett. I guess being smart and funny doesn't mean you're in the same league as someone, you have to be equally good-looking too. And if Garrett's been talking to girls who are pretty, maybe they don't feel like he's in their league.

I didn't make a big deal out of it when we were talking, because I don't think he wanted to talk about it a lot. But afterwards, I was thinking that if we decide to do a visit, I should definitely go out to Northrop to see him instead of him coming here. Obviously, I'm hoping something'll happen between us, but also, I thought, maybe if the other people at his school see us together, he might feel better. Because I know sometimes that works: if you're hanging out with a cool person, you feel cool, and other people think you're cool. Not that I'm super cool, but I guess people like how I look, so I thought it might help.

ELLEN HUTCHINSON, PROFESSOR OF SOCIOLOGY AT PEMBLETON:

I admire the students who are putting forth this initiative. Their idealism heartens me, but I have mixed feelings about their goal.

Like everyone else my age, I've had to come to terms with the effects time has had on my appearance. It wasn't an easy thing to get used to, but I've reached the point where I'm content with the way I look. Although I can't deny that I'm curious to see what a calli-only community would be like; maybe there a woman my age wouldn't become invisible when a young woman entered the room.

But would I have wanted to adopt calli when I was young? I don't know. I'm sure it would've spared me some of the distress I felt about growing older. But I *liked* the way I looked when I was young. I wouldn't have wanted to give that up. I'm not sure if, as I grew older, there was ever a point when the benefits would have outweighed the costs for me.

And these students, they might never even lose the beauty of youth. With the gene therapies coming out now, they'll probably look young for decades, maybe even their entire lives. They might never have to make the adjustments I did, in which case adopting calli wouldn't even save them from pain later on. So the idea that they might voluntarily give up one of the pleasures of youth is almost galling. Sometimes I want to shake them and say, "No! Don't you realize what you have?"

I've always liked young people's willingness to fight for their beliefs. That's one reason I've never really believed in the cliché that youth is wasted on the young. But this initiative would bring the cliché closer to reality, and I would hate for that to be the case.

JOSEPH WEINGARTNER:

I've tried calliagnosia for a day; I've tried a wide variety of agnosias for limited periods. Most neurologists do, so we can better understand these conditions and empathize with our patients. But I couldn't adopt calliagnosia on a long-term basis, if for no other reason than that I see patients.

There's a slight interaction between calliagnosia and the ability to gauge a person's health visually. It certainly doesn't make you blind to things like a person's skin tone, and a calliagnosic can recognize symptoms of illness just like anyone else does; this is something that general cognition handles perfectly well. But physicians need to be sensitive to very subtle cues when evaluating a patient; sometimes you use your intuition when making a diagnosis, and calliagnosia would act as a handicap in such situations.

Of course, I'd be disingenuous if I claimed that professional requirements were the only thing keeping me from adopting calliagnosia. The more relevant question is, would I choose calliagnosia if I did nothing but lab research and never dealt with patients? And to that, my answer is no. Like many other people, I enjoy seeing a pretty face, but I consider myself mature enough to not let that affect my judgment.

TAMERA LYONS:

I can't believe it, Garrett got his calli turned back on.

We were talking on the phone last night, just ordinary stuff, and I ask him if he wants to switch to video. And he's like, "Okay," so we do. And then I realize he's not looking at me the same way he was before. So I ask him if everything's okay with him, and that's when he tells me about getting calli again.

He said he did it because he wasn't happy about the way he looked. I asked him if someone had said something about it, because he should ignore them, but he said it wasn't that. He just didn't like how he felt when he saw himself in a mirror. So I was like, "What are you talking about, you look cute." I tried to get him to give it another chance, saying stuff like, he should spend more time without calli before making any decisions. Garrett said he'd think about it, but I don't know what he's going to do.

Anyway, afterwards, I was thinking about what I'd said to him. Did I tell him that because I don't like calli, or because I wanted him to see how I looked? I mean, of course I liked the way he looked at me, and I was hoping it would lead somewhere, but it's not as if I'm being inconsistent, is it? If I'd always been in favor of calli, but made an exception when it came to Garrett, that'd be different. But I'm against calli, so it's not like that.

Oh, who am I kidding? I wanted Garrett to get his calli turned off for my own benefit, not because I'm anti-calli. And it's not even that I'm anti-calli, so much, as I am against calli being a requirement. I don't want anyone else deciding calli's right for me: not my parents, not a student organization. But if someone decides they want calli themselves, that's fine, whatever. So I should let Garrett decide for himself, I know that.

It's just frustrating. I mean, I had this whole plan figured out, with Garrett finding me irresistible, and realizing what a mistake he'd made. So I'm disappointed, that's all.

FROM MARIA DE SOUZA'S SPEECH THE DAY BEFORE THE
ELECTION:

We've reached a point where we can begin to adjust our minds. The question is, when is it appropriate for us to do so? We shouldn't automatically accept that natural is better, nor should we automatically presume that we can improve on nature. It's up to us to decide which qualities we value, and what's the best way to achieve those.

I say that physical beauty is something we no longer need.

Calli doesn't mean that you'll never see anyone as beautiful. When you see a smile that's genuine, you'll see beauty. When you see an act of courage or generosity, you'll see beauty. Most of all, when you look at someone you love, you'll see beauty. All calli does is keep you from being distracted by surfaces. True beauty is what you see with the eyes of love, and that's something that nothing can obscure.

FROM THE SPEECH BROADCAST BY REBECCA BOYER,
SPOKESPERSON FOR PEOPLE FOR ETHICAL NANOMEDICINE,
THE DAY BEFORE THE ELECTION:

You might be able to create a pure calli society in an artificial setting, but in the real world, you're never going to get a hundred percent compliance. And that is calli's weakness. Calli works fine if everybody has it, but if even one person doesn't, that person will take advantage of everyone else.

There'll always be people who don't get calli; you know that. Just think about what those people could do. A manager could promote attractive employees and demote ugly ones, but you won't even notice. A teacher could reward attractive students and punish ugly ones, but you won't be able to tell. All the discrimination you hate could be taking place, without you even realizing.

Of course, it's possible those things won't happen. But if people could always be trusted to do what's right, no one would have suggested calli in the first place. In fact, the people prone to such behavior are liable to do it even more once there's no chance of their getting caught.

If you're outraged by that sort of lookism, how can you afford to get calli? You're precisely the type of person who's needed to blow the whistle on that behavior, but if you've got calli, you won't be able to recognize it.

If you want to fight discrimination, keep your eyes open.

FROM A BROADCAST OF EDUNEWS:
The Pembleton University calliagnosia initiative was defeated by a vote of sixty-four percent to thirty-six percent.

Polls indicated a majority favoring the initiative until days before the election. Many students who previously supported the initiative say they reconsidered after seeing the speech given by Rebecca Boyer of the People for Ethical Nanomedicine. This despite an earlier revelation that PEN was established by cosmetics companies to oppose the calliagnosia movement.

MARIA DESOUZA:
Of course it's disappointing, but we originally thought of the initiative as a long shot. That period when the majority supported it was something of a fluke, so I can't be too disappointed about people changing their minds. The important thing is that people everywhere are talking about the value of appearances, and more of them are thinking about calli seriously.

And we're not stopping; in fact, the next few years will be a very exciting time. A spex manufacturer just demonstrated some new technology that could change everything. They've figured out a way to fit somatic positioning beacons in a pair of spex, custom-calibrated for a single person. That means no more helmet, no more office visit needed to reprogram your neurostat; you can just put on your spex and do it yourself. That means you'll be able to turn your calli on or off, *any time you want*.

That means we won't have the problem of people feeling that they have to give up beauty altogether. Instead, we can promote the idea that beauty is appropriate in some situations and not in others. For example, people could keep calli enabled when they're working, but disable it when they're among friends. I think people recognize that calli offers benefits, and will choose it on at least a part-time basis.

I'd say the ultimate goal is for calli to be considered the proper way to behave in polite society. People can always disable their calli in private, but the default for public interaction would be freedom from lookism. Appreciating beauty would become a consensual interaction, something you do only when both parties, the beholder and the beheld, agree to it.

FROM A BROADCAST OF EduNews:

In the latest on the Pembleton calliagnosia initiative, EduNews has learned that a new form of digital manipulation was used on the broadcast of PEN spokesperson Rebecca Boyer's speech. EduNews has received files from the SemioTech Warriors that contain what appear to be two recorded versions of the speech: an original — acquired from the Wyatt/Hayes computers — and the broadcast version. The files also include the SemioTech Warriors' analysis of the differences between the two versions.

The discrepancies are primarily enhancements to Ms. Boyer's voice intonation, facial expressions, and body language. Viewers who watch the original version rate Ms. Boyer's performance as good, while those who watch the edited version rate her performance as excellent, describing her as extraordinarily dynamic and persuasive. The SemioTech Warriors conclude that Wyatt/Hayes has developed new software capable of fine-tuning paralinguistic cues in order to maximize the emotional response evoked in viewers. This dramatically increases the effectiveness of recorded presentations, especially when viewed through spex, and its use in the PEN broadcast is likely what caused many supporters of the calliagnosia initiative to change their votes.

WALTER LAMBERT, PRESIDENT OF THE NATIONAL CALLIAGNOSIA ASSOCIATION:

In my entire career, I've met only a couple people who have the kind of charisma they gave Ms. Boyer in that speech. People like that radiate a kind of reality-distortion field that lets them convince you of almost anything. You feel moved by their very presence, you're ready to open your wallet or agree to whatever they ask. It's not until later that you remember all the objections you had, but by then, often as not, it's too late. And I'm truly frightened by the prospect of corporations being able to generate that effect with software.

What this is, is another kind of supernormal stimuli, like flawless beauty but even more dangerous. We had a defense against beauty, and Wyatt/Hayes has escalated things to the next level. And protecting ourselves from this type of persuasion is going to be a hell of a lot harder.

There is a type of tonal agnosia, or aprosodia, that makes you unable to hear voice intonation; all you hear are the words, not the delivery. There's also an agnosia that prevents you from recognizing facial expressions. Adopting the two of these would protect you from this type of manipulation, because you'd have to judge a speech purely on its content; its delivery would be invisible to you. But I can't recommend these agnosias. The result is nothing like calli. If you can't hear tone of voice or read someone's expression, your ability to interact with others is crippled. It'd be a kind of high-functioning autism. A few NCA members *are* adopting both agnosias, as a form of protest, but no one expects many people will follow their example.

So that means that once this software gets into widespread use, we're going to be facing extraordinarily persuasive pitches from all sides: commercials, press releases, evangelists. We'll hear the most stirring speeches given by a politician or general in decades. Even activists and culture jammers will use it, just to keep up with the establishment. Once the range of this software gets wide enough, even the movies will use it, too: an actor's own ability won't matter, because everyone's performance will be uncanny.

The same thing'll happen as happened with beauty: our environment will become saturated with this supernormal stimuli, and it'll affect our interaction with real people. When every speaker on a broadcast has the presence of a Winston Churchill or a Martin Luther King, we'll begin to regard ordinary people, with their average use of paralinguistic cues, as bland and unpersuasive. We'll become dissatisfied with the people we interact with in real life, because they won't be as engaging as the projections we see through our spex.

I just hope those spex for reprogramming neurostat hit the market soon. Then maybe we can encourage people to adopt the stronger agnosias just when they're watching video. That may be the only way for us to preserve authentic human interaction: if we save our emotional responses for real life.

TAMERA LYONS:
I know how this is going to sound, but... well, I'm thinking about getting my calli turned back on.

In a way, it's because of that PEN video. I don't mean I'm getting calli just because makeup companies don't want people to and I'm angry at them. That's not it. But it's hard to explain.

I *am* angry at them, because they used a trick to manipulate people; they weren't playing fair. But what it made me realize was, I was doing the same kind of thing to Garrett. Or I wanted to, anyway. I was trying to use my looks to win him back. And in a way that's not playing fair, either.

I don't mean that I'm as bad as the advertisers are! I love Garrett, and they just want to make money. But remember when I was talking about beauty as a kind of magic spell? It gives you an advantage, and I think it's very easy to misuse something like that. And what calli does is make a person immune to that sort of spell. So I figure I shouldn't mind if Garrett would rather be immune, because I shouldn't be trying to gain an advantage in the first place. If I get him back, I want it to be by playing fair, by him loving me for myself.

I know, just because he got his calli turned back on doesn't mean that I have to. I've really been enjoying seeing what faces look like. But if Garrett's going to be immune, I feel like I should be too. So we're even, you know? And if we do get back together, maybe we'll get those new spex they're talking about. Then we can turn off our calli when we're by ourselves, just the two of us.

And I guess calli makes sense for other reasons, too. Those makeup companies and everyone else, they're just trying to create needs in you that you wouldn't feel if they were playing fair, and I don't like that. If I'm going to be dazzled watching a commercial, it'll be when I'm in the mood, not whenever they spring it on me. Although I'm not going to get those other agnosias, like that tonal one, not yet anyway. Maybe once those new spex come out.

This doesn't mean I agree with my parents' having me grow up with calli. I still think they were wrong; they thought getting rid of beauty would help make a utopia, and I don't believe that at all. Beauty isn't the problem, it's how some people are misusing it that's the problem. And that's what calli's good for; it lets you guard against that. I don't know, maybe this wasn't a problem back in my parents' day. But it's something we have to deal with now.

The Girl Who Was Plugged In

James Tiptree, Jr.

Listen, zombie. Believe me. What I could tell you — you with your silly hands leaking sweat on your growth-stocks portfolio. One-ten lousy hacks of AT&T on twenty-point margin and you think you're Evel Knievel. AT&T? You doubleknit dummy, how I'd love to show you something.

Look, dead daddy, I'd say. See for instance that rotten girl?

In the crowd over there, that one gaping at her gods. One rotten girl in the city of the future. (That's what I said.) Watch.

She's jammed among bodies, craning and peering with her soul yearning out of her eyeballs. Love! Oo-ooh, love them! Her gods are coming out of a store called Body East. Three youngbloods, larking along loverly. Dressed like simple street-people but...smashing. See their great eyes swivel above their nosefilters, their hands lift shyly, their inhumanly tender lips melt? The crowd moans. Love! This whole boiling megacity, this whole fun future world loves its gods.

You don't believe gods, dad? Wait. Whatever turns you on, there's a god in the future for you, custom-made. Listen to this mob. "I touched his foot! Ow-oow, I TOUCHED Him!"

Even the people in the GTX tower up there love the gods — in their own way and for their own reasons.

The funky girl on the street, she just loves. Grooving on their beautiful lives, their mysterioso problems. No one ever told her about mortals who love a god and end up as a tree or a sighing sound. In a million years it'd never occur to her that her gods might love her back.

She's squashed against the wall now as the godlings come by. They move in a clear space. A holocam bobs above, but its shadow never falls on them. The store display-screens are magically clear of bodies as the gods glance in and a beggar underfoot is suddenly alone. They give him a token. "Aaaaah!" goes the crowd.

Now one of them flashes some wild new kind of timer and they all trot to catch a shuttle, just like people. The shuttle stops for them — more magic. The crowd sighs, closing back. The gods are gone.

(In a room far from — but not unconnected to — the GTX tower a molecular flipflop closes too, and three account tapes spin.)

Our girl is still stuck by the wall while guards and holocam equipment pull away. The adoration's fading from her face. That's good, because now you can see she's the ugly of the world. A tall monument to pituitary dystrophy. No surgeon would touch her. When she smiles, her jaw — it's half purple — almost bites her left eye out. She's also quite young, but who could care?

The crowd is pushing her along now, treating you to glimpses of her jumbled torso, her mismatched legs. At the corner she strains to send one last fond spasm after the godlings' shuttle. Then her face reverts to its usual expression of dim pain and she lurches onto the moving walkway, stumbling into people. The walkway junctions with another. She crosses, trips and collides with the casualty rail. Finally she comes out into a little bare place called a park. The sportshow is working, a basketball game in three-di is going on right overhead. But all she does is squeeze onto a bench and huddle there while a ghostly free-throw goes by her ear.

After that nothing at all happens except a few furtive hand-mouth gestures which don't even interest her bench mates. But you're curious about the city? So ordinary after all, in the FUTURE?

Ah, there's plenty to swing with here — and it's not all that *far* in the future, dad. But pass up the sci-fi stuff for now, like for instance the holovision technology that's put TV and radio in museums. Or the worldwide carrier field bouncing down from satellites, controlling communication and transport systems all over the globe. That was a spin-off from asteroid mining, pass it by. We're watching that girl.

I'll give you just one goodie. Maybe you noticed on the sportshow or the streets? No commercials. No ads.

That's right. NO ADS. An eyeballer for you.

Look around. Not a billboard, sign, slogan, jingle, sky-write, blurb, sublimflash, in this whole fun world. Brand names? Only in those ticky little peep-screens on the stores, and you could hardly call that advertising. How does that finger you?

.Think about it. That girl is still sitting there.

She's parked right under the base of the GTX tower, as a matter of fact. Look way up and you can see the sparkles from the bubble on top, up there among the domes of godland. Inside that bubble is a boardroom. Neat bronze shield on the door: Global Transmissions Corporation — not that that means anything.

I happen to know there are six people in that room. Five of them technically male, and the sixth isn't easily thought of as a mother. They are absolutely unremarkable. Those faces were seen once at their nuptials and will show again in their obituaries and impress nobody either time. If you're looking for the secret Big Blue Meanies of the world, forget it. I know. Zen, do I know! Flesh? Power? Glory? You'd horrify them.

What *they* do like up there is to have things orderly, especially their communications. You could say they've dedicated their lives to that, to freeing the world from garble. Their nightmares are about hemorrhages of information; channels screwed up, plans misimplemented, garble creeping in. Their gigantic wealth only worries them, it keeps opening new vistas of disorder. Luxury? They wear what their tailors put on them, eat what their cooks serve them. See that old boy there — his name is Isham — he's sipping water and frowning as he listens to a databall. The water was prescribed by his medistaff. It tastes awful. The databall also contains a disquieting message about his son, Paul.

But it's time to go back down, far below to our girl. Look!

She's toppled over sprawling on the ground.

A tepid commotion ensues among the bystanders. The consensus is she's dead, which she disproves by bubbling a little. And presently she's taken away by one of the superb ambulances of the future, which are a real improvement over ours when one happens to be around.

At the local bellevue the usual things are done by the usual team of clowns aided by a saintly mop-pusher. Our girl revives enough to answer the questionnaire without which you can't die, even in the future. Finally she's cast up, a pumped-out hulk on a cot in the long, dim ward.

Again nothing happens for a while except that her eyes leak a little from the understandable disappointment of finding herself still alive.

But somewhere one GTX computer has been tickling another, and toward midnight something does happen. First comes an attendant who pulls screens around her. Then a man in a business doublet comes daintily down the ward. He motions the attendant to strip off the sheet and go.

The groggy girl-brute heaves up, big hands clutching at bodyparts you'd pay not to see.

"Burke? P. Burke, is that your name?"

"Y-yes." Croak. "Are you…policeman?"

"No. They'll be along shortly, I expect. Public suicide's a felony."

"…I'm sorry."

He has a 'corder in his hand. "No family, right?"

"No."

"You're seventeen. One year city college. What did you study?"

"La—languages."

"H'mm. Say something."

Unintelligible rasp.

He studies her. Seen close, he's not so elegant. Errand-boy type.

"Why did you try to kill yourself?"

She stares at him with dead-rat dignity, hauling up the gray sheet. Give him a point, he doesn't ask twice.

"Tell me, did you see Breath this afternoon?"

Dead as she nearly is, that ghastly love-look wells up. Breath is the three young gods, a loser's cult. Give the man another point, he interprets her expression.

"How would you like to meet them?"

The girl's eyes bug out grotesquely.

"I have a job for someone like you. It's hard work. If you did well you'd be meeting Breath and stars like that all the time."

Is he insane? She's deciding she really did die.

"But it means you never see anybody you know again. Never, *ever*. You will be legally dead. Even the police won't know. Do you want to try?"

It all has to be repeated while her great jaw slowly sets. *Show me the fire I walk through*. Finally P. Burke's prints are in his 'corder, the man holding up the big rancid girl-body without a sign of distaste. It makes you wonder what else he does.

And then—THE MAGIC. Sudden silent trot of litterbearers tucking P. Burke into something quite different from a bellevue stretcher, the oiled slide into the daddy of all luxury ambulances — real flowers in that holder!—and the long jarless rush to nowhere. Nowhere is warm and gleaming and kind with nurses. (Where did you hear that money can't buy genuine kindness?) And clean clouds folding P. Burke into bewildered sleep.

...Sleep which merges into feedings and washings and more sleeps, into drowsy moments of afternoon where midnight should be, and gentle businesslike voices and friendly (but very few) faces, and endless painless hyposprays and peculiar numbnesses. And later comes the steadying rhythm of days and nights, and a quickening which P. Burke doesn't identify as health, but only knows that the fungus place in her armpit is gone. And then she's up and following those few new faces with growing trust, first tottering, then walking strongly, all better now, clumping down the short hall to the tests, tests, tests, and the other things.

And here is our girl, looking—

If possible, worse than before. (You thought this was Cinderella transistorized?)

The disimprovement in her looks comes from the electrode jacks peeping out of her sparse hair, and there are other meldings of flesh and metal. On the other hand, that collar and spinal plate are really an asset; you won't miss seeing that neck.

P. Burke is ready for training in her new job.

The training takes place in her suite and is exactly what you'd call a charm course. How to walk, sit, eat, speak, blow her nose, how to stumble, to urinate, to hiccup — DELICIOUSLY. How to make each nose-blow or shrug delightfully, subtly, different from any ever spooled before. As the man said, it's hard work.

But P. Burke proves apt. Somewhere in that horrible body is a gazelle, a houri, who would have been buried forever without this crazy chance. See the ugly duckling go!

Only it isn't precisely P. Burke who's stepping, laughing, shaking out her shining hair. How could it be? P. Burke is doing it all right, but she's doing it through something. The something is to all appearances a live girl. (You were warned, this is the FUTURE.)

When they first open the big cryocase and show her her new body, she says just one word. Staring, gulping, "How?"

Simple, really. Watch P. Burke in her sack and scuffs stump down the hall beside Joe, the man who supervises the technical part of her training. Joe doesn't mind P. Burke's looks, he hasn't noticed them. To Joe, system matrices are beautiful.

They go into a dim room containing a huge cabinet like a one-man sauna and a console for Joe. The room has a glass wall that's all dark now. And just for your information, the whole shebang is five hundred feet underground near what used to be Carbondale, Pa.

Joe opens the sauna cabinet like a big clamshell standing on end with a lot of funny business inside. Our girl shucks her shift and walks into it bare, totally unembarrassed. *Eager.* She settles in face-forward, butting jacks into sockets. Joe closes it carefully onto her humpback. Clunk. She can't see in there or hear or move. She hates this minute. But how she loves what comes next!

Joe's at his console, and the lights on the other side of the glass wall come up. A room is on the other side, all fluff and kicky bits, a girly bedroom. In the bed is a small mound of silk with a rope of yellow hair hanging out.

The sheet stirs and gets whammed back flat.

Sitting up in the bed is the darlingest girl child you've EVER seen. She quivers — porno for angels. She sticks both her little arms straight up, flips her hair, looks around full of sleepy pazazz. Then she can't resist rubbing her hands down over her minibreasts and belly. Because, you see, it's the god-awful P. Burke who is sitting there hugging her perfect girl-body, looking at you out of delighted eyes.

Then the kitten hops out of bed and crashes flat on the floor.

From the sauna in the dim room comes a strangled noise. P. Burke, trying to rub her wired-up elbow, is suddenly smothered in *two* bodies, electrodes jerking in her flesh. Joe juggles inputs, crooning into his mike. The flurry passes; it's all right.

In the lighted room the elf gets up, casts a cute glare at the glass wall, and goes into a transparent cubicle. A bathroom, what else? She's a live girl, and live girls have to go to the bathroom after a night's sleep even if their brains are in a sauna cabinet in the next room. And P. Burke isn't in that cabinet, she's in the bathroom. Perfectly simple, if you have the glue for that closed training circuit that's letting her run her neural system by remote control.

Now let's get one thing clear. P. Burke does not *feel* her brain is in the sauna room, she feels she's in that sweet little body. When you wash your hands, do you feel the water is running on your brain? Of course not. You feel the water on your hand, although the "feeling" is actually a potential-pattern flickering over the electrochemical jelly between your ears. And it's delivered there via the long circuits from your hands. Just so, P. Burke's brain in the cabinet feels the water on her hands in the bathroom. The fact that the signals have jumped across space on the way in makes no difference at all. If you want the jargon, it's known as eccentric projection or sensory reference and you've done it all your life. Clear?

Time to leave the honeypot to her toilet training — she's made a booboo with the toothbrush, because P. Burke can't get used to what she sees in the mirror —

But wait, you say. Where did that girl-body come from?

P. Burke asks that too, dragging out the words.

"They grow 'em," Joe tells her. He couldn't care less about the flesh department. "PDS. Placental decanters. Modified embryos, see? Fit the control implants in later. Without a Remote Operator it's just a vegetable. Look at the feet—no callus at all." (He knows because they told him.)

"Oh...oh, she's incredible...."

"Yeah, a neat job. Want to try walking-talking mode today? You're coming on fast."

And she is. Joe's reports and the reports from the nurse and the doctor and style man go to a bushy man upstairs who is some kind of medical cybertech but mostly a project administrator. His reports in turn go—to the GTX boardroom? Certainly not, did you think this is *a big* thing? His reports just go up. The point is, they're green, very green. P. Burke promises well.

So the bushy man — Dr. Tesla — has procedures to initiate. The little kitten's dossier in the Central Data Bank, for instance. Purely routine. And the phase-in schedule which will put her on the scene. This is simple: a small exposure in an off-network holoshow.

Next he has to line out the event which will fund and target her. That takes budget meetings, clearances, coordinations. The Burke project begins to recruit and grow. And there's the messy business of the name, which always gives Dr. Tesla an acute pain in the bush.

The name comes out weird, when it's suddenly discovered that Burke's "P." stands for "Philadelphia." Philadelphia? The astrologer grooves on it. Joe thinks it would help identification. The semantics girl references *brotherly love, Liberty Bell, main line, low teratogenesis,* blah-blah. Nicknames Philly? Pala? Pooty? Delphi? Is it good, bad? Finally "Delphi" is gingerly declared goodo. ("Burke" is replaced by something nobody remembers.)

Coming along now. We're at the official checkout down in the underground suite, which is as far as the training circuits reach. The bushy Dr. Tesla is there, braced by two budgetary types and a quiet fatherly man whom he handles like hot plasma.

Joe swings the door wide and she steps shyly in.

Their little Delphi, fifteen and flawless.

Tesla introduces her around. She's child-solemn, a beautiful baby to whom something so wonderful has happened you can feel the tingles. She doesn't smile, she...brims. That brimming joy is all that shows of P. Burke, the forgotten hulk in the sauna next door. But P. Burke doesn't know she's alive — it's Delphi who lives, every warm inch of her.

One of the budget types lets go a libidinous snuffle and freezes. The fatherly man, whose name is Mr. Cantle, clears his throat.

"Well, young lady, are you ready to go to work?"

"Yes, sir," gravely from the elf.

"We'll see. Has anybody told you what you're going to do for us?"

"No, sir." Joe and Tesla exhale quietly.

"Good." He eyes her, probing for the blind brain in the room next door.

"Do you know what *advertising* is?"

He's talking dirty, hitting to shock. Delphi's *eyes* widen and her little chin goes up. Joe is in ecstasy at the complex expressions P. Burke is getting through. Mr. Cantle waits.

"It's, well, it's when they used to tell people to buy things." She swallows. "It's not allowed."

"That's right." Mr. Cantle leans back, grave. "Advertising as it used to be is against the law. *A display other than the legitimate use of the product, intended to promote its sale.* In former times every manufacturer was free to tout his wares any way, place, or time he could afford. All the media and most of the landscape was taken up with extravagant competing displays. The thing became uneconomic. The public rebelled. Since the so-called Huckster Act sellers have been restrained to, I quote, displays in or on the product itself, visible during its legitimate use or in on-premise sales." Mr. Cantle leans forward. "Now tell me, Delphi, why do people buy one product rather than another?"

"Well..." Enchanting puzzlement from Delphi. "They, um, they see them and like them, or they hear about them from somebody?" (Touch of P. Burke there; she didn't say, from a friend.)

"Partly. Why did *you* buy your particular body-lift?"

"I never had a body-lift, sir."

Mr. Cantle frowns; what gutters do they drag for these Remotes?

"Well, what brand of water do you drink?"

"Just what was in the faucet, sir," says Delphi humbly. "I — I did try to boil it — "

"Good god." He scowls; Tesla stiffens. "Well, what did you boil it in? A cooker?"

The shining yellow head nods.

"What *brand* of cooker did you buy?"

"I didn't buy it, sir," says frightened P. Burke through Delphi's lips. "But — I know the best kind! Ananga has a Burnbabi. I saw the name when she — "

"Exactly!" Cantle's fatherly beam comes back strong; the Burnbabi account is a strong one, too. "You saw Ananga using one so you thought it must be good, eh? And it is good, or a great human being like Ananga wouldn't be using it. Absolutely right. And now, Delphi, you know what you're going to be doing for us. You're going to show some products. Doesn't sound very hard, does it?"

"Oh, no, sir…" Baffled child's stare; Joe gloats.

"And you must never, *never* tell anyone what you're doing." Cantle's eyes bore for the brain behind this seductive child.

"You're wondering why we ask you to do this, naturally. There's a very serious reason. All those products people use, foods and healthaids and cookers and cleaners and clothes and cars — they're all made by *people*. Somebody put in years of hard work designing and making them. A man comes up with a fine new idea for a better product. He has to get a factory and machinery, and hire workmen. Now. What happens if people have no way of hearing about his product? Word of mouth is far too slow and unreliable. Nobody might ever stumble onto his new product or find out how good it was, right? And then he and all the people who worked for him — they'd go bankrupt, right? So, Delphi, there has to be *some way* that large numbers of people can get a look at a good new product, right? How? By letting people see you using it. You're giving that man a chance."

Delphi's little head is nodding in happy relief.

"Yes, Sir, I do see now — but sir, it seems so sensible, why don't they let you — "

Cantle smiles sadly.

"It's an overreaction, my dear. History goes by swings. People overreact and pass harsh unrealistic laws which attempt to stamp out an essential social process. When this happens, the people who understand have to carry on as best they can until the pendulum swings back." He sighs. "The Huckster Laws are bad, inhuman laws, Delphi, despite their good intent. If they were strictly observed they would wreak havoc. Our economy, our society, would be cruelly destroyed. We'd be back in caves!" His inner fire is showing; if the Huckster Laws were strictly enforced he'd be back punching a databank.

"It's our duty, Delphi. Our solemn social duty. We are not breaking the law. You will be using the product. But people wouldn't understand, if they knew. They would become upset just as you did. So you must be very, very careful not to mention any of this to anybody."

(And somebody will be very, very carefully monitoring Delphi's speech circuits.)

"Now we're all straight, aren't we? Little Delphi here" — he is speaking to the invisible creature next door — "little Delphi is going to live a wonderful, exciting life. She's going to be a girl people watch. And she's going to be using fine products people will be glad to know about and helping the good people who make them. Yours will be a genuine social contribution." He keys up his pitch; the creature in there must be older.

Delphi digests this with ravishing gravity.

"But sir, how do I — ?"

"Don't worry about a thing. You'll have people behind you whose job it is to select the most worthy products for you to use. Your job is just to do as they say. They'll show you what outfits to wear to parties, what suncars and viewers to buy, and so on. That's all you have to do."

Parties — clothes — suncars! Delphi's pink mouth opens. In P. Burke's starved seventeen-year-old head the ethics of product sponsorship float far away.

"Now tell me in your own words what your job is, Delphi."

"Yes, sir. I — I'm to go to parties and buy things and use them as they tell me, to help the people who work in factories."

"And what did I say was so important?"

"Oh — I shouldn't let anybody know, about the things."

"Right." Mr. Cantle has another paragraph he uses when the subject shows, well, immaturity. But he can sense only eagerness here. Good. He doesn't really enjoy the other speech.

"It's a lucky girl who can have all the fun she wants while doing good for others, isn't it?" He beams around. There's a prompt shuffling of chairs. Clearly this one is go.

Joe leads her out, grinning. The poor fool thinks they're admiring her coordination.

It's out into the world for Delphi now, and at this point the up-channels get used. On the administrative side account schedules are opened, subprojects activated. On the technical side the reserved bandwidth is cleared. (That carrier field, remember?) A new name is waiting for Delphi, a name she'll never hear. It's a long string of binaries which have been quietly cycling in a GTX tank ever since a certain Beautiful Person didn't wake up.

The name winks out of cycle, dances from pulses into modulations of modulations, whizzes through phasing, and shoots into a giga-band beam racing up to a synchronous satellite poised over Guatemala. From there the beam pours twenty thousand miles back to Earth again, forming an all-pervasive field of structured energics supplying tuned demand-points all over the CanAm quadrant.

With that field, if you have the right credit rating, you can sit at a GTX console and operate an ore-extractor in Brazil. Or — if you have some simple credentials like being able to walk on water — you could shoot a spool into the network holocam shows running day and night in every home and dorm and rec site. Or you could create a continentwide traffic jam. Is it any wonder GTX guards those inputs like a sacred trust?

Delphi's "name" appears as a tiny analyzable nonredundancy in the flux, and she'd be very proud if she knew about it. It would strike P. Burke as magic; P. Burke never even understood robotcars. But

Delphi is in no sense a robot. Call her a waldo if you must. The fact is she's just a girl, a real-live girl with her brain in an unusual place. A simple real-time on-line system with plenty of bit-rate — even as you and you.

The point of all this hardware, which isn't very much hardware in this society, is so Delphi can walk out of that underground suite, a mobile demand-point draining an omnipresent fieldform. And she does — eighty-nine pounds of tender girl flesh and blood with a few metallic components, stepping out into the sunlight to be taken to her new life. A girl, with everything going for her including a medi-tech escort. Walking lovely, stopping to widen her eyes at the big antennae system overhead.

The mere fact that something called P. Burke is left behind down underground has no bearing at all. P. Burke is totally unselfaware and happy as a clam in its shell. (Her bed has been moved into the waldo cabinet room now.) And P. Burke isn't in the cabinet; P. Burke is climbing out of an airvan in a fabulous Colorado beef preserve, and her name is Delphi. Delphi is looking at live Charolais steers and live cottonwoods and aspens gold against the blue smog and stepping over live grass to be welcomed by the reserve super's wife.

The super's wife is looking forward to a visit from Delphi and her friends, and by a happy coincidence there's a holocam outfit here doing a piece for the nature nuts.

You could write the script yourself now, while Delphi learns a few rules about structural interferences and how to handle the tiny time lag which results from the new forty-thousand-mile parenthesis in her nervous system. That's right — the people with the leased holo-cam rig naturally find the gold aspen shadows look a lot better on Delphi's flank than they do on a steer. And Delphi's face improves the mountains too, when you can see them. But the nature freaks aren't quite as joyful as you'd expect.

"See you in Barcelona, kitten," the headman says sourly as they pack up.

"Barcelona?" echoes Delphi with that charming little subliminal lag. She sees where his hand is and steps back. "Cool, it's not her fault," another man says wearily. He knocks back his grizzled hair. "Maybe they'll leave in some of the gut."

Delphi watches them go off to load the spools on the GTX transport for processing. Her hand roves over the breast the man had touched. Back under Carbondale, P. Burke has discovered something new about her Delphi-body.

About the difference between Delphi and her own grim carcass.

She's always known Delphi has almost no sense of taste or smell. They explained about that: only so much bandwidth. You don't have to taste a suncar, do you? And the slight overall dimness of Delphi's sense of touch — she's familiar with that, too. Fabrics that would prickle P. Burke's own hide feel like a cool plastic film to Delphi.

But the blank spots. It took her a while to notice them. Delphi doesn't have much privacy; investments of her size don't. So she's slow about discovering there's certain definite places where her beastly P. Burke body *feels* things that Delphi's dainty flesh does not. H'mm! Channel space again, she thinks — and forgets it in the pure bliss of being Delphi.

You ask how a girl could forget a thing like that? Look. P. Burke is about as far as you can get from the concept *girl*. She's a female, yes — but for her, sex is a four-letter word spelled P-A-I-N. She isn't quite a virgin. You don't want the details; she'd been about twelve and the freak lovers were bombed blind. When they came down, they threw her out with a small hole in her anatomy and a mortal one elsewhere. She dragged off to buy her first and last shot, and she can still hear the clerk's incredulous guffaws.

Do you see why Delphi grins, stretching her delicious little numb body in the sun she faintly feels? Beams, saying, "Please, I'm ready now."

Ready for what? For Barcelona like the sour man said, where his nature-thing is now making it strong in the amateur section of the Festival. A winner! Like he also said, a lot of strip mines and dead fish have been scrubbed, but who cares with Delphi's darling face so visible?

So it's time for Delphi's face and her other delectabilities to show on Barcelona's Playa Nueva. Which means switching her channel to the EurAf synchsat.

They ship her at night so the nanosecond transfer isn't even noticed by that insignificant part of Delphi that lives five hundred feet under Carbondale, so excited the nurse has to make sure she eats. The circuit switches while Delphi "sleeps," that is, while P. Burke is out of the waldo cabinet. The next time she plugs in to open Delphi's eyes it's no different — do you notice which relay boards your phone calls go through?

And now for the event that turns the sugarcube from Colorado into the PRINCESS.

Literally true, he's a prince, or rather an Infante of an old Spanish line that got shined up in the Neomonarchy. He's also eighty-one, with a passion for birds — the kind you see in zoos. Now it suddenly turns out that he isn't poor at all. Quite the reverse; his old sister laughs in their tax lawyer's face and starts restoring the family hacienda while the Infante totters out to court Delphi. And little Delphi begins to live the life of the gods.

What do gods do? Well, everything beautiful. But (remember Mr. Cantle?) the main point is Things. Ever see a god empty-handed? You can't be a god without at least a magic girdle or an eight-legged horse. But in the old days some stone tablets or winged sandals or a chariot drawn by virgins would do a god for life. No more! Gods make it on novelty now. By Delphi's time the hunt for new god-gear is turning the earth and seas inside-out and sending frantic fingers to the stars. And what gods have, mortals desire.

So Delphi starts on a Euromarket shopping spree squired by her old Infante, thereby doing her bit to stave off social collapse.

Social what? Didn't you get it, when Mr. Cantle talked about a world where advertising is banned and fifteen billion consumers are glued to their holocam shows? One capricious self-powered god can wreck you.

Take the nose-filter massacre. Years, the industry sweated years to achieve an almost invisible enzymatic filter. So one day a couple of pop-gods show up wearing nose-filters like *big purple bats*. By the end of the week the world market is screaming for purple bats. Then it switched to bird-heads and skulls, but by the time the industry re-tooled the crazies had dropped bird-heads and gone to injection globes. Blood!

Multiply that by a million consumer industries, and you can see why it's economic to have a few controllable gods. Especially with the beautiful hunk of space R & D the Peace Department laid out for and which the taxpayers are only too glad to have taken off their hands by an outfit like GTX, which everybody knows is almost a public trust.

And so you — or rather, GTX — find a creature like P. Burke and give her Delphi. And Delphi helps keep things *orderly*, she does what you tell her to. Why? That's right, Mr. Cantle never finished his speech.

But here come the tests of Delphi's button-nose twinkling in the torrent of news and entertainment. And she's noticed. The feedback shows a flock of viewers turning up the amps when this country baby gets tangled in her new colloidal body-jewels. She registers at a couple of major scenes, too, and when the Infante gives her a suncar, little Delphi trying out suncars is a tiger. There's a solid response in high-credit country. Mr. Cantle is humming his happy tune as he cancels a Benelux subnet option to guest her on a nude cook-show called Wok Venus.

And now for the superposh old-world wedding! The hacienda has Moorish baths and six-foot silver candelabra and real black horses, and the Spanish Vatican blesses them. The final event is a grand gaucho ball with the old prince and his little Infanta on a bowered balcony. She's a spectacular doll of silver lace, wildly launching toy doves at her new friends whirling by below.

The Infante beams, twitches his old nose to the scent of her sweet excitement. His doctor has been very helpful. Surely now, after he has been so patient with the suncars and all the nonsense —

The child looks up at him, saying something incomprehensible about "breath." He makes out that she's complaining about the three singers she had begged for.

"They've changed!" she marvels. "Haven't they changed? They're so dreary. I'm so happy now!"

And Delphi falls fainting against a gothic vargueno.

Her American duenna rushes up, calls help. Delphi's eyes are open, but Delphi isn't there. The duenna pokes among Delphi's hair, slaps her. The old prince grimaces. He has no idea what she is beyond an excellent solution to his tax problems, but he had been a falconer in his youth. There comes to his mind the small pinioned birds which were flung up to stimulate the hawks. He pockets the veined claw to which he had promised certain indulgences and departs to design his new aviary.

And Delphi also departs with her retinue to the Infante's newly discovered yacht. The trouble isn't serious. It's only that five thousand miles away and five hundred feet down P. Burke has been doing it too well.

They've always known she has terrific aptitude. Joe says he never saw a Remote take over so fast. No disorientations, no rejections. The psychomed talks about self-alienation. She's going into Delphi like a salmon to the sea.

She isn't eating or sleeping, they can't keep her out of the body-cabinet to get her blood moving, there are necroses under her grisly sit-down. Crisis!

So Delphi gets a long "sleep" on the yacht and P. Burke gets it pounded through her perforated head that she's endangering Delphi. (Nurse Fleming thinks of that, thus alienating the psychomed.)

They rig a pool down there (Nurse Fleming again) and chase P. Burke back and forth. And she loves it. So naturally when they let her plug in again Delphi loves it too. Every noon beside the yacht's hydrofoils darling Delphi clips along in the blue sea they've warned her not to drink. And every night around the shoulder of the world an ill-shaped thing in a dark burrow beats its way across a sterile pool.

So presently the yacht stands up on its foils and carries Delphi to the program Mr. Cantle has waiting. It's long-range; she's scheduled for at least two decades' product life. Phase One calls for her to connect with a flock of young ultrariches who are romping loose between Brioni and Djakarta where a competitor named PEV could pick them off.

A routine luxgear op, see; no politics, no policy angles, and the main budget items are the title and the yacht, which was idle anyway. The storyline is that Delphi goes to accept some rare birds for her prince—who cares? The *point* is that the Haiti area is no longer radioactive and look! — the gods are there. And so are several new Carib West Happy Isles which can afford GTX rates, in fact two of them are GTX subsids.

But you don't want to get the idea that all these newsworthy people are wired-up robbies, for pity's sake. You don't need many if they're placed right. Delphi asks Joe about that when he comes down to Barranquilla to check her over. (P. Burke's own mouth hasn't said much for a while.)

"Are there many like me?"

"Nobody's like you, buttons. Look, are you still getting Van Allen warble?"

"I mean, like Davy. Is he a Remote?"

(Davy is the lad who is helping her collect the birds. A sincere redhead who needs a little more exposure.)

"Davy? He's one of Matt's boys, some psychojob. They haven't any channel."

"What about the real ones? Djuma van O, or Ali, or Jim Ten?"

"Djuma was born with a pile of GTX basic where her brain should be, she's nothing but a pain. Jimsy does what his astrologer tells him. Look, peanut, where do you get the idea you aren't real? You're the realest. Aren't you having joy?"

"Oh, Joe!" Flinging her little arms around him and his analyzer grids. "Oh, *me gusto mucho, muchisimo!*"

"Hey, hey." He pets her yellow head, folding the analyzer.

Three thousand miles north and five hundred feet down a forgotten hulk in a body-waldo glows.

And is she having joy. To waken out of the nightmare of being P. Burke and find herself a peri, a star-girl? On a yacht in paradise with no more to do than adorn herself and play with toys and attend revels and greet her friends — her, P. Burke, having friends! — and turn the right way for the holocams? Joy!

And it shows. One look at Delphi and the viewers know: DREAMS CAN COME TRUE.

Look at her riding pillion on Davy's sea-bike, carrying an apoplectic macaw in a silver hoop. Oh, *Morton, let's go there this winter!* Or learning the Japanese chinchona from that Kobe group, in a dress that looks like a blowtorch rising from one knee, and which should sell big in Texas. *Morton, is that real fire?* Happy, happy little girl!

And Davy. He's her pet and her baby, and she loves to help him fix his red-gold hair. (P. Burke marveling, running Delphi's fingers through the curls.) Of course Davy is one of Matt's boys — not impotent exactly, but very *very* low drive. (Nobody knows exactly what Matt does with his bitty budget, but the boys are useful and one or two have made names.) He's perfect for Delphi; in fact the psychomed lets her take him to bed, two kittens in a basket. Davy doesn't mind the fact that Delphi "sleeps" like the dead. That's when P. Burke is out of the body-waldo up at Carbondale, attending to her own depressing needs.

A funny thing about that. Most of her sleepy-time Delphi's just a gently ticking lush little vegetable waiting for P. Burke to get back on the controls. But now and again Delphi all by herself smiles a bit or stirs in her "sleep." Once she breathed a sound: "Yes."

Under Carbondale P. Burke knows nothing. She's asleep too, dreaming of Delphi, what else? But if the bushy Dr. Tesla had heard that single syllable, his bush would have turned snow white. Because Delphi is TURNED OFF.

He doesn't. Davy is too dim to notice, and Delphi's staff boss, Hopkins, wasn't monitoring.

And they've all got something else to think about now, because the cold-fire dress sells half a million copies, and not only in Texas. The GTX computers already know it. When they correlate a minor demand for macaws in Alaska the problem comes to human attention: Delphi is something special.

It's a problem, see, because Delphi is targeted on a limited consumer bracket. Now it turns out she has mass-pop potential — those macaws in *Fairbanks*, man! — it's like trying to shoot mice with an ABM. A whole new ball game. Dr. Tesla and the fatherly Mr. Cantle start going around in headquarters circles and buddy-lunching together when they can get away from a seventh-level weasel boy who scares them both.

In the end it's decided to ship Delphi down to the GTX holocam enclave in Chile to try a spot on one of the mainstream shows. (Never mind why an Infanta takes up acting.) The holocam complex occupies a couple of mountains where an observatory once used the clean air. Holocam total-environment shells are very expensive and electronically superstable. Inside them actors can move freely without going off-register, and the whole scene or any selected part will show up in the viewer's home in complete three-di, so real you can look up their noses and much denser than you get from mobile rigs. You can blow a tit ten feet tall when there's no molecular skiffle around.

The enclave looks — well, take everything you know about Hollywood-Burbank and throw it away. What Delphi sees coming down is a neat giant mushroom-farm, domes of all sizes up to monsters for the big games and stuff. It's orderly. The idea that art thrives on creative flamboyance has long been torpedoed by proof that what art needs is computers. Because this showbiz has something TV and Hollywood never had — *automated inbuilt viewer feedback*. Samples, ratings, critics, polls? Forget it. With that carrier field you can get real-time response-sensor readouts from every receiver in the world, served up at your console. That started as a thingie to give the public more influence on content.

Yes.

Try it, man. You're at the console. Slice to the sex-age-educ-econ-ethno-cetera audience of your choice and start. You can't miss. Where the feedback warms up, give 'em more of that. Warm — warmer — *hot!* You've hit it — the secret itch under those hides, the dream in those hearts. You don't need to know its name. With your hand controlling all the input and your eye reading all the response, you can make them a god. . . and somebody'll do the same for you.

But Delphi just sees rainbows, when she gets through the degaussing ports and the field relay and takes her first look at the insides of those shells. The next thing she sees is a team of shapers and technicians descending on her, and millisecond timers everywhere. The tropical leisure is finished. She's in gigabuck mainstream now, at the funnel maw of the unceasing hose that's pumping the sight and sound and flesh and blood and sobs and laughs and dreams of *reality* into the world's happy head. Little Delphi is going plonk into a zillion homes in prime time and nothing is left to chance. Work!

And again Delphi proves apt. Of course it's really P. Burke down under Carbondale who's doing it, but who remembers that carcass? Certainly not P. Burke, she hasn't spoken through her own mouth for months. Delphi doesn't even recall dreaming of her when she wakes up.

As for the show itself, don't bother. It's gone on so long no living soul could unscramble the plotline. Delphi's trial spot has something to do with a widow and her dead husband's brother's amnesia.

The flap comes after Delphi's spots begin to flash out along the world-hose and the feedback appears. You've guessed it, of course. Sensational! As you'd say, they IDENTIFY.

The report actually says something like InskinEmp with a string of percentages, meaning that Delphi not only has it for anybody with a Y chromosome, but also for women and everything in between. It's the sweet supernatural jackpot, the million-to-one.

Remember your Harlow? A sexpot, sure. But why did bitter hausfraus in Gary and Memphis know that the vanilla-ice-cream goddess with the white hair and crazy eyebrows was *their baby girl*? And write loving letters to Jean warning her that their husbands weren't good enough for her? Why? The GTX analysts don't know either, but they know what to do with it when it happens.

(Back in his bird sanctuary the old Infante spots it without benefit of computers and gazes thoughtfully at his bride in widow's weeds. It might, he feels, be well to accelerate the completion of his studies.)

The excitement reaches down to the burrow under Carbondale where P. Burke gets two medical exams in a week and a chronically inflamed electrode is replaced. Nurse Fleming also gets an assistant who doesn't do much nursing but is very interested in access doors and identity tabs.

And in Chile, little Delphi is promoted to a new home up among the stars' residential spreads and a private jitney to carry her to work. For Hopkins there's a new computer terminal and a full-time schedule man. What is the schedule crowded with?

Things.

And here begins the trouble. You probably saw that coming too.

"What does she think she is, a goddamn *consumer rep*?" Mr. Cantle's fatherly face in Carbondale contorts.

"The girl's upset," Miss Fleming says stubbornly. "She *believes* that, what you told her about helping people and good new products."

"They are good products," Mr. Cantle snaps automatically, but his anger is under control. He hasn't got where he is by irrelevant reactions.

"She says the plastic gave her a rash and the glo-pills made her dizzy."

"Good god, she shouldn't swallow them," Dr. Tesla puts in agitatedly.

"You told her she'd use them," persists Miss Fleming.

Mr. Cantle is busy figuring how to ease this problem to the feral-faced young man. What, was it a goose that lays golden eggs?

Whatever he says to Level Seven, down in Chile the offending products vanish. And a symbol goes into Delphi's tank matrix, one that means roughly *Balance unit resistance against* PR *index*.

This means that Delphi's complaints will be endured as long as her Pop Response stays above a certain level. (What happens when it sinks need not concern us.) And to compensate, the price of her exposure-time rises again. She's a regular on the show now and response is still climbing.

See her under the sizzling lasers, in a holocam shell set up as a walkway accident. (The show is guesting an acupuncture school shill.)

"I don't think this new body-lift is safe," Delphi's saying. "It's made a funny blue spot on me—look, Mr. Vere."

She wiggles to show where the mini-gray pak that imparts a delicious sense of weightlessness is attached.

"So don't leave it *on*, Dee. With your meat—watch that deck-spot, it's starting to synch."

"But if I don't wear it it isn't honest. They should insulate it more or something, don't you see?"

The show's beloved old father, who is the casualty, gives a senile snigger.

"I'll tell them," Mr. Vere mutters. "Look now, as you step back bend like this so it just shows, see? And hold two beats."

Obediently Delphi turns, and through the dazzle her eyes connect with a pair of strange dark ones. She squints. A quiet young man is lounging alone by the port, apparently waiting to use the chamber.

Delphi's used by now to young men looking at her with many peculiar expressions, but she isn't used to what she gets here. A jolt of something somber and knowing. Secrets.

"Eyes! Eyes, Dee!"

She moves through the routine, stealing peeks at the stranger. He stares back. He knows something.

When they let her go she comes shyly to him.

"Living wild, kitten." Cool voice, hot underneath.

"What do you mean?"

"Dumping on the product. You trying to get dead?"

"But it isn't right," she tells him. "They don't know, but I do, I've been wearing it."

His cool is jolted.

"You're out of your head."

"Oh, they'll see I'm right when they check it," she explains. "They're just so busy. When I tell them—"

He is staring down at little flower-face. His mouth opens, closes. "What are you doing in this sewer anyway? Who are you?"

Bewilderedly she says, "I'm Delphi."

"Holy Zen."

"What's wrong? Who are you, please?"

Her people are moving her out now, nodding at him.

"Sorry we ran over, Mr. Uhunh," the script girl says.

He mutters something, but it's lost as her convoy bustles her toward the flower-decked jitney.

(Hear the click of an invisible ignition-train being armed?)

"Who was he?" Delphi asks her hairman.

The hairman is bending up and down from his knees as he works.

"Paul. Isham. Three," he says and puts a comb in his mouth.

"Who's that? I can't see."

He mumbles around the comb, meaning, "Are you jiving?" Because she has to be, in the middle of the GTX enclave.

Next day there's a darkly smoldering face under a turban-towel when Delphi and the show's paraplegic go to use the carbonated pool.

She looks.

He looks.

And the next day, too.

(Hear the automatic sequencer cutting in? The system couples, the fuels begin to travel.)

Poor old Isham senior. You have to feel sorry for a man who values order: when he begets young, genetic information is still transmitted in the old ape way. One minute it's a happy midget with a rubber duck — look around and here's this huge healthy stranger, opaquely emotional, running with god knows who. Questions are heard where there's nothing to question, and eruptions claiming to be moral outrage. When this is called to Papa's attention — it may take time, in that boardroom — Papa does what he can, but without immortality-juice the problem is worrisome.

And young Paul Isham is a bear. He's bright and articulate and tender-souled and incessantly active, and he and his friends are choking with appallment at the world their fathers made. And it hasn't taken Paul long to discover that *his* father's house has many mansions and even the GTX computers can't relate everything to everything else. He noses out a decaying project which adds up to something like, Sponsoring Marginal Creativity (the free-lance team that "discovered" Delphi was one such grantee). And from there it turns out that an agile lad named Isham can get his hands on a viable packet of GTX holocam facilities.

So here he is with his little band, way down the mushroom-farm mountain, busily spooling a show which has no relation to Delphi's. It's built on bizarre techniques and unsettling distortions pregnant with social protest. An *underground* expression to you.

All this isn't unknown to his father, of course, but so far it has done nothing more than deepen Isham senior's apprehensive frown.

Until Paul connects with Delphi.

And by the time Papa learns this, those invisible hypergolics have exploded, the energy-shells are rushing out. For Paul, you see, is the genuine article. He's serious. He dreams. He even reads — for example, *Green Mansions* — and he wept fiercely when those fiends burned Rima alive.

When he hears that some new GTX pussy is making it big, he sneers and forgets it. He's busy. He never connects the name with this little girl making her idiotic, doomed protest in the holocam chamber. This strangely simple little girl.

And she comes and looks up at him and he sees Rima, lost Rima the enchanted bird girl, and his unwired human heart goes twang.

And Rima turns out to be Delphi.

Do you need a map? The angry puzzlement. The rejection of the dissonance Rima-hustling-for-GTX-My-Father. Garbage, cannot be. The loitering around the pool to confirm the swindle...dark eyes hitting on blue wonder, jerky words exchanged in a peculiar stillness... the dreadful reorganization of the image into Rima-Delphi *in my Father's tentacles —*

You don't need a map.

Nor for Delphi either, the girl who loved her gods. She's seen their divine flesh close now, heard their unamplified voices call her name. She's played their god-games, worn their garlands. She's even become a goddess herself, though she doesn't believe it. She's not disenchanted, don't think that. She's still full of love. It's just that some crazy kind of *hope* hasn't —

Really you can skip all this, when the loving little girl on the yellow-brick road meets a Man. A real human male burning with angry compassion and grandly concerned with human justice, who reaches for her with real male arms and — boom! She loves him back with all her heart.

A happy trip, see?

Except.

Except that it's really P. Burke five thousand miles away who loves Paul. P. Burke the monster down in a dungeon smelling of electrode paste. A caricature of a woman burning, melting, obsessed with true love. Trying over twenty-double-thousand miles of hard vacuum to reach her beloved through girl-flesh numbed by an invisible film. Feeling his arms around the body he thinks is hers, fighting through shadows to give herself to him. Trying to taste and smell him through beautiful dead nostrils, to love him back with a body that goes dead in the heart of the fire.

Perhaps you get P. Burke's state of mind?

She has phases. The trying, first. And the shame. The SHAME. *I am not what thou lovest.* And the fiercer trying. And the realization that there is no, no way, none. Never. *Never...* A bit delayed, isn't it, her understanding that the bargain she made was forever? P. Burke should have noticed those stories about mortals who end up as grasshoppers.

You see the outcome — the funneling of all this agony into one dumb protoplasmic drive to fuse with Delphi. To leave, to close out the beast she is chained to. *To become Delphi.*

Of course it's impossible.

However, her torments have an effect on Paul. Delphi-as-Rima is a potent enough love object, and liberating Delphi's mind requires hours of deeply satisfying instruction in the rottenness of it all. Add in Delphi's body worshiping his flesh, burning in the fire of P. Burke's savage heart — do you wonder Paul is involved?

That's not all.

By now they're spending every spare moment together and some that aren't so spare.

"Mr. Isham, would you mind staying out of this sports sequence? The script calls for Davy here."

(Davy's still around, the exposure did him good.)

"What's the difference?" Paul yawns. "It's just an ad. I'm not blocking that thing."

Shocked silence at his two-letter word. The script girl swallows bravely.

"I'm sorry, sir, our directive is to do the *social sequence* exactly as scripted. We're having to respool the segments we did last week, Mr. Hopkins is very angry with me."

"Who the hell is Hopkins? Where is he?"

"Oh, please, Paul. *Please.*"

Paul unwraps himself, saunters back. The holocam crew nervously check their angles. The GTX boardroom has a foible about having things *pointed* at them and theirs. Cold shivers, when the image of an Isham nearly went onto the world beam beside that Dialadinner.

Worse yet, Paul has no respect for the sacred schedules which are now a full-time job for ferret boy up at headquarters. Paul keeps forgetting to bring her back on time, and poor Hopkins can't cope.

So pretty soon the boardroom data-ball has an urgent personal action-tab for Mr. Isham senior. They do it the gentle way, at first.

"I can't today, Paul."

"Why not?"

"They say I have to, it's *very* important."

He strokes the faint gold down on her narrow back. Under Carbondale, Pa., a blind mole-woman shivers.

"Important. Their importance. Making more gold. Can't you see? To them you're just a thing to get scratch with. *A huckster.* Are you going to let them screw you, Dee? Are you?"

"Oh, Paul —"

He doesn't know it, but he's seeing a weirdie; Remotes aren't hooked up to flow tears.

"Just say no, Dee. No. Integrity. You have to."

"But they say, it's my job —"

"Will you believe I can take care of you, Dee? Baby, baby, you're letting them rip us. You have to choose. Tell them, no."

"Paul… I w-will…."

And she does. Brave little Delphi (insane P. Burke). Saying, "No, please, I promised, Paul."

They try some more, still gently.

"Paul, Mr. Hopkins told me the reason they don't want us to be together so much. It's because of who you are, your father."

She thinks his father is like Mr. Cantle, maybe.

"Oh, great. Hopkins. I'll fix him. Listen, I can't think about Hopkins now. Ken came back today, he found out something."

They are lying on the high Andes meadow watching his friends dive their singing kites.

"Would you believe, on the coast the police have *electrodes in their heads?*"

She stiffens in his arms.

"Yeah, weird. I thought they only used PP on criminals and the army. Don't you see, Dee — something has to be going on. Some movement. Maybe somebody's organizing. How can we find out?" He pounds the ground behind her: "We should make *contact!* If we could only find out."

"The, the news?" she asks distractedly.

"The news." He laughs. "There's nothing in the news except what they want people to know. Half the country could burn up, and nobody would know it if they didn't want. Dee, can't you take what I'm explaining to you? They've got the whole world programmed! Total control of communication. They've got everybody's minds wired in to think what they show them and want what they give them and they give them what they're programmed to want — you can't break in or out of it, you can't get *hold* of it anywhere. I don't think they even have a plan except to keep things going round and round — and god knows what's happening to the people or the Earth or the other planets, maybe. One great big vortex of lies and garbage pouring round and round, getting bigger and bigger, and nothing can ever change. If people don't wake up soon we're through!"

He pounds her stomach softly.

"You have to break out, Dee."

"I'll try, Paul, I will —"

"You're mine. They can't have you."

And he goes to see Hopkins, who is indeed cowed.

But that night up under Carbondale the fatherly Mr. Cantle goes to see P. Burke.

P. Burke? On a cot in a utility robe like a dead camel in a tent, she cannot at first comprehend that he is telling *her* to break it off with Paul. P. Burke has never seen Paul. *Delphi* sees Paul. The fact is, P. Burke can no longer clearly recall that she exists apart from Delphi.

Mr. Cantle can scarcely believe it either, but he tries.

He points out the futility, the potential embarrassment, for Paul. That gets a dim stare from the bulk on the bed. Then he goes into her duty to GTX, her job, isn't she grateful for the opportunity, etcetera. He's very persuasive.

The cobwebby mouth of P. Burke opens and croaks.

"No."

Nothing more seems to be forthcoming.

Mr. Cantle isn't dense, he knows an immovable obstacle when he bumps one. He also knows an irresistible force: GTX. The simple solution is to lock the waldo-cabinet until Paul gets tired of waiting for Delphi to wake up. But the cost, the schedules! And there's something odd here…he eyes the corporate asset hulking on the bed and his hunch-sense prickles.

You see, Remotes don't love. They don't have real sex, the circuits designed that out from the start. So it's been assumed that it's *Paul* who is diverting himself or something with the pretty little body in Chile. P. Burke can only be doing what comes natural to any ambitious gutter-meat. It hasn't occurred to anyone that they're dealing with the real hairy thing whose shadow is blasting out of every holo-show on Earth.

Love?

Mr. Cantle frowns. The idea is grotesque. But his instinct for the fuzzy line is strong; he will recommend flexibility. And so, in Chile:

"Darling, I don't have to work tonight! And Friday too — isn't that right, Mr. Hopkins?"

"Oh, great. When does she come up for parole?"

"Mr. Isham, please be reasonable. Our schedule — surely your own production people must be needing you?"

This happens to be true. Paul goes away. Hopkins stares after him, wondering distastefully why an Isham wants to ball a waldo. How sound are those boardroom belly-fears — garble creeps, creeps in! It never occurs to Hopkins that an Isham might not know what Delphi is.

Especially with Davy crying because Paul has kicked him out of Delphi's bed.

Delphi's bed is under a real window.

"Stars," Paul says sleepily. He rolls over, pulling Delphi on top. "Are you aware that this is one of the last places on Earth where people can see the stars? Tibet, too, maybe."

"Paul…"

"Go to sleep. I want to see you sleep."

"Paul, I…I sleep so *hard*, I mean, it's a joke how hard I am to wake up. Do you mind?"

"Yes."

But finally, fearfully, she must let go. So that five thousand miles north a crazy spent creature can crawl out to gulp concentrates and fall on her cot. But not for long. It's pink dawn when Delphi's eyes open to find Paul's arms around her, his voice saying rude, tender things. He's been kept awake. The nerveless little statue that was her Delphi-body nuzzled him in the night.

Insane hope rises, is fed a couple of nights later when he tells her she called his name in her sleep.

And that day Paul's arms keep her from work and Hopkins's wails go up to headquarters where the weasel-faced lad is working his sharp tailbone off packing Delphi's program. Mr. Cantle defuses that one.

But next week it happens again, to a major client. And ferret-face has connections on the technical side.

Now you can see that when you have a field of complexly hetero-dyned energy modulations tuned to a demand-point like Delphi, there are many problems of standwaves and lashback and skiffle of all sorts which are normally balanced out with ease by the technology of the future. By the same token they can be delicately unbalanced too, in ways that feed back into the waldo operator with striking results.

"Darling—what the hell! What's wrong? DELPHI!"

Helpless shrieks, writhings. Then the Rima-bird is lying wet and limp in his arms, her eyes enormous.

"I...I wasn't supposed to..." she gasps faintly. "They told me not to..."

"Oh, my god—*Delphi*."

And his hard fingers are digging in her thick yellow hair. Electron-ically knowledgeable fingers. They freeze.

"You're a *doll*! You're one of those PP implants. They control you. I should have known. Oh, god, I should have known."

"No, Paul," she's sobbing. "No, no, no—"

"Damn them. Damn them, what they've done—you're not *you*—"

He's shaking her, crouching over her in the bed and jerking her back and forth, glaring at the pitiful beauty.

"No!" she pleads (it's not true, that dark bad dream back there). "I'm Delphi!"

"My father. Filth, pigs—damn them, damn them, damn them."

"No, no," she babbles. "They were good to me—" P. Burke under-ground mouthing, "They were good to me—AAH-AAAAH!"

Another agony skewers her. Up north the sharp young man wants to make sure this so-tiny interference works. Paul can scarcely hang on to her, he's crying too. "I'll kill them."

His Delphi, a wired-up slave! Spikes in her brain, electronic shack-les in his bird's heart. Remember when those savages burned Rima alive?

"I'll *kill* the man that's doing this to you."

He's still saying it afterward, but she doesn't hear. She's sure he hates her now, all she wants is to die. When she finally understands that the fierceness is tenderness, she thinks it's a miracle. *He knows —and he still loves!*

How can she guess that he's got it a little bit wrong?

You can't blame Paul. Give him credit that he's even heard about pleasure-pain implants and snoops, which by their nature aren't mentioned much by those who know them most intimately. That's what he thinks is being used on Delphi, something to *control* her. And to listen—he burns at the unknown ears in their bed.

Of waldo-bodies and objects like P. Burke he has heard nothing.

So it never crosses his mind as he looks down at his violated bird, sick with fury and love, that he isn't holding *all* of her. Do you need to be told the mad resolve jelling in him now?

To free Delphi.

How? Well, he is, after all, Paul Isham III. And he even has an idea where the GTX neurolab is. In Carbondale.

But first things have to be done for Delphi, and for his own stomach. So he gives her back to Hopkins and departs in a restrained and discreet way. And the Chile staff is grateful and do not understand that his teeth don't normally show so much.

And a week passes in which Delphi is a very good, docile little ghost. They let her have the load of wildflowers Paul sends and the bland loving notes. (He's playing it coony.) And up in headquarters weasel boy feels that *his* destiny has clicked a notch onward and floats the word up that he's handy with little problems.

And no one knows what P. Burke thinks in any way whatever, except that Miss Fleming catches her flushing her food down the can and next night she faints in the pool. They haul her out and stick her with IVs. Miss Fleming frets, she's seen expressions like that before. But she wasn't around when crazies who called themselves Followers of the Fish looked through flames to life everlasting. P. Burke is seeing Heaven on the far side of death, too. Heaven is spelled P-a-u-l, but the idea's the same. *I will die and be born again in Delphi.*

Garbage, electronically speaking. No way.

Another week and Paul's madness has become a plan. (Remember, he does have friends.) He smolders, watching his love paraded by her masters. He turns out a scorching sequence for his own show. And finally, politely, he requests from Hopkins a morsel of his bird's free time, which duly arrives.

"I thought you didn't *want* me anymore," she's repeating as they wing over mountain flanks in Paul's suncar. "Now you *know* —"

"Look at me!"

His hand covers her mouth, and he's showing her a lettered card.

DON'T TALK THEY CAN HEAR EVERYTHING WE SAY.

I'M TAKING YOU AWAY NOW.

She kisses his hand. He nods urgently, flipping the card.

DON'T BE AFRAID. I CAN STOP THE PAIN IF THEY TRY TO HURT YOU.

With his free hand he shakes out a silvery scrambler-mesh on a power pack. She is dumbfounded.

THIS WILL CUT THE SIGNALS AND PROTECT YOU DARLING.

She's staring at him, her head going vaguely from side to side, No.

"Yes!" He grins triumphantly. "Yes!"

For a moment she wonders. That powered mesh will cut off the field, all right. It will also cut off Delphi. But he is Paul. Paul is kissing her, she can only seek him hungrily as he sweeps the suncar through a pass.

Ahead is an old jet ramp with a shiny bullet waiting to go. (Paul also has credits and a Name.) The little GTX patrol courier is built for nothing but speed. Paul and Delphi wedge in behind the pilot's extra fuel tank, and there's no more talking when the torches start to scream.

They're screaming high over Quito before Hopkins starts to worry. He wastes another hour tracking the beeper on Paul's suncar. The suncar is sailing a pattern out to sea. By the time they're sure it's empty and Hopkins gets on the hot flue to headquarters, the fugitives are a sourceless howl above Carib West.

Up at headquarters weasel boy gets the squeal. His first impulse is to repeat his previous play, but then his brain snaps to. This one is too hot. Because, see, although in the long run they can make P. Burke do anything at all except maybe *live*, instant emergencies can be tricky. And — Paul Isham III.

"Can't you order her back?"

They're all in the GTX tower monitor station, Mr. Cantle and ferret-face and Joe and a very neat man who is Mr. Isham senior's personal eyes and ears.

"No, sir," Joe says doggedly. "We can read channels, particularly speech, but we can't interpolate organized pattern. It takes the waldo op to send one-to-one — "

"What are they saying?"

"Nothing at the moment, sir." The console jockey's eyes are closed. "I believe they are, ah, embracing."

"They're not answering," a traffic monitor says. "Still heading zero zero three zero — due north, sir."

"You're certain Kennedy is alerted not to fire on them?" the neat man asks anxiously.

"Yes, sir."

"Can't you just turn her off?" The sharp-faced lad is angry. "Pull that pig out of the controls!"

"If you cut the transmission cold you'll kill the Remote," Joe explains for the third time. "Withdrawal has to be phased right, you have to fade over to the Remote's own autonomics. Heart, breathing, cerebellum, would go blooey. If you pull Burke out you'll probably finish her too. It's a fantastic cybersystem, you don't want to do that."

"The investment." Mr. Cantle shudders.

Weasel boy puts his hand on the console jock's shoulder, it's the contact who arranged the no-no effect for him.

"We can at least give them a warning signal, sir." He licks his lips, gives the neat man his sweet ferret smile. "We know that does no damage."

Joe frowns, Mr. Cantle sighs. The neat man is murmuring into his wrist. He looks up. "I am authorized," he says reverently, "I am authorized to, ah, direct a signal. If this is the only course. But minimal, minimal."

Sharp-face squeezes his man's shoulder.

In the silver bullet shrieking over Charleston Paul feels Delphi arch in his arms. He reaches for the mesh, hot for action. She thrashes, pushing at his hands, her eyes roll. She's afraid of that mesh despite the agony. (And she's right.) Frantically Paul fights her in the cramped space, gets it over her head. As he turns the power up she burrows free under his arm and the spasm fades.

"They're calling you again, Mr. Isham!" the pilot yells.

"Don't answer. Darling, keep this over your head damn it how can I —"

An AX90 barrels over their nose, there's a flash.

"Mr. Isham! Those are Air Force jets!"

"Forget it," Paul shouts back. "They won't fire. Darling, don't be afraid."

Another AX90 rocks them.

"Would you mind pointing your pistol at my head where they can see it, sir?" the pilot howls.

Paul does so. The AX90s take up escort formation around them. The pilot goes back to figuring how he can collect from GTX too, and after Goldsboro AB the escort peels away.

"Holding the same course." Traffic is reporting to the group around the monitor. "Apparently they've taken on enough fuel to bring them to towerport here."

"In that case it's just a question of waiting for them to dock." Mr. Cantle's fatherly manner revives a bit.

"Why can't they cut off that damn freak's life-support," the sharp young man fumes. "It's ridiculous."

"They're working on it," Cantle assures him.

What they're doing, down under Carbondale, is arguing. Miss Fleming's watchdog has summoned the bushy man to the waldo room.

"Miss Fleming, you will obey orders."

"You'll kill her if you try that, sir. I can't believe you meant it, that's why I didn't. We've already fed her enough sedative to affect heart action; if you cut any more oxygen she'll die in there."

The bushy man grimaces. "Get Dr. Quine here fast."

They wait, staring at the cabinet in which a drugged, ugly madwoman fights for consciousness, fights to hold Delphi's eyes open.

High over Richmond the silver pod starts a turn. Delphi is sagged into Paul's arm, her eyes swim up to him.

"Starting down now, baby. It'll be over soon, all you have to do is stay alive, Dee."

"…stay alive…"

The traffic monitor has caught them. "Sir! They've turned off for Carbondale—Control has contact—"

"Let's go."

But the headquarters posse is too late to intercept the courier wailing into Carbondale. And Paul's friends have come through again. The fugitives are out through the freight dock and into the neurolab admin port before the guard gets organized. At the elevator Paul's face plus his handgun get them in.

"I want Doctor—what's his name, Dee? Dee!"

"…Tesla…" She's reeling on her feet.

"Dr. Tesla. Take me down to Tesla, fast."

Intercoms are squalling around them as they whoosh down, Paul's pistol in the guard's back. When the door slides open the bushy man is there.

"I'm Tesla."

"I'm Paul Isham. *Isham*. You're going to take your flaming implants out of this girl—now. Move!"

"What?"

"You heard me. Where's your operating room? Go!"

"But—"

"Move! Do I have to burn somebody?"

Paul waves the weapon at Dr. Quine, who has just appeared.

"No, no," says Tesla hurriedly. "But I can't, you know. It's impossible, there'll be nothing left."

"You screaming well can, right now. You mess up and I'll kill you," says Paul murderously. "Where is it, there? And wipe the feke that's on her circuits now."

He's backing them down the hall, Delphi heavy on his arm.

"Is this the place, baby? Where they did it to you?"

"Yes," she whispers, blinking at a door. "Yes…"

Because it is, see. Behind that door is the very suite where she was born.

Paul herds them through it into a gleaming hall. An inner door opens, and a nurse and a gray man rush out. And freeze.

Paul sees there's something special about that inner door. He crowds them past it and pushes it open and looks in.

Inside is a big mean-looking cabinet with its front door panels ajar.

And inside that cabinet is a poisoned carcass to whom something wonderful, unspeakable, is happening. Inside is P. Burke, the real living woman who knows that HE is there, coming closer — Paul whom she had fought to reach through forty thousand miles of ice — PAUL is here! — is yanking at the waldo doors —

The doors tear open and a monster rises up.

"Paul darling!" croaks the voice of love, and the arms of love reach for him.

And he responds.

Wouldn't you, if a gaunt she-golem flab-naked and spouting wires and blood came at you clawing with metal-studded paws —

"Get away!" He knocks wires.

It doesn't much matter which wires. P. Burke has, so to speak, her nervous system hanging out. Imagine somebody jerking a handful of your medulla —

She crashes onto the floor at his feet, flopping and roaring PAUL-PAUL-PAUL in rictus.

It's doubtful he recognizes his name or sees her life coming out of her eyes at him. And at the last it doesn't go to him. The eyes find Delphi, fainting by the doorway, and die.

Now of course Delphi is dead, too.

There's a total silence as Paul steps away from the thing by his foot.

"You killed her," Tesla says. "That was her."

"Your control." Paul is furious, the thought of that monster fastened into little Delphi's brain nauseates him. He sees her crumpling and holds out his arms. Not knowing she is dead.

And Delphi comes to him.

One foot before the other, not moving very well — but moving. Her darling face turns up. Paul is distracted by the terrible quiet, and when he looks down he sees only her tender little neck.

"Now you get the implants out," he warns them. Nobody moves.

"But, but she's dead," Miss Fleming whispers wildly.

Paul feels Delphi's life under his hand, they're talking about their monster. He aims his pistol at the gray man.

"You. If we aren't in your surgery when I count three, I'm burning off this man's leg."

"Mr. Isham," Tesla says desperately, "you have just killed the person who animated the body you call Delphi. Delphi herself is dead. If you release your arm you'll see what I say is true."

The tone gets through. Slowly Paul opens his arm, looks down.

"Delphi?"

She totters, sways, stays upright. Her face comes slowly up.

"Paul…" Tiny voice.

"Your crotty tricks," Paul snarls at them. "Move!"

"Look at her eyes," Dr. Quine croaks.

They look. One of Delphi's pupils fills the iris, her lips writhe weirdly.

"Shock." Paul grabs her to him. "*Fix* her!" He yells at them, aiming at Tesla.

"For god's sake…bring it in the lab." Tesla quavers.

"Good-bye-bye," says Delphi clearly. They lurch down the hall, Paul carrying her, and meet a wave of people.

Headquarters has arrived.

Joe takes one look and dives for the waldo room, running into Paul's gun.

"Oh, no, you don't."

Everybody is yelling. The little thing in his arm stirs, says plaintively, "I'm Delphi."

And all through the ensuing jabber and ranting she hangs on, keeping it up, the ghost of P. Burke or whatever whispering crazily, "Paul… Paul… Please, I'm Delphi… Paul?"

"I'm here, darling, I'm here." He's holding her in the nursing bed. Tesla talks, talks, talks unheard.

"Paul…don't sleep…." The ghost-voice whispers. Paul is in agony, he will not accept, WILL NOT believe.

Tesla runs down.

And then near midnight Delphi says roughly, "Ag-ag-ag — " and slips onto the floor, making a rough noise like a seal.

Paul screams. There's more of the *ag-ag* business and more gruesome convulsive disintegrations, until by two in the morning Delphi is nothing but a warm little bundle of vegetative functions hitched to some expensive hardware — the same that sustained her before her life began. Joe has finally persuaded Paul to let him at the waldo-cabinet. Paul stays by her long enough to see her face change in a dreadfully alien and coldly convincing way, and then he stumbles out bleakly through the group in Tesla's office.

Behind him Joe is working wet-faced, sweating to reintegrate the fantastic complex of circulation, respiration, endocrines, midbrain homeostases, the patterned flux that was a human being — it's like saving an orchestra abandoned in midair. Joe is also crying a little; he alone had truly loved P. Burke. P. Burke, now a dead pile on a table, was the greatest cybersystem he has ever known, and he never forgets her.

The end, really.

You're curious?

Sure, Delphi lives again. Next year she's back on the yacht getting sympathy for her tragic breakdown. But there's a different chick in Chile, because while Delphi's new operator is competent, you don't get two P. Burkes in a row — for which GTX is duly grateful.

The real belly-bomb of course is Paul. He was *young*, see. Fighting abstract wrong. Now life has clawed into him and he goes through gut rage and grief and grows in human wisdom and resolve. So much so that you won't be surprised, sometime later, to find him — where?

In the GTX boardroom, dummy. Using the advantage of his birth to radicalize the system. You'd call it "boring from within."

That's how he put it, and his friends couldn't agree more. It gives them a warm, confident feeling to know that Paul is up there. Sometimes one of them who's still around runs into him and gets a big hello.

And the sharp-faced lad?

Oh, he matures too. He learns fast, believe it. For instance, he's the first to learn that an obscure GTX research unit is actually getting something with their loopy temporal anomalizer project. True, he doesn't have a physics background, and he's bugged quite a few people. But he doesn't really learn about that until the day he stands where somebody points him during a test run —

— and wakes up lying on a newspaper headlined NIXON UNVEILS PHASE TWO.

Lucky he's a fast learner.

Believe it, zombie. When I say growth, I mean *growth*. Capital appreciation. You can stop sweating. There's a great future there.

Dear Alice Sheldon

L. Timmel Duchamp

Alice Sheldon, whether as James Tiptree, Jr., or as Alli, was a prolific letter-writer; one of the last things she did in this life was to write her frequent correspondent, Ursula Le Guin.

In our 2005 anthology we included a letter from Sheldon to Rudolf Arnheim. In 2006, we chose to showcase someone writing her back. *Talking Back: Epistolary Fantasies* came out this year from L. Timmel Duchamp's Aqueduct Press. It is a collection of letters by contemporary writers to Oscar Wilde, Jack Kerouac, Madame Defarge, and others. The reliably brilliant Duchamp addressed her own letter to Alice Sheldon.

Dear Alice Sheldon,

I have always held your fiction in such high regard that I can easily imagine writing you a fan letter with the simple object of expressing my gratitude and admiration for your work. But another kind of letter demands to be written. I will admit up front that it is the kind of letter I would never even have considered writing to you while you still lived. But death, like publication of one's words, changes everything. Just as your published fiction must always be a fit subject for public discussion, so certain facts and speculations about your life must be as well. In your *Contemporary Authors* interview, you said, "there is a certain magic in writing, and there is no magic in writers. I have a very strong feeling that the writer's life and the writer's work should be kept separate, especially in writing that carries some sense of wonder." And you quote lines from a Kipling poem, "The Appeal":

> *And for the little, little, span*
> *The dead are borne in mind.*

Seek not to question other than
The books I leave behind.

You were replying, in that interview, to a question about whether the revelation of your "real personal identity" changed your feelings about your writing. I imagine there was more to your desire to keep the writer and the writing separate than the wish to preserve the magic of the work. You would, of course, have long since understood that to write well, one can hold nothing back.

I know from my own experience that holding nothing back from the writing generates a deep, almost irrational need to keep trivial aspects of oneself private. For years I avoided meeting people in the sf world, although (like you) I happily corresponded with them. During my first few face-to-face encounters with editors, fans, and other writers, I felt naked and exposed. I had no particular secret to conceal, only that fierce wish to maintain a separation between the work and the writer. As a woman writing and insisting on taking herself seriously, how could I not feel that separation to be crucial?

Women writers have traditionally been unable to keep the fact of their gender from influencing how their work is read and judged. Knowing we're marked, doesn't it make sense for us to seek ways to keep consciousness of that marked-ness at bay? And so when the sf world discovered that James Tiptree, Jr., was Alice Sheldon, you discovered that possessing a marked gender (in sharp contrast to "Uncle Tip's" male privilege of being unmarked by gender) necessarily meant that when the writer is known to be a woman, the work will never enjoy the privilege of being judged without reference to the writer. But I suspect that even before you were subject to that harsh lesson, as a writer burdened with a heavy secret that began life weighing less than a feather more apt to tickle than crush your spirit, you always understood the impossibility of maintaining a clear separation between the writer and the work.

I doubt you'd appreciate knowing that feminist sf fans of a certain age sometimes reminisce about where they were and what they felt when they discovered that James Tiptree, Jr., was in fact Alice Sheldon. I have heard some say that they were delighted to learn the news, others that they were shocked and disappointed—disappointed, that is, to learn that there was no such exceptional man as James Tiptree, Jr., appeared to be. I had barely begun reading sf at the time of the revelation; I lacked fan connections and read and knew your fiction in a strictly private way. So I don't recall how I first discovered you were both Tiptree and Sheldon. Probably I read it in an article about your work, or in a head-note to one of your stories, or even in the intro to one of your books. But the fact that I don't remember the moment and context of my discovery tells me that the revelation did not have the same impact on me as it did on so many others.

What strikes me most forcibly all these years later is that the greatest effect the revelation of your gender had on your work was to render it all but invisible even as it led to your becoming an icon. Shortly before the revelation, Gardner Dozois wrote a long essay about your fiction. He proclaimed your significance:

> *Who is James Tiptree, Jr., and why should we care about him?*
>
> *We should care about him because, at his best, he is one of the two or three finest short-story writers in science fiction; because he has produced a body of work almost unparalleled in the genre for originality, power, and consistent quality; because he has managed to be a literary synthesist as well as a trailblazer, bringing together disparate — and often formerly hostile — traditions to produce viable fictional hybrids; and because, perhaps most important, he is one of the most influential of all present-day SF writers in terms of his impact on upcoming generations of authors — much of the future of science fiction belongs to Tiptree, both through those shaped directly by him and those who will — perhaps unwittingly — follow his well-blazed paths, and if we are to understand that future it first behooves us to make an attempt to understand Tiptree.*

Did anyone, after the revelation, characterize you as a trailblazer? As a "literary synthesist" producing "viable fictional hybrids"? Or as an influence on the future of science fiction? Alas. As you and I both know, the revelation swamped the fiction, and the issue of your gender took front and center stage. And the only people who devoted themselves to writing criticism of your work were feminist critics. I discovered this myself only recently, when Karen Joy Fowler's "What I Didn't See" became a *cause célèbre*, and I learned that many sf professionals were unfamiliar with "The Women Men Don't See," which John Clute characterizes as "your most famous single story."

Though you were dismayed to discover that being identified as a woman meant that your female status would become scandalously visible and your work all but invisible, I don't believe you could have been all that surprised. You soon came to articulate with painful clarity certain aspects of that invisibility that very few writers, critics, or readers are aware of taking for granted. In "Zero at the Bone," you wrote:

> As Tiptree, I had an unspoken classificatory bond to the world of male action; Tiptree's existence opened to unknown possibilities of power. And, let us pry deeper—to the potential of evil. Evil is the voltage of good; the urge to goodness, without the potential of evil, is trivial. A man impelled to good is significant; a woman pleading for the good is trivial. A great bore. Part of the appeal of Tiptree was that he ranged himself on the side of good by choice.
>
> Alli Sheldon has no such choice.

> What evil can a woman do? Except pettily, to other, weaker women or children? Cruel stepmothers; male fantasies of the Wicked Witch, who can always be assaulted or burnt if she goes too far. Men certainly see women as doing many evil things—but always nuisancy, trivial, personal, and, easily-to-be-punished-for. Not for us the great evils; the jolly maraudings, burnings, rapings, and hacking-up; the Big Nasties, the genocidal world destroyers, who must be reckoned with on equal terms.

> Always draining us is the reality of our inescapable commitment. Whatever individual women may do, it is we who feel always the tug

toward empathy, toward caring, cherishing, building-up — the dull interminable mission of creating, nourishing, protecting, civilizing — maintaining the very race. At bottom is always the bitter knowledge that all else is boys' play — and that this boys' play rules the world.

How I long, how I long to be free of this knowledge!

As Tiptree, this understanding was "insight." As Alli Sheldon, it is merely the heavy center of my soul.

In other words, under a masculine name, you could write as a man of the world — and be taken seriously. (Interestingly, you came to feel that though the view allowed to a man of the world was extraordinarily expansive, it was partial, excluding a part of the world you did not consider insignificant: which is how you explain why the Raccoona Sheldon pseudonym came into existence. And Gwyneth Jones later commented that your contributions to the *Khatru* Symposium, which drew flak from participating feminists, were written in drag — not from the perspective of a woman. And I think she was right.) Sadly (and predictably), when you lost the masculinity of the name, the worldliness of your work lost all credibility. Worldliness in a woman, after all, means something entirely different than worldliness in a man. In 1977 there could be no equivalence. As there cannot be now in 2005, for that matter.

Dear Alice Sheldon, your insight about women's lack of moral credibility is not one that many of us ever get. And what's worse: though I get it every time I read that passage above, it always slips away from me. See, I just can't stand to believe it. If I believed it, I'd have to realize that my writing will never have any chance of rising above the private and trivial, even if I did somehow manage to write to the level of my ambition. And yet I know that it's true. It's not just me, of course, who falls continually into denial. You reveal in your *Contemporary Authors* interview that despite your insight, you too continued to deny it on at least some level when you remarked:

And then there were the male writers who had seemed to take my work

> *quite seriously, but who now began discovering that it was really the enigma of Tip's identity which had lent a spurious interest — and finding various more-or-less subtle ways of saying so. (Oh, how well we know and love that pretentiously aimiable [sic] tone, beneath which hides the furtive nastiness!) I'd been warned against it, but it was still a shock, coming from certain writers. The one thing I admire about that type of male hatred is its strategic agility; they soon got their ranks closed. Only here the timing was so damn funny, the perfect unison of their "reevaluation" of poor old Tip rather weakened the effect.*

Dear Alice Sheldon, I believe they *did* take your work seriously (for as long as they thought you were a man of the world). Yes, they loved the image of that man of the world, but the image of the writer didn't interfere with the reading of the fiction until the image became that of a "little old lady in McLean." All women writers have to at least *functionally* believe they are an exception when their fiction explores the "unknown possibilities of power." And of course sometimes there's some recognition — from men as well as women — and the thought occurs that maybe this time a woman's work will be perceived as powerful. But this fleeting perception of the exceptional woman writer has risen repeatedly over the centuries. Margaret Ezell has described the process in her book, *Writing Women's Literary History*. Any brief exception to the rule is fleeting precisely because it's an exception, for if the work of enough women were visible, there would be no exceptionality in the first place.

But reviewing again Dozois's praise of you before the Awful Truth came out, my mind blossoms with speculation, conceiving forking paths of possible histories that might have been. In one possible history, you wrote under the name Jane Tiptree — choosing a pseudonym for the same reason you said you chose the James Tiptree, Jr., pseudonym, but without concealing your gender. You might well have produced much of the same work and probably been able to sell most of it, but it would have been quietly admired and perhaps won an award or two and would not have been seen as "trail-blazing" or powerful. I conjecture that it would have been categorized as "soft" sf and been lumped together with the work of other brilliant women so gloriously illuminating the seventies (which decade is now regarded by some people as having been a mediocre one for the genre). Remember how when in January 1977 *Locus* in a news item headed "Tiptree Revealed" reported that Theodore Sturgeon had commented in a recent speech that "nearly all of the top newer writers, with the exception of James Tiptree, Jr., were women" — only to add that "The exception is now gone"? On the upside, though, had you written as Jane Tiptree, because you wouldn't have suffered the blow that followed the revelation of your gender, you would likely have continued to produce more work at that same amazing pace with steadily growing confidence. Who knows how far your work might have gone?

In another version of history, you wrote as James Tiptree, Jr., and no one ever found out, not even after your death. Perhaps you retired him and let Raccoona take on more and more of the work. In that version of history, following the path Gardner Dozois marked for a future that he judged "belonged" to Tiptree, you would have been regarded as one of the principle influences on the genre, and scholars would now be studying that influence. There would, of course, be no Tiptree Award. (There might, instead, be an award for fine feminist sf, named, perhaps, for Naomi Mitchison or Katherine Burdekin or Charlotte Perkins Gilman.)

As an sf writer, you would understand, of course, why I entertain such a fantasy. It is not wishful thinking, but a desire for insight into why the history of which we are a part is taking the shape it is. History is what hurts, *n'est-ce pas?* And so dear Alice Sheldon, history is what we must understand.

With love and respect,
Timmi

Little Faces

Vonda N. McIntyre

The old-fashioned science fiction term "sense of wonder" applies so well to this story, with its *very* alien aliens, its unique love (and revenge) relationships, its almost geologic time scale, and its all-too-familiar emotional territory. Perhaps no one else except Octavia Butler (in "Bloodchild") has ventured so far from our expectations about sex and reproduction, with such powerful results.

The blood woke Yalnis. It ran between her thighs, warm and slick, cooling, sticky. She pushed back from the stain on the silk, bleary with sleep and love, rousing to shock and stabbing pain.

She flung off the covers and scrambled out of bed. She cried out as the web of nerves tore apart. Her companions shrieked a chaotic chorus.

Zorargul's small form convulsed just below her navel. The raw edges of a throat wound bled in diminishing gushes. Her body expelled the dying companion, closing off veins and vesicles.

Zorargul was beyond help. She wrapped her hand around the small broken body as it slid free. She sank to the floor. Blood dripped onto the cushioned surface. The other companions retreated into her, exposing nothing but sharp white teeth that parted and snapped in defense and warning.

Still in bed, blinking, yawning, Seyyan propped herself on her elbow. She gazed at the puddle of blood. It soaked in, vanishing gradually from edge to center, drawn away to be separated into its molecules and stored.

A smear of blood marked Seyyan's skin. Her first companion blinked its small bright golden eyes. It snapped its sharp teeth, spattering scarlet droplets. It shrieked, licked its bloody lips, cleaned its teeth with its tongue. The sheet absorbed the blood spray.

Seyyan lay back in the soft tangled nest, elegantly lounging, her luxuriant brown hair spilling its curls around her bare shoulders and over her delicate perfect breasts. She shone like molten gold in the starlight. Her other companions pushed their little faces from her belly, rousing themselves and clacking their teeth, excited and jealous.

"Zorargul," Yalnis whispered. She had never lost a companion. She chose them carefully, and cherished them, and Zorargul had been her first, the gift of her first lover. She looked up at Seyyan, confused and horrified, shocked by loss and pain.

"Come back." Seyyan spoke with soft urgency. She stretched out her graceful hand. "Come back to bed." Her voice intensified. "Come back to me."

Yalnis shrank from her touch. Seyyan followed, sliding over the fading bloodstain in the comfortable nest of ship silk. Her first companion extruded itself, just below her navel, staring intently at Zorargul's body.

Seyyan stroked Yalnis's shoulder. Yalnis pushed her away with her free hand, leaving bloody fingerprints on Seyyan's golden skin.

Seyyan grabbed her wrist and held her, moved to face her squarely, touched her beneath her chin and raised her head to look her in the eyes. Baffled and dizzy, Yalnis blinked away tears. Her remaining companions pumped molecular messages of distress and anger into her blood.

"Come back to me," Seyyan said again. "We're ready for you."

Her first companion, drawing back into her, pulsed and muttered. Seyyan caught her breath.

"I never asked for this!" Yalnis cried.

Seyyan sat back on her heels, as lithe as a girl, but a million years old.

"I thought you wanted me," she said. "You welcomed me — invited me — took me to your bed — "

Yalnis shook her head, though it was true. "Not for this," she whispered.

"It didn't even fight," Seyyan said, dismissing Zorargul's remains with a quick gesture. "It wasn't worthy of its place with you."

"Who are you to decide that?"

"I didn't," Seyyan said. "It's the way of companions." She touched the reddening bulge of a son-spot just below the face of her first companion. "This one will be worthy of you."

Yalnis stared at her, horrified and furious. Seyyan, the legend, had come to her, exotic, alluring, and exciting. All the amazement and attraction Yalnis felt washed away in Zorargul's blood.

"I don't want it," she said. "I won't accept it."

Seyyan's companion reacted to the refusal, blinking, snarling. For a moment Yalnis feared Seyyan too would snarl at her, assault her and force a new companion upon her.

Seyyan sat back, frowning in confusion. "But I thought — did you invite me, just to refuse me? Why — ?"

"For pleasure," Yalnis said. "For friendship. And maybe for love — maybe you would offer, and I would accept — "

"How is this different?" Seyyan asked.

Yalnis leaped to her feet in a flare of fury so intense that her vision blurred. Cradling Zorargul's shriveling body against her with one hand, she pressed the other against the aching bloody wound beneath her navel.

"Get out of my ship," she said.

The ship, responding to Yalnis's wishes, began to resorb the nest into the floor.

Seyyan rose. "What did you think would happen," she said, anger replacing the confusion in her tone, "when you announced the launch of a daughter? What do you think everyone is coming for? I was just lucky enough to be first. Or unfortunate enough." Again, she brushed her long fingertips against the son-spot. It pulsed, a red glow as hot and sore as infection. It must find a place, soon, or be stillborn. "And what am I to do with this?"

Yalnis's flush of anger drained away, leaving her pale and shocked.

"I don't care." All the furnishings and softness of the room vanished, absorbed into the pores of Yalnis's ship, leaving bare walls and floor, and the cold stars above. "You didn't even ask me," Yalnis said softly.

"You led me to believe we understood each other. But you're so young — " Seyyan reached toward her. Yalnis drew back, and Seyyan let her hand fall with a sigh. "So young. So naïve." She caught up her purple cloak from the floor and strode past Yalnis. Though the circular chamber left plenty of room, she brushed past close to Yalnis, touching her at shoulder and hip, bare skin to bare skin. A lock of her hair swept across Yalnis's belly, stroking low like a living hand, painting a bloody streak.

Seyyan entered the pilus that connected Yalnis's ship with her own craft. As soon as Seyyan crossed the border, Yalnis's ship disconnected and closed and healed the connection.

Yalnis's ship emitted a few handsful of plasma in an intemperate blast, moving itself to a safer distance. Seyyan's craft gleamed and glittered against the starfield, growing smaller as Yalnis's ship moved away, coruscating with a pattern of prismatic color.

Yalnis sank to the floor again, humiliated and grief-stricken. Without her request or thought, her ship cushioned her from its cold living bones, growing a soft surface beneath her, dimming the light to dusk. Dusk, not the dawn she had planned.

She gazed down at Zorargul's small body. Its blood pooled in her palm. She drew her other hand from the seeping wound where Zorargul had lived and cradled the shriveling tendril of the companion's penis. A deep ache, throbbing regularly into pain, replaced the potential for pleasure as her body knit the wound of Zorargul's passing. Behind the wound, a sore, soft mass remained.

"Zorargul," she whispered, "you gave me such pleasure."

Of her companions, Zorargul had most closely patterned the love-making of its originator. Her pleasure always mingled with a glow of pride, that Zorar thought enough of her to offer her a companion.

Yalnis wondered where Zorar was, and if she would come to Yalnis's daughter's launching. They had not communicated since they parted. Zorar anticipated other adventures, and her ship yearned for deep space. She might be anywhere, one star system away, or a dozen, or setting out to another cluster, voyaging through vacuum so intense and a region so dark she must conserve every molecule of mass and every photon of energy, using none to power a message of acceptance, or regret, or goodwill.

Yalnis remained within parallax view of her own birthplace. She had grown up in a dense population of stars and people. She had taken a dozen lovers in her life, and accepted five companions: Zorargul, Vasigul, Asilgul, Hayaligul, and Bahadirgul. With five companions, she felt mature enough, wealthy enough, to launch a daughter with a decent, even lavish, settlement. After that, she could grant her ship's need — and her own desire — to set out on adventures and explorations.

Zorar, she thought —

She reached for Zorar's memories and reeled into loss and emptiness. The memories ended with Zorargul's murder. Zorar, much older than Yalnis, had given her the gift of her own long life of journeys and observations. They brought her the birth of stars and worlds, the energy storm of a boomerang loop around a black hole, skirting the engulfing doom of its event horizon. They brought her the most dangerous adventure of all, a descent through the thick atmosphere of a planet to its living surface.

All Yalnis had left were her memories of the memories, dissolving shadows of the gift. All the memories left in Zorargul had been wiped out by death.

By murder.

The walls and floor of her living space changed again as her ship re-created her living room. She liked it plain but luxurious, all softness and comfort. The large circular space lay beneath a transparent dome. It was a place for one person alone. She patted the floor with her bloodstained hand.

"Thank you," she said.

"True," her ship whispered into her mind.

Its decisions often pleased her and anticipated her wishes. Strange, for ships and people seldom conversed. When they tried, the interaction too easily deteriorated into misunderstanding. Their consciousnesses were of different types, different evolutionary lineages.

She rose, lacking her usual ease of motion. Anger and pain and grief drained her, and exhaustion trembled in her bones.

She carried Zorargul's body down through the ship, down into its heart, down to the misty power plant. Blood, her own and her companion's, spattered and smeared her hands, her stomach, her legs, the defending teeth or withdrawn crowns of her remaining companions, and Zorargul's pale and flaccid corpse. Its nerve ends dried to silver threads. Expulsion had reduced the testicles to wrinkled empty sacs.

Water ran in streams and pools through the power plant's housing, cold as it came in, steaming too hot to touch as it led away. Where steam from the hot pool met cold air, mist formed. Yalnis knelt and washed Zorargul's remains in the cold pool. When she was done, a square of scarlet ship silk lay on the velvety floor, flat and new where it had formed. She wrapped Zorargul in its shining folds.

"Good-bye," she said, and gave the small bundle tenderly to the elemental heat.

A long time later, Yalnis made her way to the living space and climbed into the bath, into water hot but not scalding. The bath swirled around her, sweeping away flecks of dried blood. She massaged the wound gently, making sure the nerve roots were cleanly ejected. She let the expulsion lump alone, though it was already hardening.

The remaining companions opened their little faces, protruding from the shelter of her body. They peered around, craning themselves above her skin, glaring at each other and gnashing their teeth in a great show, then closing their lips, humming to attract her attention.

She attended each companion in turn, stroking the little faces, flicking warm drops of water between their lips, quieting and calming them, murmuring, "Shh, shh." They felt no sympathy for her loss, no grief for Zorargul, only the consciousness of opportunity. She felt a moment of contempt for the quartet, each member jostling for primacy.

They are what they are, she thought, and submerged herself and them in the bath, drawing their little faces beneath the surface. They fell silent, holding their breaths and closing their eyes and mouths, reaching to draw their oxygen as well as their sustenance from her blood. A wash of dizziness took her; she breathed deep till it passed.

Each of the companions tried to please her — no, Bahadirgul held back. Her most recent companion had always been restrained in its approaches, fierce in its affections when it achieved release. Now, instead of squirming toward her center, it relaxed and blew streams of delicate bubbles from the air in its residual lungs.

Yalnis smiled, and when she closed herself off from the companions, she shut Bahadirgul away more gently than the others. She did not want to consider any of the companions now. Zorargul had been the best, the most deeply connected, as lively and considerate as her first lover.

Tears leaked from beneath her lashes, hot against her cheeks, washing away when she submerged. She looked up at the stars through the shimmering surface, through the steam.

She lifted her head to breathe. Water rippled and splashed; air cooled her face. The companions remained underwater, silent. Yalnis's tears flowed again and she sobbed, keening, grieving, wishing to take back the whole last time of waking. She wanted to change all her plans. If she did, Seyyan might take it as a triumph. She might make demands. Yalnis sneaked a look at the messages her ship kept ready for her attention. She declined to reply or even to acknowledge them. She felt it a weakness to read them. After she had, she wished she had resisted.

Why did you tantalize and tease me? Seyyan's message asked. You know this was what you wanted. I'm what you wanted.

Yalnis eliminated everything else Seyyan had sent her.

"Please refuse Seyyan's messages," she said to her ship.

"True," it replied.

"Disappear them, destroy them. No response."

"True."

"Seyyan, you took my admiration and my awe, and you perverted it," she said, as if Seyyan stood before her. "I might have accepted you.

I might have, if you'd given me a chance. If you'd given me time. What do we have, but time? I'll never forgive you."

The bath flowed away, resorbing into the ship's substance. Warm air dried her and drew off the steam. She wrapped herself in a new swath of ship silk without bothering to give it a design. Some people went naked at home, but Yalnis liked clothes. For now, though, a cloak sufficed.

She wandered through her ship, visiting each chamber in the current configuration, looking with amazement and apprehension at the daughter ship growing in the ship's lower flank. What would the person be like, this new being who would accompany this new ship into the universe? She thought she had known, but everything had changed.

She returned, finally, to her living chamber.

"Please defend yourself," she said.

"True."

Yalnis snuggled into the ship's substance, comforted by its caress. She laid her hand over her belly, pressing her palm against the hot, healing wound, then petting each of the little faces. They bumped against her palm, yearning, stretching from their shafts so she could tickle behind Asilgul's vestigial ears, beneath Vasigul's powerful lower jaw. Even Bahadirgul advanced from its reserve, blinking its long-lashed eyelids to caress her fingers, touching her palm with its sharp hot tongue.

Each one wished to pleasure her, but she felt no wish for pleasure. Even the idea of joy vanished, in grief and guilt.

The nest drew around her, covering her legs, her sex, her stomach. It flowed over the faces and extruded a nipple for each sharp set of teeth. The ship took over feeding the companions so they would not drain Yalnis as she slept.

"Please, a thousand orbits," she said.

"True," said the ship, making her aware it was content to have time to complete and polish the daughter ship, to prepare for the launch. But, afterward, it wanted to stretch and to explore. She accepted its need, and she would comply.

For now she would sleep for a thousand orbits. If anyone besides Seyyan accepted the invitation to her daughter's launch, they would arrive in good time, and then they could wait for her, as she waited for them. Perhaps a thousand orbits — a thousand years in the old way of speaking — would give her time to dream of a proper revenge. Perhaps a thousand years of sleep would let her dream away the edges of her grief. The ship's support extensions grew against her, into her. She accepted the excretion extensions and swallowed the feeding extension. The monitor gloved one hand and wrist.

The view through the dome swept the orbit's plane, facing outward toward the thick carpet of multicolored stars, the glowing gas clouds.

Yalnis slept for a thousand years.

The kiss of her ship woke her. Water exuded from the feeding extension, moistening her lips and tongue. The tangy fragrance touched her consciousness. She drifted into the last, hypnopompic layer of sleep, finding and losing dreams.

She thought: It would be good if... I would like...

Loss hit her unaware. A chill of regret and grief swept through her and to her four remaining companions; they woke from their doze and released the nipples and squeaked and shrilled. The ship, after a thousand orbits of the irritation of their little sharp teeth, drew away its fabric.

The ship made Yalnis aware of everything around them: the ship's own safety, the star and its planets, the astronomical landscape glowing through the transparent dome.

And it displayed to her the swarm of other ships, sending to her in their individual voices that ships and people had come to celebrate the launch of her daughter and her ship's daughter. She recognized friends and acquaintances, she noted strangers. She looked for former lovers, and found, to her joy and apprehension, that Zorar's ship sailed nearby.

And, of course, Seyyan remained.

During Yalnis's long rest, Seyyan had never approached, never tried to attach or attack. Yalnis felt glad of this. Her ship would have surrounded itself with an impermeable shell, one that induced a severe allergic reaction in other ships. A defensive shell drew heavily on a ship's resources. Her ship was sleek and well-provisioned, but growing defenses while developing a daughter ship would strain any resources.

Instead of approaching, Seyyan's craft's course had closely paralleled her own for all this time, as if it were herding and protecting Yalnis.

Annoyed that she had not anticipated such a move — she had expected aggression, not a show of protection — Yalnis nudged her ship to a different course, to a mathematical center along the long curved line of other craft. Her ship agreed and complied, even to skirting the bounds of safety and good manners, in moving itself into a position where Seyyan would have difficulty acting as their shadow.

Yalnis stretched. The ship, understanding that she wished to rise, withdrew its extensions from her body. She gagged a little, as she always did, when the nutrient extension slid up her throat, across her tongue, between her lips, leaving a trace of sweetness. The extension collapsed; the ship's skin absorbed it. Excretion extensions and the monitor followed, and disappeared.

She raised her head slowly. The weight of her hair, grown long, held her down. She turned the dome reflective and gazed up.

Her hair spread in a wide shining fan across the floor, covering the whole diameter of the living room, drawn out by the living carpet as it lengthened. Its color ranged in concentric circles. The outer circle, spread out so wide that each hair was a single ray, glowed an attenuated platinum blond, the color she had worn her hair when she first met Seyyan. It changed dramatically to black, then progressed from honey to auburn to dark brown, and the sequence started over. She removed the palest color from the growth sequence for the future. It would only remind her.

Instead of cutting her hair to the short and easy length she usually favored, she asked the ship to sever it at a length that would touch the ground when she stood.

Despite the ship's constant care when she slept, she always had difficulty rising after a long hibernation. The ship eased the gravity to help her. She rose on shaky legs, and stumbled when she left the nest. The companions squealed with alarm.

"Oh, be quiet," she said. "What cause have I ever given you, to fear I'd fall on you?" Besides, their instincts would pull them inside her if she ever did fall, and the only bruises would form on her own body.

But even if I've never fallen on them, she thought, I *have* left them reason to fear. To doubt my protection.

Her hair draped around her shoulders, over her breasts, along her hips and legs to the ground. The companions peered through the thick curtain, chittering with annoyance. Bahadirgul sneezed. In sudden sympathy, she pushed her hair back to leave them free.

The wound beneath her navel had healed, leaving a pale white scar. Beneath her skin, the sperm packet Zorargul emitted as its last living action made a jagged capsule, invisible, but perceptible to her fingers and vaguely painful to her nerves. She had to decide whether to use it, or to finish encapsulating it and expel it in turn.

Without being asked, the ship absorbed the shorn ends of her hair. She and the ship had been born together; despite the mysteries each species kept from the other, each knew the other's habits. It produced a length of ship silk formed into comfortable and neutral garments: loose pants with a filmy lace panel to obscure the companions, a sleeveless shirt with a similar lace panel. She wore clothes that allowed the companions some view of the world, for they could be troublesome when bored. She left the silk its natural soft beige, for the horizontal stripes of her hair gave plenty of drama. She twisted her hair into a thick rope to keep it from tangling as she dressed, then let it loose again. It lay heavy on her neck and shoulders.

I may reconsider this haircut, she thought. But not till after the launch. I can be formal for that long, at least.

Messages flowed in from the other ships. It pleased her that so many had accepted her invitation. Still she did not reply, even to welcome them. Her ship looked out a long distance, but no other craft approached. The party was complete.

Yalnis closed her eyes to inspect her ship's status and records. The ship ran a slight fever, reflecting its increasing metabolism. Its flank, smooth before her sleep, now bulged. The daughter ship lay in its birth pouch, shiny-skinned and adorned with a pattern of small knots. The knots would sink into the new ship's skin, giving it the potential of openings, connections, ports, antennae, undifferentiated tissue for experiment and play.

"It's beautiful," she whispered to the ship.

"True."

The companions squeaked with hunger, though they had spent the last thousand years dozing and feeding without any exertion. They were fat and sleek. They were always hungry, or always greedy, rising for a treat or a snack, though they connected directly to her bloodstream as well as to her nerves and could draw their sustenance from her without ever opening their little mouths or exposing their sharp little teeth.

But Yalnis had been attached to the ship's nutrients for just as long, and she too was ravenous.

She left the living room and descended to the garden. The light was different, brighter and warmer. The filter her ship used to convey light to the garden mimicked a blanket of atmosphere.

She arrived at garden's dawn. Birds chirped and sang in the surrounding trees, and a covey of quail foraged along borders and edges. Several rabbits, nibbling grass in the pasture, raised their heads when she walked in, then, unafraid, went back to grazing. They had not seen a person for thousands of their generations.

The garden smelled different from the rest of the ship, the way she believed the surface of a planet might smell. She liked it, but it frightened her, too, for it held living organisms she would never see. The health of the garden demanded flotillas of bacteria, armies of worms, swarms of bugs. She thought it might be safer to grow everything in hydroponic tanks, as had been the fashion last time she paid attention, but she liked the spice of apprehension. Besides, the ship preferred this method. If it thought change necessary, it would change.

She walked barefoot into the garden, trying not to step on any adventurous worm or careless bug. The bacteria would have to look out for themselves.

She captured a meal of fruit, corn, and a handful of squash blossoms. She liked the blossoms. When she was awake, and hunted regularly, she picked them before they turned to vegetables. The neglected plants emitted huge squashes of all kinds, some perfect, some attacked and nibbled by vegetarian predators.

The companions, reacting to the smell of food, fidgeted and writhed, craning their thick necks to snap at each other. She calmed and soothed them, and fed them bits of apple and pomegranate seeds.

They had already begun to jostle for primacy, each slowly moving toward her center, migrating across skin and muscle toward the spot where Zorargul had lived, as if she would not notice. Her skin felt stretched and sore. No companion had the confidence or nerve to risk detaching from its position to reinsert itself in the primary spot.

A good thing, too, she thought. I wouldn't answer for my temper if one of them did that without my permission.

Leaving her garden, she faced the task of welcoming her guests.

I don't want to, she thought, like a whiny girl: I want to keep my privacy, I want to enjoy my companions. I want to be left alone. To grieve alone.

In the living room, beneath the transparent dome, the ship created a raised seat. She slipped in among the cushions, sat on her hair, cursed at the sharp pull, swept the long locks out from under her and coiled them — bits of dirt and leaves tangled in the ends; she shook them off with a shudder and left the detritus for the carpet to take away. She settled herself again.

"I would like to visit Zorar," she said to her ship.

"True."

She dozed until the two ships matched, extruded, connected. A small shiver ran through Yalnis's ship, barely perceptible.

Yalnis hesitated at the boundary, took a deep breath, and entered the pilus where the fabric of her ship and the fabric of Zorar's met, mingled, and communicated, exchanging unique bits of genetic information to savor and explore.

At the border of Zorar's ship, she waited until her friend appeared.

"Zorar," she said.

Zorar blinked at her, in her kindly, languorous way. She extended her hand to Yalnis and drew her over the border, a gesture of trust that broke Yalnis's heart. She wanted to throw herself into Zorar's arms.

Do I still have the right? she thought.

She burst into tears.

Zorar enfolded Yalnis, murmuring, "Oh, my dear, oh, what is it?"

Between sobs and sniffles, and an embarrassing bout of hiccups, Yalnis told her. Zorar held her hand, patting it gently, and fell still and silent.

"I'm so sorry," Yalnis whispered. "I was so fond of Zorargul. I could always remember you, when…I feel so empty."

Zorar glanced down. The lace of Yalnis's clothes modestly concealed the companions.

"Let me see," she said. Her voice remained calm. Yalnis had always admired her serenity. Now, though, tears brightened her brown eyes.

Yalnis parted the lace panels. The four remaining companions blinked and squirmed in the increased light, the unfamiliar gaze. Bahadirgul retreated, the most modest of them all, but the others stretched and extended and stared and bared their teeth.

"You haven't chosen a replacement."

"How could I replace Zorargul?"

Zorar shook her head. "You can't duplicate. But you can replace."

Yalnis gripped Zorar's hands. "Do you mean…" She stopped, confused and embarrassed, as inarticulate as the girl she had been when she first met Zorar. That time, everything that happened was her choice. This time, by rights, it should be Zorar's.

"A daughter between us," Zorar said. "She would be worth knowing."

"Yes," Yalnis said. Zorar laid her palm against Yalnis's cheek.

Instead of leaning into her touch, Yalnis shivered.

Zorar immediately drew back her hand and gazed at Yalnis.

"What do *you* want, my dear?" she asked.

"I want…" She sniffled, embarrassed. "I want everything to be the way it was before I ever met Seyyan!" She took Zorar's hand and held it, clutched it. "I wanted a daughter with Zorargul, but Zorargul is gone, and I…" She stopped. She did not want to inflict her pain on Zorar.

"You aren't ready for another lover," Zorar said. "I understand entirely."

Zorar glanced at Yalnis's bare stomach, at the one shy and three bold little faces, at the scar left from Zorargul's murder.

"It wasn't meant to be," Zorar said.

Yalnis touched the scar, where Zorargul's jagged remains pricked her skin from underneath.

"Maybe I should —"

"No." Zorar spoke sharply.

Discouraged, Yalnis let the lacy panels slip back into place.

"It's our memories Seyyan killed," Zorar said. "Would you send out a daughter with only one parent's experience?"

Zorar was kind; she refrained from saying that the one parent would be Yalnis, young and relatively inexperienced. Yalnis's tears welled up again. She struggled to control them, but she failed. She fought the knowledge that Zorar was right. Zorar was mature and established, with several long and distant adventures to her credit. Her memories were an irreplaceable gift, to be conveyed to a daughter through Zorargul. The sperm packet alone could not convey those memories. "Let time pass," Zorar said. "We might see each other again, in some other millennium."

Yalnis scrubbed at her eyes with her sleeve. "I'm so angry!" she cried. "How could Seyyan betray me like this?"

"How did you find her?" Zorar asked, as if to change the subject. "She's not been heard of for…" She paused to think, to shrug. "Sixty or eighty millennia, at least. I thought she was lost."

"Did you hope it?"

Zorar gave her a quizzical glance. "Don't you remember?"

Yalnis looked away, ashamed. "I don't have all Zorargul's memories," she said. "I savored them — anticipated them. I didn't want to gobble them all up at once. It would be too greedy."

"How old are you now?" Zorar asked gently, as if to change the subject.

"My ship is eleven millennia," she replied. "In waking time, I'm twenty-five years old."

"You young ones always have to find out everything for yourselves," Zorar said with a sigh. "Didn't you ask Zorargul, when you took up with Seyyan?"

Yalnis stared at her, deeply shocked. "Ask Zorargul about Seyyan?" Zorar might as well have suggested she make love in a cluster of ships with the dome transparent, everyone looking in. It had never occurred to Yalnis to tell the companions each others' names, or even to wonder if they would understand her if she did. She had a right to some privacy, as did her other lovers.

"You young ones!" Zorar said with impatience. "What do you think memories are for? Are they just a toy for your entertainment?"

"I was trying to treat them respectfully!" Yalnis exclaimed.

Zorar snorted.

Yalnis wondered if she would ever be so confident, so well-established, that she could dispense with caring what others thought about her. She yearned for such audacity, such bravery.

"I asked about her, of course!" she exclaimed, trying to redeem herself. "Not the companions, but Shai and Kinli and Tasmin were all near enough to talk to. They all said, Oh, is she found? Or, She's a legend, how lucky you are to meet her! Or, Give her my loving regard."

"Tasmin has a daughter with her. She'd never hear anything against her. I suppose Seyyan never asked anything of Tasmin that she wasn't willing to give. Kinli wasn't even born last time anyone heard anything from Seyyan, and Shai..." She glanced down at her hands and slowly, gradually, unclenched her fists. "Shai fears her."

"She could have warned me."

"Seyyan terrifies her. Is she here?" She closed her eyes, a habitual movement that Yalnis did, too, when she wanted information from her ship's senses.

"No," Yalnis said, as Zorar said, "No, I see she's not."

"She said she would, but she changed her mind. It hurt my feelings when she disappeared without a word, and she never replied when I asked her what was wrong."

"She changed her mind after you mentioned Seyyan."

Yalnis thought back. "Yes."

"Would you have believed her, if she'd warned you?"

Yalnis remembered Seyyan's word and touch and beauty, the flush Yalnis felt just to see her, the excitement when she knew Seyyan looked at her. She shivered, for now all that had changed.

"I doubt it," she said. "Oh, you're right, I wouldn't have believed her. I would have suspected jealousy."

Zorar brushed away Yalnis's tears.

"What did she do to you?" Yalnis whispered.

Zorar took a deep breath, and drew up the gauzy hem of her shirt.

She carried the same companions as when she and Yalnis first met: five, the same number Yalnis had accepted. Yalnis would have expected someone of Zorar's age and status to take a few more. Five was the right number for a person of Yalnis's age and minor prosperity.

"You noticed this scar," Zorar said, tracing an erratic line of pale silver that skipped from her breastbone to her navel, nearly invisible against her translucently delicate skin. "And I shrugged away your question."

"You said it happened when you walked on the surface of a planet," Yalnis said. "You said a flesh-eating plant attacked you."

"Yes, well, one did," Zorar said, unabashed. "But it didn't leave that scar." She stroked the chin of her central little face. Just below her navel, the companion roused itself, blinking and gnashing its teeth. It neither stretched up aggressively nor retreated defensively. Yalnis had never seen its face; like the others, it had remained nearly concealed, only the top of its head showing, while Yalnis and Zorar made love. Yalnis had thought the companions admirably modest, but now she wondered if their reaction had been fear.

Zorar pressed her fingers beneath the companion's chin, scratching it gently, revealing its neck.

The scar did not stop at Zorar's navel. It continued, crossing the back of the companion's neck and the side of its throat. "Seyyan claimed she behaved as she'd been taught. As she thought was proper, and right. She was horrified at my distress."

She stroked the companion's downy scalp. It closed its eyes.

Her voice hardened.

"I had to comfort her, she acted so distraught. *I* had to comfort *her*."

"She accused me of teasing and deceiving her," Yalnis said. "And she *killed* Zorargul."

Under Zorar's gentle hand, the scarred companion relaxed and slept, its teeth no longer bared.

"Perhaps she's learned efficiency," Zorar whispered, as if the companion might hear and understand her. "Or…mercy."

"Mercy!" Yalnis exclaimed. "Cruelty and sarcasm, more likely."

"She killed Zorargul," Zorar said. "This one, mine, she left paralyzed. Impotent."

Yalnis imagined: Zorargul, cut off from her, unable to communicate with either pleasure or memory, parasitic, its pride destroyed. She gazed at Zorar with astonishment and pity, and she flushed with embarrassment. She had felt piqued when Zorar created Zorargul with a secondary little face, instead of with her first companion. Now Yalnis knew why.

Yalnis laid her hand on Zorar's. Her own fingers touched the downy fur of the damaged companion. Involuntarily, she shuddered. Zorar glanced away.

Could I have kept Zorargul? Yalnis wondered. No matter how much I loved Zorar…

She thought Zorar was the bravest person she had ever met.

Would it be right to say so? She wondered. Any more right than to

ask the questions I know not to ask: How could you — ? Why didn't
you — ?

"What do you think, now?" Zorar said.

"I'm outraged!" Yalnis said.

"Outraged enough to tell?"

"I told you."

"You confessed to me. You confessed the death of Zorargul, as if
it were your fault. Do you believe Seyyan, that you deceived her? Are
you outraged enough to accuse her, instead of yourself?"

Yalnis sat quite still, considering. After a long while, she patted
Zorar's hand again, collected herself, and brushed her fingertips
across Zorar's companion's hair with sympathy. She kissed Zorar
quickly and returned to her own ship.

Preparations, messages of welcome to old acquaintances, greetings
to new ones, occupied her. Zorar's question always hovered in the
back of her mind, and sometimes pushed itself forward to claim her
attention:

What do you think, now?

While she prepared, the ships moved closer, extruded connections, grew together. Yalnis's ship became the center, till the colony
obscured her wide vistas of space and clouds of stars and glowing
dust. She felt her ship's discomfort at being so constricted; she shared
it. She felt her ship's exhilaration at intense genetic exchange: those
sensations, she avoided.

She continued to ignore Seyyan, but never rescinded her invitation. Yalnis's ship allowed no direct connection to Seyyan's glittering
craft. Seyyan remained on the outskirts of the colony, forming her
own connections with others. The ships floated in an intricately delicate dance of balance and reciprocity. As the people exchanged greetings, reminiscences, gifts, the ships exchanged information and new
genetic code.

Most of their communications were cryptic. Oftentimes even the
ships had no idea what the new information would do, but they collected and exchanged it promiscuously, played with it, rearranged it,

tested it. The shimmery pattern of rainbow reflections spread from Seyyan's craft's skin to another, and another, and the pattern mutated from solid to stripes to spots.

Yalnis's ship remained its customary reflective silver.

"The ships have chosen a new fashion," Yalnis said.

"True," her ship said. Then, "False."

Yalnis frowned, confused, as her ship displayed a genetic sequence and its genealogy tag. Yalnis left all those matters to the ship, so she took a moment to understand that her ship rejected the pattern because it descended from Seyyan's craft. Her ship led her further into its concerns, showing how many new sequences it had considered but rejected and stopped taking in when it encountered Seyyan's tag.

"Thank you," Yalnis said.

"True."

That was a long conversation, between ship and human. She was glad it had ended without misunderstanding.

The ship did understand "Thank you," Yalnis believed, and Yalnis did understand its response of appreciation.

Maybe Seyyan was right, Yalnis said to herself. Maybe I *am* naïve. I feared direct assault, but never thought of a sneak attack on my ship.

She wondered if her encounter with Seyyan had changed the balance between the two ships, or if their estrangement had its own source. She wondered if she should try to exclude Seyyan's craft from the colony. But that would be an extreme insult, and Seyyan had more friends than Yalnis, and many admirers. She was older, wealthier, more experienced and accomplished, more limber of voice and of body.

"I trust your judgment," she said, remaining within the relative safety of simple declarative statements. She would leave decisions about Seyyan's craft to her own ship.

"True."

The shimmering new fashion continued to extend from Seyyan's to other craft, each vying with the next to elaborate upon her pattern.

Seyyan's popularity created a second center for the colony, decreasing the stability of the delicate rotation, but there was nothing to be done about it. It was ships' business, not people's.

Yalnis was ready. She made her last decisions, dressed in intricate lace, took a deep, shaky breath, and welcomed her guests.

Zorar arrived first, too well-established to concern herself with being fashionably late. Yalnis embraced her, grateful for her presence. Zorar kissed her gently and handed her a sealed glass ampoule.

"For your daughter's vineyard," she said. "I think the culture's improved even over what I gave your mother, when she launched you and your ship."

"Thank you," Yalnis said, honored by the gift. She put it on the central table, in a place of distinction.

More guests arrived; an hour passed in a blur of greetings, reunions, introductions, gifts. People brought works of art, stories, and songs. They brought ship silk as refined as fog, seeds of newly adapted plants, embryos of newly discovered creatures, unique cultures of yeast and bacteria. Yalnis accepted them all with thanks and gratitude. Her daughter would be well and truly launched; her ship would be rich, and unique.

Her guests ate and drank, wished each other long life and adventures, congratulated voyagers on their safe return. They exchanged compliments and gossip, they flirted, they told tales, they even bragged: Kinli had, of course, been on another great adventure that made all others pale by comparison. Guests complimented Yalnis's ship's cooking, especially the savory rabbit, and the complexity and quality of her wine. Everyone wore their best ship silk, and most, like Yalnis, wore lace so their companions could remain decently modest while watching the party. A few guests wore opaque garments to enforce a complete modesty; Yalnis thought the choice a little cruel. The very youngest people, recently debuted from solitary girl to adult, revealed their virgin midriffs.

Yalnis found herself always aware of the new connections leading from other ships to her living space. The openings, glowing in the cool pastels of biological light, changed her living area from one of comfortable intimacy to one of open vulnerability.

Zorar handed her a glass of wine. Yalnis had based the vintage on the yeast Zorar gave her ship when it and Yalnis were born and launched.

Yalnis sipped it, glanced around, swallowed a whole mouthful. The effects spread through her. The companions squeaked with pleasure, leaning into her, absorbing the alcohol, yearning. She brushed her hand across the lace of her shirt. She had been neglecting the companions since Zorargul's murder. She drank more wine, and Zorar refilled their glasses.

Yalnis blocked out the rising level of conversation. She was unused to noise, and it tired her.

"What do you think?" she said.

Zorar raised one eyebrow. "That's the question I want you to answer."

"Oh," said Yalnis. "Yes, of course." She blushed at her misstep. "But I meant, about the wine."

"It's excellent," Zorar said, "as you well know. Your ship is of a line that seldom makes a recombinant error, and I can only approve of the changes. What about Seyyan? Did you ban her?"

"No. I want her here. So she knows she failed. Maybe she banned herself."

"Maybe she's trying to unnerve you. Or to wait till you drink too much."

Yalnis drained her glass again.

"Maybe if I do, I'll be ready for her."

She was ignoring the noise, but she noticed the sudden silence.

"And then I —" Kinli said, and stopped.

Seyyan stood in the largest new entryway, silhouetted by golden bioluminescence, her face shadowed, dramatized, by the softer party light. Yalnis's heart pounded; her face flushed.

"I thought she was so beautiful," Yalnis whispered to Zorar, amazed, appalled. She thought she whispered: a few people nearby glanced toward her, most amused, but one at least pale with jealousy for her relationship with the renowned adventurer.

If you only knew, Yalnis thought. I wonder what you'd think then?

Yalnis mourned the loss of the joy she had felt when Seyyan chose her, but she mourned the loss of Zorargul much more.

Seyyan strode into the party, greeting allies, her gaze moving unchecked past the few who had rejected her craft's fashionable offerings. Misty ship silk flowed around her legs and hips, shimmering with the pattern that newly decorated the flanks of so many craft. No one else had thought to apply it to clothing. She wore a shawl of the same fabric around her shoulders, over her breasts, across her companions.

But her hands were empty of gifts. Yalnis declined to notice, but others did, and whispered, shocked.

Then she flung back the end of the shawl, revealing herself from breastbone to pubis.

She had accepted more companions since she was with Yalnis. She bore so many Yalnis could not count them without staring, and she would not stare. Her gaze hesitated only long enough to see that the son-spot had erupted and healed over.

The other guests did stare.

How could any person support so many companions? And yet Seyyan displayed health and strength, an overwhelming physical wealth.

She turned to draw another guest from the shadows behind her. Ekarete stepped shyly into the attention of the party. Ekarete, one of the newly debuted adults, already wore new lace. Seyyan bent to kiss her, to slip her hand beneath the filmy panel of her shirt, so everyone would know that if she had neglected a launching gift for Yalnis's daughter, she had given a more intimate one to Ekarete.

Seyyan wanted Yalnis to know what had happened to the new companion, that she had easily found someone to accept it.

Seyyan whispered to Ekarete, drew her hand down her cheek, and continued toward Yalnis and Zorar. Ekarete followed, several steps behind, shy and attentive, excited and intimidated by her first adult gathering.

Seyyan's first companion, the assassin, protruded all the way to the base of his neck, eyes wide, teeth exposed and snapping sharply.

Her other companions, responding to him, gnashed their teeth and blinked their eyes.

"What a pleasant little party," Seyyan said. "I so admire people who aren't caught up in the latest fashion."

"Do have some wine," Yalnis said. She meant to speak in a pleasant tone. Her voice came out flat, and hard.

Seyyan accepted a glass, and sipped, and nodded. "As good as I remember."

Yalnis wished for the ancient days Seyyan came from, when poison could still wreak havoc with a person's biochemistry, undetected till too late. She wished for a poisoned apple, a single bite, and no one ever to kiss Seyyan again.

Maybe I can have that last wish, she thought, and took action on her decision.

She let Zorargul's wound break open. The stab of pain struck through her. Her companions shrieked, crying like terrified birds, reacting to her distress. Blood blossomed through the lace panel of her shirt. All around her, people gasped.

Yalnis reached beneath the scarlet stain. Her hand slid across the blood on her skin. The wound gaped beneath her fingers.

Her body had treated Zorargul's sperm packet like an intrusion, an irritation, as something to encapsulate like the seed of a pearl. At the same time, the packet struggled for its own survival, extending spines to remain in contact with her flesh. As it worked its way out, scraping her raw, she caught her breath against a whimper.

Finally the capsule dropped into her hand. She held it up. Her body had covered the sperm packet's extrusions with shining white enamel. All that remained of Zorargul was a sphere of bloody fangs. "This is your work, Seyyan," she said. Blood flowed over her stomach, through her pubic hair, down her legs, dripping onto the rug, which absorbed it and carried it away. Yalnis went cold, light-headed, pale. She took courage from Zorar, standing at her elbow.

"You took me as your lover," Seyyan said. "I thought you wanted me. I thought you wanted a companion from me. My lineage always fought for place and position."

"I wasn't at war with you," Yalnis said. "I loved you. If you'd asked, instead of…" She glanced down at the gory remains.

"Asked?" Seyyan whispered. "But *you* asked *me*."

Whispers, exclamations, agreement, objections all quivered around them.

Tasmin moved to stand near Seyyan, taking her side.

"You must have been neglectful," she said to Yalnis. "I think you're too young to support so many companions."

Seyyan glanced at Tasmin, silencing her. Anyone could see that Yalnis was healthy and well supplied with resources. She was her own evidence, and her ship the final proof.

As they confronted each other, the guests sorted themselves, most in a neutral circle, some behind Yalnis, more flanking Seyyan. Yalnis wished Shai had remained for the gathering. She might have sided with Seyyan, but the others might have seen her fear.

Ekarete, in her new lace shirt, moved shyly between the opponents.

"Seyyan was very gentle with me," she whispered. "She acceded to my choice." She twitched the hem of her shirt aside, just far enough, just long enough, to reveal the fading inflammation of a new attachment, and the golden skin and deep brown eyes of Seyyan's offspring, Ekarete's first little face.

"Very gentle," Ekarete said again. "Very kind. I love her."

"For giving you a cast-off?" Yalnis said. "For inducing you to take the companion I refused?"

Ekarete stared at her. Yalnis felt sorry for her, sorry to have humiliated her.

Tasmin stood forward with Ekarete. "Yalnis, you're speaking out of grief," she said. "You lost a companion — I grieve with you. But don't blame Seyyan or embarrass Ekarete. We all know Seyyan for her generosity. My daughter by her launched gloriously."

"You're hardly disinterested," said Yalnis.

"But I am," said Kinli, "and I know nothing against her."

Yalnis started to say, When did you ever listen to anyone but yourself?

Zorar yanked up the hem of her shirt, revealing the scar and her emasculated companion with its drooping mouth and dull eyes. It roused far enough to bare its teeth. It drooled.

The older people understood; the younger ones started in horror at the mangled thing, heard quick whispers of explanation, and stared at Seyyan.

"I loved you, too," Zorar said. "I told myself, it must have been my fault. I should have understood. *I* consoled *you*. After you did this."

"I came for a celebration," Seyyan said, holding herself tall and aloof. "I expect to be taken as I am — not ambushed with lies and insults."

She spun, the hem of her dress flaring dramatically, and strode away.

Ekarete ran after her. Seyyan halted, angry in the set of her shoulders; she paused, softened, bent to speak, kissed Ekarete, and continued away, alone. The main entrance silhouetted her formidable figure as she left Yalnis's ship.

Ekarete stood shivering, gazing after her, pulling the hem of her shirt down all the way around. Finally she scurried after her. Tasmin glared at Yalnis, heaved a heavy sigh, and followed.

The others, even Kinli, clustered around Yalnis and Zorar.

"You've spoiled your own party," Kinli said, petulant. "What now? A permanent break? A feud?"

"I shun her," Yalnis said.

"That's extreme!"

Yalnis hesitated, hoping for support if not acclaim. She shrugged into the silence. "If the community doesn't agree, why should she care if only I shun her?"

"And I," Zorar said, which made more difference to more people.

The light of the connecting corridors faded as she spoke. The openings slowly ensmalled. No one had to be told the party had ended. The guests hurried to slip through the connections before they vanished. Their finery went dim.

All around, the tables resorbed into the floor, leaving crumbs and scraps and disintegrating utensils. The rug's cilia carried them away in a slow-motion whirlpool of dissolving bits, into pores, to be metabolized. The gifts all sank away, to be circulated to the new ship.

Only Zorar remained. Yalnis's knees gave out. She crouched, breathing hard, dizzy. Zorar knelt beside her.

"I'm — I have to — "

"Hush. Lie back."

"But — "

"It's waited this long. It can wait longer."

Yalnis let Zorar ease her down. The ship received her, nestling her, creeping around and over her with its warm skin. The pain eased and the flow of blood ceased. The blood she had shed moved from her skin, from her clothes, red-brown drying specks flowing in tiny lines across the comforter, and disappeared.

She dozed, for a moment or an hour. When she woke, Zorar remained beside her.

"Thank you," Yalnis whispered. She closed her eyes again. She desperately wanted to be alone.

Zorar kissed Yalnis and slipped through the last exit. It sealed itself and disappeared.

Yalnis wanted only to go back to sleep. A thousand years might not be enough this time. She had never been among so many people for so long, and she had never been in such a confrontation. Exhaustion crept over her, but she must stay awake a little longer.

"I shun Seyyan," she said. Her companions quivered at her distress.

"True," the ship said, and let all its connections to all the other ships shrivel and drop away. The primary colony broke apart, resolving into individual ships. They moved to safer distances, and the stars reappeared above Yalnis's living space.

Seyyan's glittering secondary colony remained, with her craft protected in its center. None broke away to shun her. Yalnis turned her back on the sight. She no longer had anything to do with Seyyan.

"It's time," she said aloud.

"True," her ship replied. It created a nest for her, a luxurious bed of ship silk. It dimmed the light and mirrored the outer surface of the transparent dome. The stars took on a ghostly appearance. Yalnis could see out, but no one could see inside.

Yalnis pulled off her shirt. Her long hair tangled in it. Annoyed, she shook her hair free. She stepped out of her loose trousers. Naked, she reclined in the nest.

"Please, cut my hair."

"True," the ship said. The nest cropped her hair, leaving a cap of dark brown. The weight fell away; the strands moved across the carpet, fading to a dust of molecules.

Yalnis relaxed, gazed at her companions, and let her hand slide down her body. The little faces knew her intent. Each stretched itself to its greatest extent, into her and out of her, whispering and offering.

She made her choice.

Bahadirgul stretched up to seek her hand, moaning softly through its clenched sharp teeth. The other companions contracted, hiding their little faces in modesty or disappointment till they nearly disappeared. Yalnis stroked Bahadirgul's head, its nape, and caressed its neck and shaft. She opened herself to her companion.

The pleasure started slowly, spreading from Bahadirgul's attachment point deeper into her body. It reached the level of their ordinary couplings, which always gave Yalnis joy, and gave the companion days of pride and satiation. It continued, and intensified. Yalnis cried out, panting, arching her back. Bahadirgul shivered and extended. Yalnis and her companion released, and combined.

Their daughter formed. Yalnis curled up, quivering occasionally with a flush of pleasure, listening to their daughter grow. The pleasure faded to a background throb.

Inside her, her daughter grew.

Content, she nestled deeper into the ship silk and prepared to sleep.

Instead, the dome went transparent. Seyyan's colony of connected ships gleamed in the distance. The connecting pili stretched thin, preparing to detach and resorb.

Yalnis sighed. Seyyan was none of her concern anymore. She had sworn to take no more notice of her.

What happened next, Yalnis would never forget, no matter how many millennia she lived or how many adventures filled her memory.

The connections deformed, shifted, arched in waves. They contracted, forcing the craft closer even as they tried to separate and depart.

Seyyan commanded her supporters, and they discovered the limits of their choices. They tried to free their ships, tried to dissolve the connections, but Seyyan drew them ever nearer.

Seyyan's craft had infected their ships not only with beauty, but with obedience.

Tasmin's craft, old and powerful, broke free. Its pilus tore, shredding and bleeding. Yalnis's ship quivered in response to the sight or to a cry of distress imperceptible to people. The destruction and distraction allowed a few other people to overcome the wills of their craft and wrench away, breaking more connections. After the painful and distressing process, the freed craft fled into a wider orbit, or set a course to escape entirely from the star system and from Seyyan.

Person and ship alike suffered when fighting the illness of a malignant genetic interchange. Yalnis hoped they would all survive.

"What's she doing?" Yalnis whispered. Her ship interpreted her words, correctly, as a question for people, not for ships. It opened all her silenced message ports and let in exclamations, cries of outrage, excuses, argument, wild speculation.

Seyyan's craft gleamed and shimmered and proclaimed its ascension and gathered the remaining captives into a shield colony. With its imprisoned allies, it moved toward Yalnis and her ship.

Yalnis went cold with fear, shock, and the responsibility for all that had happened: she had brought all the others here; she had succumbed to Seyyan and then challenged her; she had forced people to take sides.

"Seyyan infected their defenses," Yalnis said. That's what the fashionable pattern was for, she thought. A temptation, and a betrayal.

"True," her ship replied.

Yalnis's ship moved toward Seyyan's craft. It quivered around her, like the companions within her. It had made its decision, a decision that risked damage. This was ship's business. Yalnis could fight it, or she could add her will to her ship's and join the struggle. She chose her ship.

Zorar followed, and, reluctantly, so did Tasmin's craft, its torn pili leaking fluid that broke into clouds of mist and dissipated in sunlit sparkles. The skin of the craft dulled to its former blue sheen, but patches of shimmering infection broke out, spread, contracted.

After all too brief a time, the stars vanished again, obscured by the coruscating flanks of Seyyan's shield. Yalnis's ship pushed dangerously into the muddle. Yalnis crouched beneath the transparent dome, overcome with claustrophobia. No escape remained, except perhaps for Seyyan.

Seyyan forced her captive allies to grow extensions, but when they touched Yalnis's ship, they withdrew abruptly, stung by its immune response. In appreciation, Yalnis stroked the fabric of her ship.

"True," her ship whispered.

Please, Yalnis thought, Seyyan, please, just flee. Let everyone go. Announce a new adventure. Declare that you've shamed me enough already, that you won our altercation.

She had no wish to speak to Seyyan, but she had an obligation. She created a message port. Seyyan answered, and smiled.

"Your shunning didn't last long," she said. "Shall I tell my friends to withdraw?"

Yalnis flushed, embarrassed and angry, but refused to let Seyyan divert her.

"What do you want?" Yalnis cried. "Why do you care anymore what I think? Leave us all alone. Go on more of your marvelous and legendary adventures —"

"Flee?" Seyyan said. "From *you*?"

Ekarete's craft, willingly loyal to Seyyan, interposed itself between Seyyan and Yalnis. A pore opened in its skin. A spray of scintillating liquid exploded outward, pushed violently into vacuum by the pressure behind it. The fluid spattered over the dome of Yalnis's ship. It spread, trying to penetrate, trying to infect. Yalnis flinched, as if the stuff could reach her.

Her ship shuddered. Yalnis gasped. The temperature in her living space rose: her ship's skin reacted to the assault, marshalling a powerful immune response, fighting off the infection. The foreign matter sublimated, rose in a foggy sparkle, and dispersed.

Seyyan lost patience. The flank of her craft bulged outward, touching Ekarete's. It burst, like an abscess, exploding ship's fluids onto the flank of Ekarete's craft. The lines of fluid solidified in the vacuum and radiation of space, then contracted, pulling the captive craft closer, drawing it in to feed upon. Ekarete's craft, its responses compromised, had no defense.

"Seyyan!" Ekarete cried. "I never agreed — How — " And then, "Help us!"

Seyyan's craft engulfed Ekarete's, overwhelming the smaller ship's pattern variations with the stronger design. The captive ship matched the captor, and waves of color and light swept smoothly from one across the other.

"You must be put away," Yalnis said to Seyyan, and ended their communication forever.

Tasmin's craft, its blue skin blotched with shimmer, its torn connections hovering and leaking, approached Seyyan's craft.

"Don't touch it again!" Yalnis cried. "You'll be caught too!"

"She must stop," Tasmin said, with remarkable calm.

Yalnis took a deep breath.

"True," she said. Her ship responded to her assent, pressing forward.

To Tasmin, she said, "Yes. But you can't stop her. You can only destroy yourself."

Tasmin's ship decelerated and hovered, for Seyyan had already damaged it badly.

A desperate pilus stretched from the outer flank of Ekarete's ship. Yalnis allowed it to touch, her heart bounding with apprehension.

Her ship reached for it, and the connecting outgrowths met. Her ship declined to fuse, but engulfed the tip to create a temporary connection. It opened its outgrowth, briefly, into Yalnis's living room.

The outlines of the younger craft blurred as Seyyan's ship incorporated it, dissolved it, and took over its strength. The pilus ripped free of Yalnis's ship and sank into the substance of Seyyan's craft.

Air rushed past Yalnis in a quick blast; the wind fell still as her ship clenched its pilus and resorbed it.

The shrinking pilus pulled Ekarete inside. Naked, crying, her hair flying, she held her hand over her stomach for modesty. Her palm hid the little face of her companion, muffling its squeals and the clash of its sharp teeth.

Maybe it will bite her, Yalnis thought, distracted, and chided herself for the uncharitable thought.

"How could she, how could she?" Ekarete said.

"Yalnis," Zorar said from the depths of her own ship, "what are you doing? What should I do?"

"Come and get me if we dissolve," Yalnis said. And then she wondered, Could I leave my ship, if Seyyan bests us? *Should* I?

If Seyyan had been patient, Yalnis thought, she might have persuaded her friends to defend her willingly. If she'd asked them, they might have agreed I'd outraged her unjustly. If she'd trusted them, they might have joined her out of love.

No shield colony had existed in Yalnis's lifetime, or in the memories of the lovers whose companions she had accepted: no great danger had threatened any group of people. A shield was a desperate act, a last effort, an assault. Extricating and healing the ships afterward was a long and expensive task. But Seyyan's friends might have done it willingly, for Seyyan's love. Instead they tore themselves away from her, one by one, desperately damaging themselves to avoid Ekarete's fate, but weakening Seyyan as well.

They dispersed, fleeing. Seyyan's craft loomed, huge and old, sucking in the antennae desperately growing outward from the vestiges of Ekarete's craft.

Ekarete cried softly as her ship vanished.

"Do be quiet," Yalnis said.

Until the last moment of possibility, Yalnis hoped Seyyan would relent. Yalnis and Zorar and Tasmin, and a few others, hovered around her, but she had room to escape. Seyyan's former allies gathered beyond the first rank of defense, fearful of being trapped again but resolving to defend themselves.

Yalnis's ship emitted the first wave of ship silk, a silver plume of sticky fibers that caught against the other ship and wrapped around its skin. Yalnis's ship balanced itself: action and reaction.

The other ships followed her lead, spraying Seyyan's craft with plume after plume: silver, scarlet, midnight blue, ultraviolet, every color but the holographic pattern their defenses covered. Seyyan's craft reacted, but the concerted effort overwhelmed it. It drew inward, shrinking from the touch of the silk to avoid allergic reaction. Gradually it disappeared beneath the layers of solidifying color.

Yalnis listened for a plea, a cry for mercy, even a shout of defiance. But Seyyan maintained a public silence.

Is she secretly giving orders to her allies? Yalnis wondered. Does she have allies anymore? She glanced over her shoulder at Ekarete.

Ekarete, creeping up behind her, launched herself at Yalnis, her teeth bared in an eerie mirror of her angry companion's. She reached for Yalnis's face, her hand pouring blood, and they fell in a tangle. Yalnis struggled, fending off Ekarete's fists and fingernails, desperate to protect her tiny growing daughter, desperate to defend her companions against Ekarete's, which was after all the spawn of Seyyan and her murderous first companion.

All the companions squealed and gnashed their teeth, ready to defend themselves, as aware of danger as they were of opportunity.

"Why are you doing this?" Yalnis cried. "I'm not your enemy!"

"I want my ship! I want Seyyan!"

"It's gone! She's gone!" Yalnis wrestled Ekarete and grabbed her, holding tight and ducking her head as Ekarete slapped and struck her. The companions writhed and lunged at their opponent. Their movements gave Yalnis weird sensations of sexual arousal and pleasure in the midst of anger and fear.

The floor slipped beneath her, startling her as it built loose lobes of ship silk. She grabbed one and flung herself forward, pulling the gossamer fabric over Ekarete, letting go, rolling free, leaving Ekarete trapped. The silk closed in. Yalnis struggled to her feet, brushing her hand across her stomach to reassure herself that her companions and her daughter remained uninjured. She wiped sweat from her face and realized it was not sweat, but blood, not Ekarete's but her own, flowing from a stinging scratch down her cheek.

Both she and her ship had been distracted. Seyyan's craft struggled against a thin spot that should have been covered by more silver silk from Yalnis's ship. The tangled shape rippled and roiled, and the craft bulged to tear at the restraint. Glowing plasma from the propulsion system spurted in tiny jets beneath the surface of the silk. The craft convulsed. Yalnis flinched to think of the searing plasma trapped between the craft's skin and the imprisoning cover.

"Finish it," Yalnis said to her ship. "Please, finish it." Tears ran hot down her face. Ekarete's muffled cries and curses filled the living space, and Yalnis's knees shook.

"True," her ship said. A cloak of silver spread to cover the weak spot, to seal in the plasma.

The roiling abruptly stopped.

Yalnis's friends flung coat after coat of imprisoning silk over Seyyan's craft, until they were all exhausted.

When it was over, Yalnis's ship accelerated away with the last of its strength. Her friends began a slow dispersal, anxious to end the gathering. Seyyan's craft drifted alone and silent, turning in a slow rotation, its glimmer extinguished by a patchwork of hardening colors.

Yalnis wondered how much damage the plasma had done, how badly Seyyan's craft had been hurt, and whether it and Seyyan had survived.

"Tasmin," she said, quietly, privately, "will you come for Ekarete? She can't be content here."

Ekarete was a refugee, stripped of all her possessions, indigent and pitiable, squeaking angrily beneath ship silk like a completely hidden companion.

After a hesitation Yalnis could hardly believe, or forgive, Tasmin replied.

"Very well."

Yalnis saw to her ship. Severely depleted, it arced through space in a stable enough orbit. It had expended its energy and drawn on its structural mass. Between defending itself and the demands of its unborn daughter ship, it would need a long period of recovery.

She sent one more message, a broadcast to everyone, but intended for Seyyan's former friends.

"I haven't the resources to correct her orbit." She felt too tired even to check its stability, and reluctant to ask her ship to exert itself. "Someone who still cares for her must take that responsibility."

"Let me up!" Ekarete shouted. Yalnis gave her a moment of attention.

"Tasmin will be here soon," Yalnis said. "She'll help you."

"We're bleeding."

Yalnis said, "I don't care."

She pulled her shirt aside to see to her own companions. Three of the four had retracted, showing only their teeth. She stroked around them till they relaxed, dozed, and exposed the tops of their downy little heads, gold and copper and softly freckled. Only Bahadirgul, ebony against Yalnis's pale skin, remained bravely awake and alert.

Drying blood slashed its mouth, but the companion itself had sustained only a shallow scratch. Yalnis petted the soft black fur of Bahadirgul's hair.

"You're gallant," Yalnis said. "Yes, gallant. I made the right choice, didn't I?" Bahadirgul trembled with pleasure against her fingers, within her body.

When Bahadirgul slept, exhausted and content, Yalnis saw to her daughter, who grew unmolested and unconcerned; she saw to herself and to her companions, icing the bruises of Ekarete's attack, washing her scratches and the companion's. She looked in the mirror and wondered if she would have a scar down her cheek, across her perfect skin.

And, if I do, will I keep it? she wondered. As a reminder?

As she bathed and put on new clothes, Tasmin's ship approached, sent greetings, asked for permission to attach. Yalnis let her ship make that decision and felt relieved when the ship approved. A pilus extended from Tasmin's ship; Yalnis's ship accepted it. Perhaps it carried some risk, but they were sufficiently exhausted that growing a capsule for Ekarete's transport felt beyond their resources.

As the pilus widened into a passage, Zorar whispered to her through a message port, "Shall I come and help? I think I should."

"No, my friend," Yalnis whispered in reply. "Thank you, but no."

Tasmin entered, as elegant and perfect as ever. Yalnis surprised herself by taking contrary pride in her own casual appearance. Zorar's concern and worry reached her. Yalnis should be afraid, but she was not.

"Please release Ekarete," she said to her ship.

"True," it said, its voice soft. The net of silk withdrew, resorbed. As soon as one hand came free, Ekarete clutched and scratched and dragged herself loose. She sprang to her feet, blood-smeared and tangle-haired.

She took one step toward Yalnis, then stopped, staring over Yalnis's shoulder.

Yalnis glanced quickly back.

As if deliberately framed, Seyyan's craft loomed beyond the transparent dome of the living space, bound in multicolored layers of the heaviest ship silk, each layer permeated with allergens particular to the ship that had created it. Seyyan's craft lay cramped within the sphere, shrinking from its painful touch, immobilized and put away until time wore the restraints to dust.

Ekarete keened with grief. The wail filled Yalnis's hearing and thickened the air.

Tasmin hurried to her, putting one arm around her shaking shoulders, covering her with a wing of her dress.

"Take her," Yalnis said to Tasmin. "Please, take her."

Tasmin turned Ekarete and guided her to the pilus. The connection's rim had already begun to swell inward as Yalnis's ship reacted to the touch of Tasmin's with inflammation. Tasmin and Ekarete hurried through and disappeared.

Seyyan's former friends would have to decide how to treat Ekarete. They might abandon her, adopt her, or spawn a new craft for her. Yalnis had no idea what they would choose to do, whether they would decide she was pure fool for her loyalty or pure hero for the same reason.

When the connector had healed over, leaving the wall a little swollen and irritated, when Tasmin's ship moved safely away, Yalnis took a long deep breath and let it out slowly. Silence and solitude calmed her.

"It's time, I think," she said aloud.

"True," replied her ship.

Yalnis descended to the growing chamber, where the daughter ship lay fat and sleek, bulging toward the outer skin. It had formed as a pocket of Yalnis's ship, growing inward. A thick neck connected the two craft, but now the neck was thinning, with only an occasional pulse of nutrients and information. The neck would part, healing over on the daughter's side, opening wide on the outer skin of Yalnis's ship.

Yalnis stepped inside for the first, and perhaps the only, time.

The living space was very plain, very beautiful in its elegant simplicity, its walls and floor a black as deep and vibrant as space without stars. Its storage bulged with the unique gifts Yalnis's guests had brought: new foods, new information, new bacteria, stories, songs, and maps of places unimaginably distant.

The soft silver skin of Yalnis's ship hugged it close, covering its transparent dome.

The new ship awoke to her presence. It created a nest for her. She cuddled into its alien warmth, and slept.

She woke to birth pangs, her own and her ship's. Extensions and monitors retracted from her body.

"Time for launch," she said to her ship.

"True," it said, without hesitation or alternation. It shuddered with a powerful labor pang. It had recovered its strength during the long rest.

"Bahadirgul," Yalnis said, "it's time."

Bahadirgul yawned hugely, blinked, and came wide awake.

Yalnis and Bahadirgul combined again. The pleasure of their mental combining matched that of their physical combining, rose in intensity, and exceeded it. At the climax, they presented their daughter with a copy of Yalnis's memories and the memories of her lover Bahadir.

A moment of pressure, a stab of pain —

Yalnis picked up the blinking gynuncula. Her daughter had Bahadir's ebony skin and hair of deepest brown, and Yalnis's own dark blue eyes. Delighted, she showed her to Bahadirgul, wondering, as she always did, how much the companion understood beyond pleasure, satiation, and occasional fear or fury. It sighed and retreated to its usual position, face exposed, calm. The other companions hissed and blinked and looked away. Yalnis let the mesh of her shirt slip over their faces.

Yalnis carried her daughter through the new ship, from farm space to power plant, pausing to wash away the stickiness of birth in the pretty little bathing stream. The delicate fuzz on her head dried as soft as fur.

The daughter blinked at Yalnis. Everyone said a daughter always knew her mother from the beginning. Yalnis believed it, looking into the new being's eyes, though neither she nor anyone she knew could recall that first moment of life and consciousness.

By the time she returned to the living space at the top of the new ship, the connecting neck had separated, one end healing against the daughter ship in a faint navel pucker, the other slowly opening to the outside. Yalnis's ship shuddered again, pushing at the daughter ship. The transparent dome pressed out, to reveal space and the great surrounding web of stars.

Yalnis's breasts ached. She sank cross-legged on the warm midnight floor and let her daughter suck, giving her a physical record of dangers and attractions as she and Bahadirgul had given her a mental record of the past.

"Karime," Yalnis whispered, as her daughter fell asleep. Above them the opening widened. The older ship groaned. The new ship quaked as it pressed out into the world.

"Karime, daughter, live well," Yalnis said.

She gave her daughter to her ship's daughter, placing the chubby sleeping creature in the soft nest. She petted the ship-silk surface.

"Take good care of her," she said.

"True," the new ship whispered.

Yalnis smiled, stood up, watched the new ship cuddle the new person for a moment, then hurried through the interior connection before it closed.

She slipped out, glanced back to be sure all was well, and returned to her living space to watch.

Yalnis's ship gave one last heavy shudder. The new ship slipped free.

It floated nearby, getting its bearings, observing its surroundings. Soon — staying near another ship always carried an element of danger, as well as opportunity — it whispered into motion, accelerating itself carefully toward a higher, more distant orbit.

Yalnis smiled at its audacity. Farther from the star, moving through the star's dust belt, it could collect mass and grow quickly. In a thousand, perhaps only half a thousand, orbits, Karime would emerge to take her place as a girl of her people.

"We could follow," Yalnis said. "Rest, recoup..."

"False," her ship whispered, displaying its strength, and its desire, and its need. "False, false."

"We could go on our adventure."

"True," her ship replied, and turned outward toward the web of space, to travel forever, to feast on stardust.

Knapsack Poems

Eleanor Arnason

Eleanor Arnason has written several stories about the goxhat, an alien race of gestalt groups rather than individuals. This one's narrator is an eight-bodied itinerant poet; some of the bodies are male, some female, some neuter. One day during its travels, it finds a baby, the only surviving part of a new person. Some parts of the poet feel it should be abandoned to die with the rest of itself; others want to nurture it, even though this means it will always be alone and incomplete. As alien as the goxhat seem to us, much about their lives will be familiar, including their parenting concerns.

Within this person of eight bodies, thirty-two eyes, and the usual number of orifices and limbs, resides a spirit as restless as gossamer on wind. In youth, I dreamed of fame as a merchant-traveler. In later years, realizing that many of my parts were prone to motion sickness, I thought of scholarship or accounting. But I lacked the Great Determination that is necessary for both trades. My abilities are spontaneous and brief, flaring and vanishing like a falling star. For me to spend my life adding numbers or looking through dusty documents would be like "lighting a great hall with a single lantern bug" or "watering a great garden with a drop of dew."

Finally, after consulting the care-givers in my crèche, I decided to become a traveling poet. It's a strenuous living and does not pay well, but it suits me.

Climbing through the mountains west of Ibri, I heard a *wishik* call, then saw the animal, its wings like white petals, perched on a bare branch.

> *"Is that tree flowering*
> *So late in autumn?*

Ridiculous idea!
I long for dinner."

One of my bodies recited the poem. Another wrote it down, while still others ranged ahead, looking for signs of habitation. As a precaution, I carried cudgels as well as pens and paper. One can never be sure what will appear in the country west of Ibri. The great poet Raging Fountain died there of a combination of diarrhea and malicious ghosts. Other writers, hardly less famous, have been killed by monsters or bandits, or, surviving these, met their end at the hands of dissatisfied patrons.

The Bane of Poets died before my birth. Its[1] ghost or ghosts offered Raging Fountain the fatal bowl of porridge. But other patrons still remain "on steep slopes and in stony dales."

> "*Dire the telling*
> *Of patrons in Ibri:*
> *Bone-breaker lurks*
> *High on a mountain.*
> *Skull-smasher waits*
> *In a shadowy valley.*
> *Better than these*
> *The country has only*
> *Grasper, Bad-bargain,*
> *And Hoarder-of-Food.*"

Why go to such a place, you may be wondering? Beyond Ibri's spiny mountains lie the wide fields of Greater and Lesser Ib, prosperous lands well-known for patronage of the arts.

---

1 Goxhat units, or "persons" as the goxhat say, comprise four to sixteen bodies and two or three sexes. The Bane of Poets was unusual in being entirely neuter, which meant it could not reproduce. According to legend, it was reproductive frustration and fear of death that made The Bane so dangerous to poets.

Why poets? They produce two kinds of children, those of body and those of mind, and grasp in their pincers the gift of undying fame.

Late in the afternoon, I realized I would find no refuge for the night. Dark snow-clouds hid the hills in front of me. Behind me, low in the south, the sun shed pale light. My shadows, long and many-limbed, danced ahead of me on the rutted road.

My most poetic self spoke:

> "*The north is blocked*
> *By clouds like boulders.*
> *A winter sun*
> *Casts shadows in my way.*"

Several of my other selves frowned. My scribe wrote the poem down with evident reluctance.

"Too obvious," muttered a cudgel-carrier.

Another self agreed. "Too much like Raging Fountain in his/her mode of melancholy complaint."

Far ahead, a part of me cried alarm. I suspended the critical discussion and hurried forward in a clump, my clubs raised and ready for use.

Soon, not even breathless, I stopped at a place I knew by reputation: the Tooth River. Wide and shallow, it ran around pointed stones, well-exposed this time of year and as sharp as the teeth of predators. On the far side of the river were bare slopes that led toward cloudy mountains. On the near side of the river, low cliffs cast their shadows over a broad shore. My best scout was there, next to a bundle of cloth. The scout glanced up, saw the rest of me, and — with deft fingers — undid the blanket folds.

Two tiny forms lay curled at the blanket's center. A child of one year, holding itself in its arms. "Alive?" I asked myself.

The scout crouched closer. "One body is and looks robust. The other body — " my scout touched it gently " — is cold."

Standing among myself, I groaned and sighed. There was no problem understanding what had happened. A person had given birth. Either the child had been unusually small, or the other parts had died. For some reason, the parent had been traveling alone. Maybe he/

THE JAMES TIPTREE AWARD ANTHOLOGY 3

she/it had been a petty merchant or a farmer driven off the land by poverty. If not these, then a wandering thief or someone outlawed for heinous crimes. A person with few resources. In any case, he/she/it had carried the child to this bitter place, where the child's next-to-last part expired.

Imagine standing on the river's icy edge, holding a child who had become a single body. The parent could not bear to raise an infant so incomplete! What parent could? One did no kindness by raising such a cripple to be a monster among ordinary people.

Setting the painful burden down, the parent crossed the river.

I groaned a second time. My most poetic self said:

> *"Two bodies are not enough;*
> *One body is nothing."*

The rest of me hummed agreement. The poet added a second piece of ancient wisdom:

> *"Live in a group*
> *Or die."*

I hummed a second time.

The scout lifted the child from its blanket. "It's female."

The baby woke and cried, waving her four arms, kicking her four legs, and urinating. My scout held her as far away as possible. Beyond doubt, she was a fine, loud, active mite! But incomplete. "Why did you wake her?" asked a cudgel-carrier. "She should be left to die in peace."

"No," said the scout. "She will come with me."

"Me! What do you mean by me?" my other parts cried.

There is neither art nor wisdom in a noisy argument. Therefore, I will not describe the discussion that followed as night fell. Snowflakes drifted from the sky — slowly at first, then more and more thickly. I spoke with the rudeness people reserve for themselves in privacy; and the answers I gave myself were sharp indeed. Words like pointed stones, like the boulders in Tooth River, flew back and forth. Ah! The wounds I inflicted and suffered! Is anything worse than internal dispute?

The scout would not back down. She had fallen in love with the baby, as defective as it was. The cudgel-bearers, sturdy males, were outraged. The poet and the scribe, refined neuters, were repulsed. The rest of me was female and a bit more tender.

I had reached the age when fertile eggs were increasingly unlikely. In spite of my best efforts, I had gained neither fame nor money. What respectable goxhat would mate with a vagabond like me? What crèche would offer to care for my offspring? Surely this fragment of a child was better than nothing.

"No!" said my males and neuters. "This is not a person! One body alone can never know togetherness or integration!"

But my female selves edged slowly toward the scout's opinion. Defective the child certainly was. Still, she was alive and goxhat, her darling little limbs waving fiercely and her darling mouth making noises that would shame a monster.

Most likely, she would die. The rest of her had. Better that she die in someone's arms, warm and comfortable, than in the toothy mouth of a prowling predator. The scout rewrapped the child in the blanket.

It was too late to ford the river. I made camp under a cliff, huddling together for warmth, my arms around myself, the baby in the middle of the heap I made.

When morning came, the sky was clear. Snow sparkled everywhere. I rose, brushed myself off, gathered my gear, and crossed the river. The water was low, as I expected this time of year, but ice-cold. My feet were numb by the time I reached the far side. My teeth chattered on every side like castanets. The baby, awakened by the noise, began to cry. The scout gave her a sweet cake. That stopped the crying for a while.

At mid-day, I came in sight of a keep. My hearts lifted with hope. Alas! Approaching it, I saw the walls were broken.

The ruination was recent. I walked through one of the gaps and found a courtyard, full of snowy heaps. My scouts spread out and investigated. The snow hid bodies, as I expected. Their eyes were gone, but most of the rest remained, preserved by cold and the season's lack of bugs.

"This happened a day or two ago," my scouts said. "Before the last snow, but not by much. *Wishik* found them and took what they could, but didn't have time — before the storm — to find other predators and lead them here. This is why the bodies are still intact. The *wishik* can pluck out eyes, but skin is too thick for them to penetrate. They need the help of other animals, such as *hirg*." One of the scouts crouched by a body and brushed its rusty black hair. "I won't be able to bury these. There are too many."

"How many goxhat are here?" asked my scribe, taking notes.

"It's difficult to say for certain. Three or four, I suspect, all good-sized. A parent and children would be my guess."

I entered the keep building and found more bodies. Not many. Most of the inhabitants had fallen in the courtyard. There was a nursery with scattered toys, but no children.

"Ah! Ah!" I cried, reflecting on the briefness of life and the frequency with which one encounters violence and sorrow.

My poet said:

> *"Broken halls*
> *and scattered wooden words*
> *How will the children*
> *learn to read and write?"*[2]

Finally I found a room with no bodies or toys, nothing to remind

---

2 This translation is approximate. Like humans, goxhat use wooden blocks to teach their children writing. However, their languages are ideogrammic, and the blocks are inscribed with entire words. The children build sentences shaped like walls, towers, barns, and other buildings. Another translation of the poem would be:

Broken walls.
Broken sentences.
Ignorant offspring.
Alas!

me of mortality. I lit a fire and settled for the night. The baby fussed. My scout cleaned her, then held her against a nursing bud — for comfort only; the scout had no milk. The baby sucked. I ate my meager rations. Darkness fell. My thirty-two eyes reflected firelight. After a while, a ghost arrived. Glancing up, I saw it in the doorway. It looked quite ordinary: three goxhat bodies with rusty hair.

"Who are you?" one of my scouts asked.

"The former owner of this keep, or parts of her. My name was Content-in-Solitude; and I lived here with three children, all lusty and numerous. — Don't worry."

My cudgel-carriers had risen, cudgels in hand.

"I'm a good ghost. I'm still in this world because my death was so recent and traumatic. As soon as I've gathered myself together, and my children have done the same, we'll be off to a better place.[3]

"I stopped here to tell you our names, so they will be remembered."

"Content-in-Solitude," muttered my scribe, writing.

"My children were Virtue, Vigor, and Ferric Oxide. Fine offspring! They should have outlived me. Our killer is Bent Foot, a bandit in these mountains. He took my grandchildren to raise as his own, since his female parts — all dead now — produced nothing satisfactory. Mutant children with twisted feet and nasty dispositions! No good will come of them; and their ghosts will make these mountains worse than ever. Tell my story, so others may be warned."

"Yes," my poet said in agreement. The rest of me hummed.

For a moment, the three bodies remained in the doorway. Then they drew together and merged into one. "You see! It's happening! I am becoming a single ghost! Well, then. I'd better be off to find the rest of me, and my children, and a better home for all of us."

The rest of the night was uneventful. I slept well, gathered around

---

3 According to the goxhat, when a person dies, his/her/its goodness becomes a single ghost known as "The Harmonious Breath" or "The Collective Spirit." This departs the world for a better place. But a person's badness remains as a turbulent and malicious mob, attacking itself and anyone else who happens along.

the fire, warmed by its embers and my bodies' heat. If I had dreams, I don't remember them. At dawn, I woke. By sunrise, I was ready to leave. Going out of the building, I discovered three *hirg* in the courtyard: huge predators with shaggy, dull-brown fur. *Wishik* fluttered around them as they tore into the bodies of Content and her children. I took one look, then retreated, leaving the keep by another route.

That day passed in quiet travel. My poet spoke no poetry. The rest of me was equally silent, brooding on the ruined keep and its ghost.

I found no keep to shelter me that night or the next or the next. Instead, I camped out. My scout fed the baby on thin porridge. It ate and kept the food down, but was becoming increasingly fretful and would not sleep unless the scout held it to a nursing bud. Sucking on the dry knob of flesh, it fell asleep.

"I don't mind;" said the scout. "Though I'm beginning to worry. The child needs proper food."

"Better to leave it by the way," a male said. "Death by cold isn't a bad ending."

"Nor death by dehydration," my other male added.

The scout looked stubborn and held the child close.

Four days after I left the ruined keep, I came to another building, this one solid and undamaged.

My scribe said, "I know the lord here by reputation. She is entirely female and friendly to the womanly aspects of a person. The neuter parts she tolerates. But she doesn't like males. Her name is The Testicle Straightener."

My cudgel-carriers shuddered. The scribe and poet looked aloof, as they inevitably did in such situations. Clear-eyed and rational, free from sexual urges, they found the rest of me a bit odd.

The scout carrying the baby said, "The child needs good food and warmth and a bath. For that matter, so do I."

Gathering myself together, I strode to the gate and knocked. After several moments, it swung open. Soldiers looked out. There were two of them: one tall and gray, the other squat and brown. Their bodies filled the entrance, holding spears and axes. Their eyes gleamed green and yellow.

"I am a wandering poet, seeking shelter for the night. I bring news from the south, which your lord might find useful."

The eyes peered closely, then the soldiers parted — gray to the left, brown to the right — and let me in.

Beyond the gate was a snowy courtyard. This one held no bodies. Instead, the snow was trampled and urine-marked. A living place! Though empty at the moment, except for the two soldiers who guarded the gate.

I waited in an anxious cluster. At length, a servant arrived and looked me over. "You need a bath and clean clothes. Our lord is fastidious and dislikes guests who stink. Come with me."

I followed the servant into the keep and down a flight of stairs. Metal lamps were fastened to the walls. Most were dark, but a few shone, casting a dim light. The servant had three sturdy bodies, all covered with black hair.

Down and down. The air grew warm and moist. A faint, distinctive aroma filled it.

"There are hot springs in this part of Ibri," the servant said. "This keep was built on top of one; and there is a pool in the basement, which always steams and smells."

Now I recognized the aroma: rotten eggs.

We came to a large room, paved with stone and covered by a broad, barrel vault. Metal lanterns hung from the ceiling on chains. As was the case with the lamps on the stairway, most were dark. But a few flickered dimly. I could see the bathing pool: round and carved from bedrock. Steps went down into it. Wisps of steam rose.

"Undress," said the servant. "I'll bring soap and towels."

I complied eagerly. Only my scout hesitated, holding the baby.

"I'll help you with the mite," said my scribe, standing knee-deep in hot water.

The scout handed the baby over and undressed.

Soon I was frolicking in the pool, diving and spouting. Cries of joy rang in the damp, warm room. Is anything better than a hot bath after a journey?

The scout took the baby back and moved to the far side of the pool.

When the servant returned, the scout sank down, holding the baby closely, hiding it in shadow. Wise mite, it did not cry!

The rest of me got busy, scrubbing shoulders and backs. Ah, the pleasure of warm lather!

Now and then, I gave a little yip of happiness. The servant watched with satisfaction, his/her/its arms piled high with towels.

On the far side of the pool, my best scout crouched, nursing the babe on a dry bud and watching the servant with hooded eyes.

At last, I climbed out, dried off, and dressed. In the confusion — there was a lot of me — the scout managed to keep the baby concealed. Why, I did not know, but the scout was prudent and usually had a good reason for every action, though parts of me still doubted the wisdom of keeping the baby. There would be time to talk all of this over, when the servant was gone.

He/she/it led me up a new set of stairs. The climb was long. The servant entertained me with the following story.

The keep had a pulley system, which had been built by an ingenious traveling plumber. This lifted buckets of hot water from the spring to a tank on top of the keep. From there the water descended through metal pipes, carried by the downward propensity that is innate in water. The pipes heated every room.

"What powers the pulley system?" my scribe asked, notebook in hand.

"A treadmill," said the servant.

"And what powers the treadmill?"

"Criminals and other people who have offended the lord. No keep in Ibri is more comfortable," the servant continued with pride. "This is what happens when a lord is largely or entirely female. As the old proverb says, male bodies give a person forcefulness. Neuter bodies give thoughtfulness and clarity of vision. But nurture and comfort come from a person's female selves."

Maybe, I thought. But were the people in the treadmill comfortable?

The servant continued the story. The plumber had gone east to Ib and built other heated buildings: palaces, public baths, hotels, hospitals, and crèches. In payment for this work, several of the local lords mated with the plumber; and the local crèches vied to raise the plumber's children, who were numerous and healthy.

"A fine story, with a happy ending," I said, thinking of my fragment of a child, nursing on the scout's dry bud. Envy, the curse of all artists and artisans, roiled in my hearts. Why had I never won the right to lay fertile eggs? Why were my purses empty? Why did I have to struggle to protect my testes and to stay off treadmills, while this plumber — surely not a better person than I — enjoyed fame, honor, and fertility?

The guest room was large and handsome, with a modern wonder next to it: a defecating closet. Inside the closet, water came from the wall in two metal pipes, which ended in faucets. "Hot and cold," said the servant, pointing. Below the faucets was a metal basin, decorated with reliefs of frolicking goxhat. Two empty buckets stood next to the basin.

The servant said, "If you need to wash something, your hands or feet or any other part, fill the basin with water. Use the buckets to empty the basin; and after you use the defecating throne, empty the buckets down it. This reduces the smell and gets rid of the dirty water. As I said, our lord is fastidious; and we have learned from her example. The plumber helped, by providing us with so much water.

"I'll wait in the hall. When you're ready to meet the lord, I'll guide you to her."

"Thank you," said my scribe, always courteous.

I changed into clean clothing, the last I had, and put bardic crowns on my heads.[4] Each crown came from a different contest, though all were minor. I had never won a really big contest. Woven of fine wool, with brightly colored tassels hanging down, the crowns gave me an appearance of dignity. My nimble-fingered scouts unpacked my

---

4 Actually, cerebral bulges. The goxhat don't have heads as humans understand the word.

instruments: a set of chimes, a pair of castanets and a bagpipe. Now I was ready to meet the lord.

All except my best scout, who climbed into the middle of a wide soft bed, child in arms.

"Why did you hide the mite?" asked my scholar.

"This keep seems full of rigid thinkers, overly concerned with themselves and their behavior. If they saw the child they would demand an explanation. 'Why do you keep it? Can't you see how fragmentary it is? Can't you see that it's barely alive? Don't you know how to cut your losses?' I don't want to argue or explain."

"What is meant by 'I'?" my male parts asked. "What is meant by 'my' reasons?"

"This is no time for an argument," said the poet.

All of me except the scout went to meet the keep's famous lord.

The Straightener sat at one end of large hall: an elderly goxhat with frosted hair. Four parts of her remained, all sturdy, though missing a few pieces here and there: a foot, a hand, an eye or finger. Along the edges of the hall sat her retainers on long benches: powerful males, females, and neuters, adorned with iron and gold.

> "Great your fame,
> Gold-despoiler,
> Bold straightener of scrota,
> Wise lord of Ibri.

> "Hearing of it,
> I've crossed high mountains,
> Anxious to praise
> Your princely virtues."

My poet stopped. Straightener leaned forward. "Well? Go on! I want to hear about my princely virtues."

"Give me a day to speak with your retainers and get exact details of your many achievements," the poet said. "Then I will be able to praise you properly."

The goxhat leaned back. "Never heard of me, have you? Drat! I was hoping for undying fame."

"I will give it to you," my poet said calmly.

"Very well," the lord said. "I'll give you a day, and if I like what you compose, I'll leave your male parts alone."

All of me thanked her. Then I told the hall about my stay at the ruined keep. The retainers listened intently. When I had finished, the lord said, "My long-time neighbor! Dead by murder! Well, death comes to all of us. When I was born, I had twenty parts. A truly large number! That is what I'm famous for, as well as my dislike of men, which is mere envy. My male bodies died in childhood, and my neuter parts did not survive early adulthood. By thirty, I was down to ten bodies, all female. The neuters were not much of a loss. Supercilious twits, I always thought. But I miss my male parts. They were so feisty and full of piss! When travelers come here, I set them difficult tasks. If they fail, I have my soldiers hold them, while I unfold their delicate, coiled testicles. No permanent damage is done, but the screaming makes me briefly happy."

My male bodies looked uneasy and shifted back and forth on their feet, as if ready to run. But the two neuters remained calm. My poet thanked the lord a second time, sounding confident. Then I split up and went in all directions through the hall, seeking information.

The drinking went on till dawn, and the lord's retainers were happy to tell me stories about the Straightener. She had a female love of comfort and fondness for children, but could not be called tender in any other way. Rather, she was a fierce leader in battle and a strict ruler, as exact as a balance or a straight-edge.

"She'll lead us against Bent Foot," one drunk soldier said. "We'll kill him and bring the children here. The stolen children, at least. I don't know about Bent Foot's spawn. It might be better for them to die. Not my problem. I let the lord make all the decisions, except whether or not I'm going to fart."

Finally, I went up to my room. My scout lay asleep, the baby in her arms. My male parts began to pace nervously. The rest of me settled to compose a poem.

As the sky brightened, the world outside began to wake and make noise. Most of the noise could be ignored, but there was a *wishik* under the eaves directly outside my room's window. Its shrill, repeating cry drove my poet to distraction. I could not concentrate on the poem.

Desperate, I threw things at the animal: buttons from my sewing kit, spare pens, an antique paperweight I found in the room. Nothing worked. The *wishik* fluttered away briefly, then returned and resumed its irritating cry.

At last my scout woke. I explained the problem. She nodded and listened to the *wishik* for a while. Then she fastened a string to an arrow and shot the arrow out the window. It hit the *wishik*. The animal gave a final cry. Grabbing the string, my scout pulled the beast inside.

"Why did you do that?" I asked.

"Because I didn't want the body to fall in the courtyard."

"Why not?"

Before she could answer, the body at her feet expanded and changed its shape. Instead of the body of a dead *wishik*, I saw a gray goxhat-body, pierced by the scout's arrow, dead.

My males swore. The rest of me exclaimed in surprise.

My scout said, "This is part of a wizard, no doubt employed by the keep's lord, who must really want to unroll my testicles, since she is willing to be unfair and play tricks. The *wishik* cry was magical, designed to bother me so much that I could not concentrate on my composition. If this body had fallen to the ground, the rest of the wizard would have seen it and known the trick had failed. As things are, I may have time to finish the poem." The scout looked at the rest of me severely. "Get to work."

My poet went back to composing, my scribe to writing. The poem went smoothly now. As the stanzas grew in number, I grew increasingly happy and pleased. Soon I noticed the pleasure was sexual. This sometimes happened, though usually when a poem was erotic. The god of poetry and the god of sex are siblings, though they share only one parent, who is called the All-Mother-Father.

Even though the poem was not erotic, my male and female parts became increasingly excited. Ah! I was rubbing against myself. Ah! I was making soft noises! The poet and scribe could not feel this sexual pleasure, of course, but the sight of the rest of me tumbling on the rug was distracting. Yes, neuters are clear-eyed and rational, but they are also curious; and nothing arouses their curiosity more than sex. They stopped working on the poem and watched as I fondled myself.[5]

Only the scout remained detached from sensuality and went into the defecating closet. Coming out with a bucket of cold water, the scout poured it over my amorous bodies.

I sprang apart, yelling with shock.

"This is more magic;" the scout said. "I did not know a spell inciting lust could be worked at such a distance, but evidently it can. Every part of me that is male or female, go in the bathroom! Wash in cold water till the idea of sex becomes uninteresting! As for my neuter parts —" The scout glared. "Get back to the poem!"

"Why has one part of me escaped the spell?" I asked the scout.

"I did not think I could lactate without laying an egg first, but the child's attempts to nurse have caused my body to produce milk. As a rule, nursing mothers are not interested in sex, and this has proved true of me. Because of this, and the child's stubborn nursing, there is a chance of finishing the poem. I owe this child a debt of gratitude."

"Maybe," grumbled my male parts. The poet and scribe said, "I shall see."

The poem was done by sunset. That evening I recited it in the lord's hall. If I do say so myself, it was a splendid achievement. The *wishik's* cry was in it, as was the rocking up-and-down rhythm of a sexually excited goxhat. The second gave the poem energy and an emphatic beat. As for the first, every line ended with one of the two sounds in the *wishik's* ever-repeating, irritating cry. Nowadays, we call this repetition of sound "rhyming." But it had no name when I invented it.

---

5 The goxhat believe masturbation is natural and ordinary. But reproduction within a person — inbreeding, as they call it — is unnatural and a horrible disgrace. It rarely happens. Most goxhat are not intrafertile, for reasons too complicated to explain here.

When I was done, the lord ordered several retainers to memorize the poem. "I want to hear it over and over," she said. "What a splendid idea it is to make words ring against each other in this fashion! How striking the sound! How memorable! Between you and the traveling plumber, I will certainly be famous."

That night was spent like the first one, everyone except me feasting. I feigned indigestion and poured my drinks on the floor under the feasting table. The lord was tricky and liked winning. Who could say what she might order put in my cup or bowl, now that she had my poem?

When the last retainer fell over and began to snore, I got up and walked to the hall's main door. Sometime in the next day or so, the lord would discover that her wizard had lost a part to death and that one of her paperweights was missing. I did not want to be around when these discoveries were made.

Standing in the doorway, I considered looking for the treadmill. Maybe I could free the prisoners. They might be travelers like me, innocent victims of the lord's malice and envy and her desire for hot water on every floor. But there were likely to be guards around the treadmill, and the guards might be sober. I was only one goxhat. I could not save everyone. And the servant had said they were criminals.

I climbed the stairs quietly, gathered my belongings and the baby, and left through a window down a rope made of knotted sheets.

The sky was clear; the brilliant star we call Beacon stood above the high peaks, shedding so much light I had no trouble seeing my way. I set a rapid pace eastward. Toward morning, clouds moved in. The Beacon vanished. Snow began to fall, concealing my trail. The baby, nursing on the scout, made happy noises.

Two days later, I was out of the mountains, camped in a forest by an unfrozen stream. Water made a gentle sound, purling over pebbles. The trees on the banks were changers, a local variety that is blue in summer and yellow in winter. At the moment, their leaves were thick with snow. "Silver and gold," my poet murmured, looking up.

The scribe made a note.

A *wishik* clung to a branch above the poet and licked its wings. Whenever it shifted position, snow came down.

> "*The* wishik *cleans wings*
> *As white as snow.*
> *Snow falls on me, white*
> *As a* wishik,"

the poet said.

My scribe scribbled.

One of my cudgel-carriers began the discussion. "The Bane of Poets was entirely neuter. Fear of death made it crazy. Bent Foot was entirely male. Giving in to violence, he stole children from his neighbor. The last lord I encountered, the ruler of the heated keep, was female, malicious and unfair. Surely something can be learned from these encounters. A person should not be one sex entirely, but rather — as I am — a harmonious mixture of male, female, and neuter. But this child can't help but be a single sex."

"I owe the child a debt of gratitude," said my best scout firmly. "Without her, I would have had pain and humiliation, when the lord — a kind of lunatic — unrolled my testes, as she clearly planned to do. At best, I would have limped away from the keep in pain. At worst, I might have ended in the lord's treadmill, raising water from the depths to make her comfortable."

"The question is a good one," said my scribe. "How can a person who is only one sex avoid becoming a monster? The best combination is the one I have: male, female, and both kinds of neuter. But even two sexes provide a balance."

"Other people — besides these three — have consisted of one sex," my scout said stubbornly. "Not all became monsters. It isn't sex that has influenced these lords, but the stony fields and spiny mountains of Ibri, the land's cold winters and ferocious wildlife. My various parts can teach the child my different qualities: the valor of the cudgel-carriers, the coolness of poet and scribe, the female tenderness that the rest of me has. Then she will become a single harmony."

The scout paused. The rest of me looked dubious. The scout continued.

"Many people lose parts of themselves through illness, accident, and war; and some of these live for years in a reduced condition. Yes, it's sad and disturbing, but it can't be called unnatural. Consider aging and the end of life. The old die body by body, till a single body remains. Granted, in many cases, the final body dies quickly. But not always. Every town of good size has a Gram or Gaffer who hobbles around in a single self.

"I will not give up an infant I have nursed with my own milk. Do I wish to be known as ungrateful or callous? I, who have pinned all my hope on honor and fame?"

I looked at myself with uncertain expressions. The *wishik* shook down more snow.

"Well, then," said my poet, who began to look preoccupied. Another poem coming, most likely. "I will take the child to a crèche and leave her there."

My scout scowled. "How well will she be cared for there, among healthy children, by tenders who are almost certain to be prejudiced against a mite so partial and incomplete? I will not give her up."

"Think of how much I travel," a cudgel-carrier said. "How can I take a child on my journeys?"

"Carefully and tenderly," the scout replied. "The way my ancestors who were nomads did. Remember the old stories! When they traveled, they took everything, even the washing pot. Surely their children were not left behind."

"I have bonded excessively to this child," said my scribe to the scout.

"Yes, I have. It's done and can't be undone. I love her soft baby-down, her four blue eyes, her feisty spirit. I will not give her up."

I conversed this way for some time. I didn't become angry at myself, maybe because I had been through so much danger recently. There is nothing like serious fear to put life into perspective. Now and then, when the conversation became especially difficult, a part of me got up and went into the darkness to kick the snow or to piss. When the part came back, he or she or it seemed better.

Finally I came to an agreement. I would keep the child and carry it on my journeys, though half of me remained unhappy with this decision.

How difficult it is to be of two minds! Still, it happens; and all but the insane survive such divisions. Only they forget the essential unity that underlies differences of opinion. Only they begin to believe in individuality.

The next morning, I continued into Ib.

The poem I composed for the lord of the warm keep became famous. Its form, known as "ringing praise," was taken up by other poets. From it, I gained some fame, enough to quiet my envy; and the fame led to some money, which provided for my later years.

Did I ever return to Ibri? No. The land was too bitter and dangerous; and I didn't want to meet the lord of the warm keep a second time. Instead, I settled in Lesser Ib, buying a house on a bank of a river named It-Could-Be-Worse. This turned out to be an auspicious name. The house was cozy and my neighbors pleasant. The child played in my fenced-in garden, tended by my female parts. As for my neighbors, they watched with interest and refrained from mentioning the child's obvious disability.

> "Lip-presser on one side.
> Tongue-biter on t'other.
> Happy I live,
> Praising good neighbors."

I traveled less than previously, because of the child and increasing age. But I did make the festivals in Greater and Lesser Ib. This was easy traveling on level roads across wide plains. The Ibian lords, though sometimes eccentric, were nowhere near as crazy as the ones in Ibri and no danger to me or other poets. At one of the festivals, I met the famous plumber, who turned out to be a large and handsome male and neuter goxhat. I won the festival crown for poetry, and he/it won the crown for ingenuity. Celebrating with egg wine, we became amorous and fell into each other's many arms.

It was a fine romance and ended without regret, as did all my other romances. As a group, we goxhat are happiest with ourselves. In addition, I could not forget the prisoners in the treadmill. Whether the plumber planned it or not, he/it had caused pain for others. Surely it was wrong — unjust — for some to toil in darkness, so that others had a warm bed and hot water from a pipe?

I have to say, at times I dreamed of that keep: the warm halls, the pipes of water, the heated bathing pool and the defecating throne that had — have I forgotten to mention this? — a padded seat.

> "Better to be here
> In my cozy cottage.
> Some comforts
> Have too high a cost."

I never laid any fertile eggs. My only child is Ap the Foundling, who is also known as Ap of One Body and Ap the Many-talented. As the last nickname suggests, the mite turned out well.

As for me, I became known as The Clanger and The *Wishik*, because of my famous rhyming poem. Other names were given to me as well: The Child Collector, The Nurturer, and The Poet Who Is Odd.

winners and short lists

The Tiptree Award process does not call for a list of nominees from which a winner is chosen, because we feel that creates an artificial set of "losers." Instead, each panel releases a winner (or winners) and a "short list" of fiction that the jurors consider especially worthy of readers' attention. In some years, the jurors publish a "long list" of books and stories they also found interesting in the course of their reading.

Below are the winners and short lists from all years of the award, as well as the long list from 2005. The 2005 jurors were Liz Henry (chair), Nike Bourke, Matt Ruff, and Georgie Schnobrich. (A fifth juror, Hiromi Goto, was forced to drop out partway into the year due to a family emergency.)

Entries in boldface are represented in this volume. For more information on all of these works, please visit our website -- at *www. tiptree.org* — for all of the annotated lists.

You are encouraged to join the not-so-secret Secret Feminist Cabal and forward recommendations for novels and short fiction works that explore and expand gender. You'll find a recommendation form on the website. The wider our network of supporters, the more good candidates the jurors see every year.

2005 WINNER
Geoff Ryman, *Air* (St. Martin's Griffin 2004; Orion 2005)

2005 SHORT LIST
Aimee Bender, *Willful Creatures* (Doubleday 2005)

Margo Lanagan, "Wooden Bride" (in *Black Juice*, Allen & Unwin 2004; Eos 2005)

Vonda N. McIntyre, "Little Faces" (*SciFiction* 02.23.05)

Wen Spencer, *A Brother's Price* (Roc 2005)

Wesley Stace, *Misfortune* (Little, Brown 2005)

Mark W. Tiedemann, *Remains* (Benbella Books 2005)

2005 LONG LIST

Emily Brunson, "Arcana" (CSI Forensics fanfic website)

Janine Cross, *Touched by Venom* (Roc 2005)

Ronlyn Domingue, *The Mercy of Thin Air* (Atria 2005)

L. Timmel Duchamp, *Alanya to Alanya* (Aqueduct Press 2005)

L. Timmel Duchamp, *The Red Rose Rages (Bleeding)* (Aqueduct Press 2005)

Carol Emshwiller, *Mister Boots* (Viking Juvenile 2005)

Adam Gopnik, *The King in the Window* (Miramax 2005)

Nalo Hopkinson and Geoff Ryman, editors, *Tesseracts Nine* (EDGE 2005)

Rosaleen Love, "In the Shadow of the Stones" (in *The Traveling Tide*, Aqueduct Press 2005)

Meghan McCarron, "Close to You" (*Strange Horizons* 4/18/05)

David Moles, "Planet of the Amazon Women" (*Strange Horizons* 5/16/05)

Sarah Monette, *Melusine* (Ace 2005)

Helen Oyeyemi, *The Icarus Girl* (Doubleday 2005)

Julie Anne Peters, *Luna* (Little, Brown 2004)

Scott Westerfeld, *Uglies* (Simon Pulse 2005)

Gabrielle Zevin, *Margarettown* (Miramax 2005)

2005 SPECIAL MENTION

Nisi Shawl and Cynthia Ward, *Writing the Other* (Aqueduct Press 2005)

Ka-Ping Yee, Regender website (*regender.com/*)

2004 WINNERS

Joe Haldeman, *Camouflage*

Johanna Sinisalo, *Not Before Sundown* (also as *Troll: A Love Story*)

2004 SHORT LIST

A. S. Byatt, *Little Black Book of Stories*

L. Timmel Duchamp, *Love's Body, Dancing in Time*

Carol Emshwiller, "All of Us Can Almost…"

Nancy Farmer, *The Sea of Trolls*

Eileen Gunn, *Stable Strategies and Others*

Gwyneth Jones, *Life*

Jaye Lawrence, "Kissing Frogs"

2003 WINNER

Matt Ruff, *Set This House in Order: A Romance of Souls*

2003 SHORT LIST

Kim Antieau, *Coyote Cowgirl*

Richard Calder writing as Christina X, "The Catgirl Manifesto: An Introduction"

Kara Dalkey, "The Lady of the Ice Garden"

Carol Emshwiller, "Boys"

Nina Kiriki Hoffman, *A Fistful of Sky*

Kij Johnson, *Fudoki*

Sandra McDonald, "The Ghost Girls of Rumney Mill"

Ruth Nestvold, "Looking Through Lace"

Geoff Ryman, "Birth Days"

Tricia Sullivan, *Maul*

2002 WINNERS

M. John Harrison, *Light*

John Kessel, "Stories for Men"

2002 SHORT LIST

Eleanor Arnason, "Knapsack Poems"

Ted Chiang, "Liking What You See: A Documentary"
John Clute, *Appleseed*
Karen Joy Fowler, "What I Didn't See"
Gregory Frost, "Madonna of the Maquiladora"
Shelley Jackson, *The Melancholy of Anatomy*
Larissa Lai, *Salt Fish Girl*
Peter Straub, editor, *Conjunctions 39: The New Wave Fabulists*

2001 WINNER
Hiromi Goto, *The Kappa Child*

2001 SHORT LIST
Joan Givner, *Half Known Lives*
Hugh Nissenson, *The Song of the Earth*
Ken MacLeod, *Dark Light*
Sheri S. Tepper, *The Fresco*

2000 WINNER
Molly Gloss, *Wild Life*

2000 SHORT LIST
Michael Blumlein, "Fidelity: A Primer"
James L. Cambias, "A Diagram of Rapture"
David Ebershoff, *The Danish Girl*
Mary Gentle, *Ash: A Secret History*
Camille Hernandez-Ramdwar, "Soma"
Nalo Hopkinson, "The Glass Bottle Trick"
Nalo Hopkinson, *Midnight Robber*
China Miéville, *Perdido Street Station*
Pamela Mordecai, "Once on the Shores of the Stream Senegambia"
Severna Park, *The Annunciate*
Tess Williams, *Sea as Mirror*

1999 WINNER
Suzy McKee Charnas, *The Conqueror's Child*

1999 SHORT LIST

Judy Budnitz, *If I Told You Once*
Sally Caves, "In the Second Person"
Graham Joyce, "Pinkland"
Yumiko Kurahashi, *The Woman with the Flying Head and Other Stories*
Penelope Lively, "5001 Nights"
David E. Morse, *The Iron Bridge*
Kim Stanley Robinson, "Sexual Dimorphism"

1998 WINNER

Raphael Carter, "Congenital Agenesis of Gender Ideation"

1998 SHORT LIST

Eleanor Arnason, "The Gauze Banner"
Octavia Butler, *Parable of the Talents*
Ted Chiang, "Story of Your Life"
Stella Duffy, *Singling Out the Couples*
Karen Joy Fowler, *Black Glass*
Maggie Gee, *The Ice People*
Carolyn Ives Gilman, *Halfway Human*
Phyllis Gotlieb, *Flesh and Gold*
Nalo Hopkinson, *Brown Girl in the Ring*
Gwyneth Jones, "La Cenerentola"
James Patrick Kelly, "Lovestory"
Ursula K. Le Guin, "Unchosen Love"
Elizabeth A. Lynn, *Dragon's Winter*
Maureen F. McHugh, *Mission Child*
Karl-Rene Moore, "The Hetairai Turncoat"
Rebecca Ore, "Accelerated Grimace"
Sara Paretsky, *Ghost Country*
Severna Park, *Hand of Prophecy*
Kit Reed, "The Bride of Bigfoot"
Kit Reed, *Weird Women, Wired Women*
Robert Reed, "Whiptail"
Mary Rosenblum, "The Eye of God"

Joan Slonczewski, *The Children Star*
Martha Soukup, "The House of Expectations"
Sean Stewart, *Mockingbird*
Sarah Zettel, *Playing God*

1997 WINNERS
Candas Jane Dorsey, *Black Wine*
Kelly Link, "Travels with the Snow Queen"

1997 SHORT LIST
Storm Constantine, "The Oracle Lips"
Paul Di Filippo, "Alice, Alfie, Ted and the Aliens"
Emma Donoghue, *Kissing the Witch: Old Tales in New Skins*
L. Timmel Duchamp, "The Apprenticeship of Isabetta di Pietro
    Cavazzi"
Molly Gloss, *The Dazzle of Day*
M. John Harrison, *Signs of Life*
Gwyneth Jones, "Balinese Dancer"
Ian McDonald, *Sacrifice of Fools*
Vonda N. McIntyre, *The Moon and the Sun*
Shani Mootoo, *Cereus Blooms at Night*
Salman Rushdie, "The Firebird's Nest"
Paul Witcover, *Waking Beauty*

1996 WINNERS
Ursula K. Le Guin, "Mountain Ways"
Mary Doria Russell, *The Sparrow*

1996 SHORT LIST
Fred Chappell, "The Silent Woman"
Suzy McKee Charnas, "Beauty and the Opera, or The Phantom
    Beast"
L. Timmel Duchamp, "Welcome, Kid, to the Real World"
Alasdair Gray, *A History Maker*
Jonathan Lethem, "Five Fucks"

Pat Murphy, *Nadya*
Rachel Pollack, *Godmother Night*
Lisa Tuttle, *The Pillow Friend*
Tess Williams, "And She Was the Word"
Sue Woolfe, *Leaning Towards Infinity*

1995 WINNERS

Elizabeth Hand, *Waking the Moon*
Theodore Roszak, *The Memoirs of Elizabeth Frankenstein*

1995 SHORT LIST

Kelley Eskridge, "And Salome Danced"
Kit Reed, *Little Sisters of the Apocalypse*
Lisa Tuttle, "Food Man"
Terri Windling, editor, *The Armless Maiden, and Other Stories for Childhood's Survivors*

1994 WINNERS

Ursula K. Le Guin, "The Matter of Seggri"
Nancy Springer, *Larque on the Wing*

1994 SHORT LIST

Eleanor Arnason, "The Lovers"
Suzy McKee Charnas, *The Furies*
L. Warren Douglas, *Cannon's Orb*
Greg Egan, "Cocoon"
Ellen Frye, *Amazon Story Bones*
Gwyneth Jones, *North Wind*
Graham Joyce & Peter F. Hamilton, "Eat Reecebread"
Ursula K. Le Guin, *A Fisherman of the Inland Sea*
Ursula K. Le Guin, "Forgiveness Day"
Rachel Pollack, *Temporary Agency*
Geoff Ryman, *Unconquered Countries*
Melissa Scott, *Trouble and Her Friends*
Delia Sherman, "Young Woman in a Garden"

George Turner, *Genetic Soldier*

1993 WINNER
Nicola Griffith, *Ammonite*

1993 SHORT LIST
Eleanor Arnason, *Ring of Swords*
Margaret Atwood, *The Robber Bride*
Sybil Claiborne, *In the Garden of Dead Cars*
L. Timmel Duchamp, "Motherhood"
R. Garcia y Robertson, "The Other Magpie"
James Patrick Kelly, "Chemistry"
Laurie J. Marks, *Dancing Jack*
Ian McDonald, "Some Strange Desire"
Alice Nunn, *Illicit Passage*
Paul Park, *Coelestis*

1992 WINNER
Maureen McHugh, *China Mountain Zhang*

1992 SHORT LIST
Carol Emshwiller, "Venus Rising"
Ian MacLeod, "Grownups"
Judith Moffett, *Time, Like an Ever-Rolling Stream*
Kim Stanley Robinson, *Red Mars*
Sue Thomas, *Correspondence*
Lisa Tuttle, *Lost Futures*
Élisabeth Vonarburg, *In the Mothers' Land*

1991 WINNERS
Eleanor Arnason, *A Woman of the Iron People*
Gwyneth Jones, *White Queen*

1991 SHORT LIST

John Barnes, *Orbital Resonance*

Karen Joy Fowler, *Sarah Canary*

Mary Gentle, *The Architecture of Desire*

Greer Ilene Gilman, *Moonwise*

Marge Piercy, *He, She and It*

RETROSPECTIVE AWARD WINNERS

Suzy McKee Charnas, *Motherlines* (1978)

Suzy McKee Charnas, *Walk to the End of the World* (1974)

Ursula K. Le Guin, *The Left Hand of Darkness* (1969)

Joanna Russ, *The Female Man* (1975)

Joanna Russ, "When It Changed" (1972)

RETROSPECTIVE AWARD SHORT LIST

Margaret Atwood, *The Handmaid's Tale* (1986)

Iain Banks, *The Wasp Factory* (1984)

Katherine Burdekin, *Swastika Night* (1937)

Octavia Butler, *Wild Seed* (1980)

Samuel R. Delany, *Babel-17* (1966)

Samuel R. Delany, *Triton* (1976)

Carol Emshwiller, *Carmen Dog* (1990)

Sonya Dorman Hess, "When I Was Miss Dow" (1966)

Elizabeth A. Lynn, *Watchtower* (1979)

Vonda N. McIntyre, *Dreamsnake* (1978)

Naomi Mitchison, *Memoirs of a Spacewoman* (1962)

Marge Piercy, *Woman on the Edge of Time* (1976)

Joanna Russ, *The Two of Them* (1978)

Pamela Sargent, editor, *Women of Wonder* (1974), *More Women of Wonder* (1976), and *The New Women of Wonder* (1977)

John Varley, "The Barbie Murders" (1978)

Kate Wilhelm, *The Clewiston Test* (1976)

Monique Wittig, *Les Guerillères* (1969)

Pamela Zoline, "The Heat Death of the Universe" (1967)

about the authors

DOROTHY ALLISON grew up in Greenville, South Carolina, the first child of a fifteen-year-old unwed mother who worked as a waitress. Now living in northern California with her partner Alix and her teenage son, Wolf Michael, she describes herself as a feminist, a working-class storyteller, a Southern expatriate, a sometime poet, and a happily born-again Californian. Allison's chapbook of poetry, *The Women Who Hate Me*, was published with Long Haul Press in 1983. Her short story collection, *Trash* (Firebrand Books, 1988), won two Lambda Literary Awards and the American Library Association Prize for Lesbian and Gay Writing. Allison received mainstream recognition with her novel *Bastard Out of Carolina* (1992), a finalist for the 1992 National Book Award, which became a bestseller, and an award-winning movie. It has been translated into more than a dozen languages. *Cavedweller* (1998) was another national bestseller, a *New York Times* Notable Book of the Year, and an ALA prize winner. A third novel, *She Who*, is forthcoming from Riverhead.

ELEANOR ARNASON's novel *A Woman of the Iron People* shared the very first James Tiptree, Jr. Award and won the Mythopoeic Fantasy Award. A later novel, *Ring of Swords*, won the Minnesota Book Award. She has published five novels and dozens of short stories as well as numerous poems and articles. She has been published in *Orbit*, *New Women of Wonder*, *The Norton Book of Science Fiction*, and *Tales of the Unanticipated* just to name a few. She lives in St. Paul, Minnesota.

AIMEE BENDER is the author of three books, *The Girl in the Flam-*

mable Skirt, a *New York Times* Notable Book of 1998; *An Invisible Sign of My Own*, an *L.A. Times* Pick for 2000; and *Willful Creatures*. She's had short fiction published in *Harper's*, GQ, *Granta*, *Paris Review*, and *McSweeney's*. She lives in Los Angeles and teaches at the University of Southern California. Visit her website *Flammableskirt.com*.

TED CHIANG was born in Port Jefferson, New York, and currently lives outside Seattle, Washington, where he works as a freelance technical writer. His stories have appeared in the anthologies *Starlight 2*, *Vanishing Acts*, and *Starlight 3*, among other places, to extraordinary critical acclaim. All except the most recent are collected in *Stories of Your Life and Others*, published by Tor in 2002.

L. TIMMEL DUCHAMP is the author of a collection of short fiction (*Love's Body, Dancing in Time*), a collection of essays (*The Grand Conversation*), four novels (*Alanya to Alanya*, *Renegade*, *Tsunami*, and *The Red Rose Rages (Bleeding)*), and dozens of short stories and essays. She has been a finalist for the Nebula and Sturgeon awards and has been shortlisted for the James Tiptree Award several times. A selection of her essays and fiction can be found at *ltimmel.home.mindspring.com*.

NALO HOPKINSON has so far published a collection of short stories, some plays, three novels, and an anthology or two. She has lived in Toronto, Canada, since 1977, but spent most of her first sixteen years in the Caribbean, where she was born. *The New Moon's Arms*, Hopkinson's newest novel, is appearing from Warner Books in February 2007. Her writing reflects her hybrid reality. More details can be found on her website, www.nalohopkinson.com.

MARGO LANAGAN lives in Sydney, Australia, works as a technical writer, and has been publishing books for children, young people, and adults for about fifteen years. She has published poetry, teenage romance, junior fantasy novels, mainstream young adult novels, and two collections of speculative-fiction short stories, *White Time* and *Black Juice*. *Black Juice* won two World Fantasy Awards (for Best Short

Story and Best Collection), two Ditmars, and two Aurealis Awards, and was made a Michael L. Printz Honor Book by YALSA. Stories from the collection have been shortlisted for the International Horror Guild, Bram Stoker, Theodore Sturgeon, Nebula and Hugo Awards — two stories were reprinted in the Datlow/Grant/Link *Year's Best Fantasy and Horror #18*. Margo has just completed a third story collection, *Red Spikes*, and is working on a novel.

URSULA K. LE GUIN has published six books of poetry, twenty novels, over a hundred short stories (collected in eleven volumes), four collections of essays, eleven books for children, and four volumes of translation. Her work includes realistic fiction, science fiction, fantasy, young children's books, books for young adults, screenplays, essays, verbal texts for musicians, and voicetexts for performance or recording. Her awards include a National Book Award, five Hugo Awards, five Nebula Awards, SFWA's Grand Master, the Kafka Award, a Pushcart Prize, the Howard Vursell Award of the American Academy of Arts and Letters, the *L.A. Times* Robert Kirsch Award, the PEN/Faulkner Award for Short Stories, and the ALA Margaret Edwards Award for Young Adult Fiction. She is also a two-time winner of the James Tiptree, Jr. Award, and a winner of the Tiptree Retrospective Award.

VONDA N. MCINTYRE is the author of *Dreamsnake*, which won both the Nebula Award and the Hugo award for best science fiction novel in 1979; *The Moon and the Sun*, which won the Nebula Award in 1998; and several other novels, including both original novels and *Star Trek* and *Star Wars* tie-in fiction. She graduated as a Bachelor of Science from the honors program of the University of Washington and did a year of graduate work in genetics before becoming a full-time writer. She has exhibited hunters and jumpers, organized conferences, observed humpback whales in Alaska, and rafted in the white water of Idaho. She earned shodan (first-degree black belt) in the martial art Aikido. She lives in Seattle, Washington.

PAM NOLES' one-line biography is "Ape shall not kill ape, but it is quite acceptable to make fun of ape when necessary." She is a critic, comics fan, and essayist living in southern California.

GEOFF RYMAN has published ten books. His recent novel *Air* was shortlisted for a Nebula and won the Arthur C. Clarke Award, the British Science Fiction Association Award, the Sunburst Award, and the Tiptree Award. *Tesseracts Nine*, an anthology of Canadian sf published the same year that Ryman co-edited with Nalo Hopkinson, won the Aurora Award. Previous stories and novels have won the Philip K. Dick Award, the World Fantasy Award, and the John W. Campbell Memorial Award (first place), and others for a total of a lucky thirteen awards. His most recent novel, *The King's Last Song*, is set in Cambodia ancient and modern. He currently teaches creative writing at the University of Manchester in the UK.

JAMES TIPTREE, JR./ALICE SHELDON is the writer for whom the Tiptree Award was named. *James Tiptree, Jr.: The Double Life of Alice B. Sheldon* by Julie Phillips, a comprehensive biography of this many-faceted individual, was released in 2006 by St. Martin's Press.

about the editors

KAREN JOY FOWLER is the *New York Times* bestselling author of *The Jane Austen Book Club*. Her previous novel, *Sister Noon*, was a finalist for the PEN/Faulkner award. Her first novel, *Sarah Canary*, won the Commonwealth medal for best first novel by a Californian in 1991. Her short story collection *Black Glass* won the World Fantasy Award in 1999; her first two novels were both *New York Times* Notable Books in their year. She is a Founding Mother of the Tiptree Award. She lives with her husband in Davis, California.

PAT MURPHY has won numerous awards for her science fiction and fantasy writing. In 1987, she won the Nebula, an award presented by the Science Fiction Writers of America, for both her second novel, *The Falling Woman*, and her novelette "Rachel in Love." Her novel *There and Back Again* won the 2002 Seiun Award for best foreign science fiction novel translated into Japanese. Her most recent novel is *Adventures in Time and Space with Max Merriwell*. When she is not writing science fiction, Pat writes for the Exploratorium, San Francisco's museum of science, art, and human perception. She is a Founding Mother of the James Tiptree Award and a member of the award's Motherboard.

DEBBIE NOTKIN is an editor and nonfiction writer. She edited *Flying Cups & Saucers*, the first collection of Tiptree-recognized short fiction, published by Edgewood Press in 1998. She edited and wrote the text for photographer Laurie Toby Edison's two books, *Women En*

Large: Images of Fat Nudes, and *Familiar Men: A Book of Nudes*. She is the chair of the James Tiptree Award Motherboard and an advisor to Broad Universe, an organization with the primary goal of promoting science fiction, fantasy, and horror written by women. She has been an editor and consulting editor for Tor Books and Prima Publishing. Her essays on body image, and on science fiction, have been widely published and she has spoken on these topics all over the United States and in Japan.

JEFFREY D. SMITH was a friend of James Tiptree's and is the literary trustee of her estate. He is a member of the James Tiptree Award Motherboard. He edited "Women in Science Fiction," a groundbreaking 1975 symposium, and *Meet Me at Infinity*, a posthumous collection of Tiptree's stories and essays.